D1195162

THE CROWN OF SILENCE

THE CROWN OF SILENCE

STORM CONSTANTINE

TOR®

A TOM DOHERTY ASSOCIATES BOOK
NEW YORK

THE CROWN OF SILENCE

Copyright © 2001 by Storm Constantine

A Tor Book
Published by Tom Doherty Associates, LLC
175 Fifth Avenue
New York, NY 10010

Tor® is a registered trademark of Tom Doherty
Associates, LLC.

ISBN 0-312-87329-8

Printed in the United States of America

This book is dedicated to Paul Weston,
Reiki Master and master quester par excellence.

THE CROWN OF SILENCE

EXPERIENCE OF WAR

WHEN SHAN WAS fifteen years old, dark soldiers came out of the west, like a cloud of evil boiling over the soft hills of his homeland. They commanded terrible beasts, which killed with hooked claws like scythes and cold eyes that dripped icy fire. The soldiers wore helmets that looked like fiends, tusked and snarling and sneering.

Shan was just an ordinary boy. His mother was dead, and his father, Hod, gathered crops in the fields for a local farmholder. In the winter, Hod harvested wood from the rustling forests that surrounded the fields. Shan worked at his father's side, with no ambition ever to do anything else. They lived in a one-room cottage on the outskirts of Holme, a village filled with peasant folk, whose lives were those of toil and scant ambition. There was a squire, Sir Rupert Sathe, to whom they paid tithes and who occasionally funded village celebrations. Once a year Sir Rupert attended God's chapel for the harvest festival, but other than that, he was mostly invisible in the villagers' lives. His sons and daughters spent most of their time, along with their mother, in the city of Dantering, far down the Great Western

Road. Country life held no attractions for Sir Rupert's family, so there were no winsome, blue-blooded maids to fire the hearts of local boys, nor rakehellion sons to make the village girls tremble in their beds.

Shan was as happy as any person in his position could be. He was fed adequately, the cottage snug and secure against wolves in winter and cool in the summer. He and his father grew vegetables in the small patch that surrounded their home, and there was a single apple tree that always bore good fruit. His aunt came regularly to make sure he and his father didn't live like pigs, which left alone they probably would. Once a week they worshipped in the chapel of the God who had no name, and laid offerings of forest flowers at the altars of His three daughters, the virgin, the mother and one without child. Though devout in their conventional worship, they also made more furtive offerings to the folk of the forest, to ensure that their livestock were free from blight, and their produce without bane. Also, most importantly, they revered the guardians of the land, those invisible spirits whose benevolence ensured the seasons gave forth their appointed bounty. The god might enable a person's soul to walk the airy road beyond death into the heaven of heavens, but all the villagers knew who really held power in the realm of the living; the fertile earth, the running stream, the water-bearing clouds. The guardians cared not for human souls; they were the life of the land, and were treated with respect rather than worshipped.

News came slowly down the Great Western Road, or not at all. The people of Holme knew nothing of politics. When the great city of Dantering fell to the Magravands, nobody heard. Messengers might have fled from the burning walls with dire news for other cities, but the villages were hidden among the hills. Who would bring news to them in time? They were unaware Dantering had been their last defense against whatever might come prowling from the west.

The soldiers came at sundown, first to the manor house. Sir Rupert, dining alone, was dragged roaring from his dinner table and summarily beheaded before the astonished servants, who had been rounded up like sheep. Then the male servants were hung, the women raped and beaten. A commanding officer of the invading army went into the dining room and there sat down with his staff to finish the squire's dinner. All the time they ate, they must have been able to hear the screams of the women, the pleading moans of the men.

While their officers were making inroads into the port wine, the rest of the troupe rode down toward Holme, their beasts flapping and scrabbling before them. The guardians of the land sank down into the deep earth at their approach, sensing a power so dark their own was in danger of being snuffed out. Their absence left the landscape without spirit, its inhabitants more vulnerable to attack.

Men do terrible things in war. To fighting men, people are no longer people. The soldiers displayed the head of Sir Rupert high upon a pole, as they poured like oil over the hills and into Holme. The villagers were taken by surprise, and offered no resistance to speak of, yet still their cottages were put to the torch, their women ravished, and the men cut down like wheat. It was a senseless atrocity. The schemes and aspirations of men in power meant nothing to the people of Holme. They cared only for their daily toil, the bread upon their tables, the roofs over their heads. The soldiers could just have told the villagers who their new masters were and ridden on. Whoever sat in the manor house would still need his land tended, after all.

When it happened, Shan was sitting by the willow pool at the back of the cottage. He heard the noises—strange and terrible—and for a moment sat very still. His instincts told him at once that something bad was happening, something very bad. He smelled smoke, and it was not the sweet smell of wood burning. His father came out of the cottage and looked at him where he was squatting by the water, tense and alert as a young dog. They exchanged a glance, and then Hod went out to the road and looked down it. Shan heard the sound of galloping hooves. Someone was coming, a great many someones. He wanted to tell his father to move, that they should run into the woods in the next field, but it all happened too quickly. Later, he thought about how if he'd shouted out this intuitive suggestion the moment Hod had looked round the cottage wall, they might both have been saved, and for many years punished himself for those minutes of indecision.

The riders were accompanied by two of the terrible black beasts, which lunged ahead of them down the road, scratching up sparks.

They fell upon Shan's father before he could defend himself or attempt to escape. The razor claws slashed and the poisonous eyes dripped smoking ruin. It did not take them long to reduce a human body to a mess of meat no longer recognizable as a man.

Shan was frozen in horror by the pool. He wondered what he and his father could have done wrong. Who were these people? His stasis was mercifully brief and once it released him, he surrendered to the instinct to flee. At first, his limbs moved sluggishly, as in a nightmare. He struggled in what seemed painful slowness toward the back gate. The flesh over his spine contracted, waiting for a blow. Had they seen him? The fact that his father had just been gored to death had not sunk in. Self-preservation was his only thought. Suddenly, everything became faster. He vaulted over the gate like a deer, and his legs were pumping madly as he cut a path through the long grass of the field beyond.

He had almost reached the shadows of the trees, whose labyrinth he knew so well and in which he would undoubtedly have managed to lose his pursuers, when the riders caught up. There were only two, and the beasts were not with them. This was clearly to be different sport. They set their horses prancing round Shan in a circle. He could not see their faces, because of the demonic helmets, but he heard their laughter, muffled by metal. They swung swords that still dripped blood. He tried to keep running, but they left him no avenue of escape. He cowered in the grass before them, hoping that death would be quick.

One of the riders dropped lightly from his saddle, his leather armor creaking. He was hot in his leathers, for Shan could smell him strongly. The soldier said something in a language Shan did not know, but he could tell it was a rhetorical question from the tone: something like, "What have we here?"

"I haven't done anything," Shan squealed, but perhaps they didn't understand him.

The things those men made him do and did to him, Shan later blotted from his memory. They were without compassion and so full of mirth at their obscene attack, it was beyond the worst human evil.

They hurt Shan badly, and perhaps thought they'd killed him, because after a while, they got back onto their horses and rode away again.

Shan lay in the crushed grass, unable to see properly. His head was full of a buzzing sound and lights pulsed before his eyes. Carrion flies landed on his face and feasted on the crusts of blood and saliva and semen. He thought his body was broken beyond repair and dared not move. Every muscle felt wrenched and torn.

The moon rose above him, hung about with a pall of bitter smoke. He heard a vixen cry, and the contemplative hoot of an owl. Wide white wings crossed the clouds above his head. He heard their rattling whisper. Perhaps some of the forest folk would insinuate themselves into the night and come ghosting through the trees toward him. They might take pity on him, and remember the sweet-smelling posies he had left among the mossy roots for their pleasure. But no one came, and the land was quiet, holding its breath, its guardians still affronted and buried far deep beneath the soil.

Shan expelled a careful sigh. Must he wait to die? How long would it take? He thought he could hear ominous sounds in his body, as of vital fluids flowing through the wrong channels, pooling in dangerous places. Through his blurred vision, he saw his father standing over him, and thought that perhaps he'd been wrong about seeing him slaughtered. "You must get up, lad," said Hod and his face was a mask of grief.

"Dada," murmured Shan through his torn lips and tried to reach out with his bloodied fingers. But his father wasn't there at all. For only a moment, he thought someone else stood close to him, a young man, still and silent. He tensed in terror, but there was only the sky above him, and a few stalks of broken grass hanging over his face. The tears came then, although he couldn't give in to them because the sobbing would hurt his bruised chest. He set his face into a rictus of despair and the tears rolled coldly, but he was otherwise immobile.

He lay in the field all night, occasionally dozing, when horrendous dreams would fill his mind and slap him back to feverish wakefulness. The dawn came beautifully over the land, in a roll of mist that conjured every scent from the trees and the wild flowers and eclipsed the stink of burning. Some of the spirit of the landscape was creeping back, tentatively, in fragments. Shan turned onto his side and for a few moments hung poised on his elbows, panting. How was it possible to ache this much and not be dead? Would it take days to die? His clothes were torn to rags and stained with blood. Shakily, he got to his feet and then discovered, with some surprise, that he could walk, albeit stiffly. He could see immediately that the cottage was no more than a smoking tumble of charred beams and boulders. The willows too had been mostly burned and the pool was covered with an oily, ashy scum. What of the willow women, the spirits who lived within the trees? Had they fled or been destroyed? Shan made his way slowly to the gate and leaned there, suddenly terrified of facing whatever might be lying in the road. He hadn't the strength to bury what was left of his father. Would Hod's spirit understand?

Skirting the back of the ruined cottage, Shan peered up the road toward Holme. He felt he must go there, see if anyone was left alive. All was silent, and thin skeins of black smoke rose lazily into the dawn sky. He knew the soldiers and their beasts had gone. There was no sense of their presence.

Holme was no more. The village had stood for hundreds of years but had been destroyed utterly in only a couple of hours. Shan stumbled toward the old green, which was now a patch of mud and black ashes. Bodies lay everywhere, but Shan could not recognize them. He heard sobbing coming from the ruins, so not everybody was dead. Presently, some women, who had been crouched in a building that was still half standing, saw him motionless there, staring blankly at the carnage. Two of them came limping out to him, their bodies bent almost double, like those of very old women, though only yesterday they had been young. Their gowns were rags and their faces black with soot, streaked with tear trails. They were still weeping uncontrollably and the sight of Shan's half-naked body, his lower parts swathed in blood, made them weep all the more and put steepled hands against their mouths. For a few moments, sound faded from the world, and he was faced with a silent image of the lamenting women, their agonized postures, their twisted faces. The buzzing noise rose to a crescendo in his head, then abated, leaving a gleaming calm that tasted of metal in his throat. He realized in later years he had been lucky; the soldiers had thought him pretty enough to be an object of lust rather than simply fodder for their swords.

For three days the survivors lived numbly in the ruins. Nobody had the strength or will even to think about rebuilding, and in their shock they were cut off from the spirit of the land that gave them vigor. Those few men who had survived by running away came slinking back and buried all the bodies they could find. A few of the women went up to the manor house, but found only corpses blackening in the yard. The doors hung open; already wild animals had gone inside, and had eaten whatever edible things they'd come across. The manor seemed haunted now; the villagers did not stay, even though its untouched walls would have provided shelter for everyone left in Holme.

Back in the village, the survivors all ate raw vegetables from the fields, unable to face killing even a rabbit for meat. Blood scared them now. The god of blood had come visiting and put his mark upon them. He had murdered the God with no name and desecrated His chapel. The priest had been sodomized with a holy relic and left for dead. In his last agonized moments, one of the soldiers' beasts had chewed off his arms. Most of the villagers would never be able to take meat again. Few could talk about what had happened, and many sat rocking in the rubble with blank eyes, hugging their violated bodies, their faces masks of ash and pain.

On the first day, Shan went to wash himself in the river. He lay on his back in the water, with no thoughts in his head. If he closed his eyes, the sounds came back; cruel laughter, grunts and screams. At the same time, his nose would fill with the stench of sweat-soaked leather. He could not see how he would ever sleep again and stared up at the sky, his eyes watering because he was trying not to blink. He pictured the images of the three daughters of God hanging over him like clouds. They were not weeping, but serene, impassive. They are only clouds, Shan thought.

On the second day, dressed in clothes too big for him, scavenged from a house of the dead, he went back to his home. The men had removed his father's body and had buried it beside the willow pool.

There was a dark stain on the road where he'd been killed. Apathetically, Shan kicked through the rubble of the cottage, but could find nothing to salvage. For a long time he sat on the porch stone, which had survived intact. The sun beat down and conjured a heat haze in the dust. Behind him, the cooling charred joists creaked and popped. Birds were singing in the trees again, and cattle wandered aimlessly across the meadows. The future was meaningless. Shan was living utterly in the moment, and each that came was empty.

On the third day, a rider on a yellow horse came out of the east. He rode into the ruins of Holme and pulled his mount to a halt where the inn had once stood. "Do not be afraid," he called to the scuttling presences that had fled to hide themselves at his approach. "I mean you no harm."

He was very patient, and did not dismount, or say anything more. He drank from a water leather and leaned forward in his saddle, resting his hands on the pommel. It was difficult to see his face because he wore a hat with an enormous brim, but hazel-colored hair streamed out down his back. Eventually, a few of the villagers slipped shyly from their hiding places and watched him without getting too close. He nodded to them and lifted his head so that they could see his smile. His jaw was clean and well shaped. He looked to be a rich man.

"The demon of death has ridden through this land," he told them clearly but in a strange accent. "You are not the only ones to have suffered."

A woman dared to speak then. "What of Bischurch, Axenford and Willows?"

The rider lifted his shoulders in a shrug. "All gone. Like Holme."

A sob drifted out from the ruins. Some had had relatives in these villages.

"Why has this happened?" asked the woman who had dared to speak.

"There is no reason," answered the rider, "really. Greed, power . . ." He raised his hands, which were elegant and expressive. "You must carry on—as others have. The Magravands are your lords and masters now—unless you have the courage to fight them."

Few knew what he meant exactly, although some had heard of Magravandias. It was a distant country. "What do the Magravands want with us?"

"Land," said the rider, "more and more of it, until all the world bears the black and purple banner of their abominable emperor."

More of the survivors were slinking from their hiding places and among them was Shan. He stood looking at the rider, and experienced a hot pang of envy. How clean he looked, how content. Whatever he might say about the soldiers, it was clear he had not suffered personally at their hands. What right had he to come and talk to them so casually in their grief and despair? Shan picked up a stone the size of his hand, and threw it at the stranger. As it flew from his fingers, some of his anger went with it.

The horse reared and uttered a cry, for the stone had caught it on the wither. The rider nearly fell off, but managed to control both his posture and the animal before his dignity was entirely lost. For a few seconds, he looked very angry, and his fierce eyes scanned the crowd. "Too late for that!" he snapped. "It is not I you should assault with missiles! Did any of you raise your hands to the demons that destroyed your homes? I think not. You ran, you hid, you crouched and whimpered! Only a coward would attack a lone stranger who wishes you no ill."

"Go away!" someone yelled.

Shan had another stone in his hand, and was ready to throw it. It was conceivable the whole episode could have got entirely out of hand, because other survivors were now looking at the stony ground intently, their fingers flexing, images of their recent assault brimming through their minds. It would take only a couple more of them to find their courage and the stranger would be surrounded.

The rider must have known this, and maybe regretted his bald words. Perhaps he realized he had told them things they did not want to hear. They were scarred and grieving victims, ready to lash out only when they thought the odds were at last stacked in their favor. The rider scanned the crowd swiftly, then fixed Shan with a steady eye. He did not look angry now. Gathering up his reins, he urged his horse forward.

Before Shan realized what was happening, he had been grabbed and hauled up across the front of the saddle. Because he still ached so much, he could not struggle.

The rider wheeled his mount around in a circle a few times and addressed the astonished onlookers. "You will hear of this boy again," he said, and with these words, kicked his horse into a gallop, and careered off up the road toward the east.

THE RIDER'S NAME WAS Taropat and he lived in a high narrow house in the middle of a forest, approached by a winding track. He was, Shan quickly realized, a wizard. The journey took two days, and during this time, Shan tried to escape on several occasions. It was then he discovered that Taropat was no ordinary man, because all he had to do to halt the runaway was raise his hand and say a few words, and Shan would come tumbling down as if someone had cast a rope around his ankles. Taropat was a light sleeper, and no matter how quietly Shan tried to slip away at night, his attempts always failed. It did not stop him trying, however.

"Boy, give up," said Taropat, smiling, after the fifth abortive escape bid. He never bound Shan, or punished him. He did not have to.

Shan could not speak to him and only snarled and spat. He wondered if Taropat would do to him what the soldiers had done. This time he would die fighting. But Taropat did not come near him, except for the times when they rode the horse together, during which their proximity was unavoidable. As they rode, Taropat would ramble on, talking about distant lands, and demons and emperors and armies. Shan wanted to tell him to shut up, he did not care, but something had happened to his voice. It had flown away from him as if it had been a bird captive in his throat. Sometimes he could feel the ghost of its fluttering wings, but no matter how hard he tried, no sound would come out. Taropat did not seem concerned about this. "We will soon be there," he said, and then explained where "there" was. "No one can find my house, it is so safely hidden. It will be your sanctuary for a while." Shan did not question why Taropat had abducted him. It had simply happened.

The forest around the high, narrow house was very beautiful and very old, and the spirits of the trees were strong. As Shan and Taropat made the final stage of the journey along the winding path, ancient oaks seemed to reach out to them with gnarled hands. They were not angry hands, or cruel, but welcoming and curious. Shan felt as if they were riding through a silent, watchful crowd. Sunlight came down softly through the high crown of the forest; the deep green moss around the tree roots shone like crushed velvet. The forest was tranquil; birdsong was muted, but in the distance there was a chime of running water. Small purple flowers sequinned the short apple-colored grass that grew between the trees. Squirrels leapt across the path, but far over the travellers' heads, so that the heavy branches swayed and rustled. Shan could sense the presence of forest folk very near, although they didn't show themselves. He felt comforted. In such a place, he might heal, although his conscious mind did not realize that.

Shan grinned when the house appeared through the trees. It was such a ridiculous shape, he could not see how it remained standing. It stood in its own glade, which was dominated by a large pool fed by a rushing stream that fell over a lip of rock, braceleted with ferns. The house was attached to a water wheel, and rose above it in a crooked spire, crowned by an immense weather vane that spun round madly even though there was no wind.

"We are here," said Taropat and swung down out of the saddle.

Shan had been in a daze during the journey, but now they had reached their destination, a crashing wave of weakness broke over him. He felt exhausted, used up and withered and could not even find the strength to slip to the ground. He thought, I will never see my father again. It seemed impossible. How could life change so much so quickly?

Taropat lifted him off the horse and carried him toward the house. "You must sleep now," he said, "for three full days. In that time I shall conjure nymphs of respite to comb your mind with their cool fingers. When you wake, your grief will be raw and immediate, but at least there will be a wound to heal."

Shan wanted to say that he could not sleep properly, but his voice had not flown back to him. All he saw of the house, as Taropat carried him through its dim-lit rooms, were picture fragments: a high-backed chair; a tilted painting of a frowning face; the gleam of a crystal ball on a cluttered table; a tattered cloth hung from the ceiling; cracked paint on the walls beside the stairs. He was taken to a room where the light was green because ivy grew over nearly all of the narrow window. The air smelled of earth and ancient dust. Taropat laid him on a bed that was too soft; the billowy mattress seemed to swallow Shan up. His eyes felt gritty and it was becoming increasingly difficult to keep them open. He could not bear the thought of dreams and in anguish reached out and caught hold of Taropat's wrist, forcing all of his feelings into his reddened eyes. *Don't let me sleep! Don't make me!*

"Be not afraid," said Taropat gently, and his hand came down upon Shan's face like a swooping wing. The fingers were cool and soothing and Shan could do nothing but close his eyes. "I have put a charm on you," said Taropat. "Your eyes shall see nothing evil from within or without. If you dream, it will be of the distant past or the best moments of the future."

Shan did dream. He saw lands spread out below him, as if he were as big as a god. He saw the pageant of banners, horses, and castles steepled with a hundred flagpoles. The panorama of life revolved about him in a swirl of color and feeling. But all of this he forgot once he awoke. Only one dream stayed with him.

He saw himself as a very young child, sitting upon his mother's knee in the cottage garden, his head resting against her bosom. She was an apple woman, all rosy and ripe, in the time before the sickness took her breath. "Now, Shan, you be a good boy for your mammy. Keep yourself clean and always be polite—even to rude people. You have a secret eye inside your head that sees into people's hearts. Learn how to open it, for you will need it." She tickled his stomach to make him laugh, and Shan could hear his own merriment ringing out in the summer air. Then his mother turned her head to the road and said, "Oh, I have a visitor." She put Shan down beside her chair, where a bowl of podded peas was lying. He saw her walk to the wicket gate and there was a tall dark figure, who had come to put his mark upon her. She came back frowning. "Now that's a strange thing. I saw a man standing by the fence, but then he was gone."

He is still with you, Shan thought, and could see a shadow hovering tall behind his mother's body.

When Shan woke, the dream seemed so real, he wondered if it had ever really happened. As the images faded, he became aware of his surroundings and knew he was in a room that now belonged to him. He didn't know it, yet it was familiar, and he felt at home in its ambience. It was dark, but cozy like a den, and cluttered with items he might have collected himself: strange stones, pieces of gnarled wood, bright feathers from magical birds, twisted rods of metal that might be the spears of lightning gods. After this awareness had settled, Shan's grief made itself felt. It seemed to have been waiting next in line. Shan was too appalled to weep. He felt ashamed, terrified, and in indescribable pain, both in mind and body. His own cruel ordeal, the utter injustice of the death of Holme, the brutal waste, were beyond his comprehension. The soldiers were not a conquering army but a plague, striking people down at random. Shan knew little of war, but understood that it was the commerce of kings and generals. What had simple villagers to do with it? And surely war meant fighting on both sides? No one in Holme had had the chance to fight. They had been murdered, the victims of a lust that could only be sated by blood and pain. What kind of people were the Magravands? He remembered the two soldiers who had raped him in the field: their demon helms high above him as they circled their horses, the red sunset gleaming on their black leather armor, and the smells of leather, sweat and blood. Firmly, he forced this image from his mind. He did not want to remember any more.

Then Taropat came into the room carrying an enormous bowl of porridge. Shan's body responded immediately; his stomach growled and his mouth filled with saliva. He had not eaten properly since before the soldiers came.

"Now you are ready to begin again," said Taropat, sitting down on the bed and offering Shan the bowl.

Shan took a mouthful of the porridge, then felt sick. He was hungry yet couldn't eat.

"Force yourself," said Taropat firmly, "or I shall have to sit on your chest and feed you myself."

Shan opened his mouth and a croak came out, the sound that an injured crow might make.

"That's better," said Taropat. "Now eat. I shall let you do so in private. Then, when you are ready, you will find clothes in the chest, and you may dress yourself and come downstairs. You have slept long enough."

Left alone, Shan took small mouthfuls of the sweet porridge and although it took him nearly an hour, cleaned the bowl. It made his mouth feel dry and his stomach swollen, but there was a new strength in his body.

On top of the chest against the far wall was a large cracked bowl and a jug of cold water. Shan drank some of the water, poured the rest into the bowl and washed his face and hands with it, then he went to the window and looked out. The waterwheel was turning slowly, making a grinding noise. Beneath it, the pool looked deep and dark and watchful, vibrating with unseen life. Bright blue birds flashed in the sunlight, flying so fast Shan could not make out their shapes. Perhaps they weren't birds at all. The yellow horse was tethered below his window, cropping the lush grass. Beyond, the soughing green shadows of the forest hugged the house in its glade like giant hands. The air seemed to shimmer with the immanence of the guardians of the land. It was an idyllic scene. Shan wondered then what Taropat wanted from him. Was he seeking an apprentice, or had he just felt pity for the grubby urchin scrabbling through the ruins of Holme? What made people perform acts of kindness? Perhaps Taropat wasn't really kind. It was difficult to tell. He could be fattening Shan up to eat him. Shan remembered his mother's words in the dream. He wanted to open his inner eye that could read the hearts of men.

2

THE HİGH ΠARRΦW HOUSE

TAROPAT HAD A FAMILIAR, a grim named Gust. When Shan first came downstairs into the kitchen and caught sight of the creature, he started gasping and panicking. Gust was squatting on top of the stove, hunched like a gargoyle. Taropat, who was sitting smoking a clay pipe next to the hearth, his stockinged feet resting on the hot-stones, sat bolt upright and uttered a few words that somehow forced Shan to calm down. "Don't be afraid of old Gust," he said. "He may look a bit fearsome, but he's a pleasant enough beast."

Gust was black all over and had gleaming red eyes. His face wasn't human at all, and he had long, shining claws, leathery wings and a tail. He was the size of well-built child. Later, Shan discovered he could disappear from one place and appear somewhere else at will. It became a game of his to hide in the rafters of the rooms and drop objects down onto Shan, such as bobbins, and saucers and gobbets of mud. But in those first few moments, Shan saw only a demon in the hearth and feared that his suspicions about Taropat's nature had proved correct.

"Sit down," Taropat said. "You cannot speak, so I must ask myself a question aloud that I know is in your heart."

Casting nervous glances at Gust, Shan sidled across the room and sat down on a wooden seat at the table, some distance away from Taropat's upholstered chair. Gust watched him unblinkingly, occasionally letting a string of drool fall from his jaws.

Taropat took a draw from his long, narrow pipe, his teeth clicking against the baked clay. "You must be wondering why you are here." He glanced at Shan quizzically.

Shan kept his face expressionless, made no sound.

"You must not be afraid. Nothing here will harm you. All I want is that you should heal. The body is one thing, the heart another."

Shan still felt unable to react, but this did not appear to bother Taropat.

"When you are ready, I will talk to you about the future, but in the meantime get to know my home and find the part of you that fled your body in Holme. Now, will you send to me the shape of your name?"

Shan frowned, but immediately as Taropat had spoken, he couldn't help thinking of his own name.

"Shan," said Taropat. "A good name."

This man must be very powerful, thought Shan. It still puzzled him why Taropat had chosen him from all the survivors, and despite appearances and soothing words, there might still be a sinister reason behind what seemed to be charity. Yet in his heart, he felt safe. Perhaps for now he could dare to believe he was.

For two weeks, Taropat left Shan on his own for most of the time. The wizard often shut himself away in a room that was an extension to the house at ground level. Shan never went into this room. For the first few days, he was nervous of leaving the glade, for the spirit presences among the trees beyond were far more powerful than any he'd sensed before. The house had a number of sheds and outhouses, which Shan explored. They were full of interesting items, some broken, that kept him amused. Gust seemed curious about him, and followed him around, always keeping a distance between them. After a few days, Shan got used to the grim's strange appear-

ance, and began to welcome his company. Gust was like an animal.
He did not expect Shan to talk, but seemed simply to like being with
him. Shan remembered his aunt's cat, and how it would follow her
around. It never liked to be picked up or fussed, but was always near
her. Something that felt like a spike of iron pierced Shan's heart. He
realized it was the first time he'd thought of his aunt since before the
soldiers came. She had not been among the survivors, yet he'd not
even looked for her body. She'd simply disappeared from his memory.
He too had been like an animal for a while, dehumanized by the
horror of his experiences. Shan sat down in the dust and wept, for
his father and for his aunt. The grief hurt so much he could hardly
breathe. His gut-deep sobs were inadequate expressions of his feelings.
His face pressed against his knees, Shan became aware of something
warm and living touching him. He looked up and saw Gust's grotesque face very close to his own. The claws of one hand were resting
lightly on Shan's shoulder. Gust made a noise, a mournful whining
growl. His long forked tongue flicked out and licked Shan's cheek.
Perhaps he liked the salt taste of tears. Shan reached up and gently
ran the fingers of one hand down Gust's arm. The hide felt alien, hot
and scaly. He had never touched anything like it before. All his life,
he'd sensed the presence of spirits and forest folk, but Gust was the
first nonhuman sentient creature he'd seen. Living in Taropat's house,
he might see more.

Shan didn't know whether he was allowed to bathe in the mill
pool or not, but as Taropat was hardly ever around, decided to do
so anyway. Sometimes, when he ventured into territory which he
shouldn't, Gust would somehow let him know by becoming agitated,
or hissing. As Shan stripped off his clothes beside the pool, Gust
merely crouched on the waterwheel, nibbling his claws, which Shan
took as a kind of permission.

The water was incredibly cold, very clear and had a wonderful
taste that was almost sparkling. Shan imagined it was what an elden
draught would taste like, that magical potion the elden sometimes gave
to human folk to give them wondrous dreams by which they were
ensnared. Shan had been scared by stories of the elden as a younger
child. His aunt had comforted him by saying that there were no elden

haunts by Holme. She knew that because the villagers never found changelings in their children's beds and no one went missing mysteriously. The elden were very beautiful, but were so different from men and women, it was impossible for humans to comprehend their abstract morals. "To them, we are like animals," said his aunt. "If a man or a woman loved a cow, that would be most unnatural, which is why I don't believe any of the stories of people having elden lovers. It just wouldn't happen. They do like to steal people, though, and make them dance to death, or drink peculiar philters that do strange things to the mind. They also find human babies fascinating. I've heard they always get bored of them after a while, as some people get bored of puppies, and then they leave them to die." She had frowned. "I don't know many humans who'd leave a puppy to die, but still, elden are not like us."

If there was a place where the elden had a haunt, the forest around Taropat's house was it. As Shan floated in the chilly water, he shivered, suddenly aware of the rich, mysterious ambience of the glade, its deep-breathing watchfulness. His aunt's cat had always warned her of unseen presences by staring at places where there was nothing to be seen. Shan decided that Gust would perform the same function, and at present the grim was still happily engrossed in cleaning his claws.

Shan put his head beneath the water and exhaled a plume of bubbles. As they cleared, he caught a glimpse of a sly pointed face in the depths below that was arrowing toward him. He'd never moved so fast, and was back on the bank in moments, hugging himself, staring at the deceptive waters. Perhaps it was not a good place to bathe after all.

At night, lying drowsily awake, with the moonlight falling through his open window, Shan would hear Taropat's muffled voice somewhere in the house below him. It would sound as if the man were chanting, or reciting something. Spells, thought Shan, afraid and thrilled. Once he had a strange dream, where it seemed he woke up and went to his window. Out in the glade, Taropat was walking toward the trees. Shan could see him clearly in the moonlight. A pale, flickering shape like a marsh light was hovering through the forest, and presently emerged as a young female thing, who burned white like a flame, with smoking blue hair. Then its form shimmered and it changed into something else, a human boy with pale hair. It's an eld, thought Shan, ducking behind the curtains. Had Taropat been bewitched? Would Shan be left here alone? He dared to peer out again, and the glade was empty. A fist of panic thumped him in the stomach, and then he was waking up, lying in his bed. It had not been real. He heard the eerie strands of Taropat's chanting voice drifting up the stairs.

Although Shan did not try to speak aloud, he chattered to Gust constantly in his head, supposing that the grim could hear. After a week or so, he dared to venture into the forest. Gust scrambled up trees and jumped through the branches. Everywhere was unbelievably green, even the great trunks of the oaks and the beeches. Once Shan was sure he saw a group of aspen women dancing in a glade. When he crept forward to spy on them, he saw it was only a shimmering rainbow dancing over a waterfall. Perhaps.

Another time, Gust offered him a red, fleshy flower, which he had plucked from high in a tree. He gestured that Shan should eat the petals. Filled with a sense of daring, Shan did so, and after a while, began to see spirits everywhere. Panicking, he tried to run blindly back to the narrow house, and got lost. Taropat found him some time later, huddled amongst a nest of tree roots, his hands over his eyes.

"I'd advise you not to eat anything Gust offers to you again," was all he said, then led Shan home. There, he gave him a foul-tasting drink and presently reality reasserted itself. Gust crouched on the stove looking slightly abashed. Shan could not feel angry with him. He felt that Gust had only tried to give him something he sensed Shan wanted, something for which he was not quite ready.

If Gust became Shan's friend, the same could not quite be said for Taropat. In the mornings, Shan would come downstairs and find that some breakfast had been left for him, and he would eat alone in the kitchen. Sometimes, Taropat would be present at midday, when he'd nibble a frugal lunch, but he'd always have his nose in a book, and hardly seemed to notice that Shan was there. In the evenings, he became a little more companionable, and would read to Shan from history books, although the history was bizarre, and rarely involved human folk. Shan supposed they were just stories, although Taropat would say it had all really happened. At these times, Shan wished he had a voice because his mind would be full of questions. He discovered that the inner voice is easier to ignore than the spoken word. If he formed questions in his head, Taropat would rarely answer them properly, although it was clear he knew what was on Shan's mind.

One morning, Shan woke up with dry eyes, and instead of feeling a painful hard lump in his chest, he was filled only with a wistful melancholy. He thought about how all the memories of his father and aunt were happy. Other children in the village had had stern parents, and had been beaten, but his own recollections were of laughter and warmth. He had worked hard, and it felt strange now to be so idle, but his life had been simple and good. It was gone forever, and whatever future he had would be far larger than any he could have expected in Holme. It was as if he had to wrap it up in leaves and bury it among the roots of a tree, like an offering to the guardians. It was over.

Feeling strangely elated, he washed and dressed and went downstairs, thinking that he and Gust could go further afield in the forest today. The morning felt so enchanted, something marvellous was bound to happen. He was surprised to find Taropat sitting by the hearth smoking his pipe, just as he had been on the first morning Shan had awoken in the house.

"Sit down," Taropat said, and his voice was stern. "Now I must talk to you."

Shan did so, filled with apprehension.

"The whole of history is made up of stories, you know," continued Taropat airily. "Everything has a beginning, a middle and an end. Like life. You understand that?"

Shan nodded slowly.

"Well, the beginning of your story is nearly over, and soon you will reach the really interesting part. The middle is always the longest bit." He paused. "Do you follow?"

Shan shrugged uncertainly.

"Stories happen around us all the time. Some are marvellous, some poignant, while others are tragic. Some are long and last for centuries, while others endure only for an hour. Who can tell when a story really ends?"

Shan wriggled uncomfortably and wished Taropat would get to the point.

"The Magravands are part of a long and gory epic. It might have happened that their story never touched you—but that was unlikely." He pointed at Shan with his pipe. "In any case, now you *are* a part of it, whether you like it or not."

"No," said Shan, a shaky word. Its arrival surprised him more than it appeared to surprise Taropat, who made no comment.

"Yes," he said softly. "That day I found you, I was looking for a boy, a particular boy. It was important to me that he did not miss his destiny. Why do you think the soldiers wanted to kill everybody? It wasn't just blood-lust, no." He stood up. "Come with me. I want to show you something."

Shan followed Taropat to another room. This was clearly his study or workroom, being an extension to the main building at ground level that was the largest room in the house. Its length was filled with tables and bookcases and strange mechanisms whose purpose were not immediately obvious. Taropat sauntered into the room, and reached out with one hand to set an astrolabe spinning. "This is my temple," he told Shan.

Taropat paused at a table midway down the room, and sorted through the clutter that covered it. "Ah, here . . ." He summoned Shan to his side. "Do you know what this is?"

"No," croaked Shan, looking at what appeared to be a quantity of black ink confined between two sheets of glass and surrounded by an ornate wooden frame. The liquid flowed back and forth as Taropat tilted the frame.

"It is a portable scry mede. Very useful." Taropat cleared a space on the table between them and laid the object on it. "Now look. If you concentrate, pictures will form in the medium. That is how I learned the fate of the villages around Holme."

Shan glanced at Taropat in amazement, then stared down at the scry mede. Try as he might, no pictures came. "I can't see . . ." he said.

"Well, it takes practice," Taropat said, seemingly amused. "The trouble with this type of information is that you never get the whole story, just tantalizing fragments. For instance, I learned that Magravandias is on the move again, after what we must suppose was a winter break. At first, I didn't know where they'd strike, but they'd been moving close to Breeland with every year's campaign. Then, I discovered that the emperor's magi believed that a threat lay in our humble land, which must be destroyed at once. A potential leader had been born—always a bother. Hence, I suspect, the genocidal sweeps." Taropat paused and straightened up. "I went out to find this person, to save them from the slaughter." He sighed. "Unfortunately, I was unsuccessful. The Magravand magi were too thorough. By the time I reached Hambone, the boy was already dead. Doubly dead, you might say, and the sight was not pretty. So, the hero is dead and the legend is over." He smiled in a private kind of way, the light in his eyes turned inward. "But then I thought, it doesn't have to be. I shall throw myself into the arms of chaotic forces. I will roll a die at every crossroads to choose my direction. This led me to Holme. When you threw the stone at me you happened to fulfill a prophecy I had made up during the journey. I said to myself that whoever, out of all the wretched people I saw, presented to me some kind of spirit, they would be the one. I let fate sniff out the potential." He put a hand on Shan's shoulder and spoke theatrically, his large dark eyes rolling. "You, my boy, are that potential."

Shan stared up at Taropat in terror. The man was mad. It was all the more horrifying because he clearly believed absolutely in what he was saying. "Not me," said Shan. "No."

Taropat put his head on one side and cupped his well-shaped jaw in one hand. "Hmm. Perhaps. However, what I forgot to mention in the other room is that the endings of stories can be changed by clever individuals, and whether you are a potential hero or not, I intend to make you one."

"Why?"

Taropat laughed. "The standard answer, I suspect, is 'because I can.' Do I have a great love for this country? Not particularly. I could ply my arts anywhere, perhaps even in the court of the emperor, which would be a great irony. I am not a flag-waving sort, although I don't approve of brutality, especially if I have to witness or experience it." He sighed. "I suppose, like you, I have been chosen for a role. It was not my idea in the first place."

"Then whose?"

Taropat's eyes took on a sparkle. "Ah, that would be telling. Let's just say it was the voice of a god in my head. I have to do what he wants, otherwise he'll become affronted and might make things inconvenient for me." Taropat sighed. "Ah, you look so stricken. Don't worry. The fact is, if the Magravands believed they have killed a future leader, we might as well give them another one. It amuses me to inconvenience the empire."

"You be this hero, then."

"Me?" Taropat chuckled. "No. I excel at arcane arts and like telling people what to do, but I hate responsibility. Training you will be an interesting project, a gamble, if you like. Who knows where it may lead?" He began to walk up and down beside the table, gesturing. "The Magravands' story has to have an end, because every one does. Empires rise and fall; that is the way of the world. They become too big at the top and topple over. When that begins to happen, an enterprising soul can take advantage of the situation. It won't happen yet, but it will. We have to play a long game." He stopped prowling and cupped his chin again. "Come, come, there is something else you must see."

Shan followed him to another table further down the room. Here, the aqueous light of the mill pool outside fell into the room in mysterious rays, illuminating what seemed to be an enormous game spread out on the tabletop. There was a map, divided into hundreds of countries, all of which were covered in different-colored beads. "Help me scoop up the men," Taropat said. "Sort them into colors."

Shan did as he was bid, until all the beads were separated. Taropat sifted through the largest pile, which was black, with his long fingers. "Now watch." He scooped up the black beads and dumped them onto one of the larger countries. "That is Magravandias and her armies, all

clustered together in a hideous mound. Ah, they are on the march!"
He placed some of the beads on adjoining lands. "Now, they have to
keep a strong garrison in these places to keep hold of what they've
gained. Never know what might be rising up from the rubble! But
that means they have fewer men at home to send further afield." He
spread all the beads out on the board. "Now do you see? The armies
are spread thin, and easier to pick off."

"They'll all group together, though," Shan said, getting into the
spirit of the idea. "Then they'll squash the new leader in the first
country he takes."

"If he was stupid enough to remain there, perhaps," Taropat said,
"but if the Magravands panicked and did that, it would leave other
captured lands even more vulnerable, wouldn't it?"

"Then the leader would have to have a scry-mede like yours,
only powerful enough to tell him what the Magravands were doing
all the time." Shan's eyes took on a feverish gleam. He pointed to
the board, to the central country where only a single black bead
remained. "The weakest land would be Magravandias herself, right in
the heart of the empire!"

"Well done!" said Taropat. "Time for lunch. Are you hungry
again yet?"

Shan nodded, then laughed. "I can talk again," he said.

"Can you?" said Taropat, and ushered him from the room.

They ate thick white bread and strong peppery cheese at the
kitchen table, while Gust munched on a piece of coal atop the stove.
"How old are you, boy?" asked Taropat.

"Fifteen, nearly sixteen," Shan answered. He felt excited by Taropat's ideas. It was all so unreal, just like a game.

Taropat nodded. "Hmm, that gives us a few years to play with."

Shan grinned. He couldn't believe Taropat was so serious. "How
will you train me?"

Taropat fixed him with dark eyes. "Well, we shall start small.
You need to be educated, because there are few things worse than an
uncultured barbarian. I shall pass certain aspects of my wide knowledge on to you—in a discerning manner, of course—and then we
shall see about the rest. Fighting and leadership are not just about

athletic skill and brute force, or even cunning strategy. My task, as I see it, is to build your character and your spirit. There will be other teachers for you afterwards. There always are."

Shan chewed thoughtfully for a moment, then laid down his bread. "I haven't thanked you," he said. "You saved me."

Taropat's face darkened. "If I'd really saved you, I'd have come before you lost your innocence in that vile way."

Shan reddened. He had a feeling Taropat had seen what had happened to him in the scry mede.

"Never doubt," said Taropat in a low, terrifying voice. His eyes looked wild, insane. He leaned toward Shan, who shrank away. "I have seen the harvest of Magravand lust a thousand times. It took from me all that was human, all that could feel. There is a debt to pay, a debt of the soul. I cannot lead an army, and fighting disgusts me, but destiny, or the forces of chaos, saw fit to equip me in other ways." He bunched a fist before his face, the knuckles straining white. "Nothing happens by chance. Nothing. Especially not if you put your will into living."

Shan swallowed with difficulty, feeling slightly light-headed. He sensed then that Taropat was a man with a great hurt deep within him that only vengeance might allay.

"Whatever!" Taropat leaned back again, apparently relaxed, and took a bite of cheese. "Every experience, however disgusting, builds character and is the will of the gods. Would you like some ale with that bread?"

Shan nodded, once again mute, but this time from fear. If Taropat believed people could change the end of stories, why did he believe in the will of the gods? Shan couldn't ask. He drank the ale that was given to him and stared back at Gust, who was flaring his nostrils on the stove.

3

BASILISK HUNTING

LIVING WITH TAROPAT by the mill pool, Shan lost
track of time. Perhaps it didn't pass at all and they existed in a
strange reality beyond the world of men. Sometimes, when Shan
awoke in the morning, he had the strangest sensation he'd been asleep
for weeks. Most days, Taropat would take Shan with him into his
workroom, so that Shan could watch him working. Taropat spent
hours concocting peculiar philters with the most arcane equipment
imaginable, which often created only an abysmal stinking fluid that
had to be poured away. The more successful mixtures Taropat kept
in labelled jars on a shelf, then apparently left them there forever. He
began to teach Shan about the properties of plants, the phases of the
moon and the movement of stars. He would take the boy into a bare
room off the main chamber, where he usually performed magical rituals, and there instruct Shan in the use of the scry-mede. Try as he
might, Shan could never see anything in it but darkness. He was never
invited to attend one of Taropat's rituals, for which he was grateful.
He was sure he would be terrified.

As well as this more esoteric training, Taropat introduced Shan to the wonders of books. Shan could already read and write, albeit rather ineptly, but he had never read a whole book before. The experience amazed him. Lost in someone else's words was like living another life. It made him realize how big the world was, and that an infinite number of things were going on all the time beyond his limited perception. If I owned a thousand books, thought Shan, I need never leave this house. Everything in the world could be seen through the eyes of those who'd written the stories and histories, who'd lived them. He mentioned this to Taropat, who only smiled. "One day, perhaps, you will write your own." Shan didn't want to think about that. He was happy with his life of study. He didn't want to leave the tall narrow house and its surrounding forest, ever.

One morning, Taropat announced after breakfast that the day had come for Shan to take his education further. "You will go to a friend of mine who lives nearby," he said. "His name is Master Thremius and he is a great magus."

Shan was surprised by this. He'd believed they lived far from anyone else and said so.

Taropat laughed. "This forest is like a vast brain full of little cells, and in each cell is a thought. The thoughts are witches, sorcerers and mystics. It is an odd community, and it took me a while to get used to it myself. I have kept people away from you because you needed time to be alone."

Shan did not like the idea of having to meet other people. He enjoyed his simple existence with Taropat. Nothing much was happening, true, certainly nothing to do with the great destiny Taropat claimed to have created for him, but privately Shan was relieved about that. He'd believed that if he kept quiet and obedient, cut wood, tidied the house and helped tend the garden, it might never be mentioned again.

"Don't worry," Taropat said. "Thremius has an apprentice, a girl near your own age. It's about time you started making friends again."

NIP WAS SEVENTEEN years old and lived with Master Thremius in the hollow of an ancient oak. Their dwelling was extended by a lean-to of mud and sticks. When Shan first visited the place, he couldn't believe how an old man and a young woman could live together in such a small space. Then he discovered that there were rooms underground, beamed with arthritic tree roots.

"The rooms go so far down," Nip explained, "that they lead into tombs and the palaces of kings who were buried by earthquakes."

Shan very much wanted to believe these tales, and hoped that he would one day see the evidence for himself.

Gust had taken him to the glade and he'd first seen Nip sprawled along a wide lichened branch, picking at her toenails with a short knife. At first, he thought she was a boy. When she spotted Gust, she said, "Hello, grim thing. How are you today?" and made some coaxing noises one might utter to a cat or a dog in order to make friends. Then she caught sight of Shan. "Oho, what's this?" Her voice suggested she looked forward to sport of some kind.

"Taropat sent me," Shan said. "I'm here to see Master Thremius. He's going to teach me."

"You'll have to wait," Nip said. "He's busy. Sit down. What's your name?"

Nip appeared to be an almost unnaturally open person. In no time at all, she had told Shan a great deal about herself, while displaying not the slightest curiosity about him. Shan kept quiet, eyeing the great tree nearby and wondering whether Thremius would make an appearance in a puff of smoke. Nip was a gamine creature, with a pixielike mien, her hair hacked short and sticking up in rather greasy spikes. Shan couldn't decide whether she was pretty or not. Taropat had told him Nip was close to his own age, but then Taropat had probably forgotten how only two years' difference might as well be a decade to people in their teens. It was clear from the outset that Nip considered Shan to be a mere child in sore need of education. She dressed like a boy, ragged trousers rolled up to the knees and a grubby oversized shirt, and scorned girlish pastimes, yet she was quite sure she would be a witch when she was older, which to Shan seemed an essentially feminine career. It would be easy for her to work magic, she said, because she was not quite human.

"Not human in what way?" Shan inquired, involuntarily wrinkling up his nose.

"My grandfather was an eld," she announced with due reverence.

"How do you know?"

"My grandmother got lost in the wood one day, and even though everyone looked for her, she was nowhere to be found. She returned some months later and was heavy with child. She could remember nothing of what had happened to her. My family drew their own conclusions."

Shan could think of infinitely more mundane explanations for this event, but held his tongue.

Then Master Thremius came grumbling out of the tree and laid about him with his staff. Nip clawed her way swiftly up the gnarled trunk, while Shan froze.

"Brats," said Master Thremius and eyed Shan from his great height with a less than tolerant expression.

Thremius looked more like a wizard than Taropat did. He had a long beard and hair, which was probably grayish white under normal circumstances, but had been dyed by the juices of root and stem into a dirty green color.

"What are you here for?" he demanded.

"Taropat sent me," Shan replied, adding, "Sir."

"I don't want any more brats," said the magus, "be off with you." He went back inside the tree.

Shan looked up into the spreading branches and saw a brown face grinning down at him. Presently, Nip dropped onto the grass beside him.

"Let's go hunting," she said and without waiting for a response set off down a dark and tangled path behind the old tree.

"What are we hunting?" Shan asked, catching up.

"Basilisk," replied Nip. "I hunt nothing else."

"What is basilisk?"

"You'll know when you see one," Nip said. "Don't tromp along so loudly. They'll hear us."

Shan wondered what he was doing following this strange girl.

Taropat had sent him to Master Thremius to learn, even though Shan had no idea what that education might entail. He supposed that was the way of magical men. They liked to confuse you. Still, Thremius clearly had no intention of doing any kind of educating. Perhaps Shan should go back to the narrow house now, find Taropat and explain. He couldn't quite bring himself to suggest this to Nip, however.

Presently, they came to a glade in the wood that had a horrid furtive ambience and a brown stain in the middle where the grass didn't grow. Shan shivered. He sensed watching eyes. Birds did not shun the place but those that did rustle the high branches uttered calls like spiteful children. Nip prowled around the edge of this natural circle, occasionally sniffing the air. Perhaps this was the haunt of basilisks. It seemed to Shan as if the sun was suddenly much lower in the sky and the shadows of the trees were hungrier. He wanted to leave but lacked the courage to say so.

"Shh!" commanded Nip.

Shan neither breathed nor spoke.

Nip stood straight, hands on hips. "Yes, they were here again last night. I can always tell."

"Who?" Shan murmured.

"Elden," Nip said. "They know I look for them, but they are capricious. They hide. No doubt my grandmother lay with an eld of great status. They resent me for that."

The mood in the glade was broken. Shan crossed the dark stain. "I thought we were looking for basilisks."

"We are. You just walked across the spoor. Elden roast basilisk. It is the rarest, most delicate meat. They will have been hunting here, like me. But last night, I don't think they caught anything."

"What does a basilisk look like?"

"That depends," said Nip. "They can look like bristling hogs, a thorny bush or a bird whose feathers are made of claws. They are kin to the snake and the vulture."

"Have you ever seen one?"

She hesitated. "I will, one day."

"Are they dangerous?"

"Sometimes. They are timid, mostly." Nip grinned rather cruelly. "Haven't you learned anything living with the renowned Taropat?"

"I haven't lived with him long," Shan said. "He hasn't taught me much yet except . . ." He couldn't speak.

"What?" Nip's voice was softer. She clearly detected a sorrow.

Shan shrugged. "My family is dead. Taropat took me away. It was when the Magravands came."

Nip nodded. "Oh yes. I know of that." She put an arm around Shan's shoulder and he could smell her scent of sweat and leaves. "But we're safe here, very safe. This great forest is like a special temple. No Magravands could breach it. It would separate them, confuse them, devour them. They are creatures of fire because they worship the god Madragore. Doesn't earth contain and smother fire?"

Shan laughed shakily. "I hope so."

"But it is true! We have the potential to be far more dangerous than soldiers."

"Through magic?"

Nip uttered a scornful sound. "Magic! Is that what you call it? It is the true temperament of the world, that's all, the true science, the true will of nature."

Shan could tell these ideas were not Nip's own. "Master Thremius taught you that?"

She nodded. "It was the first thing he taught me."

Shan sighed. "Now I have to report to Taropat that the master will have nothing to do with me."

"What do you mean?"

"You know. He hit me with a stick and told me to clear off. I've learned nothing."

Nip's laugh was a wild free sound that filled the glade. "You ninny! Are you really that stupid? You've already learned a lot."

"Like what?"

Nip pulled a ridiculous wild-eyed face at him. "Basilisks? Magic? What an air brain you are!"

"You think you've been teaching me?"

"Well, who taught me?"

"I don't think that was what Taropat had in mind."

"You mean you don't think my knowledge, which I've learned from Thremius, is as valid as the words coming from his own mouth." She laughed again. "You have so much to learn, village boy!"

Nip was obviously very proud of her knowledge, and Shan had no doubt that she knew far more than he did, but wasn't there a higher source? Nip was young, like he was. One thing Shan was wise enough to be aware of was that he had limited experience, simply because he was young. His father had once said to him that knowledge came from experience. This was when one of their goats had become ill. Shan had panicked, unable to help, but Hod had known what the problem was right away. Why? Because he'd seen and dealt with it before. Nip didn't think like that. She thought she knew everything.

As they walked back through the forest, Nip chattering all the time, Shan thought about what he'd learned from the devastation of Holme. Could he deal with a situation like that if it should happen again? He could run away sooner, maybe, or be more alert for danger. He shouldn't take security and peace for granted. Was that knowledge or simply fear? Shan was confused. Perhaps Taropat would discuss it with him, although he doubted the possibility.

"You must come again tomorrow," Nip said, once they'd reached the hollow tree again.

"So you can teach me?" Shan asked archly.

Nip ignored the tone of this remark. "Have you got anything better to do?"

"I'll talk to Taropat."

"He'll tell you," Nip said. "You'd best get back now. An innocent like you should not be alone in this part of the forest after dark."

Shan stared at her for a moment. "I'm not as innocent as you think," he said.

Nip had the grace to look away. "It was fun today. I get bored on my own sometimes. See you tomorrow." She went into the tree and Shan heard a low voice mumble a rebuke. Master Thremius no doubt.

––––––––

BACK AT THE NARROW house, Taropat had dinner ready. "Well?" he asked, the moment Shan came in through the door.

Shan sighed and with some embarrassment described his day.

Taropat only nodded. "Thremius will do what he thinks best. Go along with the girl. It can't do any harm. You can maybe teach her too."

"I don't think you understand," Shan said. "Thremius wants nothing to do with me. If Nip is to be my teacher, my education will be long. I don't think she really knows that much more than me yet."

Taropat laughed. "Thremius is being clever, that's all. He's not a bad old goat at heart."

"But what am I supposed to be learning? How to hunt for basilisks?"

Taropat became still, and for a moment Shan saw the most unspeakable expression of grief in his eyes. "You are learning about yourself," he said. "Such knowledge can defend you better than a sword or armor. Such knowledge gives you arrows of the mind. It is the most important thing."

That night, Shan awoke to a sound. He thought at first that Taropat was chanting again. The sound reverberated through the whole fabric of the house, shook it on a level that was almost beyond human perception. It was the sound of weeping. Shan lay in his bed, utterly chilled. That sound contained all the fear in the world, all the misery. Was that the sound of the magician's self-knowledge?

4

TALE OF THE DRAGON LORD

S HAN RETURNED TO the hollow tree shortly after sunrise. Taropat had not been evident that morning, but Gust had been hanging around the kitchen making odd mooing sounds. Shan had suggested the grim should accompany him again. Now the creature rustled the undergrowth some yards from where Shan stood, looking at Thremius's tree house.

"Hello?" Shan called.

Silence reigned. Birds were motionless in the branches above. A sense of abandonment pervaded the scene. Shan was torn between going to investigate the innards of the tree or returning to the mill house. He walked around the glade, gazing up at the fabulously gnarled bark. The tree was so ancient it seemed sentient, watchful. Shan touched the trunk. A growling sound erupted behind him. He turned to see Master Thremius rushing out of his house, brandishing his staff. His eyes seemed to spit flames. Shan shrank away in terror.

"Still here?" snapped Thremius. His staff whistled close to Shan's ear. At that moment, Gust erupted, flapping, from a nearby stand of thorns, uttering outraged screams. Thremius adjusted his aim and beat at the grim in fury. Shan called out to Gust, thinking they should both flee the place as quickly as possible, but then Nip came sauntering down one of the forest paths, sucking nonchalantly on the stem of a flower. She smiled a little when she saw what was happening and clapped her hands. Thremius paused in his attack. "Ah, there you are, girl," he said. "What is the assumption today?"

Nip put her hands in her pockets and came to a halt before her teacher. "That we can assume nothing," she replied. "We should live in a state of constant wonder."

Thremius's heavy brows beetled together. "A simplification," he announced. "I have ordered this whelp from my presence, yet he remains. I can only assume he is a numskull."

"He is just persistent," Nip said. "You should be flattered."

Thremius bared his teeth at Shan and went back into the tree.

Shan felt in a state of shock. He could only stare at Nip. Gust still appeared to believe he was under attack because he was fighting air ten feet above the ground. Nip looked up and whistled. Did the air shimmer? Gust calmed himself and alighted beside Shan, purring in concern.

"Ready for a walk?" Nip said.

THEY WENT TO A place where small hard fruit grew on low spindly trees. The forest felt different there, more approachable. The colors of the foliage were predominantly strange bluish greens. Nip did not comment on what had taken place back at Thremius's glade and Shan, for some reason, could not bear to question her about it. He felt peculiarly shamed. Nip made soothing noises and balmed a graze on the grim's shoulder with spit on her finger. Gust had sprung to Shan's defense. He had taken wounds.

"Taropat wept in his bed last night," Shan said, unsure what had impelled him to reveal such a thing.

Nip raised her eyebrows. "He is a puzzlement," she said, putting her finger back into her mouth. She applied another ointment of saliva to the grim, who squatted motionless before her. "I think he's a fabulously handsome man, who I could fall in love with, yet at the same time he does not seem like a man at all. I'm quite sure he'd never love me back. I like going to his house on Thremius's errands, just so I can look at him, but he's never noticed me."

Shan was quite awed by the fact that Nip considered a man like Taropat should find her attractive. He couldn't imagine it himself, but felt he ought to offer some sympathetic remark. "Perhaps he doesn't notice anyone in that way."

"Mmm," said Nip. "Thremius won't tell me much, no matter how hard I pester him, but once he did tell me that Taropat carries a wound in his heart that has gone quite black."

"I think so too. Sometimes you can see it in his eyes."

Nip nodded. She seemed overly concerned with the grim, who to Shan did not appear that badly hurt.

After a pause, Shan said, "Do you know why Taropat brought me here? Has he spoken to Thremius about it?"

Nip flicked him a glance. "One magus is not required to inform another why he takes an apprentice."

"It's not just that," Shan said. He wondered whether he should tell Nip everything, but perhaps that would be unwise. He didn't know her.

Nip frowned and knotted her hands in her lap. "Thremius has said only that Taropat wants a weapon against the Magravands. Maybe that's you."

"Me? It's ridiculous. It's ridiculous to think that any one person could be that."

Nip shrugged. "Perhaps. But everyone has to do what they feel is right in life. Taropat has personal motivations. I can't tell you what they are, because even if Thremius knows, he hasn't let it slip to me."

"Don't you think I should know?"

"Yes. Probably. But that is up to Taropat." She leaned forward. "And yourself, of course. You are a willing conspirator in his dreams. Understandably. He offered you sanctuary when you sorely needed it. He wants to train you for a purpose, this is clear. And if you go along with that, without knowing all the facts, that is the fault of your silence rather than Taropat's secrecy, surely."

Shan felt glum. "I don't think he'd tell me anything if I asked.

Taropat and Thremius aren't like ordinary men." He reflected for a moment on how Nip seemed to exert a certain measure of control over her cantankerous mentor. "How was it between you and Thremius when you first went to him?"

Nip smiled. "I was confused for over a year, thinking I was stuck inside a particularly horrible nightmare. Thremius was a monster, in all senses. Sometimes he didn't even look human."

"Why is he like that if he wants to pass his knowledge on?"

"Perhaps he's resentful of that need. He's an insular creature, yet is aware his knowledge is too great to die with him. My mere presence reminds him he is mortal, although I expect he will live the equivalent of four lifetimes before he finally succumbs to death." She laughed. "He cannot always practice what he preaches. That is the unfortunate nature of knowledge. It is better to learn than to know, because even when you know, you cannot always live by it." She patted Gust's shoulder; he purred and rubbed his scaly cheek against her hand. "A creature like this has more chance of being himself than you or I. We are imperfect creatures, the hybrid offspring of gods and humans, or so Thremius told me. We have the aspirations of the divine, yet the instincts of beasts. It is why we are always fighting each other and ourselves."

"I saw nothing divine in the Magravands."

Nip shook her head. "But you are wrong. They are creatures of the great god called Madragore." She lay down on her stomach before him, her chin cupped by her hands, her legs kicking the air behind her. "I can tell you what I know. The Magravands are ruled by a sun king, an emperor, whose name is Leonid Malagash. He has many sons, who are all rivals, and a Dragon Lord called Valraven Palindrake leads his armies. This Palindrake is supposed to be a very handsome man, though of course I have never seen him myself. He is married to an imperial princess, Leonid's only daughter, and is said to be a lover of Prince Bayard the Golden, one of the emperor's sons. He comes from a magical land called Caradore. There is a wonderful legend attached to it. Palindrake is a singular creature."

"You sound as if you approve of him," Shan interrupted. "How can you? He must have led the army that killed my people. My father was gored to death by a war beast. All the men were slaughtered, the women violated. I don't even know what happened to my aunt. I was . . ." He shook his head, close to tears, choking on the remembered stench of leather and sweat.

Nip reached out quickly to touch Shan in reassurance. "Oh, I didn't mean to hurt you. I'm really sorry. I'm stupid sometimes, insensitive, perhaps too much like Thremius at times."

Shan rubbed his eyes, embarrassed. "It's all right."

Nip hesitated for only a moment, then pressed on. "Let me tell you about Caradore. Can I?"

Shan nodded.

"Hundreds of years ago, the Palindrake family communed with the sea dragons, who live in caves around the coast. They were heirs to a great heritage, and magic ran in their veins. But then, Caradore was conquered by Magravandias. The Magravands knew that they could never control the world unless the land of the sea dragons was firmly under their control. The dragon heir, the first Valraven, who was only a boy at the time, was forced to make allegiance with the empire, and one of his sisters was married to a son of the emperor. The Magravand magi used their arts to make him do as they decreed. He was only a boy, poor thing, but through his action, the link with the sea dragons was lost to the Palindrakes. Caradore was put in chains. Isn't that terrible? Every firstborn male of the Palindrake family has been named Valraven ever since, probably as a reminder. A gruesome mixture of shame, anger, resentment and sorrow must flavor their lives. Imagine it!"

Shan was silent for a moment. "Whatever some magi did hundreds of years ago, it's seems a poor excuse for someone to be a butcher now."

"Maybe it isn't a poor excuse," Nip said. "Maybe the Dragon Lord is as much a victim as . . . other people."

Shan considered this, surprised to find her words didn't anger him. "You clearly believe so."

Nip hesitated a moment. "I don't think the world is a place of black-and-white truths. It's more complex than that. Think about it. If you were a Magravand, you'd believe with your whole heart that you were an avatar of good and that everyone else in the world was ignorant, dangerous and destructive. You have to remember that while the empire sweeps across the land, it seeks to impose a divine order."

Shan shook his head angrily. "I can't accept that. You didn't see what happened in Holme. It was pointless cruelty. They revelled in it."

Nip nodded thoughtfully. "I have no doubt of that, and it appalls me too. But Shan, in order to be wise, you have to rise above the world and look down. See things from a wider perspective. You could say that the emperor is not entirely responsible for what happens in the furthest corners of his empire. All he has is his dreams, his beliefs, but they become diluted or warped as they filter down through the ranks. The Magravands are human, the soldiers perhaps more so than those who control them. War does strange things to men. It is the smell of blood. It makes them more beastlike. They crave it. They do not see fellow humans before their weapons but simply something they must destroy, dismember and defeat. The emperor himself does not walk upon the battlefield. He lives in his gilded palace, dreaming of a perfect world."

"Then he is a fool."

"Foolish," Nip corrected. "Deluded. Thremius once said to me that Leonid has unleashed a power in the Dragon Lord over which he has no control."

"How do you know all this?" Shan asked. He was thinking about how Nip lived deep in the forest, far from anywhere. Did Master Thremius go out into the world to gather news, or did he employ an arcane art like Taropat, a scrying tool? Shan still had difficulty believing valid information could be acquired that way.

Nip wrinkled up her nose and clasped her knees with her arms. "It is our business to know," she said, "because it affects us. If something happens in Magravandias, we can feel it here. The power that men crave is related to the power of nature. It is simply that they do not understand it. It is not a tool to wield, but a state of being."

"How do you know, Nip?" Shan repeated gravely.

"Spies," she answered, and jumped to her feet. "I'll show you a spot where the power gathers. Come along, grim thing!"

Shan followed her down a narrow forest path, rugged with tree roots, while Gust leapt from branch to branch overhead. Spies? He was unsure of this answer. Nip spoke with so much authority and eloquence, and seemed far older than her years. This was clearly the consequence of education. She must have lived with Thremius nearly all her life.

The path began to slope downward, pitted by channels where in winter and early spring water would run. Nip sprang nimbly down the path, while Shan was more cautious, stepping sideways. Gust flew before them, uttering unrestrained gibbers of delight. Stones shifted beneath Shan's feet. The slope was long. It would be painful to roll all the way down it.

At the bottom, they came to a glade where a natural spring rose up through the earth. Tiny snaking rivulets stole through the grass and the ground was marshy. Nip jumped from tussock to tussock, leading the way to a deep pool overhung by willows. Gust settled himself in a tree and began preening himself.

Nip, much to Shan's embarrassment, began to pull off her clothes. "Come on," she said. "Into the water."

Shan was reluctant to undress himself in front of the girl. He stood some distance back. Nip's body was nut brown, as skinny as a boy or an elden maid. She ran into the water, throwing up a spray. "Come on!" she urged. "Are you so bashful? What's the matter with you. I've seen a thousand naked boys."

Shan could not believe this assertion. He laughed nervously. "You haven't."

"Of course I have. Thremius is a healer. We treat people every day. We take off their clothes." She grinned at him. "Shan, you mustn't be shy of yourself. That is another lesson." With these words, she plunged beneath the water's surface, and presently Shan saw her head bobbing some distance away, below a fringe of willows. Stiffly, he undressed himself and gingerly entered the water. It was freezing cold. Nip was nowhere to be seen, but then her body erupted from the pool only inches from Shan's face. He yelped and winced away. Nip laughed. "That's better. Can't you feel the power here?"

"It feels very cold," Shan said. "Is that a sign?"

She shook her head. "No. Water attracts the life force and spring water more than most. Bathing in this pool can heal a hundred hurts. Just lie back and try to feel it."

"What's it supposed to feel like?"

"Tingling," she said, floating beside him, her face turned to the sky. "All through you."

That's just the cold, he thought, but let his body hang in the water as hers did. It was silent now, but for the soft chuckle of the pool and the breeze in grass and leaves. Nearby, a lone bird released a stream of shrill notes. In response, a squirrel chattered, high overhead. Shan closed his eyes. There was an ache behind them. He felt slightly disoriented, as if something were pressing hard against his head. It didn't feel pleasant. He opened his eyes, gasping.

"There," said Nip. "You felt it, I can tell."

"I feel pressure," Shan said. "It's horrible."

"You're not used to it," Nip said. "You will be, one day. That feeling is the building block of magic, your body's experience of the life force."

Shan still wasn't convinced his experience wasn't simply an effect of the cold. He began to swim around, trying to bring some warmth back to his limbs.

"You know what I think?" Nip called, still floating on her back in the middle of the pool.

Shan trod water some distance away. "What?"

She swam toward him. "If you ever hear Taropat weeping again, which you will, you must go to him. That would be the time to ask questions. His guard would be down then."

"That seems sneaky."

"Only if you look at it that way," Nip said loftily. "Another way of looking at it is that Taropat has needed someone to talk to for a long time. You could help him. Hasn't he helped you?"

SHAN AND GUST RETURNED home just as the sun was sinking into the arms of the forest. The glade was filled with a beautiful ruddy bronze light that made the yellow horse, who stood dozing under the eaves of the house, appear to be made of pure gold. The tiles of the roof looked as if they'd been painted red, while, incongruously, the trees and grass seemed to shine with a green light. Taropat had laid out supper on a wooden trestle in the garden. As Shan emerged from the forest, Taropat came out of the house carrying a big tureen, his hands shielded by tea-cloths. He whistled a greeting to Gust, who flew over to him and enclosed his master's shoulders with his leathery wings. Shan's heart ached as he gazed upon this scene. He would remember it always.

"Had a good day?" Taropat said as Shan sat down at the table.

"Yes, Nip and I went swimming. She doesn't have much modesty, does she?"

Taropat laughed. "I wouldn't count that as one of her attributes, no." He ladled out some fragrant carrot soup into bowls. "Here, eat this. Although I say it myself, it is nectar of the gods, enlivened by a dozen different herbs."

"Nip thinks you're fabulously handsome," Shan said, unable to quell the devilish urge to tell tales.

Taropat laughed. "Does she now?"

"Yes. Do you think she's pretty?"

"Nip would bite off my nose if I called her pretty," Taropat said.

"Do you like her though?"

"Not my type," Taropat said, "but you don't have to tell her that. Now shut up and eat."

Shan had wanted to use this bit of gossip about Nip as a path to more pressing topics, such as what else Nip had revealed to him that day. But Taropat clearly intended to dominate the conversation, perhaps because he sensed some of what was on Shan's mind. Shan ate quietly, as Taropat regaled him with tales of Nip's and Thremius's eccentric behavior. "He once hung upside down for a week and made Nip speak to him backwards. It's no wonder she's a bit odd."

Shan normally enjoyed listening to Taropat's tales, but as time went on, he felt increasingly tense. Unspoken words bulged in his throat. Halfway through the main course of roast pheasant and succulent vegetables, he blurted, "Nip talked to me about Magravandias today."

Shan sensed immediately a stillness come into Taropat, which the man sought to disguise. "Did she?"

"Yes, she told me the story of Caradore, about the Dragon Lord." Taropat laid down his knife and fork and spoke in a slow, steady voice. "Those are subjects which I suppose it is essential you know about eventually."

"She seems to think Valraven Palindrake is a victim. I think she wanted me to think we were similar in some way."

Taropat's face had gone very white. He stared at his food as if it were poison.

Shan wished at once that he could retract the words, because he could tell he'd said something terrible. "I don't agree with her," he stammered. "I mean, I don't know anything. It was just what she said."

"Valraven Palindrake," said Taropat as if the name burned his mouth, "is a monster in every sense. You must never, ever think otherwise. I shall have to speak to Thremius about this. What is he thinking of letting that wretched girl think that way? I can't have such obscenities spoken to you."

Shan had the impression Nip's opinions derived from Thremius's own, but decided it would not be a good point to make. "I didn't believe her," he said, then couldn't help asking cautiously, "but is it true about Caradore, the sea dragons and everything?"

"Caradore exists," Taropat said fiercely, "and perhaps the dragons did too, at one time. But the Palindrakes are foul creatures. They are immoral, corrupt and bestial. No one other than Valraven Palindrake could lead the Magravandian army. He is its heart. He is like Bayard, Leonid's degenerate son, who is equally demonic. They deserve one another."

Shan considered these words. Taropat clearly knew a lot about the subject, perhaps more than Nip did. He realized these people, mere names to begin with, were somehow coming alive for him. He was desperately curious about them. "But did it happen the way Nip said, about the first Valraven and what the Magravandian magi did to him?"

"It happened," Taropat said. He picked up his knife and gripped it firmly as if he wanted to stab something. "But the Palindrakes now are very different from their ancestors. They were stripped of their nobility and goodness. What lives in Caradore today is evil incarnate. It was the most beautiful country in the world, but now it is ruined. It began a long time ago but Bayard finished the job. Caradore has become a ghost country, a sad memory."

Shan said nothing more. It was clear he'd touched upon a topic personal to Taropat. There would be no point in pushing him further, because Taropat would only get angry. Shan sensed he was close to the secret he knew existed in Taropat's heart, but also knew he must wait to discover it. He remembered Nip's advice. There would come a time.

IN THE NIGHT, Shan awoke to the sound of a voice singing softly. It came from outside. He slipped from his bed and went to the window where the curtains hung open. The moon was a slim sickle above the trees, but clear starlight illumined the glade below. A pale, glowing figure hovered at the edge of the forest, crooning a song that could break the heart. Shan stared out of the window. He wouldn't run away this time. He should go down to the glade and confront this creature. If it was an eld, he wanted to see it.

Swiftly, he pulled on his trousers, and still half-dressed, hopped down the stairs to the dark and silent kitchen. It was only when he reached the door that he saw Taropat was already out in the garden. The man was making the most peculiar sounds, wordless cries of anger and despair. He shook his fists in the air, apparently addressing the pale form half hidden among the trees.

Shan hurried forward softly. He was just behind Taropat when the strange figure appeared to notice him. It uttered a threatening hiss and then streaked off through the trees. Taropat leaned down to rest his hands on his knees, his head hanging between them.

"Taropat," Shan said. "What was that?"

For some moments, Taropat neither answered nor straightened up. When he finally looked at Shan, his face was wet with tears.

"What was it?" Shan repeated, awkwardly.

"A torment," Taropat answered. He collapsed onto the grass, where he sat with his head in his hands, his shoulders shaking.

This is the moment, Shan thought, but didn't know how to proceed. He'd never had to deal with a stricken adult before. It seemed wrong to see a grown man weeping, not because it was unnatural, but because it was so much more powerful and frightening than the grief of a child.

Self-consciously, Shan squatted beside his mentor and gingerly patted his back. Should he speak, remain silent, what?

After some moments, Taropat raised his head, which he shook slowly. "This should not still be happening. I hoped you being here would stop it all."

"Stop what?" Shan asked.

"Today," Taropat said, "when you spoke of Palindrake, it revived unwelcome memories. Nip had a tale to tell, but so have I. She thinks Palindrake is a victim, does she? She's wrong. What you just saw here is a small part of it, a legacy."

"Tell me," Shan said bravely. "I must know."

Again, Taropat shook his head. "It would burn out my voice to speak of it."

"No, it wouldn't," Shan said. "I think you've needed to speak for a long time. Trust me, Taropat. Please. Let me help. If I am to be what you want me to be, I must know everything."

Now, Taropat nodded. "You are right. I must remember who I am, what I believe." He stared at Shan for some moments. "If I tell you this tale, it might shock you. It will change your view of me, I think."

Shan shrugged, unable to think of anything to say that didn't sound trite.

Taropat rubbed his face, then stood up. "Very well. Let's go back to the house. I'll open some port, because the story is long. Can you stand a night without sleep?"

"Yes," Shan said.

Taropat put his arm around Shan's shoulder. "It begins," he said, "with the story of another man of Caradore. He was a friend of Valraven Palindrake, married to his sister in fact. Like Palindrake, when he came of age, he was forced to go to Magrast, the capital of Magravandias, in order to train in the imperial army. His name was Khaster Leckery. I will tell you the story of his death."

5

THE ANCIENT WOUND

KHASTER WAS DRUNK when he went to the Soak. He'd not been back long from Caradore, and on his return to Magrast, his Magravandian friends had commented on his strange mood. He drank more than he usually did—far more—and his performance suffered accordingly in the training yards. It was noted that Khaster no longer spent any time with Valraven Palindrake, but then neither did Prince Bayard. What had happened in Caradore? Khaster, Valraven and Bayard had left Magrast together, to spend some rest time at Valraven's ancestral home. Yet they had all returned separately. Whispers had started up. People speculated that it was something to do with Khaster's wife, Pharinet Palindrake. She was a wild one. Had to be. She was Valraven's sister after all. Everyone knew how highly Valraven regarded her. Perhaps too highly? He'd always spoken about Pharinet more than he ever did about his own wife, Khaster's sister, Ellony.

One evening, in the sumptuous, wood-panelled lodge attached to the barracks, where all the officers would gather before going out into the city, a strange meeting between Bayard and Khaster had been witnessed. The prince had come in, his eyes as hot as fever, and had approached Khaster at one of the gaming tables. He had leaned down, muttered urgently in Khaster's ear. Later, all present had confessed they'd thought a fight would ensue, but Khaster had merely looked up, as white as a corpse, and hissed, "You lie!"

"I do not," Bayard said. "Ask him."

Ask who what? They all wanted to know, but Khaster had said nothing. He'd stormed out of the building and no friendly hand could bar his passage. His mouth had been a grim line and it did not change after.

Bayard had shrugged and grinned and ordered merlac from the bar.

"What did you say?" someone was brave enough to ask.

"The truth," Bayard had answered, taking a sip of the stinging liquor. "But he didn't want to hear it."

What Bayard had done, in fact, was merely confirm a painful suspicion that Khaster had harbored even while still in Caradore. He would not speak of it, he couldn't. He couldn't even think of it. But clearly rumors had leaked through. Only two days later, someone had asked him, grinning, "Wife playing up, then?"

Khaster merely gibbered a dark response. He hadn't told them that Pharinet was only half of his problems. Betrayal was one thing, grief another. His sister, Ellony, had died while he'd been at home. He hadn't told anyone about it, or the circumstances surrounding it. It was supposed to have been an accident, but Khaster didn't believe it. He was sure Bayard had Ellony's blood on his hands, but couldn't prove it. And wasn't Khaster himself stained with it? He'd been weak, unable to take action, unable to save Ellony from her fate. For that, he despised himself.

A week or so later, a group of the young blades of his regiment approached him. It was clear they felt sorry for him. By that time, information had filtered down from Prince Gastern's office concerning the death of Ellony Palindrake. An accident had occurred. Valraven's wife had drowned on the wild beach beneath the family castle.

The officers said to Khaster: "We're going to the Soak later. Come with us. Drown your sorrows."

Khaster, whose mood was so black he felt as if he himself had become an incarnation of evil, said, "Yes. I will."

Previously, he had avoided jaunts into this area of the city with his colleagues. The officers of the Magravandian army were all high-born young men, and the Soak was where the lowest scum of the city floated upon the many putrid canals, hid beneath the rotting walkways, cackled in the dimly lit taverns. Highbreds went there because they wanted to be daring. They wanted to sample a Soak urchin, on a stinking tarpaulin under the awning of a barge.

Khaster knew his friends were surprised he'd agreed to go with them, and that amused him. They'd always thought him to be prim and prudish, but had forgiven him these sins for his generosity, his good humor, and, because that was the way of Magravandian bravos, his beauty. But he was someone else now. A man had left Magrast, a naive foolish idiot, and a crawling demon had returned, bile dripping from its heart. Valraven would be proud of him. He'd seen nothing of Valraven since leaving Caradore. Khaster had ridden back to Magrast separately, on a fast horse, which had been virtually dead on its feet by the time he'd spurred it through the great black gates of the city, where colossi of the god Madragore snarled down upon any who approached his sacred center. Blood had stained Khaster's boots. His horse had wheezed and frothed and shivered as he leapt from its back in the stable-yard. The grooms had looked at him askance. What had happened? Khaster was a mild, polite man who cared for his horses. The grooms had glanced at one another. Something terrible had occurred.

Khaster had never experienced such enduring rage before. He was consumed by it. He had become it. Alcohol dulled it, and sensation, crude sensation. The Soak now seemed his natural environment. He had never been there before, but when the carriage drew to a halt at the Penthion Bridge, and his companions tumbled out laughing raucously, Khaster felt, with a masochistic satisfaction, that he was coming home. His condition confused him, because in his heart, he knew he had done nothing himself to create it. His wife had, the harlot Pharinet. Valraven himself had, and his repulsive catamite, Prince Bayard. They were the evil cabal. It was they who had caused the death of Khaster's sister, who had plotted together, drunk on power and lust. He despised them. Hated them. Hated himself, for his weakness, because inside his heart was bleeding. He wanted things to be different.

Rufus Lorca, Khaster's closest companion, if any Magravandian could own such a distinction, draped an arm around his shoulders. "Buck up, Khas," he said. "Forget your troubles. The Soak awaits us with its vile pleasures." He laughed, gesturing widely at the darkness ahead of them, the labyrinth of streets and canals lit by a thousand sick yellow lamps. Khaster could smell it, the age, the dissolution. At one time, it had been a fashionable district, being the great docks of the Leonid Canal that curved from the city, through a couple of foreign lands to the sea. Magravandias was landlocked, but earlier emperors had expanded upon the existing canal network. The main flow was as wide as the great river of Mewt. The present emperor's father had commissioned a new docks area on the outskirts of the city. Magrast had grown over the centuries and it was considered both savory and convenient that the docks should be far away from the residential districts. The old docks were too small a warren in any case. Some of the larger ships couldn't squeeze in between the spongy jetties. The Soak was earmarked for redevelopment, but so far it hadn't happened. The emperor had other things to squander his re-sources on, such as war and conquest. Now, it was home to the lowlife of the city. Past glories moldered in the shadows. Any illegal com-merce took place there. It was in the Soak that the lethal drink, harm, was brewed, known as the Red Witch, the Blood Stealer. Harm was one of the primary reasons the highbreds went to the Soak. It could be purchased easily enough from the back cupboards of fashionable city taverns, but somehow consuming the stuff in the cradle of its creation was more decadent, more dangerous. Under its consciousness-altering effects, any young bravo could be robbed or even murdered by a sly Soak whore.

"So will you talk of your troubles?" Rufus asked Khaster, who had squirmed away from the friendly embrace. "Come on, now, we've known each other a time, tell me."

"Do you want me, Rufus?" Khaster asked coldly. "If so, forget it. You needn't bother showing concern for my well-being."

Rufus laughed uneasily. "Someone has burned you, haven't they? You should tell me. I will help you plot revenge."

Khaster broke away from the group, staggering backward, arms spread wide. "*This* is my revenge," he cried. "The Soak and all her filthy guises. I will sample them all." He released a hysterical laugh and began to run, but because he was stumbling dangerously close to the poisonous waters of the Eel Stream, a minor tributary of the Leonid, his companions dragged him back into their midst.

"Has the Red Witch warmed his belly already?" someone asked, only half in amusement.

Rufus shook his head. "No, only my father's good merlac. We had a snifter or five before we joined you."

"He's left his head in Caradore," another said.

"Or his heart," Rufus added.

"Don't break yours," someone said. "He's a strict mother's boy." Such was the term Magravandian bravos used for men who sampled only the carnal delights of women.

The group meandered along the narrow alleys, where the commerce of the night was already in progress. Khaster had to pause to throw up into a stream. Rufus made worried noises, glancing over his shoulder because the rest of their group had been diverted into an inn by the imprecations of harlots on the street outside.

"Stand up, Khas. They've gone inside. It's not safe out here."

"Who cares," said Khaster, wiping his mouth. "Your father's merlac was bad. Look what it's done to me."

"It was the three bottles of wine you had before the merlac," Rufus said dryly. "Come on, Khas. Do you want to get us robbed and flayed?"

The Old Drake was an establishment typical of its kind. Once across the threshold, patrons were engulfed by a damp, hot smoke of cooking meat, steam from the wine cauldrons and the effluent from smokers' pipes. Bodies heaved and milled among the tables. At the back of the room, two thin girls danced to a jig performed by five musicians with fiddles. The floor was wet with vomit and liquor, but on the walls shiny brass lamps spilled a mellow light. Velvet drapes looped across the ceiling, dangling tassels that were sticky and blackened. The smell was sweet, perfume cast over rot. Khaster slumped onto a chair and rested his elbows on a table, his head between his hands. Through his fingers, he could see the Drake was full of soldiers and the sons of city lords. The only locals were the servers, the whores and the entertainers. After some moments, Rufus came to the table. "There's a private room free, though it cost us a wallet. Come on, Khas, you can't stay out there." Already some of the whores were sidling close, like predators, their fingers itching. They could smell easy prey.

Khaster staggered to his feet and let Rufus drag him through the crowds. People called out greetings to them, spangled girls with dirty fingernails pawed their coats, but then they were through and a glass-panelled door was open before them. Rufus pushed Khaster through it. Beyond, their companions were already seated around a table, in the ghoulish light of a lamp with a green glass globe from which a gilded fringe depended. The matron of the inn, Dame Sally, stood dressed in red satin beside the table. In her hands, she held the tools with which she would conjure delights for her customers. She grinned at the new arrivals. "He looks done for already, sir. Are you sure you'll risk the Witch on him?"

Rufus deposited Khaster in a chair, from which he nearly fell. "Perhaps a measure of Waters of Life to clear his senses."

"No," snarled Khaster. "Give me the Witch."

"Khas . . ."

"I'm all right. Give it to me."

"After one, he'll be on the floor," someone said. "Let him have it, Rufe."

Sally removed the glass globe from the lamp, using a thick velvet cloth to protect her hands from the heat. Once the wan flame was revealed, she poured out the harm into a shallow silver dish. This she held over the flame with tongs. Presently a steam arose from the liquor and a tart reek. Sally threw crystals of dark resin into the bowl and the steam took on a more aromatic note. "Ah, she's hungry for you, my bold lads," Sally said. "When she perfumes herself so swiftly, it's a good sign." She poured the liquor into five silver cuplets. These were downed, one after the other, in quick succession.

The cruel bitterness of the drink drew claws down Khaster's throat. He craved that feeling. It was as if a creature were captive in his brain, punching his skull, trying to get out. But he did not fall as his companion had suggested. The Red Witch cleared his sight. Every sense felt honed, alert, precise. Perhaps the Witch, with her magical spirit, was preparing him for what would happen that night. He would need his senses, his strength.

Even as Sally was preparing the second draught, the door to the room flew open. Everyone looked round in annoyance. Some got to their feet, about to remonstrate. Then they sat down again, ducking their heads, muttering respectful greetings. Another group of men had come to the door, led by Prince Bayard himself. Bayard was feared above all others. He was capable of anything. He had the Dragon Lord in his bed—or used to. There had been rumors of an estrangement, but Bayard would not speak. Valraven too held his silence, but had barely been seen since he'd returned from Caradore. Now, all the company speculated on what had taken place in that wild country. What would happen now, with Khaster Leckery and the prince together in one small room?

"Ah, a party," drawled Bayard. He was like the light of the sun itself, so beautiful and golden. But, like the sun, his heat was fierce and merciless. He was powerful enough to give life, but could take it too.

Khaster had not looked round. He only became aware of Bayard's presence when he heard the voice. Now, he froze. His first instinct was to attack. The Witch suggested he should do it, but he knew that would be foolish. The others would have him off within seconds. He clasped his hands together on the table, staring at the white knuckles.

"Well, well, well," said Bayard, sauntering across the room. "The cuckold is here. How are you, Khaster? Well, I trust?"

The Witch clenched her claws in his brain. Be cool, he told her. He smiled and turned round. "Very well, my lord. And you?"

Bayard eyed him coldly through narrowed eyes. "In top form."

He rubbed his hands together and beamed at the proprietress. "We've come to sample your naughty red lady, Sal. Have we enough chairs?"

"I'll see to it, my lord," Dame Sally said, curtseying low. "At once."

While this was being attended to, Bayard sat down on the remaining available chair and his cronies began to chat with Khaster's friends. Khaster could feel the blood beating in every inch of his veins. He could see its red bubbling behind his eyes.

"Khaster," said Bayard, and his voice was low, confiding, without the usual barbed edge.

Khaster feared that tone very much. He looked up, said nothing.

Bayard was stuffing a pipe with zeg weed, a narcotic import from Mewt. "It is not my wish for us to be enemies."

"Nor mine," said Khaster, thinking: why? Bayard had never really spoken to him before, other than on that night in the officers' lodge. Then, Bayard had only made contact to inform Khaster that his wife, Pharinet, was guilty of infidelity. "She is making a fool of you," Bayard had said coldly. "You should know about it. She and Val have been lovers since before you were married to her."

The fact that Pharinet's secret lover was her own brother was disgusting enough, but Bayard had also taken obvious pleasure in telling Khaster he'd bedded Pharinet himself. He'd made it clear he'd despised the Leckery breed. Was this unexpected approach now an indication of the estrangement with Valraven? Was Bayard seeking information or, Madragore forbid, an ally?

"I was not responsible for what happened," Bayard said, lighting his pipe. "It was the Palindrakes. They are tainted." He raised a hand. Perhaps some fire had come into Khaster's eyes he could not feel. "I do not wish to insult your wife, of course, but . . ."

"Why not?" Khaster said. "I don't care about it. Say what you like."

Bayard again eyed him speculatively, perhaps thinking that here was a new creature to snare, to use. Bayard always needed plenty of creatures to deal with the intrigues at court.

"The Palindrakes are inconstant. We cannot rely upon their loyalty. This we have learned in a hard manner. Perhaps we have both been foolish."

Do not include me in your ranks, Khaster thought. You are scum, as bad as they are. He smiled. "I would prefer to forget the whole incident."

"I have been thinking of sending something to your mother, for condolence over poor Ellony," Bayard said.

Khaster was surprised the prince remembered his sister's name. "That is a kind thought."

"Not much comfort, really, of course, but I feel a gesture should be made. Your family has long served the empire. I am so sorry that . . ."

"Please," Khaster said, "there is no need." He could not bear to talk about it, could not stand hearing his sister's name upon this monster's lips.

Bayard nodded. "I understand." He took a draw off his pipe. "My brother, Almorante, tells me you are up for promotion. That is swift ascension. You are well thought of."

And could be more so, Khaster thought. But what will be the price? He shrugged. "I do my duty."

Dame Sally had returned to brew more harm. The company was convivial and conversation flowed freely around the table. Laughter became louder. Khaster writhed in his seat. Bayard's presence scorched him. He hated the false intimacy, the insincere concern.

The prince's group had a teenage boy with them, a girlish creature, clearly a carnal toy. He was a pretty thing with long white blond hair and the eager, willing manner of a puppy. He smiled, laughed, pushed back his hair flirtatiously. Khaster stared at him in disgust, imagining him old and withered, burdened with a thousand regrets.

"Sing for us," someone said. "Sing a love song."

"Sing a lust song," Bayard said. "Sing it for me."

Khaster noticed the boy hesitated, just a brief moment, and an expression came over his features that was much like fear. But it was quickly smothered. He knew his part and opened his mouth to sing a sweet song, of love and of lust also. The men started to sing along with him, then Bayard's arms snaked out and dragged the boy onto his lap. Khaster saw the panic in the boy's eyes, the urge to struggle, to escape, hampered by the knowledge it was a prince who held him. If Bayard wanted him, he must comply. That was his function. Khaster swallowed hard. He did not want to see this. It sickened him.

"Come now, Tay, don't be coy," Bayard said. "I've always coveted you. You know that, don't you, hiding as you do behind Almorante's bed curtains. He's not here now. Give me a kiss."

The boy glanced at one of the prince's companions, and Khaster divined this must be the person responsible for the boy's presence there that night. He saw the man shrug slightly. He would not interfere. How could he?

"My lord," the boy said, his hands flat against the prince's chest, pushing himself away. "I cannot . . ."

"Oh, you can," Bayard drawled. "Just a little kiss. Almorante won't know, will he, lads?"

The company all assured him he wouldn't.

"There, you see. We are effectively alone. We can do anything and no one will see. They are blind to us." His hand dived between the boy's legs, squeezed hard, conjuring a pained yelp. Bayard laughed.

Khaster found he was on his feet. What was he doing? This was madness. "Let him go," he said.

Bayard looked up, grinning. "Why? Do you want him?"

The Witch cackled in Khaster's brain. Now that he was standing, he realized how drunk he was. He couldn't take Bayard on. "Maybe I do," Khaster said.

Bayard expelled an immense laugh. "You? I don't think so." He eyed Khaster for a moment longer, then took the boy's face in his hand and kissed him savagely.

Khaster rubbed his hands over his face. He could not bear the sounds, which were like the cries of a puppy alone, afraid, in pain. "Stop it!" he said. "Are you so depraved?"

"No," said Bayard. "This is Almorante's rutting cushion. He's used to it."

The boy broke away from Bayard's kiss and appealed to Khaster with his eyes. "Help me." The words were barely spoken, a silently mouthed plea.

"Valraven has broken your heart," Khaster said. "But that is no reason to hurt another. If you must inflict pain, find your Dragon Lord, do it to him." The Witch controlled his tongue. He was too drunk to speak so clearly, so eloquently.

Bayard's beautiful face had become hard. "You know nothing of my affairs."

"I know he's shut the door on you," Khaster said. "You are right. We are both fools, but perhaps you more than me. Val is like me. He's Caradorean. However you seduced him, the glamour's gone now. You'll never have him back. He'll be repulsed by you, mourning for his wife, who but for you would still be alive. Val is devastated about her. Your perversity could never replace a wife's love. I know this. I know him better than you do." It wasn't true, of course. Khaster suspected Valraven had never loved Ellony at all, and Bayard himself must think that too, but Khaster knew his words would still hit the mark.

The room had fallen silent. They were all terrified, Khaster thought. No one could predict how Bayard would react to this. He might leap up, skewer Khaster with a dagger. He might order his cronies to do it. But no, he merely laughed, although his eyes remained cold. "It was thoughtful of you to tell me this in front of so many."

"Let the boy go," Khaster said. "You are forcing him against his will."

"Creatures such as him have no will," Bayard said, sneering, but he pushed the boy from his lap, without even glancing at him. "Maybe you are turning, Khaster. Maybe you're not as chaste and holy as you like to think. It'll do you good. You bored Pharinet half to death. She needed real men in her bed. Take the boy. Let him fuck you. It might even make a man of him."

I have to escape, Khaster thought, feeling so weak and sick he could not even consider Bayard's insults. He had to get out of the room. The boy scrambled to his feet and took hold of Khaster's arm.

"Come, my lord," he whispered, and then Khaster was being propelled out through the door, through the pressing crowds into the night of the Soak. Here, he collapsed on the muddled pavement.

"Stand up," said the boy. "Walk. He may come after. Or send someone."

"Leave me," Khaster said. "Make your escape."

"He'll kill you," the boy said. "Believe me, I know he can."

Khaster laughed weakly. "Too late. He's already done that. Just run, boy. Get away."

"I am Tayven," said the boy, pushing back his hair. "I have a name. Get to your feet. I'll not walk back through this place alone."

"I'm no use to you."

"Rot. You wear the uniform. It's respected. It'll afford us some protection, even though we lack numbers."

Khaster allowed himself to be hauled upright. What a spectacle. He needed more to drink. He needed oblivion. Tayven, however, would not hear of entering another Soak establishment, and hired a water taxi to take them to Penthion Bridge. Khaster felt too tired to argue. Once back in the city proper, he could go to the Shining Cup, an inn that was close to the barracks. He'd rid himself of the unwelcome responsibility of Tayven, and drink until the dawn. Khaster felt weak, afraid. He was sure Bayard would make him pay for what he'd done.

Once they reached the Shining Cup, however, Tayven refused to leave Khaster's side, no matter how much Khaster protested.

"If you want to drink yourself into a catalepsy, then I will take you home afterwards," Tayven said.

The Cup was a far quieter establishment than the inns of the Soak; spotlessly clean, the lighting neither too dim nor too bright, the air redolent of the familiar odors of ale and smoke. It was very late, so the place was nearly empty. A few elderly men sat together at a table playing a sedate game of cards, while in a corner, a group of girls, apparently bird-catchers from the nets hanging at their waists, conducted an urgent, furtive conversation in low tones.

A row of wooden booths were set against the left wall, where patrons could hide themselves behind slatted doors and have some

privacy. Khaster virtually fell into one of these and for some moments
rested his face on the table. A girl came over to take their order and
Tayven requested a mild wine. When it arrived, Khaster found the
strength to lift his head.

"I owe you so much," Tayven said, pouring wine into two
wooden cups. "I was foolish to go out with Narin tonight. I should
have guessed it was one of Bayard's schemes. He's been after me for
months. I hate him. I am a fool."

"I am the fool," Khaster said, dragging one of the wine cups
toward him, and spilling a great deal of the contents in the process.
"I will tell you about it. I married the most beautiful woman on earth.
She is the sister of the Dragon Lord. Did you know that?"

Tayven ducked his head. "I know of your wife," he said. "Bayard
has talked about it."

Khaster growled. "Did he tell you about her love for her brother,
how close it was? Did he tell you that?"

"He's told everyone," Tayven said. "In Magrast, it's hardly
shocking news. You should know that."

"He's had her himself," Khaster said. "He told me. Had them
both at the same time. My best friend and my wife."

Tayven nodded. "I know."

"The three of them killed my sister."

Tayven said nothing.

"Didn't tell you that, then?"

Tayven shook his head. "No. Are you sure?"

Khaster gulped wine, spilled it. "Oh yes. They drove her mad.
She ran into the sea. It was some filthy ritual they were doing. Why
did they have to be down on the beach at dawn, the four of them?
What were they up to?" He closed his eyes. "Poor lovely Ellie. She
was innocent. They killed her. Black-hearted Pharinet, jealous of my
sister. Killed her. Valraven. Never loved her. Used her. Killed her."
The cup fell onto the table and the rest of its contents pooled around
Khaster's limp hands.

Tayven stood up. "Let's get you home," he said.

As Tayven hauled him up the stairs to his quarters, Khaster
couldn't stop laughing. The guard on the door had seen him, stag-

gering home with a pretty boy. That would start gossip. His legs
wouldn't work. Everything was too ridiculous. He sat down several
times on the stairs, so that Tayven nearly lost his temper begging him
to get up.

"Leave me, then," Khaster said. "Bugger off."

"No. I'll get you home. I want to."

Khaster vomited copiously and Tayven swore beneath his breath.

Khaster's rooms were on the second floor of the building. They
were not overly luxurious, but as well as a large bedroom, which
doubled as a sitting room, he had a tiny bathroom and kitchen. His
valet cooked breakfast for him there. Tayven maneuvered Khaster
into the bathroom, where he was sick again. Khaster hung over the
toilet, loathing himself, his insides roiling and heaving. The Red
Witch still twittered in the corners of his mind. Why had he done
this to himself? It was senseless. Tayven gave him some water to
drink, but wouldn't let him sleep on the bathroom floor. Instead, he
dragged Khaster into the bedroom. Khaster crawled onto the bed and
lay on his back, arms outflung. The ceiling bubbled above him as if
with storm clouds. His skin burned. Tayven sat beside him and offered
more water. "It'll flush you out," he said. "Drink."

"I can see the stars," Khaster said, staring with unblinking eyes
at the white ceiling.

"I'm not surprised. Come on, drink."

"No more drink, no." He put his hands over his eyes. In the
darkness, colors wove patterns that looked like dragons. He had forgotten about Bayard. All he could think of was the knot of tender
flesh that comprised his heart. The pain was physical. It would never
leave him. He felt Tayven lift his hands from his eyes. The light was
dim in the room, but it felt like spears of sunlight.

"This has to stop," Tayven said. He had the face of a judgmental
angel, beautiful and because of that terrifying.

"Then make it stop."

Tayven shook his head and the lamp light spun webs in his
swinging hair. "It's been noticed, the way you are. Almorante is concerned. He likes you, Khaster. He would be your patron."

"As he is yours?" Khaster managed a weak, cruel laugh.

Tayven briefly closed his eyes. "You know that's not what I mean. Bayard is a dangerous enemy. You would be wise to cultivate Almorante. He is very powerful."

"He can't help me."

Tayven expelled a sound of annoyance. "I remember how you were, before you went to Caradore last time. You are different now. It can't be! The person you were still lives inside you. You must find him."

"I've never seen you in my life before," Khaster said.

"I know. You wouldn't have noticed me. Why should you? You're not interested in beautiful boys, and you would believe I have no other virtue. But I've been there when you've attended Almorante's gatherings. I've watched you."

"Why?"

"Because you're different. I know you despise me, yet the fact you can view me in that way is strangely refreshing. I'm used to the other kind."

"You will grow old one day. It will happen without you realizing it. You'll lose all that you are."

"I know. I'm cursed."

Khaster shivered involuntarily. "Then leave Magrast."

Tayven sat up, sighed. "I wish I could." He clasped his knees and rested his head upon them. "I wish I had somewhere to go, but my life is cut out. I was sent to Almorante, and he will use me as he sees fit until my beauty fades and another is installed in my place."

"What then?"

"Then . . . I will be taken into the family business. My father has factories that make weapons."

"Oh."

Tayven's shoulders heaved again and the sigh gasped round the room like a lamenting spirit. A greater sigh had never been expressed. Khaster was moved by it. How much we are all victims of who we are, he thought. The Red Witch shrilled in his brain: "You are doomed, all of you. What is the point of life, of so much suffering, for brief, butterfly moments of sweet intensity that are as fragile as their powdery wings?"

"Have you ever loved, Tayven?" Khaster asked.

The shoulders heaved a little, but Tayven did not lift his head. "No," he said. "I don't want to."

"Nor I," said Khaster. "Nor I."

Tayven looked up then, and for a moment looked like poor, drowned Ellony. Khaster saw the same confusion he used to see in his sister's face, the total bewilderment with what was, rather than what should be. But even in that expression, there was an untouched core of courage and generosity. Tayven was so young, and the strength that shone from him was more pathetic than total vulnerability, because he'd had to learn it, breathe it, sleep it.

"Come here," Khaster said, lifting an arm from the bed that felt like the limb of a golem, solid and heavy.

Tayven frowned, half smiled. "What?"

"Come here. Hold me. I need it."

"Khaster, you're drunk, very very drunk. And you're addled by harm. Think about what you're saying."

"It doesn't matter. What are we but despairing souls trapped in lumps of flesh? I need to feel warmth."

Tayven sighed again and lay down beside him. Khaster hugged him close. The world felt so big around them, too overwhelming. We are just small, Khaster thought, inconsequential, unnoticed by gods. He felt exhausted, but he wanted to talk. He told Tayven about Caradore, about his family, his home, Norgance, about Pharinet and Valraven, how they used to be. He talked about himself. Tayven listened without commenting, his head resting on Khaster's chest, his fingers gently stroking it. Eventually, Khaster ran out of things to say. He felt he'd emptied his mind. "Your touch is healing," he said. "My heart beats peacefully. I can't feel any pain."

"That is probably because of all the harm you've had," Tayven said.

"No," said Khaster. "I know what it is. An old feeling." He frowned. "I've felt like this before. Drained, yet cleansed. I know. It was my wedding night. When I told Pharinet about her brother, what he was becoming here."

"Hush," said Tayven. "I can feel your heart. It's beginning to beat fast again."

Khaster lifted Tayven's head with one hand, stroked his thumb along the jaw. "Why didn't I notice you?"

Tayven pulled away, sat up. "Khaster, be careful. Remember why you didn't notice me, exactly why."

"It seems ridiculous now."

"You will regret this."

"I won't. Would you?"

Tayven laughed. "Me? Why do you think I noticed you so much? This is a dream come true for me, but then it isn't at all. I can't change you."

"Maybe . . ."

"No! Listen to yourself."

"I don't care. Kiss me. That's all. I want to find out how it feels." How was it possible to own such power? Khaster knew Tayven wanted him, so he couldn't refuse. Was this any better than what Bayard had done earlier? He couldn't tell. He just wanted to taste those lips. And then they were there against him, yellow hair hanging over his face. He was sinking down into a comfortable nest of dark feathers, where the blackness closed over him.

KHASTER'S VALET CAME in late the following morning. It was a rest day, so he was used to letting his master sleep longer than usual. Khaster was awoken by the man's embarrassed "excuse me" and the swift closing of the door. He half rose, about to speak, but a vise of pain tightened around his head and he had to lie down again. For a moment, he lay with one hand pressed against his eyes, and then recollection stole like treacle through his mind. He looked to the side, saw a naked shoulder above the sheet, the lush spill of bright hair. For a while, he stared at this sight, totally numb. Then he poked the boy roughly, said, "Wake up."

Tayven rolled over, stretching, smiling like the sun, like a cat.

Khaster tried to swallow, but his mouth was too dry. He could taste ashes and sickness. Tayven slithered toward him, embraced him, kissed him. Khaster was so stunned by this he could barely react, but then managed to push the boy away. This did not appear to discomfort Tayven, nor warn him of what was to come. "You feel terrible, don't you," he said. "That is the Witch's legacy."

Khaster continued to stare for a few moments, then said, "Tayven, what happened last night?"

Tayven sat up. "Then the Witch is a kind benefactress, it seems. Do you remember nothing?"

"Not much."

"You were a mess. You were sick on the stairs."

"After that," Khaster said carefully. "Did we . . ."

"Did we what?"

"You know what." Khaster sat up quickly, his head reeling. "By Madragore, I can't believe this." He punched the bed.

Tayven regarded him warily. "You've done nothing you should be worried about."

"Why are you in my bed? Why are you naked? Why am I, for that matter?"

Tayven frowned. "You passed out. I undressed you, and stayed because I thought you might throw up in your sleep and suffocate."

"You just kissed me."

Tayven shrugged. "Last night you did not mind."

"You said nothing happened!" Khaster was aware his voice was becoming hysterical. His valet would hear him.

"It was a kiss, nothing more. Khaster . . ."

Khaster turned away from the expression on Tayven's face. He looked too much like Ellony again, as if someone had just slapped him hard about the head. "Did you initiate it? You must tell me. What did you do?"

"I would not have done anything. I respect you. It was you. Just before you went to sleep. We just kissed."

Khaster shook his head. "This mustn't happen again. Never. That's the last time I drink like that."

There was an uncomfortable silence, then Tayven said, "Are you angry with me?"

"No." Khaster rubbed his face. "It's my fault. I was out of my mind." But it wasn't true. He was angry. A boy shouldn't look like that, feel like that. It was wrong, horribly wrong. "You'd better go," he said.

Tayven hesitated. "Khaster, don't punish yourself. You've done nothing to be ashamed of. You just needed comfort, that's all. It says nothing about who you are. Don't worry."

"Let's just say Magrastian comfort differs greatly from Caradorean comfort," Khaster said. "I don't want the taint of Magrast to touch me." He hated the prim tone to his voice, but he hated what he had done more. How he'd reviled Valraven for succumbing to Magravandian practices, now he was no better himself. People would laugh about this. And Bayard would exact revenge. Almorante, too, might not be pleased. This was his boy, after all. The mess was unbelievable, yet Tayven just sat there and told him he had nothing to worry about.

Tayven slid out from beneath the covers to reveal his sinuous pale body. Khaster looked away.

"Thank you for what you did for me," Tayven said, pulling on his clothes. "I'll not forget."

Khaster could no longer speak. He kept his back turned until the sounds had finished and someone walked to the door. He knew Tayven hesitated, waiting, for at least a good-bye. The boy had some pride. He did not speak himself.

The door closed. Khaster slumped back on the bed. He wanted to writhe in shame, scrub his body with salt. How could he have done that, kissed a boy? Was he insane? No matter how drunk he was, or how lovely the boy. He'd prided himself on being aloof from Magravandian customs. He would not let them seduce him. And yet they had. One by one. The drink to start with, then the more insidious Red Witch. He had friends among people he'd once scorned. And now this. He hadn't wanted to come here. He'd wanted to stay at home and tend his father's estates. He'd wanted to be Pharinet's husband, and her a faithful wife. He'd wanted children, running free in the wild, heady air of Caradore. He wasn't a soldier, certainly not an officer. He simply didn't care enough about the emperor's ambitions. Why should he? He was Caradorean, son of a conquered race. He

was little more than a slave. Not like Val. Val had surrendered himself
entirely to Magravandias, in body and soul. Now he was no longer
the boy with whom Khaster had explored the forests above Norgance.
Now he was the Dragon Lord, part of the emperor's inner circle,
where Khaster would never be invited. Almorante was a powerful
man, yes, but there were others far more powerful. Prince Gastern,
the heir to the throne, the emperor's vizier, his mage-priests, his generals. Khaster didn't want to think about making allies, yet part of
him knew he should. What did it matter? His life, as he could see it,
was doomed to be one he didn't want to live. He would never be
free, never truly be home. Caradore was lost to him, ruined, because
of what had happened there. He would be forever lonely. He could
not imagine finding a wife in Magrast, not one of those aloof,
shrouded women, or the alternative, a brazen, shrill whore. But he
needed a woman, desperately now. He needed to reassert himself, cast
off the taint that had touched him.

A short while later, Khaster's valet presented himself at the door
once more. The smell of cooking insinuated itself around him. "Will
your guest require breakfast too?" he inquired, clearly making a great
effort not to look round the room.

"I have no guest," Khaster said. People would think he'd had sex
with Tayven. He would not be able to convince them otherwise. A
person should never think his situation can't get worse. It always can.
Always.

6

RED WİTCH

FROM THAT MORNING FORWARD, Khaster shut him-
self away. He applied himself to his training with savage zeal
that left him exhausted and scarred. He would not drink. In just a
few short weeks he'd be sent to Cos, and maybe there he would die.
He was too much of a coward to kill himself, but there would be
plenty of opportunity for the Cossic guerrillas to have him. He'd make
sure of it. Rufus Lorca came every day to inquire as to his state of
mind. He wouldn't give up, no matter how offhand Khaster was with
him. After a few days, Rufus said hesitantly, "You mustn't hide away
because of Bayard. He won't touch you. Almorante will make sure
of it."

Khaster uttered a snarl. "Almorante? I doubt it. He will be under
the impression I have made free with his property. I probably have
two enemies now."

Rufus frowned. "What are you talking about?"

"That wretched boy. He virtually had to carry me home, then
stayed with me because I passed out. But who will believe that?"

"Well, everyone," Rufus said, shrugging. "Tayven told Almo-

rante what happened. He has sung your praises about court. You have
nothing to fear from that corner. Anyway, Almorante wouldn't mind
even if you had screwed the boy. Tayven isn't a slave, Khaster. Almorante is fond of him. They have an understanding."

"I was led to believe differently."

"I can't imagine you were."

Khaster growled. "It doesn't matter, in any case. I don't want to
get in that state again. I'm not hiding from Bayard, Rufus, I'm simply
avoiding dissolution."

Rufus shook his head, laughed. "You are a singular creature,
Khaster. Will you at least come hunting with us tomorrow?"

"All right," Khaster grumbled.

The following day, part of him harbored the ridiculous fear that
Tayven would be in the hunting party. He wasn't. I am flooded by
relief, Khaster thought, but the relief felt odd and strangely like disappointment.

On the night before the rest days, Khaster dreamed of Tayven.
It wasn't a particularly disturbing dream, the boy just haunted its
borders, radiating joy that Khaster could not reach or absorb. In the
dream, he thought to himself, I have dreamed of him every night. I
just haven't remembered. He awoke with a furious resolve. He would
avoid his friends later. He would find himself a woman. It had to
happen. He couldn't bear the way Tayven's presence still seemed to
hang around his rooms like the stink of a hidden dead rat. Only, it
didn't smell bad really. That just made it worse.

He decided he would visit one of the high-class whorehouses in
the city. No more Soak encounters. The thought of actually going
into such a place and voicing his request filled him with dread. He
couldn't do this sober. So he went out into the city, to a liquor
merchant. The shop was cavernous and dim. A thousand bottles
glinted on the shelves, filled with exotic fluids that had come from all
corners of the world. Khaster browsed, wondering whether to buy a
flagon of wine or go for expensive merlac. Then a tall red bottle
caught his eye. It looked like a gigantic perfume bottle, its neck slender, its belly softly curved. Harm, called in this place by its proper
foreign name, Etropia. Khaster stared at it. Should he? No, no. But

he couldn't take his eyes off it. He could taste it again, the bittersweet resinous perfume. The craving washed over him like a wave. Could he become addicted so swiftly? No, surely not. He simply craved the oblivion the Red Witch imparted. He took down the bottle from the shelf. This he carried to the counter, where the merchant praised his selection. "Only the best, from the Mewtish border with Elatine. She's travelled a long way, this one." He patted the bottle affectionately as he wrapped it in dark red tissue. "Will you be requiring any of the essential tools, sir?"

"Everything," Khaster muttered, embarrassed. He felt he was the only person in Magrast who was ever embarrassed. They all took everything for granted, sex, narcotics, drink. This man probably drank harm with his mother after dinner.

Khaster didn't want to examine the array of bowls, tongs, and resin bags. "Anything," he said curtly. "The cheapest will do."

Disappointed, the merchant put the paraphernalia back in its drawers. "Which resin do you require? Prime?"

"Yes." Khaster got out his money. No doubt the merchant was now wishing he'd just suggested the most expensive tools as well.

Back in his quarters, Khaster arranged the equipment on his table with shaking hands. It felt sordid, doing it alone like this. He had no idea how much resin to put into the fluid, nor how long to heat it. The first measure he drank was so fiery and fierce he thought he would choke. Dame Sally's brew had been smoother. Clearly, this would take practice. Khaster drank three measures, and by the time he left his quarters, his blood was on fire. The whole world looked red to him, shadows were crimson, the sunset above the spires of the city an incredible blaze of infernal hues. He felt as if a sober part of himself still resided in his brain, observing the behavior of the part of him controlled by the Witch. He watched as this person went into a flaming doorway, where inside it was like a genteel hotel. No grubby whores on display. The women who occasionally glided across the lobby all looked like duchesses.

Somehow, he came to be in a room with a female who wore small, carefully curled feathers in her hair. Her makeup was precise and perfect. Her manners were impeccable. She made polite conversation as she undid Khaster's trousers and put her hands inside. Before she did anything else, she let down her shinning yellow hair, and it made her look younger, mischievous.

Khaster sprawled on a sofa, his head thrown back, his eyes closed, while the woman knelt before him, skillfully pleasuring him with her mouth. He couldn't feel anything. He was hard, so something must be going right, but it was as if he was apart from his body. It was clearly enjoying the experience, but his mind wasn't participating. Was that possible? He raised his head, blinking at the ruddy light in the room. He looked down. The yellow hair, so lustrous, like silk, like sheaves of corn. He reached down to touch it, mesmerized. The woman raised her eyes to him, smiled around his cock, and then it was Tayven kneeling there. A shudder passed through Khaster's body. His mind woke up. Intense feelings pulsed through him, unbearable delight. He uttered an ecstatic yet mournful cry that turned into sobbing as an orgasm squeezed every muscle in his body into a painful knot.

The woman drew away. "You taste of the Red Witch," she said. "Would you like more?"

He hardly dared to look at her, but when he did it was the gracious whore kneeling there, not anyone else. Her eyebrows were raised and she seemed to be smothering a smile. He shook his head. "No. Thank you."

She stood up. "Is there anything else you require, sir?"

Khaster could barely move. Could he ask her to help him up? Perhaps another measure of the Witch would restore him. He felt sick, feverish. "Your offer of the Red Witch. Yes. Give me that."

The woman smiled and nodded. She had the equipment in the room. He watched her deft preparations. Perhaps he should talk to her now. She would be wise, offer advice and comfort. He could pay her to do anything. Be my wife, be my mother, take me home. In the event, she gave him the drink, then made it clear his time was up. But the Witch had worked her magic. He could walk now, function.

Back in his quarters, he wept. He'd taken too much of the Witch. Nothing was real anymore. He saw animals crouched in the corners

of his room, a shadowy writing shape upon the bed. He wanted to
tear out his eyes. He knew people had done things like that under
the Witch's spell. He'd never felt so alone. "I won't do this again,"
he said aloud, and then he saw the spirit of the Witch sitting across
from him in a place where there was no chair to sit. She looked like
Pharinet, a wicked smiled surrounded by a halo of shining black hair.
She grinned at him, her head tilted to the side. "Will you not?" she
said and laughed.

"I want you," Khaster told the vision, who was becoming more
like Pharinet with every moment. "I want Val. I want you back, both
of you. Where are you?"

The vision vanished. Everything vanished. He was alone in a
black void.

Khaster had to spend the next day in bed. He only got up once
to pour the rest of the harm down his toilet. He dared not have it in
the room. He didn't trust himself, because he felt so ill only another
measure of the Witch could cure him. He would suffer this through,
cleanse himself. The actions he'd taken last night hadn't solved anything. He wouldn't do that again, not under the Witch's influence
anyway.

Rufus Lorca turned up late in the afternoon. He could see immediately that Khaster was ill and voiced concern. Khaster didn't tell
him what was wrong. He wouldn't be able to bear the fact that Rufus
would be pleased. "A secret acolyte of the Witch," he would say,
"how wonderfully sly of you, Khaster."

"It's a pity you're out of sorts," Rufus said, "because Almorante
has invited you to a gathering at the palace this evening. It's a personal
invitation, which he's asked me to deliver. You won't just be one of
the crowd this time."

Khaster groaned and put a pillow over his head.

"Yes, I can see you're disappointed. Can't you raise yourself,
take a bath, eat something? You might feel better. This is a good
opportunity for you, Khas. You should make the effort to attend."

"I would rather eat my own limbs."

"The cuisine will be quite exquisite. Far nicer than raw meat."

Khaster removed the pillow. "I'm not going this time, Rufus. It's got nothing to do with how I feel physically. Please convey my apologies to the prince. You can tell him I am ill."

"He won't take no for an answer, Khas, rest assured of that. When Almorante gets an idea, he pursues it until it's brought to ground."

"What idea?"

"He wants to cultivate you. You are Caradorean, and a kinsman by marriage of the Caradorean who holds the emperor's right hand."

"You mean Valraven? We are not close friends."

"Not anymore, no. That only makes you more valuable."

Khaster sat up, intrigued in spite of himself. "What is Almorante up to? Why does he need me?"

Rufus idly picked up a lump of Caradorean serpentine that Khaster kept on the windowsill. "Oh, you know what the court is like. Everyone needs allies, and the princes more than most, seeing as there are so many of them. Valraven has become very powerful. I don't know what happened the last time you two went home, and I don't expect you to tell me, but it's clearly affected you both very strongly. Valraven hardly leaves the imperial palace now. Leonid treats him like a son. You can appreciate Almorante's concern."

"He's only second in line. What does Gastern feel?"

"Gastern wants Valraven. Not in the sense Bayard does, but politically. Gastern is his father's favorite, but he's no fool. He knows that once Leonid goes, all hell will break loose. He'll need strong allies then. No Caradorean has ever been as close to the emperor as Valraven. You are a spiky lot. You do your duty, but you're always fighting the bit. Not Palindrake. He can be ridden without a bridle."

There was a silence. Rufus put down the serpentine, rubbed his hands together.

"Almorante is wrong about me," Khaster said. "I'm of no use to him. I have absolutely no interest in what goes on at court. They can slaughter each other for all I care."

"Oh, don't *care*," Rufus said. "Don't even think about it. But take up a hand, play the game. It's called survival."

"Maybe I don't want to survive."

Rufus snorted. "Oh, do stop whipping yourself, Khaster. It's boring. You're alive, so just get on with it."

THE NEXT MORNING, very early, a page from Almorante's palace presented himself at Khaster's door. He held in his hands a letter written in Almorante's own hand. Khaster opened it. His heart sank. It was a summons, not an invitation. He could not disobey.

"I'll wait while you get ready," said the page sitting down at Khaster's table. "Then I'll take you to the prince."

Khaster didn't like the way the boy looked at him. His expression was amused yet calculating. Khaster had the sudden dread that the page knew Tayven, had spoken with him about the events of the previous week. There was a conspiracy afoot. He could smell it. "Wait outside," he snapped.

Slowly, insultingly, the boy got up and left the room.

Almorante's palace was part of the great imperial building, which dominated the center of the city, as big as a town itself. All the royal sons, who were of age, had an establishment of their own, as did the empress Tatrini. Palaces within palaces, cells in a gargantuan body, where the inhabitants brewed their intrigues and plotted scandals. The military buildings surrounded the palaces like a protective wall, yet it still took nearly an hour for Khaster to walk from his own quarters to those of the prince. He walked through fabulous colonnades, up innumerable steps, beneath ceremonial arches hung with flags. Bells tolled in the lofty campaniles, proclaiming the hour. Birds clattered up in great flocks, cawing and wheeling around the towers. Somewhere nearby, Valraven sat with the emperor. What was he feeling now?

The page led Khaster directly into Almorante's presence, then closed the doors upon them and departed. The prince's morning room was warm and comfortable. A fire roared in the hearth and upon a table stood the remains of Almorante's breakfast. Like all the imperial princes, Almorante was an arresting and imposing man. He was very tall, and for a Malagash, his hair was unusually dark, falling in a straight curtain about his shoulders. His face was handsome in a hawk-ish sort of way, the forehead high, the eyes deep-set. His hands were long, the fingers unnaturally mobile. He stood up when Khaster entered the room, and Khaster bowed to him. Not for the first time, he thought that Almorante should really be the heir to the throne. He was far more regal than Gastern.

"Thank you for coming," Almorante said. His voice was deep and hoarse, as if he smoked zeg weed at every waking moment. "I wish to talk with you."

"I'm sorry I couldn't attend your gathering last night. I was ill."

"I know. Rufus Lorca conveyed your apologies. A shame. It was a pleasant evening, and you were missed."

Khaster's heart had begun to beat faster. He hoped Almorante would get to the point quickly.

"Please sit down," Almorante said, gesturing at a chair before the fire. "Would you care for a beverage?"

"Thank you, my lord."

Almorante pulled a bell cord and sat down opposite Khaster. He steepled his fingers before his chin and shook his head. "So, here you are, the remains of poor Khaster Leckery. Such a sorry state."

Khaster was so shocked by these intimate remarks, he uttered, "What?"

Almorante smiled. "I have made a mission of you, Khaster. It is my pleasure to mend you."

"My lord, I . . ." Khaster's mouth dried up.

"Please don't stand on formality. I want us to be friends. You should hold yourself in higher esteem. Others think well of you, while you only hate yourself."

"How do you know these things?" Khaster asked. He could not remember speaking intimately to anyone in Magrast. Was Almorante merely making accurate assumptions?

"I have my methods," Almorante said. "You should stay away from the Red Witch, my friend. She's a dangerous mistress. And whores talk, too. You should not visit them when you're distressed. They like nothing better than to gossip about those of higher stations than themselves."

Khaster, who was adept at feeling embarrassed, had never felt so ashamed in his life. What had he said to the whore? Nothing that he could remember. Unless the Witch had completely addled his brain.

"I don't want to see you squirm," said the prince. "I'm not judging you, Khaster. You have been damaged, haven't you. Your sister, your wife . . ." He gestured widely. "I need say no more. We understand each other, don't we?"

"Is that why I'm here? Because of Bayard?"

"Bluntly put," said Almorante dryly. A servant came in then, carrying a tray of steaming drinks. Almorante waited for him to depart. "You're here mainly because I hate to see waste. I like to create. I like to repair. Also, Tayven Hirantel has spoken strongly in your favor. Your friends are concerned for you."

"Tayven is not a friend of mine," Khaster said before he could stop himself. "I want no one's concern." At that moment, memory came crashing back, and he remembered how he'd talked to Tayven for hours that night after the Soak. So that was Almorante's source. Yet another reason to regret that debauched behavior.

Almorante sighed. "I know about you," he said. "You don't want to be here in Magrast. You have no interest in fighting for the imperial army, let alone partly leading it. But that is your fate. You fight against it by making yourself an undesirable commodity. That is not wise, Khaster. You should think more about how you can achieve what you want from life. You should be clever."

"Your remarks are accurate," Khaster said. "But I cannot achieve what I want. It is impossible."

"Erase that word from your vocabulary," Almorante said. "You want to live in Caradore, then at least aspire to it. Nothing in life remains the same."

"My father wanted it all his life. He died wanting it on a battlefield in Cos."

"You are of the next generation. You do not have to live your father's life."

"Then tell me how it can be different. What do you want from me?"

"I want your loyalty, that is all. If you give it me willingly and wholly, I will repay you, when the time comes. But you must trust me."

Khaster was silent for a moment. He shook his head. "I don't understand your interest in me. I am unremarkable, a failure. I am riddled with anxiety and I'm a coward. It cannot be disputed."

"If you insist," said Almorante, "but that too can be changed. You are admired, even among your self-indulgent colleagues, for your honesty, your compassion and your integrity. These men, they lack all those qualities, yet they respect them in you. Why? Why don't they just laugh at you, when you muddle and fuddle your way through life here? You call yourself a coward, yet you were the only one courageous enough to stand up to Bayard and curb his excesses. People were in awe of that. Then, you had the most coveted boy in Magrast in your bed and you cast him out with a curse. Normally, this would invoke only savage hysteria. But no. When Khaster Leckery behaves like a frigid virgin, people only worry and wonder what to do." Almorante shook his head again. He leaned forward. "Don't let past hurts rule your life. Learn to live again. Forget the Palindrakes for now. And Bayard. Find yourself. Then the time may come when you can avenge your hurts." He paused. "One day I will give you Caradore, Khaster. I promise you this. Trust me."

"I am overwhelmed," Khaster said. "This is too much to take in."

"I disagree. Get used to it."

Khaster watched the prince warily as he took a drink from his cup. Almorante's remarks, though vague, suggested he thought that one day he would be emperor. This was treason. How could Almorante trust him with these intemperate words? Because the prince had a keen instinct concerning men, which he could depend upon implicitly? That must be it. The promise he had given was the one thing Khaster wanted more than anything. Almorante knew a Caradorean's price. He had named it. That's why he trusted Khaster. And Khaster, in his heart, knew he could trust Almorante too. He smiled.

"Yes?" said the prince.

"Yes," said Khaster flatly. "That is the answer. Yes."

Almorante nodded. "I am gratified and you will not be sorry."

He put down his cup. "Tayven dearly wants to see you. Might I send for him?"

Khaster paused. "No. That is something that cannot be changed."

"I am intrigued. What is your objection?"

"His gender."

"But your other friends are male. What's the difference?"

"There is one, you know there is. I can't look upon a boy in the same way you do."

"Well, of course I cannot argue with that. But what troubles me is that if you are so rigorously strict in your affections, why won't you see the poor creature? He is wretched. He feels he's wronged you."

"By repeating everything I said to him to you? That doesn't matter. I just don't want to see him."

"Tayven did not come sneaking to me, spilling secrets. I knew there was something wrong. I had to prize it out of him. I think, Khaster, that you desire this boy and you cannot bear it, because it goes against your moral code. Your hatred of love between men is racist. You hate it mainly because Magravands don't, and you loathe everything Magravandian."

"If you think this of me, then why . . . ?"

"Oh, be quiet. I know your feelings for my country and my people. I don't blame you. I'd probably feel the same in your position. But you're never going to progress in life until you can conquer certain aspects of yourself, which have been carried in the blood of Caradoreans for generations. You make yourself a slave. Open your eyes. Wake up. Cast off the shackles. You can start with one small thing. It would be the first step to a greater freedom. If you want the boy, have him. How can it harm you?"

"I don't want him."

"I can see it would be easy to become very annoyed by you," Almorante said. "So I'll withdraw from this argument. However, it is my wish that you attend my next gathering in a week's time. You will be there, of course."

"Yes, my lord. I will be there."

"Good. Finish that drink and go. I have work to do."

Khaster drained his cup and stood up. He bowed. "Thank you, my lord. I cannot believe it, but you have given me hope."

"Such was my intention."

Khaster inclined his head and went to the door. As he opened it, Almorante said, "Tayven is a celebrity in Magrast, because of his association with me. Uttering his name at the moment of climax was bound to amuse the whore. You do not desire him, of course. You know best. Until the rest days, Khaster. Fare thee well."

THREE DAYS LATER, Khaster celebrated his twenty-fifth birthday. Rufus bought him a new jacket for the occasion. From Valraven there was no word. Nor did Pharinet make contact, but why should she? Khaster's mother, Saskia, sent a long, despairing letter, saying how much she missed him, and that Norgance was a tomb, devoid as it was of its menfolk. She lamented about "her baby," Khaster's younger brother, Merlan, who was at the college in Magrast. Khaster thought she hardly need worry. Merlan, unlike his elders, was not destined to lead men into battle. He was a scholar, and had already been tagged by the imperial government for a post abroad, in an administrative capacity. He was still only thirteen. Reminded by the letter, Khaster went to see his brother. Merlan was a knowing boy and assessed Khaster quickly in the cloisters of the college. "You are making news," he said. "Gossip concerning Khaster Leckery flies around the city."

Khaster's heart sank. "No word to our mother, Merlan. You must swear it."

"Will you take me to the palace with you soon?"

"Why?"

"I wish to make contacts."

Khaster eyed his brother wearily. He had never been like Merlan, aware, clever, ambitious. "I'm sure you'll need no help from me."

"I want to come. I want to meet Prince Almorante and his mages. He has a strong presence in Mewt, and since that's where I'll be sent in a couple of years . . ."

"Merlan, can't you just concentrate on being a child?"

Merlan narrowed his eyes. "Khaster, I've had to do the growing up for both of us, it seems. Can I come to the palace? A letter to our mother depends on it."

"All right. I'll see what I can do."

In the event, Khaster decided it might be safer for him to take Merlan with him to Almorante's next gathering. He was sure he'd never dare do anything indecorous in front of his younger brother. Despite the boy's young age, he was astute and alert. As Merlan was rather bookish, and certainly no slinkingly disturbing creature like Tayven, Khaster knew he would be safe from the amorous intentions of any of Almorante's entourage. A letter was sent to Almorante's steward inquiring whether Khaster could bring his brother as a guest. Not really to Khaster's surprise, because by now he knew Almorante was keen to please him, a reply was received in the affirmative.

The brothers climbed the steps to Almorante's palace ten minutes late—at Merlan's insistence because he said he knew the etiquette of these things. Khaster found it hard to believe Merlan was still so young. Dressed as a man, and with all the poise of someone at least six years older, he had learned quickly from his Magravandian class-mates. Khaster felt he could see into the future at that point, and observed Merlan doing very well for himself. He clearly had no res-ervations about working for the emperor. He wanted to succeed in life, at whatever cost. "Have you seen Val recently?" Merlan asked, as a servant took their coats from them in the outer hall.

"No. We're no longer on good terms." Khaster wasn't sure how much Merlan knew of what had happened in Caradore.

"Do you think he'll be here tonight?"

"Certainly not. He's not part of Almorante's circle."

"I thought he was. He used to be, didn't he?"

"Things change, Merlan. This way. Hurry up."

"I think it's important to put our money on the right horse, don't you?" Merlan said as they walked along a gilded corridor. Music could be heard faintly from a room at the far end.

"Explain what you mean."

"Well, the princes all have their own cliques and areas of power. When Leonid dies, someone else will be emperor. What we have to decide is who that will be, and make them our friend. At the moment, I'd put my money on Almorante, wouldn't you?"

"Gastern will inherit, you know that."

Merlan gave his brother a condescending glance. "Either you're stupid, or you think I am."

"Don't talk like that here. Be careful." As if the warning was needed.

"People at school talk about how the empress favors Bayard. She too has great power. Have you ever met her?"

"Not personally, no. As you're no doubt aware, I'm as far from Bayard's clique as it's possible to get."

"Things are available to you that are not available to him. He won't like that."

"I've a suspicion about what you mean by that remark, which I shall ignore." They had come to the great doors, beyond which lay a splendid salon. As Khaster and Merlan walked into the gathering, Khaster reflected on how different social occasions were in Magrast than they were in Caradore. For a start, there were no women present. In the upper classes, the social mingling of sexes was sporadic, but appearances were deceptive. Merlan was right. Tatrini, the empress, was a powerful woman. She might not attend all male gatherings, but it was no secret she knew everything that transpired at them. Khaster missed his womenfolk, even more so because he felt they were removed from him forever, even those who still lived. How could he go home again now? He was married to Pharinet, yet he couldn't bear to see her. She too no doubt dreaded the possibility of him taking his next leave in Caradore. Perhaps he should write to her, try to salvage something from the situation, some kind of civilized understanding. This thought cheered him, so that his smile was genuine when Almorante gestured for him to approach.

"So this is your younger brother," the prince said, inclining his head to Merlan. "You look alike."

Khaster glanced down at Merlan. Surely not? Yet the young man beside him now was far from the scruffy student with ink-stained fingers.

"I have been looking forward to meeting you, my lord," said Merlan, full of confidence.

"You are to be stationed in Mewt, I hear," said Almorante, who had no doubt researched Khaster's family in the very recent past.

"That is true, my lord. I look forward to it. They say Mewt is an amazing land."

"It is indeed. And you are fortunate tonight, because Lord Maycarpe is with us. He is the governor in Akahana, home for a short visit. I will introduce you to him presently." He turned his attention to Khaster. "And you look well, my friend. I am pleased to see it."

"The last time you saw me I was in the grip of a vicious hangover," Khaster said.

Almorante raised an eyebrow. "I would like you to sit by me at dinner this evening. It will be served shortly." He clicked his fingers so that a servant scuttled over with a tray of drinks. "Enjoy yourself in moderation, Khaster. Mingle. Be sociable." He smiled and departed.

Merlan took a glass of wine off the tray and handed one to his brother. He shook his head. "I can't believe it. You were always in Valraven's shadow, now this. You must have worked hard. A favorite of an imperial prince. I'm in awe."

"I am not a favorite," Khaster said. "And it's happened by accident rather than design."

"He must think you'll be useful," Merlan said. "If you're sensible, you'll make sure you are."

Khaster sighed. "Our roles should be reversed. You'd thrive on this."

Merlan laughed, then said, "We have great opportunity for our family here. The Leckerys have always been secondary to the Palindrakes in Caradore. We can change that. Valraven has made mistakes."

"No, he hasn't," Khaster said, "Don't make too many assumptions. We have to tread carefully."

"That's the spirit!" said Merlan.

Two of Almorante's younger brothers were present, Celetian and Roarke. In the scheme of things, only three of the imperial sons had desire for leadership, Almorante, Gastern and Bayard. The others—

for the moment at least—were content to ally themselves with the powerful sibling they most admired. Of the emperor's eleven sons, three were still only children. Bayard had only one fraternal ally, Prince Wymer, who was rumored to be as dissipated as Bayard himself. Of the rest, Princes Eremore and Pormitre were of Gastern's circle. Relations between Gastern and Almorante, and their respective cliques, were warmer than those between Bayard and anyone else. Members of the Malagash family were suspicious and paranoid about one another. Privately, Khaster found it farcical, while being aware that because the Malagashes *were* powerful, their tantrums and preferences could affect a great many others.

As Almorante had promised, he introduced the Leckerys to Lord Maycarpe, who was a tall, saturnine man in his late thirties. His skin was bronzed by the hot sun of Mewt and his fingers were adorned with rings bearing the lion-serpent motifs of that exotic country. Merlan behaved impeccably, at once polite, assertive and respectfully curious. He encouraged Maycarpe to talk about Akahana, flattering the man discreetly. Khaster could not help but admire his brother's cool manipulation of the situation. It would help ensure things went well for him when he was finally stationed abroad. Khaster had never been one for such behavior. Maybe Merlan was right. Khaster had been in Valraven's shadow since they'd been small children. It had crushed him. And for what? Ultimate betrayal.

The gathering moved into an adjoining room, where a long table gleamed with silver cutlery in the light of a thousand candles. Almorante sat at the head of the table and gestured for Khaster to sit on the first seat to his right. So far, there had been no sign of Tayven Hirantel. Perhaps Almorante was being considerate of Khaster's feelings. If so, this accommodation seemed to be going too far. What was the prince's motive? Merlan was seated some distance away, next to Lord Maycarpe, and some other dignitaries from the imperial government in Mewt. He was clearly in his element and had forgotten his elder brother was present. In Caradore, Merlan might be regarded as precocious, a prodigy perhaps, but one that needed to be kept in his place. Not here. The Magravandians were aware of the boy's talent and intellect.

Khaster sat among a clutch of princes, two of whom he'd barely spoken to before. Now, whether voluntarily or not, Roarke and Celetian realized the sense of being pleasant to him. They always had half an eye on Almorante, like dogs currying favor.

"You seem more at peace with yourself," Almorante said to Khaster.

"Truce might be a better word."

Almorante laughed. "Better than none."

Course after course was brought in; dishes smothered in rich sauces, and spices imported from Mewt. Almorante indulged in polite conversation, never once touching upon any sensitive subject, either personal or political. He invited Khaster to other events in the future, even a soiree with the empress, which should be interesting. Khaster had no fear that Valraven would be there, but Bayard certainly would be. Carefully, he mentioned this to Almorante.

"Don't worry about Bayard," the prince said. "He is an effete hedonist, with pretensions to power. He has far too little self-control ever to have it. He is a great one for foot-stamping, and always has been. Mother has indulged him, of course, which hasn't helped. He is the gilded one, the pretty one. Our father barely acknowledges his existence."

"Our father is embarrassed by him," said Prince Celetian.

"Enough of that," said Almorante quietly. "It is time for entertainment, I think." He made a discreet signal. While servants moved soft-footed around the room, removing the remains of the meal, others lit dim lamps around a raised platform opposite to where Khaster sat. A troupe of musicians came in, carrying harps, drums and wind instruments. "I hope you will like this," Almorante said.

Khaster was alerted by the tone of the prince's voice. "Why?"

Almorante put a finger to his lips. The musicians started to play, a rhythmic yet languid tribal dance. A figure appeared among them, swathed in a long dark cloak, and a face mask of dangling silver disks: the garb of a Cossic mystic. The Magravandians were fond of reproducing the entertainments of their conquered lands. The cloaked figure sat down cross-legged upon the floor in front of the musicians, and began to sway. Then a voice purred out, singing a haunting incantation. Khaster knew that voice. Tayven's. He half rose from his seat, but Almorante's right hand flicked out and grabbed his left wrist in a painfully strong grip. "Sit still," he said. Khaster remained rigid. Almorante would not let him go. The song changed, became more conventional, and the words burned into Khaster's mind. Could they possibly be addressed to him? The song was about the stupidity and waste of self-hatred, about realizing the wonder of life, of becoming free from fear and misery. Khaster had the feeling this had all been staged. His first instinct was to be angry, but then Almorante murmured, "Ah Khaster, do you not see? It is up to you entirely how you react to this. That is your control over the outcome."

"Did he ask you to let him do this, or was it your suggestion?" Khaster asked.

"He asked me," Almorante said with a shrug. "He wants nothing more than to tell you his thoughts. After the way you treated him, he deserves nothing less."

The song ended with the words. "I forgive you."

"Let me go," said Khaster.

Almorante released his wrist. "I apologize, but you would have bolted, wouldn't you?"

"Probably."

"Are you really so afraid?"

"What is it to you, my lord?"

Almorante shrugged again, and took out his pipe. "Tayven would be good for you. He possesses rare qualities. He could heal you utterly. Just his light, his presence. He is a balm to me, but I am not a greedy man. He does not love me as a lover should, nor I him. Yet he deserves love. He has so much to give."

And in thrall to Tayven, Khaster would be so much more malleable for Almorante. "I thought I explained myself to you before."

"You did, but there is more to love than physical gratification, isn't there?"

On the platform, Tayven removed his mask of glittering disks and threw back the hood of his cloak, which he then removed. Beneath it, he was dressed in the soft tunic and trousers of a Cossic. The gathering cheered and clapped his performance, but it seemed to give him no joy. His face appeared strained. There was a furrow between his eyes. Yet how fair he was, how perfect. Khaster felt a pang, an uncomfortable stab of memory, of lying on a bed with that boy, holding him in his arms.

"Look at him," Almorante said, shaking his head. "He is in torment. How can you be so cruel?"

Khaster laughed lightly. "He hardly knows me. How can he feel that way so quickly? It's a boy's infatuation. He'll get over it. How do you feel the next campaign will proceed in Cos?"

Almorante refused to drop the subject. "It may well be infatuation, but at such an age all feelings are intense and painful."

Khaster affected a pained yet amused expression. "My lord, how old is he?"

Almorante smiled, took a sip of wine. "Sixteen. A sweet age."

Khaster rolled his eyes, but didn't speak for fear his sentiments would offend the prince.

"It is my wish for Tayven to join us," Almorante said. "Can I count on your courtesy?"

"Yes," said Khaster, resigned. He reached for a decanter of wine. Almorante gave him a sharp glance, but made no comment.

Almorante gestured to Tayven, who hesitated a moment before approaching the table. Celetian and Roarke were quick to offer their appreciation for his performance, but Tayven seemed buffeted by their good humor. He would not look at Khaster. Almorante took his hand. "So pale of cheek, Tay," he said. "Have some wine. Sit down. Enjoy yourself."

The depth of their relationship was indicated by the way Tayven pulled a sour face at him. They were like brothers. Still, he sat down next to the prince on a stool that a servant had hurriedly placed there.

"Look, Khaster is here," Almorante said. "Be civilized. Greet one another."

Khaster smiled thinly. He had resolved not to let Almorante humiliate him. "You sang well," he said.

"Thank you," Tayven murmured. He looked around the room, as if seeking an excuse to escape.

Strangely, Khaster felt quite comfortable. It was Tayven who was clearly ill at ease. The princes were all smirking at one another, enjoying the situation. Khaster felt sorry for Tayven. Perhaps Almorante had been right and the song had been enough. Perhaps this enforced proximity was excruciating to the boy.

"Will you sing again later?" Almorante suggested. "He should, shouldn't he, Khaster?"

"Well, yes . . ."

"No," said Tayven and stood up. "I'm tired. I have to go." He began to walk away swiftly.

Almorante made a gesture to Khaster. "For Madragore's sake, go after him."

Khaster hesitated.

"Go on. Make peace. I have to live with this."

Khaster got to his feet. "I will do as you wish, my lord, although I'm not sure I can offer him peace. Surely a person can only find that for themselves?"

"A polite gesture is all that's required," Almorante said. "I appreciate your cooperation."

Khaster found Tayven on the salon beyond the dining hall, dragging his feet. Had he expected pursuit? Khaster called his name. He stopped, but did not turn. "Almorante wants peace between us," Khaster said.

Tayven nodded. He turned then and blurted out, "I'm sorry. I'm sorry. What more can I say?"

"Sorry for what?"

"What I did to you. I made it all worse. I made you hate yourself more. I . . ."

"Be quiet," Khaster said.

Tayven shook his head. "No. I know what I am, and what you are. You are more than us."

"No, I'm not. Shut up. You're being ridiculous. Have you forgotten the sentiments of your song already?"

Tayven shook his head again, furiously. "You were right, that's all."

Khaster put his hands in his pockets. He wasn't sure how to deal with this. He didn't want to deal with it. "Look, you know I have problems, but they're nothing to do with you. I reacted badly that morning, and I'm sorry if you've suffered for it. You offered me only kindness. I'm not angry with you, Tayven, and I don't blame you. I'm here now, in Almorante's company, because of you, aren't I?"

Tayven swallowed, nodded, his brow deeply furrowed. "Yes, but you'd made a good impression already. Your pedigree had."

"I know that." Khaster patted Tayven awkwardly on the arm. "Please, don't be sad."

"I can't help it. I'm sorry."

"Almorante wants us to be friends, so we'll be friends. Let's meet tomorrow. Would you like that?"

"You mustn't play with me," Tayven said. "I can't stand it."

"I'm not playing," Khaster said, his patience fraying.

"You've been drinking. You'll change your mind tomorrow."

"I'm not drunk. I won't change my mind." Impulsively, he leaned forward and kissed Tayven's cheek. "There, you see? We are not enemies."

Tayen regarded him warily. "Being a friend to me might set you on a path you'll regret."

Khaster forced a smile. "I can control myself."

"That's not what I meant," Tayven said darkly.

"Dire prophecy," Khaster said. He couldn't suppress a smile.

"Perhaps it is," Tayven answered.

Khaster held out a hand. "Shall we return to the company?"

Tayven turned away. "No. I've had enough of it. I want my sanctuary." He turned round again, his expression almost fierce. "You could come with me, if you like."

Khaster was aware of the challenge in Tayven's tone. "All right. Where are you going?"

"You'll see."

They ventured into the winding, silent corridors of the palace. Only a few yards away from Almorante's gathering, the building seemed empty. "It'd be easy to lose yourself in this labyrinth," Khaster said quietly. It seemed inappropriate to speak at normal volume.

"People have," Tayven replied. "Foreign guests, especially. They will insist on exploring. Almorante has a retinue of palace scouts employed solely to retrieve missing people."

Khaster laughed. "I don't believe that."

"It's true," Tayven said. "Some have never been found." He was comfortable enough to smile now.

"I expect you know this place," Khaster said.

"When I first came here, I mapped it," Tayven replied. "Well, most of it. I found some secret spots." They had walked the length of a bare corridor that appeared to be used only by servants, if anyone. Cobwebs hung from the dim lamps on the walls. At the end, Tayven lifted aside a curtain to reveal a low door.

"A turret room?" Khaster said.

"Not quite." Beyond the door was a narrow, spiralling staircase of cold stone. At the top, they emerged into another corridor, then climbed more stairs. Eventually, Tayven opened the door onto what appeared to be an attic. The walls sloped steeply, but on one side they were completely paned in stained glass.

"Amazing," Khaster breathed. "But what a strange, isolated spot for it. Why was it put here?" He turned round in a circle. "This could never have been widely used, surely?"

"I can't find out how it got here," Tayven said, "but I like to think it was once commissioned in secret, by a princess or a queen. This was their secret place, where they came to escape."

"Where you do," Khaster said.

"Yes. Come here." Tayven went to the windows and operated a series of levers to crank the great panes open. "There is a terrace beyond." He climbed out through the gap and Khaster followed.

Below them, the city glowed in the darkness. They could see nearly all of it. Sulphurous steams rose into the sky from the alchemists' quarter, while dull red fires burned along the canals of the Soak. The great cathedral was bathed in light, monstrous against the stars. "An incredible view," Khaster said.

Tayven went to the edge of the terrace and leaned on the blackened balustrade. "I've never brought anyone here before," he said.

Khaster stood beside him. "Thanks for showing it to me."

Tayven was silent for a moment, then said, "Have you ever been to the puppet market?"

"No," Khaster said. "What's that?"

"What it sounds like," Tayven said. "I could take you there tomorrow. It's a strange and colorful place. Some of the puppets are terrifying."

"I'll finish my training sessions at four," Khaster replied. "Meet me at the yard."

Tayven nodded. "I'll be there."

Khaster examined him covertly for some moments. He could sense Tayven's tension, as if he thought Khaster might bolt at any moment. This was such a peculiar situation. Khaster wasn't sure how he felt about it, or whether he knew what was really happening. A friend such as Rufus Lorca would never suggest a visit to a market, however weird its merchandise.

"I should go back to the dining hall," he said. "My brother's there. I don't want to leave him alone for too long."

"I'll show you the way back," Tayven said.

He sounded resigned, if not disappointed. Perhaps he hoped his secret hideaway would kindle some romantic response in his companion. But that was too obvious.

"I think there's something you're not telling me," Khaster said.

Tayven stared at him, silent for a while. Then he said, "I can be your ally, Khaster. You should look beneath the surface."

Khaster laughed uneasily. "That's a perilous course in Magrast. Sometimes, you find more than you bargained for."

"And that's not always a bad thing." Tayven began to walk toward the open window, the darkness beyond.

7

THE SEVEN LAKES

K HASTER DID NOT WANT his brother Merlan to learn
of his friendship with Tayven, and kept it as clandestine as
possible. There was little to keep secret. Despite whatever Tayven
might want from the relationship, Khaster was unable to develop it
physically. Under the influence of alcohol, inhibitions went to the
winds, but Khaster was afraid of that and kept sober. He met Tayven's
family, a moneyed, well-to-do clan, who lived in the most esteemed
area of Magrast. The Hirantels were pleased Tayven had found what
they presumed was a new patron. Obviously, they had feared that
Almorante's interest might have been brief.

Khaster took Tayven with him to the opera and gatherings at the
palace. They were seen together everywhere, and more than once
Bayard's hard gaze could be seen across a room. He was not pleased.
Khaster once even bumped into Valraven at a function. They faced
one another as strangers, uttering stilted greetings. Valraven was like
an automation, distant and aloof. Once, he and Khaster had been like
brothers.

The days were ticking away toward the time when Khaster would journey once more to Cos. The emperor had gathered more funds for a further offensive into the mountain territory held by the guerillas who remained faithful to Ashalan, the exiled Cossic king. Khaster admired the Cossics. They had held on to the most impenetrable areas of their land with grim determination. They had done better than the Caradoreans had done several centuries before, but no doubt their defeat was nigh. Magravandias was an inexorable force. The great red, purple and black banners of Madragore surged across the world, bringing war and devastation in the names of peace and God.

Two weeks before Khaster was due to leave, he attended a soiree in the apartments of the empress, Tatrini, as Almorante's guest. He had dreaded bumping into Bayard, but it appeared Tatrini knew that certain of her sons and their friends should be kept apart, because the prince was absent. Almorante, courteous and attentive toward his mother, made a point of introducing Khaster to her. A tall and imposing woman, dressed in dark gold, she absorbed him in a glacial stare. "You are related to Valraven Palindrake, I believe," she said.

"Through marriage, your majesty," Khaster answered. He was sure that Tatrini knew this already, as well as recent events.

She confirmed this quickly. "I have heard of the death of Valraven's wife—your sister, of course. I remember now." She turned to Almorante. "When a person has suffered bereavement, they need a special place in which to heal. I know this because of my own suffering when your little brother, Clavelly, died." Once again, she turned to Khaster, with a fluid motion like that of a dancer. "My husband sent me to the family retreat at Recolletine. I have always loved the place. It has special restorative properties, I feel." She smiled, somewhat tightly. "Leonid signed the place over to Almorante as part of his twenty-first birthday present."

Almorante cleared his throat, obviously discomforted. "Are you suggesting, mother, that I send Khaster to Recollectine?"

The empress laughed dryly. "I am transparent, I know. Have you seen the Seven Lakes, Khaster?"

Khaster shook his head. "No, ma'am."

"It is the most beautiful area of Magravandias," she said. "That sadness in your eyes will drain away there. I guarantee it. The lakes will absorb your unspent tears. What do you think, 'Mante'?"

Almorante shrugged. "Would you like a holiday, Khaster? You will be leaving for Cos soon."

"Very like Caradore," said the empress. "Lakes, mountains, wild clean air. It would do you good."

Khaster couldn't help feeling a conspiracy was afoot. He had never met the empress before, yet she seemed unaccountably concerned for his well-being, intent on shipping him off to this place called Recolletine. "I will do whatever you think best," he said to Almorante.

Almorante slapped Khaster's shoulder. "Then a holiday it is. You can take Tayven with you."

"Yes, take Tayven with you," said the empress. "He knows the place well, because Almorante used to take him there often."

Khaster detected a barb in this comment, but couldn't interpret its meaning. He doubted very much whether Tatrini, empress of Magravandias, would disapprove of her son's morals or conduct. It was something else.

THE SEVEN LAKES of Recolletine were named for gods, who by the time Madragore's name had first been spoken in the land were already no more than dim memories in the minds of its people. As they made the final approach, in a carriage lent to them by Almorante, Tayven recited the sacred names. Anterity, god of war; Oolarn, god of knowledge; Ninatala, the sun king; Uspelter, goddess of love; Malarena, jealous goddess of the night; Rubezal, the hag of madness and inspiration and finally, Pancanara, the celestial lady, goddess of the cycle of the universe.

"The lakes are mystical," Tayven said. "Each has its own properties."

Tayven knew a lot about the countryside, because he'd been there with Almorante several times before. Khaster shrank from asking too many questions. He didn't want to dwell on what must have transpired between Tayven and the prince while they were there.

The retreat, a sprawling three-story wooden building of high, pointed eaves and shuttered windows, clung precariously to a steep, partly forested hillside overlooking the first of the lakes, Anterity. Khaster and Tayven arrived late in the afternoon, as the sun set fitfully in a sky of bulging clouds. Long ruddy rays touched the surface of the lake, where black swans haunted the shores, shrouded among rigid spears of reeds. The swans sang to the approaching night, and to Khaster it sounded like a lament for the end of the world.

Two servants, a husband and wife who lived in a small cottage farther down the hill, cared for the retreat. Their names were Porvo and Marien, and they greeted Tayven like an old friend. He let himself be enfolded by the capacious bosom of Marien and returned the less encompassing embrace of Porvo with equal warmth. Khaster stood a short distance away while this was occurring, his head thrown back to examine the building. The great eaves of the house were stippled with wind-sparrow nests. As dusk crept on, the birds filled the air with warbling shrieks.

Inside, immense fireplaces dominated every room, because in winter the place was cold, although Tayven said that Almorante didn't visit it that often then. While Tayven went to the kitchen with Marien and Porvo, Khaster explored the silent rooms with their slowly ticking clocks. The building was fascinating, full of intriguing nooks and crannies, its rooms filled with curios from a hundred lands. It was an ideal place in which to relax, because all the chairs and sofas were huge and enveloping, the library was stocked with interesting literature, and the views from the many windows were inspiring. But Khaster couldn't help thinking that these same rooms must have witnessed terrible things; namely the antics of Almorante and his cronies freed from the albeit limited restrictions of the palace in Magrast. He imagined them, drunk, lewd and greedy, indulging their hedonistic desires to capacity. He couldn't help seeing Tayven there, wearing the mask of a smile, while all the time feeling the way he had done at the Drake in the Soak, when Bayard had pawed him. As he thought this, Khaster heard Tayven's laughter ringing through the house, as if he'd come home to a family he'd sorely missed. It made him shudder.

That night, as Khaster lay awake in a wide canopied bed, he listened to the sounds outside. The window was open, and the long curtains swayed as if someone hid among them. This place was not like Caradore; the feeling was entirely different. Caradore was raw, as if the mountains were still young. Recolletine seemed older, more serene. It could be a place of healing, yes, but Khaster did not feel his spirit stir to the insistent throb of energy in the earth. There were no stark pure winds here, no high dreaming sky.

The following morning, Khaster rose early and went to stand in the sunlight by the open window. This was not Caradore, but he had to admit it was still a beautiful place. The air seemed to possess a supernatural clarity, sparkling before his eyes. Below the hill, Anterity's surface shone like metal. Bent and wizened trees surrounded it, and there was an island in its center, covered in what looked like ancient thorn. At its far end, a tier of weathered crags rose toward the sky, where feathery clouds hung motionless against the aching blue. It was not a pretty spot, in a traditional sense, being somehow stark and cold, but Khaster could sense its power. Pharinet would appreciate this place. He pushed the thought from his mind.

After breakfast, Tayven suggested they go for a walk. "There are waterfalls above Anterity," he said. "The next lake, Oolarn, is a few hours' walk away, but there are lots of mountain pools and cascades nearby."

Merien packed them some bread, cheese and a stone flagon of beer wrapped in damp cloths, which Tayven stowed in a backpack. They did not go down to the shore of Anterity, but took a narrow path up through the crags and the mountain meadows that lay above the retreat.

"We should see a few of the lakes while we're here," Tayven said. "You may not get the chance again."

"Have you visited all of them?" Khaster asked.

Tayven nodded, then pulled a rueful face. "Yes and no. I've been to all but one, because Pancanara is inaccessible. It is supposed to be hidden high in the peaks. Some people doubt it even exists."

"You seem very at home here."

Tayven smiled. "I am. I would live here forever if I could."

"Then ask Almorante if you can. He seems prepared to indulge your every whim."

Tayven laughed. "A nice idea, but even if he agreed, the retreat would never totally be mine. He could throw me out at any time."

"As if that's likely."

"Oh, it's likely, Khas," Tayven said. "Don't ever think otherwise. I'm just glad I'm here again now."

Khaster sighed. Sometimes, there was sadness in Tayven, but never bitterness. How wonderful to feel that way, not to care.

They climbed a particularly steep slope, grasping at grass and rocks to keep from falling, but then they reached the top and, through a frame of trees, they could see a waterfall rushing down through a series of fern-curtained channels into a small pool. Tayven put down his backpack. "This may not be one of the mystical lakes, but I love this spot."

"When did you first come here?" Khaster asked.

Tayven would not look at him, stared ahead at the pool. "Some years ago."

Khaster detected a tension. "How many?"

Tayven shrugged. "Three or four. I forget."

Khaster knew that Tayven did remember, and sensed it had been a significant time. A surge of hot anger flowed through him. He walked quickly toward the falls, where the sound of his own thoughts might be drowned. At the water's edge, where white foam scudded on the surface of the pool, he knelt down. The grass was damp and spongy beneath his knees.

Three or four years. It was unspeakable. Then Merlan's voice was in his head. "We must be clever. If you want to go home, you must keep your silence, play the Magravandians' game." He gazed into the pool, almost blinded by a fury he could not name. He blinked and saw a school of tiny bright blue fish twisting and turning in the hectic currents. Their scales flashed like fire beneath the foam. Beautiful. Then he saw they were clustered around a drowned water nymph fly, tearing it to pieces with minuscule teeth.

Tayven squatted down beside him. There was a flush along his cheekbones. "Don't judge me. I had no choice."

Khaster nodded. "What do you feel about it, though? If you'd had the choice, what would you have done?"

"I've never been forced into anything against my will, if that's what you mean," he replied. "I'm not that much of a victim."

"You're contradicting yourself." Khaster stood up. Why should he care? Because he wanted Tayven to become like him, scornful of Almorante and the rest? "You must have fond memories of this place," he said, wanting to wound, but when there was only silence and he turned around, Tayven wasn't there. That must be his resolve now: to walk away from Khaster's cruel words. Khaster slumped down again. He was fond of Tayven, but always wanted to hurt him with words, resenting his past, his secret life now. They were here for a reason. Almorante believed he could manipulate things that much. He couldn't. Khaster wouldn't let him.

Khaster stayed out on the mountainside until dusk and the sun sank in a sea of blood behind the jutting pines. Birds mourned in low voices and the grasses rustled with nocturnal life. He walked back to the retreat, noticing the single light burning in the attic room. There Tayven lay awake, he was completely sure. He would be lying on his back, with his hair spread out on the pillow, looking like a saint or an effigy. Khaster went into the house and directly to his own room, which was lit only by the owl-light of the moon.

The following morning, Tayven was out by the time Khaster awoke. His sleep had been disturbed by nightmares of Pharinet. All he could remember of them on waking was her cruel laughter. She had always despised him, seen him as weak in comparison to Valraven. She was right. He was weak in every sense. What was it Almorante thought he saw in him? Whatever it was, the man must be deluded. Filled with these self-hating thoughts, Khaster gloomily ate a breakfast, watched over by Marien, who seemed to observe him with knowing eyes. Tayven's absence obviously meant he was angry with Khaster, and that was unlike him. He was such a serene creature, fits of temper or melancholy on Khaster's part barely touched him.

Tayven was a being of light, and now Khaster craved those healing rays. He could see how it might be easy to become addicted to Tayven's presence. It was all that Almorante had promised.

He found Tayven high above the retreat at the waterfall they had visited the day before. It had been easy to follow his trail, for he had left a path through the dew-soaked grass. No one else would be walking here. Khaster called Tayven's name and it echoed from hill to hill. There was no response. He walked past the water, and imagined a ghost of himself there, squatting down, staring at the fish.

The trail led to a hole in the rock, where Khaster ducked down and walked along a narrow tunnel. What was Tayven doing here? For a moment he feared finding the boy dead. Died for love, they would say, of a broken heart. What kind of person did that make him, to think such a thing? He emerged into a cave, where light streamed down through a wide chimney in the stone. Tayven stood there, bathing in its rays. The scene looked utterly contrived. Tayven had heard him coming.

"The artist will be along later," Khaster said.

Tayven glanced at him, frowning. "What?"

Khaster shook his head. "Nothing. Are you angry with me?"

Tayven's frown deepened. "No. Should I be?"

"You weren't at breakfast. I haven't seen you since yesterday afternoon."

Tayven shrugged. "You need time alone."

"You lured me here."

"No. I was just looking at that." He pointed toward the wall. A ball of spiralling water nymphs hung there, like living jewels.

"They're beautiful."

"They're eating an owl."

Khaster looked closer. The bird was dead, its body a hollow shell, the wings drooping down. Nymphs were pulled beneath the waters of the lake to be devoured by fish, but they killed too. Everything beautiful had a core of evil. Nature itself.

"This place isn't affecting me the way you and Almorante wanted it to," Khaster said.

Tayven laughed. "You are so conceited, Khas. You think everybody spends all their time worrying about you and your problems. They don't. Almorante has you now. He's passed you to me for rehabilitation, haven't you noticed? But that job's not full-time for me. I have my own concerns."

Khaster nearly responded heatedly, then changed his mind. "I feel like I've been asleep all my life, and have only just woken to a horrible reality."

Tayven nodded. "I can see that." He beckoned. "Come here, Khas. Consider this."

Khaster stood next to him in the fan of light that came down through the roof. "Here we are in darkness," Tayven said, "and for us, if we did not know better, this light would be all that existed. But we do know better. We know that outside the cave the world is bathed in light."

Khaster swallowed with difficulty. He knew that at one time Almorante had stood here and said that to Tayven. Was the image therefore spoiled or a secret to be passed on? He imagined himself in years to come, in this very spot, and there was a nebulous presence beside him, waiting for the words to be spoken. He shivered. Time had stopped.

"You are mistaken about me," Tayven said. "I don't want you to want me, but only to want yourself. We won't know each other for long."

"How do you know that?"

"A feeling came to me here."

Khaster made a sound of annoyance. "This is too melodramatic," he said. "Let's go outside."

Tayven studied him for a moment, then shrugged. "I wonder whether you can," he said.

They strolled beside the river, up the mountain path toward the next lake, Oolarn. Tayven had a satchel with him, in which Merien had again placed a packed lunch. The sun had warmed the chill air by the time they emerged through a grove of trees to face another body of water. It was small and secretive, barely more than a pool, surrounded by sheer cliffs from which spindly trees depended. "Is this Oolarn?" Khaster asked.

Tayven shook his head. "No, this is just another minor site. I don't even know its name. You shouldn't visit Oolarn until you've properly experienced Anterity."

"And what's that supposed to mean?"

"It's a tradition. The lakes are a kind of mystical quest."

"And how do I experience Anterity, exactly?"

"By meditating at the site, of course." Tayven laughed. "Don't you know anything?"

"I'm not really impressed by that kind of thing," Khaster said stiffly. "Bayard is interested in ritual and mysticism, isn't he?"

"He might think he is," Tayven said. "You'd find that the reality is quite different."

"I'm a tourist, not a mystic," Khaster said. "And I like to think I can appreciate the lakes just as well, if not better, from that perspective."

Tayven said nothing, but concentrated on spreading out their lunch on a rock. They ate in silence for a while. Khaster felt disorientated. He wondered why he was there. It felt contrived, yet unreal.

"So, what are your concerns?" he said. "You mentioned you had them."

Tayven sighed. "Bayard is my main concern," he said.

Khaster was slightly surprised this information had been offered so willingly. "You're afraid of him? What about Almorante's patronage? Surely you're safe?"

Tayven observed him speculatively. "You're completely unaware of how much Bayard resents you, aren't you?"

"We have never been allies. I was beneath his notice at one time."

"Bayard is wounded, and unable to heal himself. He strikes out in bewilderment and disappointment. What happened in Caradore?"

"I told you."

"Some of it, yes. What happened?"

"Just what I said. Bayard, Valraven, Pharinet and Ellony performed a kind of ceremony on the beach. As far as I can gather, it sent Ellony mad and she ran into the sea. She was so strong in her madness that she took a grown man with her, who was trying to restrain her. He died too."

Tayven nodded. "This war will be won or lost through magic."

"What war?"

"The personal one, between the royal brothers and their allies. Bayard will kill me."

"Don't be ridiculous, Tay. Why should he? He wouldn't want to risk upsetting Almorante that much, and I don't believe you mean that much to Bayard. He had a slight fancy for you, that's all. We both know it's Valraven he worships."

"I'm a symbol," Tayven said. "You won't understand or accept this, I know, but if I am sacrificed, power will come from the act. Almorante himself would kill me if the moment was right, and I would sacrifice myself willingly, if it would do any good."

"I can't believe you'd countenance such rubbish," Khaster said. "You tell me to wake up and live my life, and now you say this. It's insane. The Malagashes are insane, Almorante especially, if he's filled your head with these things."

Tayven smiled sadly. "I knew you wouldn't understand, but you asked, and I told you. One day, you'll discover, painfully, how right I am. It's inevitable. What will happen will happen, regardless of what we think or do."

I won't let myself believe this, Khaster thought, and yet the strange ambience of the environment, the imminence shivering in the air, made him think that here was a moment of destiny. If he looked up now, there would be a star in the daytime sky, a messenger of the gods. But when he did look up, there was only Tayven. "I won't let you die," Khaster said. "Not because of Bayard."

Tayven nodded slowly, but would not smile. He stared into the water. "Almorante will send me to Cos with you."

"You mustn't come. It's a terrible place."

"It's a beautiful place," Tayven said, "but filled with enemies. I'll have to come. I can't let you go there alone. I don't trust you."

"Bayard will be with us, and Valraven Palindrake. Almorante will not. If only a little of what you fear is correct, it would be too dangerous for you to come. I would welcome your company, of course, but think you should stay here."

"Khaster . . ." Tayven shook his head. "This is difficult." He pushed back his hair. "I feel I'm bound to you. We were meant to meet and all that will happen from this moment on is also meant."

Khaster laughed softly. "You're talking about feelings," he said, "not a greater destiny."

"I think they're the same. All my life I've been groomed for something. I was sent to Almorante's court when I was ten years old." He raised a hand to silence Khaster's outraged remarks. "No, not for that. Almorante has always respected me. He's taught me many things, not least that we are all small parts of a great design. Formless powers compete for control around us, and we are their pawns. We did not choose to be born Magravandian, but that is our fate. The emperor creates change in the world. There are always emperors." He reached out and took Khaster's hand. "A few years ago, Almorante brought me to Recolletine. He told me I was light, and took me to each of the lakes in turn, except for the last. At every place, we evoked the spirit of the mountains in a different way. Almorante called light down into me. He set me on a path."

"You slept with him then. Was that the first time?"

Tayven nodded. "Yes. But it was not what you think. He cosseted me. It was almost innocent."

"And when did it stop being so innocent?"

Tayven looked away. "I wish it wasn't important to you."

"I can't help it. To me, what Almorante did to you was abuse. You're so young."

"Is that it? My age? Just that?"

"Mostly, I suppose, yes."

Tayven dropped Khaster's hand and stood up. "By Madragore, you're so blind. I'm as old as these mountains! Can't you feel that?"

"I believe your soul is old," Khaster said, "but that is not an excuse for a man to violate so young a body. Nothing can make me change my mind about that."

"I'm here for my birthday," Tayven said, "Almorante's gift to me was to send you here, let me come with you."

"His mother suggested it actually."

Tayven shook his head. "No, Almorante knew what I'd want. I'm seventeen tomorrow."

"Why didn't you tell me?"

"I wasn't sure whether I would or not. Your patronizing attitude makes me angry sometimes. Will you still see me as a child in the morning? It would have annoyed me if suddenly I was allowed to have feelings and lovers, due to the passing of one second before midnight to the next."

"I don't mean to treat you badly."

Tayven sighed. "You don't. It's just your way. I don't have to be here now. It's my choice."

There was a long and significant pause, then Khaster said, "Did you bring wine with you?"

"No, I did not!" Tayven growled in his throat. "I'll not give you that excuse." He jumped off the rock and began to run back the way they had come.

Khaster glanced at the remains of their meal and then went after him. Tayven hadn't run very far. Khaster found him weeping on the path, his face in his hands. "Tay, I'm sorry," Khaster began and put his hands on the boy's shoulders.

Tayven pushed him away. "Don't. Why do I let myself react like this? It's futile. I must just accept what is." He wiped his eyes fiercely and shook his head. "I'm learning something new—that sometimes the love you send out receives nothing in return. I should never have let it happen. We spoke about it. Do you remember? Love makes you weak and vulnerable. It's like a disease. I hate this feeling. It's making me something I'm not."

Khaster stood there helplessly. What could he say? Tayven was far wiser than he was. At seventeen, Khaster had known nothing about the ways of the world or of human feeling. He hadn't been in love with Pharinet when he'd married her. His mother had told him he should do it. It had been expected, as it had been for Valraven to take Ellony as a wife. An alliance of houses. Only homesickness, once he'd come to Magrast, had made him feel that he loved Pharinet. Perhaps he never had. All the anger and hatred he felt was because he'd been betrayed by a woman he'd been led to believe would be faithful to him, in every sense. That's what wives did. It was their role, and Pharinet was supposed to have adopted it. Why should she, though? It was simply tradition, and within that, no scope for individuality. Pharinet, more than anyone he knew, craved freedom. Why had they gone through with it? It seemed ridiculous now. "We expect so little from life," Khaster said. "We look at the ground when we should be looking at the sky."

Tayven looked at him warily, clearly perplexed because he hadn't intuited the train of Khaster's thoughts. Then, he grimaced and nodded. "You're right. I am looking at the ground. I should remember I am light, and look up. I shouldn't burden you with my feelings, because they can never be yours." He smiled sadly. "Thanks, Khas. What you said has actually helped."

"Good, although that wasn't what I meant at all. I'm not that subtle."

"What did you mean then?"

"It doesn't matter. Let's go back and finish our lunch. I want to see more sites before sundown."

Back at the rock beside the pool, a flock of small brightly colored birds was occupied with devouring the scattered food. They flew off in a whirring shrieking cloud as Tayven jumped onto the rock. "Spoiled," he said. "Are you still hungry?"

Khaster climbed up beside him. "No." He put his hands on Tayven's shoulders, sensed the boy's spine stiffen in discomfort, and withdrew as if scalded. "How far to the next pool?"

"Not far." He turned around. "Khas, I do have wine."

Khaster stared into his eyes. Feelings and urges warred within him. "No," he said. "It's too early."

"Before midnight?"

"That's not what I meant."

"Explain it to me. Tell me why you'll kiss me if you're drunk and not when you're sober. What do you feel? Is it repulsion? Is it fear? What? I'm like a guilty secret of yours, something to hide. You're ashamed of what you want to do when you're drunk."

This was the first time the matter had been addressed openly. Tayven looked belligerent, but Khaster knew he deserved answers. "I feel I have a wall around me when I'm sober," Khaster said. "Even when I went to the whore in Magrast, I had to get drunk. It's because of what happened in Caradore. My wife preferred to sleep with her brother rather than me. When I found out about all that, when Bayard told me, I thought about how Pharinet must have felt sick every time I came home. She *endured* me. It did nothing for my confidence."

"Is she beautiful?"

"Yes, like Valraven."

"Did you love her so much?"

"She was beautiful, Tay. I never knew her, not really. I was just a child, more so than you've ever been. I believed life would be one thing, then it was another. The life I knew had never existed. People weren't who I thought them to be."

"You must let it go," Tayven said. "Don't let it cripple you. Soon, you may be fighting for your life. Your despair weakens you physically. I can see it in you."

"I've decided not to drink here. That's a start, isn't it?"

"I wish I could reach you."

"You do." Khaster reached out and touched Tayven's hair. "I know you better than I ever knew Pharinet. You are so alive."

Tayven uttered a sorrowful sound and pulled Khaster into his arms. Khaster rested his chin on Tayven's head, breathing in his scent. The air was still, the only sound the lap of water against the rocks. "We will live through everything," Khaster said. "Almorante will help us. I'll do whatever he asks of me, and then he will give me freedom. I'll take you to Caradore, to the wildest places."

"Away from your family," Tayven murmured.

Khaster was silent for a moment, then, "Yes, away from them."

Khaster felt a great lightness in his heart. He felt renewed. The wall was breaking. Soon, he might step through it completely.

They returned to the retreat in the dusk, and ate the meal the servants had left out for them. As night fell, a tautness came into the room. Khaster sat in a chair before the window, staring out at the mountains. Tayven went up to him and kissed the top of his head. "I'm going to bed now. Don't sit here all night brooding. Get some sleep."

"Good night, Tay," Khaster said. He squeezed Tayven's hand, which lay on his shoulder. "I have to think. Some things became clear today."

"Sleep on it."

"I will."

Khaster watched the moon arc across the sky. The air in the room was chill, for the fire had burned away. Khaster shivered. He stood up and went to the stairs, his mind strangely numb. On the first landing, he paused, his hand on the door to his room. He looked up the next flight of stairs, where watchful ghosts seemed to cluster in the shadows. No light burned up there. He climbed the stairs carefully, making no sound. In the room at the top, the curtains were open and the last of the moonlight fell across the bed. Tayven, no longer lying on his back with outspread hair like a beautiful effigy, was a shapeless mound beneath the blankets. Khaster crept across the threshold and crossed the room. He stood staring at the bed, unsure why he was there, what he would do. Then Tayven said, "I'm not asleep, Khas." He emerged from the blankets with his hair over his eyes. Khaster knew he had been expected.

"Is it midnight yet?" Tayven asked.

Khaster pulled off his shirt. "No," he said. "Nowhere near."

TAYVEN WOKE KHASTER up in the twilight before dawn. "Come down to the lake with me," he said softly but urgently. "Now."

Khaster blinked, befuddled by sleep. "Why?"

"It's important. I don't care what you feel about magic, you must experience the power of Anterity. It is the lake of the warrior, and you need that force within you."

"I'll do it for you," Khaster said.

Tayven was already out of bed.

The air outside was cold, and Khaster wished he'd bothered to put on his boots. The grass was icy wet against his feet. Tayven hurried ahead of him down the path from the retreat, pausing every now and then to look back, to make sure Khaster was following. What was the urgency?

At the lakeside, Khaster stood yawning, scratching his hair. He felt physically replete and at peace. He could not believe he could feel that way. Perhaps he and Tayven could bathe in the water together.

"I had a dream," Tayven said, "about you and the lakes. I know you are meant to undertake the quest."

"What quest?" Khaster said. "Why?"

"I saw you here, invoking the spirit of Anterity. I saw you at every lake."

"Even the last?"

"I was with you at the last. Perhaps this is our chance at salvation, at survival."

"You said it was inaccessible, perhaps didn't even exist."

"Will you try? We could visit each lake and perform the invocations, as I did with Almorante. If we are to succeed, we'll find the seventh lake. It will just happen."

"Tayven, I'm not really interested in this kind of thing."

"Will you do it?" Tayven insisted.

Khaster had never seen him so fierce. He sighed. "If you really want me to."

"I do. You don't know how much."

"But what's the point, what's to be gained?"

"Knowledge and strength," Tayven said. "Sit down."

Grumbling beneath his breath, Khaster did so.

Tayven sat down beside him. "Close your eyes," he said. "I'll explain what we have to do."

Tayven's voice was no more than a whisper in the cold air. He told Khaster how to breathe correctly to induce a meditative state. Khaster felt himself drifting. He could so easily slip back into sleep now.

"I call upon the spirits of Anterity," Tayven said. "Reveal yourselves to us. Enter the heart of Khaster Leckery, impart your knowledge to him."

To Khaster he said, "Concentrate on the image of the lake as you last saw it. Imagine the spirits are coming to you. They can take any form. It will be personal to you. If any images appear before your mind's eye, you must tell me."

"It's just fog," Khaster murmured. He could imagine what the lake looked like, but nothing more.

"Relax," Tayven said gently. "This is the lake of the element of metal, the warrior's sword, the spear. Concentrate on that aspect."

As soon as Tayven finished speaking, Khaster saw an image of a sword. "Yes, I see it. A sword. Is that right?"

"What else?" Tayven urged.

Khaster frowned in concentration. He'd seen the sword because Tayven had suggested it. He hadn't generated the image himself. He couldn't conjure any more. "Nothing," he said, and then a clear, precise picture splashed across his mind. He saw Valraven crowned and throned as a king and holding up the great sword. In a flash, he pointed this weapon toward Khaster and said, "You are a champion of mine. One day, you'll return to me. We are one." The experience of the image was so real, it was as if Khaster had seen it with his physical eyes, heard it with his ears. More than a dream.

"No!" Khaster opened his eyes and was instantly relieved to see only the soft-focus dawn landscape around him.

"What is it?" Tayven asked. "What did you see?"

"Nothing," Khaster said. Why had his mind shown that to him? He hated Valraven. There could be no reconciliation. Valraven was not, and never could be, his king. The idea was obscene. He got to his feet. "I'm cold. I want to go back."

"Khas, you saw something. I know you did. What was it? I have to know before we go to the next lake."

"We're not going to," Khaster said. "I'm sorry, Tay. This isn't for me. I don't like the tricks the mind plays on us."

"Khas, what did you see?" Tayven asked, more insistently, but Khaster was already walking away from him, back toward the retreat.

He heard Tayven running up behind him and paused.

"It's so important," Tayven said. "I want you to have what I have."

Khaster turned around and cupped Tayven's face with his hands.

"You already have more than I ever thought could be given. Please don't push for more."

Tayven dropped his gaze. "I've bullied you," he said. "But that's because there may not be another chance."

"You have my body, you have my heart, you even have my mind, but the spirit's another matter. We're on different levels there."

"We don't have to be."

"Enough, Tay," Khaster said. "You must leave it. Let's enjoy what time we have together here."

Tayven knew enough to leave it be, but the furious frustration in his eyes, the certainty that a vital tide had been missed, haunted Khaster for the rest of their stay in Recolletine.

8

THE WAR IN COS

THE GOING WAS HARD because the wagons were hampered by mud. Whips cracked across the flanks of the straining,
steaming horses. Rain fell down in sheets. Men caught fever of the
lungs and died along the way. It was merciless, the country's assault
on those who would chase her children from her landscape.

Back in Magravandias, the weather had been perfect as the troops
filed through the city beneath the royal balcony on the outer wall of
the palace, away to war. Their armour had shone, and the pelts of
the horses. Petals and confetti had been strewn down upon them. The
foot soldiers wore flowers in their helmets. The empress Tatrini and
Leonid the emperor had stood upon the balcony, surrounded by those
of their family who were in residence: Almorante, Roarke, Celetian,
and the young princess, Varencienne. Valraven led the army beneath
them, beautiful upon a high-stepping black stallion, whose mane
flowed like the hair of Pharinet, dense and lush and fragrant. Valraven
stared straight ahead, his face pale like a sculpture. Bayard rode nearly
abreast of him, gilded, with the emblem of Madragore emblazoned on
his cloak. Banners surrounded them, and pennants, fluttering from a

forest of lifted spears, carried by a company of mounted holy knights, the Splendifers. Behind came the officers, Khaster among them, and Rufus Lorca and several others well known to him, leading in procession the cavalry, the artillery, the infantry. They were followed by the supply wagons and those that carried the beasts of war, which snarled and gibbered in darkness, beneath heavy coverings. The parade was the wealth of the capital, leaving it behind, flowing out to be squandered, and perhaps lost, in a foreign land.

People lined the streets and cheered. Leonid stood with arms upraised, beaming down upon his warriors. The empress lifted a hand and smiled faintly, while Almorante stood behind her, his expression contemplative. Khaster looked up to him as he passed, but Almorante caught no one's eye. Tayven rode behind the officers, with the other squires. He had an official position with Khaster now.

The army travelled east overland to the narrow coastal county of Petrussia and the port of Ornac on the shores of the Ranquil Sea. Here, great ships braved the tumultuous waves and carried the vast company to the western shore of Cos, where all the ports were firmly under Magravandian control. Diluente, the coastal town, was very ancient. Crumbling walls, adorned by basalt demons designed to frighten away invaders, cupped the vine-cloaked marble villas and temples. The sea gods might now wear the yoke of Madragore, but the docks were garlanded with offerings of fresh gobbets of beef bound with wheat, designed to appease the hunger of the water denizens.

The Magravandian company seethed ashore, creating chaos in the docklands. Horses neighed and stamped, cargo creaked upon its ropes, pulleys screamed with strain, men shouted orders impatiently. Native Diluentians gathered to watch the army disembark, their patrician faces haughty and scornful. Bayard made haste to a high-class inn to enjoy a final session of expensive food and drink, while Valraven stood like a stern gargoyle at the edge of the docks, overseeing the unloading, oblivious to the curious local onlookers who all knew his name.

Even then, purple thunderheads were gathering in the east. Some said renegade Cossic priests had called upon the goddess, Challis Hespereth. She had power over all the elements. By the time the army left the farmland beyond Diluente and ventured into the wilder areas of the foothills of the Rhye, the rain had begun to fall. It was relentless, punishing. It drowned the land.

Mid-country was where the troubled nested. A great range of mountains, the Rhye, effectively split Cos in two. In the past, Cossic emperors had ordered thoroughfares to be blasted through the living rock, but these were high, treacherous paths, hardly more than tunnels through the earth, where it was easy for Cossic snipers to make sport with anyone passing below. Valraven ordered Mewtish scouts to haunt the higher paths, in the hope of guarding his precious troops. It was true they flushed out several knots of resistance, but still the cliffs were immense and pocked with caves and tunnels. Cossic terrorists could move like ghosts, leaving no spoor, so there were casualties.

Every night, Khaster held Tayven to him, but sensed a distance in him. He presumed the boy was afraid of Bayard, or perhaps he missed the comforts of home. When questioned, Tayven would make an effort to be cheerful, but Khaster knew this was a sham.

Two weeks into the Rhye, the scouts reported a possible trap ahead. The army travelled a high pass that swept down into a deep, lush river valley. At its far end the cliffs formed what was virtually a natural amphitheater. The scouts were sure that the Cossics had stationed their best men here. They could attack the Magravandians from on high, as if shooting at rabbits in an empty field. Valraven gave the order to make camp at the western end of the valley. Mist steamed off the swift-moving river, but at least the rain had eased.

Khaster had felt oddly removed from reality all the way from Magrast, but now, seated on a stool outside his tent, while Tayven attended to their belongings inside, he listened to the eerily muffled sounds around him and began to feel deep unease. Was Valraven confident of victory here? The Cossics had a superb line of defense ahead, and they were driven by outrage and a lust for survival. Khaster stared through the mist at the barely visible cliff face at the other end of the valley. He could see nothing suspicious, but knew in his heart that they were being observed very closely. The Magravandians would set up their war machines and bombard the cliffs in an attempt to debilitate the enemy. But the Cossics would see that coming, wouldn't they? In the distant past, Khaster's own people had once tried to repel the Magravandians. They had failed, because of the empire's sheer force of numbers. But the Cossics were more tenacious. Khaster considered that the Caradorean soul contained an element of melancholic doom, which had perhaps contributed to their downfall. And yet, they made good soldiers, because they were able to anticipate the moves of an enemy. They were clever strategists and rode into battle with a sense of destiny, even if that destiny was to die. Khaster was confused about his own destiny. In Magrast, it hadn't been too hard to believe in Almorante's dream, but out here, in the cold hostile world, the intrigues of the court meant nothing. Even Bayard seemed different to how he behaved at home, his energy focused entirely on the task at hand. Or so it seemed.

There was no sign of life in the crags that night, but the men barely slept. In the morning, at Bayard's directive, foot soldiers dragged out the cannons and arranged them in a line to face the rocks. Bayard enjoyed a spectacle of fire and explosions. Valraven was not wholly behind Bayard's move, because he thought the Cossics had long fled the area, deterred from attack by the sheer force of Magravandian numbers. Bayard, however, insisted that the scouts had seen figures moving among the rocks. Still, Valraven must have thought they had little to lose, for only two hours after dawn the Magravandians directed the full blast of their artillery against the cliffs. There was no responding fire. Afterward, all was silent. Birds had fled. It seemed too easy. Nimble scouts scaled the smoking cliffs to count the dead. And dead there were in abundance. Unfortunately, they turned out to be the troops from a Magravandian garrison situated some miles to the north, recognizable mainly by their commander, who was found impaled in a cave nearby. They had been tied up among the rocks. It could only be surmised the garrison was no more.

Valraven seemed unaffected by the carnage and didn't even criticize Bayard's action, which surprised the other officers. He decided the Cossics would let the Magravandians press onward toward the city of Synticula, high in the mountains, long considered invincible. No doubt they expected to make short work of the exhausted Magravan-

dian army there. But no city was invincible to Valraven. Before a
siege was attempted, however, Valraven wanted to retake the garrison
to the north, so as not to allow the Cossics a secure area from where
to launch further attacks. Valraven himself would take his elite
troops to undertake this task. Meanwhile, Bayard would remain with
the rest of the men in the valley, guarding the pass to the west.

During the days that followed, parties went into the hills to hunt
for Cossic camps. Trained beasts of war would sniff them out. These
ventures were occasionally successful, and prisoners were even taken.
Some later died under torture. Khaster conducted some of these mis-
sions, wracked by doubt. Was he doing this to secure his own future
or because he believed in the cause? The Cossic king was no saint
himself. Given the opportunity, Ashalan would be in Leonid's position, emperor of a hundred lands. In previous generations, Cos had
owned vast territory, which they'd taken by force. Some people might
even say that the Magravandians were deliverers. This was one of the
reasons the land of Mewt was so amenable to its new conquerors. It
might still be occupied by foreigners, but at least the race that had
destroyed its own empire was now being routed. Before Cos, Mewt
had conquered a large part of the world. It was man's desire to carve
empires.

In addition to these greater concerns, Khaster continued to worry
about Tayven. Sometimes, he disappeared for hours. Was he trying
to avoid Bayard? The prince appeared to have forgotten the incident
in Magrast, or at least recognized it was trivial in comparison to
current concerns. Tayven would not talk about it. He performed his
duties, but the light in him, which Khaster loved and craved, seemed
shrouded. They still enjoyed physical intimacy, but rarely laughed
together now. Khaster yearned to return to Magrast. He lived like an
automaton, following orders, waiting for a time to come alive again.

One evening, Khaster dined with Rufus Lorca and a couple of
other officers in Rufus's tent. Tayven was also invited, but, as often
happened now, was mysteriously absent when the time came for Khaster to leave their tent. Over dinner, the men were relaxed, confident
that the camp was well guarded. Beasts snarled at the perimeters and
scouts prowled through the high rocks around them.

"I've a feeling we'll do all right," Rufus said, pouring wine.

Khaster smiled at him thinly. "Meaning?"

"This time, we'll win through to Synticula and Ashalan will be paraded through the streets tied to an ass."

Khaster smiled. "Is that an informed deduction or a gut feeling?"

Rufus shrugged. "Perhaps both. Don't you feel it?"

Khaster drank some wine. "I feel uneasy."

Rufus laughed. "You expect an attack here? Is that it?" He lit his pipe.

Khaster shook his head. "Not that. Something. This land is very old. It's alive. It listens."

"You Caradoreans, you're all superstitious," said another officer. "You see ghosts in every shred of river mist."

"What *are* you talking about, Khas?" Rufus asked, laughing, but his eyes were wary.

Khaster shrugged. "I really don't know. What's in that wine you're giving me?"

Rufus slapped his shoulder. "Perhaps you're worried about Valraven taking the garrison."

Again, Khaster shook his head. "Valraven will be victorious. It's not that. There's something *here*."

Rufus frowned. "What?"

Khaster took a few moments to answer. "I don't know."

For a few moments, contemplative silence filled the tent, then someone said, "Once Valraven returns, we'll take what's ours. That's the only feeling I have or want to have."

"Here, here!" others rejoined, and whatever strange moment had paralyzed the company had passed.

Presently, giving in to a pressing urge of nature, Khaster went outside. The night was silent, watchful. Now that the cannons were silenced, the birds had come back. An unidentified creature crooned sibilantly among the rushes; its voice had a disturbingly human tone. Amphibians chirred on the wet rocks along the banks and ancient willow trees swayed in a breeze Khaster could not feel. He shivered. What was it about this place? He felt something was happening; something he should know already, deep within, yet his senses failed him.

On the cliff face above, a blue-white light flared briefly. Khaster jumped instinctively, but then there was nothing there at all. Perhaps the light had alerted others, though. He heard the sound of running feet, drawing closer and closer. At first, he thought a phantom was upon him, because he could see nothing among the shadowy canopies of the camp. Then an orange light bobbed into view—someone running with a lamp. Khaster recognized the livery of a messenger. Had news come from the garrison? Khaster did up his trousers and stepped out into the path of the messenger. He opened his mouth to speak, but already the other was speaking, gabbling. "My lord, your presence is desired most urgently."

"Where?" Khaster demanded.

"The pavilion of his highness, Prince Bayard."

"What has happened?" Khaster asked. "Come inside with me and tell my comrades."

"No, my lord," said the messenger. "This message is for you alone."

Khaster hesitated. His whole being seemed to fill with a strange, buzzing power. This was the moment. This was it. "Give me the message in full."

"I was told only to request your presence."

Tell Rufus, a voice urged inside him. Don't go. Tell the others first. He heard his companions laughing together behind him, and for some reason, this diluted the need to confide in them. "Very well," he said. "Light the way for me."

Bayard's pavilion was situated in the center of the camp, near to Valraven's. Khaster was taken to a chamber within, where gilded couches were arranged in a circle. No one was sitting on them. Bayard stood in the middle of the chamber, surrounded by his cronies. Tonight, there was no feast laid out. The room seemed strangely austere. When Bayard noticed Khaster's arrival, his face was grave, but Khaster knew a smile lurked beneath his stern countenance. Khaster bowed. "You sent for me, my lord."

"Ah yes," said Bayard, as if reminded of an order he had forgotten. "I have some difficult news."

It isn't Valraven, Khaster thought. He felt a coldness come into him that might turn his limbs to stone. He didn't speak. He would provide no cues.

Bayard gestured with one hand. "As you know, we have taken a number of captives over the last week. We have interrogated them, of course. Now, it seems, we have an unexpected piece of information."

Again, Khaster did not seek to fill the pause. He remained expressionless, waiting.

"I'm afraid your squire, Tayven Hirantel, has been communicating with the enemy."

Khaster did not move. "That is impossible."

"Not at all. One thing you should know. There are schemes within schemes within schemes. My brother, Almorante, sent Hirantel here, under the guise of being your—assistant. But there were other motives. Almorante picks his people well. You should not be fooled by external appearances."

"I have no idea what you mean."

"Do you not?" Bayard laughed dryly. "A certain group of Cossic renegades are primed to assassinate me. The informant tells us this was directly engineered by my brother. Hirantel was the contact. Are you so blind?"

"I do not believe this," Khaster said, "and neither do you."

Bayard stared at him hard. "I know your thoughts," he said, "but you are wrong. I do not expect you to believe me. I am telling you how it is. Who knows what secret deals take place? In the future, it might well be useful for my brother to have tame allies in Cos. At that time, it might also be useful if I was no longer around." He turned away abruptly, apparently to examine some papers on a table. "Hirantel has been taken into custody. I thought it only fit to inform you of this. You will be required to answer questions also, although I know enough about you, Leckery, to believe you are not a part of this. It is beyond your capabilities. You were merely a screen for my brother's activities, to get his little spy onto Cossic soil for a legitimate reason—to accompany his feckless lover." He turned back to Khaster and smiled. "Didn't Almorante tell you he was concerned for you? Hasn't he foisted Hirantel upon you? Wake up, Leckery. At least be slightly outraged."

Khaster could barely take the information in. He had to struggle for a response. Eventually, after Bayard had waited with quiet relish, he said, "It was not Almorante's decision for Tayven to come to Cos."

Bayard rolled his eyes and sneered. "Of course it wasn't!" He sighed theatrically. "Oh, I can imagine what happened. That boy, with those liquid eyes, promising faith and loyalty." His expression hardened. "He's not what you think he is. But he's been found out and will be punished."

Khaster shook his head. "You cannot do this."

Bayard raised an eyebrow. "I understand this revelation must be hard for you to accept. Unfortunately, you have no alternative but to face the unpleasant reality."

Khaster was silent for a moment, then said. "What do you intend to do?" Bayard would have to wait for Valraven to return before he could take any action. He wouldn't dare do otherwise.

"You know as well as I do that the penalty for treason is extreme."

"I know also that any Magravandian accused of such a crime is given a fair hearing in Magrast. You will, of course, be sending Tayven home."

Bayard was perfectly still for a moment, then nodded. "That would seem to be the most appropriate course of action." He toyed idly with a tassel hanging from one of the canopy poles. "Naturally, once back in Magrast, Hirantel will be firmly once again beneath Almorante's wing. I find that rather irksome."

Khaster swallowed, tried to calm his panicked mind. "You cannot take the law into your own hands. Valraven will not permit it."

Bayard expelled an exaggerated yawn. "I cannot help but feel Almorante has taken the law into *his* own hands. Formal rulings do not apply to this situation."

Khaster felt as if he were being sucked underwater by a furious whirlpool. He had to clutch at reeds, but they were slippery and scarce. "What has Tayven to say about this accusation?"

Bayard snorted in amusement. "Do you really need to ask that?"
"I would like to see him."

Bayard shook his head. "At the moment, I will not allow it."

Khaster stared numbly at the prince. In a way, which sickened
him, he felt relieved. Now, at least he knew the nature of the sense
of doom that had hung over him: it had been the imminence of this
ridiculous charade. How could he appeal to this selfish, cruel man?
What had he to bargain with? "May I speak with you alone?" he
said.

Bayard again shook his head. "No."

Khaster's remaining equilibrium cracked. "I *beg* you . . ."

"No. Return to your pavilion. Two of my guards will escort you.
Please remain there until you have further word from me."

Men stepped toward Khaster, brandishing their muskets. "This is
a lie," Khaster said. "You know it."

Bayard merely gazed at him, his eyes strangely expressionless. He
raised a hand and the two soldiers took hold of Khaster and marched
him outside.

In his own tent, Khaster paced the confined space. Soon, Rufus
would discover what had happened. Valraven would return. Soon. It
must be soon. As dawn twilight stole through the camp, Khaster realized this was what Tayven had feared. Could Bayard's accusations possibly be true? Surely not. And yet, Tayven had been behaving
strangely in Cos. Stop it, Khaster told himself. Don't let Bayard convince you. Tayven is your friend. Bayard is not. This is all a scheme.

Khaster was confined to his tent alone for three days. After that, the
guards told him that Valraven had returned victorious to the camp.
Khaster had received no word of what had happened to Tayven. Not
even Rufus Lorca had been able to bribe entrance into Khaster's temporary prison. The Dragon Lord himself, however, could be turned
away by no one. In the late afternoon of his return to the camp,
Valraven Palindrake presented himself at Khaster's threshold.

At the sight of his erstwhile friend and mentor, Khaster was almost knocked over by an irrepressible surge of hope. However
blighted their relationship now was, they had known each other all
their lives. They were compatriots. And Valraven's power was total.

Khaster got up from the bed where he'd been sitting. He held out his hands in mute appeal. "Thank you for coming, Val," he began.

Valraven raised a hand to interrupt him. "This is a sorry state, Khas. It is a situation you should not be involved in." Unspoken, the rebuke that, unlike himself, Khaster was not clever enough to consort with the Magravandian princes.

Khaster did not allow himself to feel anger. He could not afford to. He lowered his hands and spoke calmly. "This accusation against Tayven is a lie. Bayard has his own reasons for wanting to hurt Tayven. You know that, surely."

Valraven's expression was impassive. "I have spoken to the informant they captured. His testimony is convincing. I'm sorry, Khas, but there does seem to be some substance to the allegation."

"I would know if there was," Khaster said. "The informant is no doubt on Bayard's payroll. This is the truth. I know it."

Valraven nodded shortly. "I understand your feelings. My personal belief is that if Almorante had indeed planned such a scheme, he would not have been found out. He is not so careless."

"Exactly," Khaster said. "Release Tayven, Val."

"I cannot do that. There has to be a trial."

"Here in Cos? Send the boy home, then."

Valraven studied him for a moment. "You have changed," he said, shaking his head. "It seems inconceivable to me that we are having this conversation."

"I have always been loyal," Khaster said, unable to keep a sting from his tone. "Tayven is a friend, unjustly accused. I can't stand by and do nothing."

"In my opinion, you must. You have been drawn into something, by unscrupulous people, whose last concern is your own welfare. Have you ever asked yourself why Almorante has suddenly taken an interest in you?"

Once again, they were children, Valraven the more astute. Khaster felt himself burn. He couldn't let this happen anymore. "I've asked it and answered it," he said. "But that is my business."

"You might think so," Valraven said, "but whatever you have become, it is not what you are meant to be. I intend to do what I can to have you sent home to Caradore. It would be the best thing for you, and perhaps this unfortunate incident will give us an avenue to accomplish that."

"Use Tayven's suffering as a convenient way home?" Khaster said. "Do you think I want that?" He paused and snarled, "Anyway, there is nothing for me to go home for."

Valraven did not even flinch. "It would be safer if you returned to Caradore—for all of us."

"What do you mean by that?"

"Almorante is using you. Your presence in Magrast—or even here—is a danger."

"To who? To you? To Bayard?"

"Yourself," Valraven answered. "Our families. It is a delicate time, Khas, you don't know how much. Caradore must be seen to ally with the most powerful prince, which for the time being means all of them."

"And you can do that so much more effectively than me," Khaster said bitterly.

"You are driven by personal concerns. You do not have a clear head."

"And whose fault is that?"

"We are all in control of our own destiny," Valraven answered coldly. "If we surrender that, it is no one's fault but our own."

Khaster shook his head. "How little you think of me, Val. Was it always this way?"

"Magrast has changed us both," Valraven said. "Many things have. We labor beneath a hard destiny. It is our legacy. We must do what we can to survive and ensure the safety of those who rely upon us."

"I know that," Khaster said. "And for this reason, I ask you to send Tayven back to Magravandias. You can do this. I know you can. It's all I ask. I can look after myself."

Valraven nodded shortly. "I will offer Bayard my advice, but I will not become embroiled in any schemes between the Malagash princes. Ultimately, it would be detrimental for me to show too much of an interest in their personal affairs."

"This is hardly a personal affair," Khaster said. "Someone's life may be at stake. You have power and must intervene. Whatever has passed between us, the Valraven I knew was just and honorable. You are the only person Bayard will listen to."

Valraven ignored these remarks. "My advice to you is to extricate yourself from Almorante's designs," he said. "Even if this one exists only in Bayard's mind, you must remember that everyone in this private royal war is expendable, but for the princes themselves."

"I am aware of that," Khaster said.

"Princes can make promises," Valraven said, "but they believe themselves to be superior to all others. The promises they make to those beneath them are worthless."

"I know that," Khaster said. "I'm not stupid. Has it ever occurred to you I'm not who you think I am?"

"Oh yes," Valraven said softly, "which is why I'm speaking to you in this way now."

Khaster turned away from him. "Thank you for coming," he said. "I realize you did not have to."

"I was obliged to, Khaster. We are still of the same family."

Khaster winced inwardly at that. "How long am I to remain under house arrest?"

"There is no house arrest. I do not believe you to be involved in any assassination attempt. Your participation, if any, was made in ignorance."

Khaster turned back to him. "There was no assassination attempt."

Valraven did not answer this. "Khaster, you need to order your thoughts. Put this matter from your mind. We are here in Cos to deal with Ashalan's renegades, and they will soon make their attack. Very soon. We must be ready."

"I don't believe it. The Cossics would not be so foolish."

Valraven shook his head. "Don't underestimate them. I've had to leave a substantial amount of men at the garrison, and the Cossics know this territory better than we do. They are desperate. It is essential we crush them now, otherwise they'll continue to harass our progress." He paused, then said, "You are, for now, an officer of the

Magravandian army with responsibilities. Whatever your thoughts concerning me and my family, think of your own now—your mother, who has lost her husband, your brothers and sisters. Survive, Khaster. For them. Once we have secured Synticula, I will do what I can to precipitate your return to Caradore. One day, you will thank me for it." He bowed curtly and marched out of the tent.

THE NEXT DAY was born in fog, an ideal condition for the Cossics to make their attack. Soft hooting sounds drifted from the invisible crags around the camp, advertising the presence of the renegade forces. There might only be a handful of them, intent on unnerving the Magravandians, or there could be a horde ready to fall upon the camp. Valraven positioned troops around the valley, behind heavy shields.

The officers gathered around the Dragon Lord, beneath his banner at the center of the camp. "They will employ the usual tactics," Valraven said. "Bowmen first, to draw us out." The Cossic bowmen were renowned for their accuracy and an almost animal ability to fire effectively from the most precarious locations.

Bayard, standing close to Valraven, laughed. "This will be suicide for them. Why do they even bother?"

"They believe this to be their country," Valraven answered smoothly. "They will continue to fight for it until Ashalan is dead— and perhaps even beyond that."

"You should have sent Mewtish agents to capture his sister, Helayna," Bayard said. "Ashalan would soon be waving the white flag, then."

Valraven ignored this remark. The Princess Helayna, if anything, was more of a threat than her brother. It was doubtful that even the most accomplished of Mewtish agents could get near her, and if they did, whether they'd survive the meeting. "The weather conditions are with them," Valraven said. "We may take heavy casualties, but we'll send the cavalry out first as usual." He addressed the other officers. "Have your musketeers ready. We'll have only one chance at this."

Presently, a deadly rain of slim Cossic arrows hissed out of the fog. Lightly armed, the bowmen could swiftly draw back, and as Valraven had said, they clearly intended to draw out the Magravandian cavalry, who could then be attacked quickly by pikes and spears. So little could be seen from behind the ranks, but the scream of horses could be heard, muffled through the fog, and the cries of men. The Magravandian musketeers advanced behind the cavalry. At the point when the Cossic bowmen drew aside to allow their hidden pikemen to charge forward, the Magravandian cavalry must also peel away, in order for the musketeers to have clear shots at the enemy, but the fog made it difficult to anticipate the right moment. Valraven, unlike the other officers, rode forward with the cavalry, as he always did. It was he who gave the order for the horsemen to gallop to the side. He did it by instinct, as he always did. And the musketeers began to fire.

The Magravandians did take casualties, perhaps more than usual, but the outcome of the battle was no different from any other the Dragon Lord had led in Cos. The remaining Cossics retreated behind the lizard gray rocks of the lower valley. Between their camp and that of the Magarvands was a muddy, bloody arena of carnage. Mist combined with gun smoke and the air smelled of death and horror.

Khaster went to his tent, where there was no Tayven to attend to his wounds. Not that he'd accrued many, just a scratch here and there. Like Valraven, and other Caradorean officers on the field, he'd taken part in the battle himself, albeit once the musketeers had done their work. He'd fought off his rage and his frustration. Each blow of his sword into leather and flesh had been a release. Men had died because of it. The enemy. But they were men, who like Khaster's own ancestors, had fought bravely for their land against impossible odds. Somewhere, hidden in the Rhye, their women and children must wait in ragged camps for news of their husbands, fathers and brothers. Tonight, the crags would ring with their laments. Exhausted, Khaster did not care. He lay on his couch, staring at the canopy overhead, where insects clustered around the swinging lamp. It was hard to recapture now the feelings he'd experienced in Recolletine, a sense of hope and freedom, a chance for the future. Now, he felt nothing except trapped, functioning without feeling. Perhaps this was what had happened to Valraven.

He heard running feet and the rasping breath and knew they came to his threshold. He wanted to sit up, but couldn't. The entry curtain was raised and there was a face, red, anguished. He didn't recognize it. "You must come, my lord. You must come."

It didn't seem real. Khaster slowly managed to raise his body, experiencing a dozen aches and twinges in his muscles. "What is it?"

"You must come."

"You must tell me where."

"Prince Bayard . . ."

"Has he summoned me?"

The messenger shook his head. No. He looked afraid.

Khaster nodded and got to his feet. For a moment, the world tilted. This is the end, he thought. He could run now. Vanish. Hide. He followed the messenger out of the tent. "Who sent you?"

The boy shook his head. "No one. But you must come. You must stop it."

"Stop what?"

The messenger shook his head, eyes screwed up. "We were friends, Tayven and I. I can't let this happen."

Khaster began to run, ignorant of the messenger's thin cries behind him. He was driven by instinct, a terrible knowledge deep within. He could hear them before he reached the prince's pavilion. Laughter, cries. The guards at the canopy made a cursory attempt to stop him, and no doubt could have done so. If he'd been more aware, he'd have realized this, but Khaster just plunged past them. He didn't even have a weapon. He was unprepared. Bayard was in the main chamber with half a dozen or so of his cronies. Khaster saw the prince first, standing with arms folded to the side of the group, his face composed in a restrained smile. He noticed Khaster's arrival and his expression did not change. One of the cronies stood erect, flicked back his hair and delivered a kick at something that lay on the ground between them, a figure curled up, bloodied pale hair spread over its face. Khaster's entire body went cold. He was frozen. Then, release, and he leapt forward, tearing at clothes, pushing bodies aside. For a moment, he saw Tayven lying at his feet, his hands over his head, trying to protect himself. Strong arms grabbed Khaster from behind, pulled him back, and Bayard moved toward him. "You should not be here," he said, and Khaster knew then that Bayard had sent for him deliberately. Khaster must be contained, not react in the way Bayard would expect. He knew that the wrong words or action now might end in Tayven's death.

"My lord, you are breaking the law," he said in the steadiest voice he could manage. "When Valraven hears . . ."

"Valraven?" Bayard laughed. "This has nothing to do with him. Hirantel tried to escape, to reach the Cossic lines. No doubt all our plans would have been revealed to the enemy."

"Plans? What are you talking about? Tayven knows nothing. He's just my squire."

Bayard shook his head. "You deluded fool." He marched to where Tayven lay and lifted his head by the hair. Tayven's eyes were swollen shut. They had beaten him badly. Perhaps he was not even aware Khaster was there. "He says nothing," Bayard sneered. "Is that the action of an innocent? He will not even defend himself."

"Look at the state of him!" Khaster cried. "He cannot speak. He's barely conscious."

"That was not the case earlier."

"This is torture. Remember Tayven is a favorite of Almorante's."

Again, Bayard laughed. "Who knows that more than I? I have no fear of my brother. He is guilty and will not want this matter to become public. Our father would be furious if he knew. He wants us all to get along, as loyal subjects of our brother, Gastern."

"Is there a price on this?" Khaster said.

Bayard studied him for a moment. "Are you trying to buy my favor?"

"Yes."

The prince drew in his breath slowly. "The price is Hirantel's confession. I want him to confess to me and then to my father in Magrast."

"Is that why I'm here?"

"He might well listen to you."

"If he confesses, he will be executed. How can I be party to that? I am not convinced he has anything to confess. I need to speak to him privately first."

Bayard sighed. "Your argument is reasonable, but I am not prepared to let the little snake win you around. You are too gullible." He gestured to one of his friends. "Throw water on the wretch. Revive him. There are other methods."

"No!" Khaster cried.

"Then tell him the right thing to do. Will you countenance his suffering otherwise?"

Khaster rubbed his hands over his face. "This must be mediated. Send for Valraven."

"No. He will not want to be concerned with this."

"I disagree. He spoke to me yesterday."

Bayard raised his eyebrows, but did not seem particularly surprised. "Whatever he might have said to you, Palindrake will not give you his support openly. Not against me. I know this as I know the beat of my own heart. He has too much to lose—the favor of my mother being the main concern. We are out in the wilderness. There are no laws here, and courtly behavior does not apply."

Khaster shook his head. "Then I will go to him myself." He tried to pull away from the men who held him, but after a brief gesture from Bayard they only increased their grip.

"Revive the boy," Bayard said.

The whole scene seemed suddenly to freeze in Khaster's mind. A memory came back to him, as vivid and pure as a lucid dream. Long ago, when he and Valraven had been youths, Khaster had ridden his gelding to one of the high pastures above Norgance, the Leckery estate, for he had agreed to meet Valraven there. They had been young teenagers, first experimenting with life. The annual summer horse fair in the village of Greenriver, nearby, had attracted a number of travelling clans to the area. Travelling girls were free and wild. They were happy to dally with handsome youths from the great houses. They liked receiving presents. They liked excitement. It had been Valraven's plan for Khaster and himself to visit the camps that afternoon and see what would happen next. Neither of them had experienced a woman and Valraven thought it was time they did. Khaster always did everything that Valraven told him. He felt nervous but also full of anticipation. Valraven was late. No doubt Pharinet had detained him, with that sixth sense she had for when he was up to mischief. She would want to come too and Valraven would have to be clever to put her off. Khaster sat on the fence kicking the wood, chewing on a sweet grass stem. The sun shone on the glossy backs of the mares and foals that grazed among the flowers. He was quite content to wait for his friend, fantasizing about what might transpire later in the afternoon.

Presently, the sound of loud male voices could be heard emanating from the nearby forest and a group of youths strolled into view. They were older than Khaster, and he immediately felt wary of them, then considered that they must be traveller lads. They wouldn't make trouble. The travellers were too fond of extracting money from the rich landowners of Caradore and that circumstance required a respectful relationship between the two tribes.

The youths jumped over the fence on the far side of the field, pushing each other around, laughing crudely, shouting. Khaster shifted uncomfortably on his perch. Where was Valraven? He looked behind, but no rider galloped along the long road from Caradore Castle. As the rowdy group drew nearer, Khaster realized they weren't traveller boys at all. Their attire lacked the flamboyance associated with travellers and they did not have the typical rangy, forest folk appearance common to the wandering tribes. But then many people were drawn to the horse fair, some from bigger towns over the border in Magravandias. Some of these people weren't interested in horses at all, but in the other delights that could be sampled at the fair. Merchants from all over Magravandias brought their wares to display. Intoxicating beverages were on sale, and in the evening people would dance and drink themselves insensible in the balm of Caradorean summer air. It was clear to Khaster that, despite the early hour, the youths before him had already been sampling some of liquor merchants' wares. To his horror, they began to chase the animals in the field, waving their arms and yelling, then doubling over with laughter as the creatures fled, terrified. Khaster saw foals separated from their mothers, screaming in fear. He saw one bulky youth run after a lone foal and throw himself upon it, bringing it to the ground. The animal uttered a piercing cry and its mother ran toward it, but a couple of the other youths, who carried sticks, beat her away. Khaster jumped down from the fence and ran into the field. He knew, because Valraven had often told him, that he was not a particularly brave person, but he could not countenance what he was seeing. He shouted out in fury, and for a moment, the gang froze and stared at him. Only for a moment. Then they were laughing again, pulling stupid faces at him, making obscene gestures. The bulky youth stood up and the foal got shakily to its feet, almost too terrified to move. Khaster felt helpless. He had initiated something he could not handle. Where could he go from here? The gang would beat him senseless, perhaps worse. They were advancing toward him, their eyes full of a hideous hunger Khaster had never seen before. It was the lust to harm. He felt his legs go weak. Then he was running back toward the fence, where his horse was tethered. He must reach it, gallop away. He could hear the thud of heavy feet behind him, the delighted catcalls of the gang. He would never get away in time. But then, miraculous wonder. A black stallion was galloping toward the fence, Valraven upon it, his black hair flying back from his head. The stallion cleared the obstacle in one soaring leap. Valraven pulled it to a rearing halt for a moment as he surveyed the situation. Then he urged it forward, uttering a scream of rage.

The stallion pounded past Khaster, and in seconds Valraven was among the gang, his mount rearing and kicking, its rider lashing out with a long stick. He needed a crop to control the horse, which was notoriously willful. The gang did not fight back. They were stunned, overwhelmed. They ran away, saying nothing. They just ran.

Khaster looked after them, full of an awareness of his own incapability. Valraven rode back to him and pulled the sweating beast to a snorting halt. He jumped down and put his arm round Khaster's shoulders. "There," he said.

That was that. He needed to say no more. Both of them knew that Khaster without Valraven was powerless, only half a creature.

That was how Khaster felt now. It was not a young foal before
him, but a boy he loved. What Bayard was doing to him was beyond
terrible and Khaster could do nothing. The men had thrown water
over Tayven's head to revive him. They had stripped him naked.
Khaster expelled a sound that did not sound human even to his own
ears. He found his strength, but it was not the strength to intervene.
He broke free of his captors, who were too interested in what was
going on before them anyway. He ran, stumbling, out of Bayard's
pavilion, out into the night that stank of death. The camp seemed
strange to him, he did not know it, but somehow he found his way
to Valraven's pavilion. The guards at the entrance made some effort
to detain him, but he was too driven to stop. He clawed his way
inside, beat at the canvas to find his way to the only person who
could ever help him.

There was an uncanny stillness in the inner chamber. Khaster
found Valraven there, sitting before a small table, upon which lay a
cup of water and a plate containing the remains of an austere meal.
Nearby, Valraven's squire moved silently and discreetly around the
chamber, attending to his master's battle gear. The boy looked up
when Khaster burst into the room and stealthily left the room between
some curtains. Valraven did not look up. His face was pinched, turned
in on itself. He had a knife in his hand, which he held point first
against the tabletop. It was almost as if he'd been waiting for Khaster
to come to him.

"Val," Khaster gasped. "Help. I need . . . Val, you must stop
them."

At that point, Valraven looked at him. What Khaster saw in his
eyes was an immense and eternal black void. There was no emotion
there. No response.

"They are killing Tayven. You must stop them. I beg you. Go
to Bayard. He'll listen to you. You know he will. Val, do anything,
but stop them. Please!" Khaster was weeping now, the same tears he
had wept a thousand times in boyhood, when he'd curled himself into
a dark corner, overcome by feelings of inadequacy and fear. Valraven
had always found him, brought him out into the light, filled him with
strength.

Now, Valraven only shook his head.

"Val!" Khaster went to the table, leaned upon it, almost retching with despair.

Valraven sighed deeply. "I can't," he said.

"Why? This is *me*, Val. Remember everything. Remember it now. Forget the anger between us. I'd give you my soul for your help. I beg you. I beg you."

"I can't," Valraven said again. He was luminous with a strange indigo light. He was inhuman, like a demon.

Khaster fell to his knees, clasped his hands upon the table, as if in prayer. "What can I do? Tell me. I'll do anything. Forgive me. Help me."

"Go," said Valraven. "I cannot help you. I am not the man you knew." He spread out his left hand on the tabletop and raised the knife. "This is who I am now." He plunged the blade into the back of his hand, skewering it to the wood.

For a moment, Khaster stared at this sight, then at the dark pulsing countenance of the man before him. He was physically repelled by the black force that emanated from those eyes. He did not know this man. It was not even a man. Something else.

Khaster ran from the pavilion. He was like a spirit cut free from reality. He was adrift, helpless, insubstantial. His only thought, born of desperation, was to offer his own life in place of Tayven's. Somehow, without remembering how he got back there, he was in Bayard's pavilion, on his knees before the prince. There was activity around him. He could hear Tayven's guttural moans of agony. He was praying.

Bayard was a blade of radiant light, the power of the sun. Yet he was serene, controlled. He listened to Khaster's outpourings in stillness, perhaps fascinated. Then he raised a hand and murmured, "Stop."

Behind Khaster, there was a thump as the two men who held Tayven dropped him to the floor. A third man stepped away, tidying his clothing. Khaster could hear choking, rasping breath, like a death rattle. He raised his head, implored with his eyes, but there was no compassion in Bayard's face, just a watchful, calculating chill.

"I have never seen anything like this," Bayard said. "It is . . . strange. I almost do not want this power—to make a man an animal." He smiled faintly. "Tayven Hirantel, look at this man." His cold shining eyes snapped toward his followers. "Raise him. Make him look."

Khaster could not look away. He was nothing more than a shuddering nerve of pain, and he had no right to be, for he had not suffered like Tayven. He heard Tayven groan as they lifted him.

"Tayven Hirantel, denounce this man," Bayard said softly. "Cast him from your life, and I will give you leniency. I will send you back to Magrast."

Tayven expelled an indistinguishable sound that may have been a word.

"I cannot hear you," Bayard said. "Speak more clearly. Say, 'Khaster Leckery, you are worthless scum. You are nothing. You cease to exist in my sight' "

Khaster could not look at Tayven, as haltingly, brokenly the words came out of him with bubbles of blood. Khaster looked only at the floor, where the blood dripped down. Hearing them, these strange confessional words, Khaster felt flooded with an almost beatific relief. What he was hearing was truth, a truth he'd always known in his heart. The experience was religious. The condemnation, wrenched from a scapegoat, was a divine judgment.

Eventually, there was only silence, but for the heaving breath of the boy.

Bayard nodded thoughtfully. "It is done," he said. He stretched his arms languorously, yawned. "I am bored of this."

Khaster let his shoulders slump. Bayard had what he wanted, perhaps what he'd desired all along: revenge. But it didn't matter. Khaster's martyrdom had been restored to him. His life was nothing. He was nothing. For a few scant moments, this revelation was spiritual in its purity and simplicity. He felt release.

"Finish it," Bayard said.

Khaster looked up at him, uncomprehending. Then, he heard Tayven cry out. The men had lifted him again, laughing. "No," Khaster said.

Bayard raised an eyebrow. "So trusting, aren't you," he murmured. "Will you stay to watch?"

They didn't detain him. They let him run, chasing him only with their laughter. Tayven was screaming in a hideous, monotonous way. He would be ripped apart. Khaster ran through the night once more. He ran among the dark tents, only barely conscious of the faces that turned to him as he stumbled past. He lurched out toward the battlefield, and someone called his name. Called him back. He did not heed it. He ran among the corpses, not yet hauled away from the ground made muddy by blood. He fell upon half-buried blades, lacerating his hands and knees. He trod upon mutilated, lifeless faces and dismembered limbs. He slipped in the entrails of a horse. And still he ran. Toward the Cossics, toward conclusion. The enemy was his redeemer. In the darkness beyond life, pain would end. As he ran, he stripped off his uniform, unaware of the cold. The Magravandian cloth and leather burned him like gall. It was a symbol of all that had destroyed him.

For what seemed like many days and nights, Khaster fled from life, out of the valley, down the narrow pass that led to wider vistas and beyond. He could not stop running; a supernatural strength gripped his body. Strange, pulsing symbols appeared before his eyes, oozed past him. He neither ate nor drank nor slept, but still his strength did not diminish. It was almost as if something called to him, drawing him onward. The otherworld, perhaps. In his flight, a detached part of his mind wondered if he was already dead, and this was the hinterland, which would lead to the extinction of consciousness he craved. But there were no answers, only the drive to keep moving.

One morning, in the dawn, he found himself lying on his belly upon a rocky platform, looking down on a land exquisite in its beauty. He realized he must have slept at last, falling exhausted in his tracks. Below him, he saw green forests, swelling hills, cascading water. It was a paradise. But he knew he was still alive. He stared at his bloody hands, furious he could not escape the prison of flesh and attain oblivion. Where were the terrorists so eager to take Magravandian lives? Perhaps he should have kept his uniform. He was anonymous now, a naked body. How long would it take to starve to death? He was thirsty, but revelled in the discomfort of it. He would not drink. He would run no more, for there was nowhere to run to. He would just lie here and wait for death, however long it took. He rolled onto his back and closed his eyes.

At first, he thought he had imagined the sound. It was faint beneath the murmur of water, the hiss of wind in the leaves. A human sound, weak but full of entreaty. Khaster listened to it for a while, until he came to his senses enough to realize it meant someone nearby was in need of help. He could not ignore it. Stiffly, he rose to his feet and, swaying, looked about him. The sound came from beyond the rock face behind him. There was a narrow path to the left and Khaster followed it, squeezing between the dark stones to emerge into a flat area, where a ring of shivering birches surrounded a pool. Water fell from a rocky lip above and the ground was a soft carpet of short green grass. The scene was idyllic but for one aspect. Half lying in the pool was the body of an old man, and it was from here that the sounds were coming.

Khaster went over to the pool and knelt down. Even despite his own pain and bitterness, his heart was touched with sympathy. The man's legs were immersed in the water. His bearded face was ashen with the approach of death, yet still retained the remnants of a handsome countenance. His clothes were not of expensive cloth, but something about him spoke of nobility. He had no weapons, no possessions Khaster could see. Perhaps he had been attacked and robbed, but he did not seem to have any obvious injuries. He might have been lying there for a long time, weakly calling for help. His pale eyes blinked at Khaster, their expression bewildered, as if he dared not believe someone had come to his aid.

In silence, Khaster took the man's head in his hands and rested it on his lap. He leaned forward and scooped a palmful of water from the pool, which he dribbled between the cracked lips.

"You have come," croaked the man, in a voice that was at once feeble and surprisingly strong. "I was afraid you would not. I have waited for you, willed you speed."

"You do not know me," Khaster said. "Where do you live? I can help you home."

The man smiled wearily. "You have come, as I have prayed for." He reached up with long shaking fingers and lightly touched Khaster's cheek. His hand was hot and dry and slightly rasping like the hide of a snake. "Empty of all, you are. My vessel." He beckoned with his fingers. "Lean close to me. I cannot raise myself and there is little time. I have hung on with all my strength, but I can feel it leaving me. I must give it to you. Come close."

Khaster thought the old man had some further nonsense to mutter so leaned down and placed his ear close to the shuddering lips. But then the man grabbed hold of his hair with an unexpectedly strong grip and pulled Khaster's face toward him. He expelled a gust of foul breath that somehow forced itself into Khaster's mouth. It was a hot and writhing wind, like a gaseous serpent, that seemed to have a life of its own.

Khaster was unable to utter a sound. He felt at once paralyzed and overwhelmingly nauseous. He had been violated, infected, but why?

The old man sighed, his narrow chest seeming to cave in before Khaster's frozen eyes. "Take it all," he murmured. "I am yours, my friend."

The air became very still. A birch leaf fell down from a branch overhead and landed on the old man's open left eye. He was dead.

Khaster sat numb, the corpse still resting on his lap. He felt strange stirrings within his body, as immense as the cracking of mountains, as small as the nip of a flea.

The sun arced across the heavens, seeking repose in the west. Khaster became aware of cold and stiffness. He gently eased the old man's body from his lap and staggered erect. The light was red around him, full of imminence. I am in Breeland, he thought, a county of Cos. How do I know that?

Because you are Taropat, murmured a voice in his mind, and he knows all.

9

THE FACE IN THE MEDE

S HAN FOUND HIMSELF outside the tall narrow house and could not remember how he had got there. The forest, the sward, even the water in the pool, were blue in the twilight before dawn. The air was cold and damp, smelling faintly of wood smoke, the beginning of autumn. Dew shimmered in the spiderwebs beneath the eaves of the house, upon each blade of grass. Shan staggered out toward the mill pool. Nausea burned the back of his throat. So many memories had come back, and not just mentally. He could smell hot leather, hear their laughter.

By the water, he collapsed upon the wet grass and wept, not just for Taropat, but for himself. How small, how fragile a human being was. No matter how powerful you might feel, whether magically or physically, ultimately others, in concert, could always stamp out your life. Shan was consumed by the desire to attack the Magravandian empire, to destroy it. There must be a way. There had to be a vulnerable chink in its armor. And yet, hadn't Taropat's story indicated clearly that evil was not just peculiar to Magravandians, but to all humans? To rid the world of one empire merely made room for another. Did evil have more provenance in this world than justice? Would it always be that way?

By the time Shan heard Taropat venture out of the house, the sun was higher and birdsong filled the garden. Taropat's steps came shushing over the grass, and eventually he stopped, his presence uncomfortably real, looming over Shan, who lay on his stomach beside the pool. "The world is not the place we want it to be," Taropat said. "It never will be."

Shan rolled onto his back. "Then why bring me here? Why talk of rebellion, of heroes, of victory?"

Taropat shook his head. "I thought that I could make a weapon of you. It was not my desire to make you a force for the good particularly, just a force for effect."

"But all I've learned in the forest is beyond such human concerns. I've learned little bits of the knowledge of a magus. Not enough to be powerful, but enough to hook me, hold me, make me hungry." He sat up. "I know now why Thremius rejected me. He disagrees with your plans. He knows what inspires them." He shivered and murmured, "It's all so clear to me. You wanted to make me Tayven, send me back as an avenger."

"You will never be Tayven," Taropat said shortly, which made Shan flush.

"I meant . . . you know what I meant."

"Perhaps you are right," Taropat said. "Now you know the truth." He sighed. "I have deluded myself. You should go back to your people." Without further words, he went back into his house and closed the door.

Shan sat on the grass, shivering. It would still take some time for the sun to warm the air. Autumn was coming with its invitation to winter. Did he want to go home? He stared into the gloom of the forest, perceiving the subtle moves of animals and even the unseen flicker of less material creatures. He had changed. He was not the person he'd been. How could he go back now, with only half an education of this new unknown world? He would tell Taropat this. The man must accept some responsibility. He couldn't cast Shan off now.

Shan got to his feet. He examined the door to the narrow house for a while, wondering whether he should go back inside. Because of what he knew about Khaster, he was afraid Taropat might damage himself in some way. Taropat had been right: the story had changed Shan's attitude toward him. He knew now that he and Taropat were more alike than he'd thought. But in other ways, more distant than he'd ever believed. He didn't understand how Khaster had become Taropat, because the story had ended before Taropat explained exactly what had happened with the old man in the pool. Listening, Shan had been too sickened to feel curiosity. He'd wanted to shut his ears from the moment Taropat had begun to tell of Tayven's suffering. He could smell it, taste it. He'd just wanted to escape, run into clear air.

Perhaps Taropat should not be left alone now. Perhaps they should talk more. Yet something impelled Shan's feet toward the forest path that led to Thremius's tree. Gust was nowhere in sight. It seemed he'd fled the scene of human emotion, perhaps distasteful of it, or afraid.

Shan found both Nip and Master Thremius outside their dwelling, cooking fish on an open fire. He heard their voices long before he saw them, and stole silently along the path, curious. Between the branches of an elder tree, he saw Nip squatting before her mentor, who was adding fuel to the fire. Nip was chatting away, and occasionally Thremius would answer her, snap out a question. She would respond and he'd nod, smiling to himself. Shan felt excluded from this scene. He and Taropat had never enjoyed such easy friendship. It also surprised him to see how close Nip and Thremius were. He considered turning away, then almost involuntarily fought his way through the bush into the glade. He had to speak to Nip. He did not care what Master Thremius might think.

Nip looked up, momentarily surprised, and Thremius twisted around to see. His face changed, from animated to expressionless.

"Shan!" Nip cried. "What's wrong?"

Shan knew he'd been right not to turn away. It seemed as if a warm wave of affection surged toward him. He went to her, knelt down, embraced her. She curled her arms about him and for some moments said nothing. Then Shan raised his head. "I have spoken to Taropat," he said.

Nip's brow was furrowed. She shook her head, her mouth pursed.

"He told me his story," Shan said.

Nip just stared at him, as if searching for words, but Thremius said gruffly, "You've come here to unburden yourself of it." Then his voice softened. "But first you must share our breakfast."

Nip nodded. "Yes." She sniffed, rubbed her nose and began to arrange plates before her. Shan noticed, with interest, that there were three plates. He noticed also that Nip was close to tears and knew in his heart that Thremius had told her he would come, perhaps even some of what Taropat had revealed to him.

They ate the fish with bread, and drank smoky milk, warmed over the fire. Shan's heart felt like a bloated weight within his chest. He sensed more unspent tears clogging the clarity of his mind, yet there was comfort in being aware of this. At one time, he wouldn't have understood these sensations within his body.

After the meal was consumed, Thremius lit his pipe and Shan knew it was time to talk. He expelled the story without pausing, and neither of his companions interrupted him. Sometimes, it felt as if he was telling his own story, and he realized that mixed up with the tragedy of Khaster were images and feelings from when the Magravandians had sacked Holme. When he related Tayven's violation, he spoke in the first person. Yet it was so different.

At the end of it, he felt exhausted and drained. The only sound in the glade was the popping of the embers in the fire. Then Thremius said sharply, "You are forgetting yourself, girl. Do what you must."

Nip settled herself opposite Shan and put her hands on his head, her fingers pressing against his temples. He felt her hands grow unnaturally hot and, for several minutes, basked in a lazy, healing energy that flowed through her hands. When she drew away, his whole body was cold and shivery, although he no longer felt so diminished.

"Thank you," he said.

"Pleasure," said Nip, and put some more milk into the pan on the fire.

Shan rubbed his face. "It's only half the story," he said. "What happened to Khaster? How did he become Taropat? I couldn't ask him. I should have done." He paused. "Now, I am afraid it is too late."

"No, no!" Nip exclaimed.

Thremius raised a hand to silence her. His teeth clicked against the stem of his pipe. "I have known Taropat for a long time," he said. "If you are afraid this release of pain will induce him to take his own life, have no fear. Khaster's suffering is not Taropat's. He can remember it, and even feel it, but not as acutely as you do now."

Shan frowned. "How is it possible? How could he become someone else?"

"He is not. He is all he ever was, and more. Taropat is a great magus. He has lived through many lifetimes. He is also a proud creature and feels his knowledge is too valuable to be lost. Unlike me, he has no faith in apprentices, because he feels that once he is dead, they can do whatever they like with the precious skills he has given to them. Therefore, he chose a different way. He finds himself an avatar and teaches them from within." Thremius sighed. "A tiring path. I, for one, will not be sad to relinquish this barbaric world when the time comes."

Nip made a sarcastic sound. "Yet you've held on to this life for considerable time."

"My tasks are not complete. I own certain responsibilities."

Nip glanced at Shan, while cocking her head toward her mentor. "He is very old, you know, older than your great grandfather would be if he was still alive."

Shan was not surprised by this information, but he had not come here to discuss Master Thremius. "Why did Taropat choose Khaster, though?"

"It was not a choice exactly," Thremius said. "Taropat simply asked the great powers of the universe to send him an avatar and one came. He'd had an inkling of it for some time, as he received an image of the lakes in Recolletine in his scry mede. He saw Khaster there and knew he would be the one. I remember he was very puzzled about it, and more than a little perturbed. It was not a choice he'd have made himself. By the time Khaster came to him, he was very damaged, as you know. This exasperated Taropat. He's had to expend a lot of time healing the mind of his avatar. I don't believe the job's yet finished."

Shan was confused by the image of Taropat and Thremius conversing about the matter, as if Khaster wasn't there. But of course he had been, on every occasion. Khaster's own mouth had talked about this ailing, weakened being inside him. It was bizarre.

"But what does Taropat really think about me?" he asked. "It was Khaster who abducted me, Khaster's desires for revenge that inspired him."

"Khaster and Taropat are one," Thremius said. "It is hard to grasp, I know, but there is really no division."

"You talk as if there is."

Thremius shook his head. "No. You misunderstand."

"You don't approve of what he's done, though, do you? You wouldn't teach me."

Thremius laughed. "And what a disappointment that must have been. You've learned well enough, boy. All that you should have." He got to his feet and picked up his staff, with which he tapped Shan upon the shoulder. "But now is the time for you to walk upon the steeper path."

"You will teach me yourself?"

"You should not believe someone is so much wiser just because they are old," Thremius said. "Some wisdom can be learned only from the young. I know this, because I do so constantly." He tapped Shan again. "Get up, boy. Go home."

Shan frowned. "To Holme?"

Thremius raised an eyebrow disapprovingly.

"To Taropat," Shan said.

"Return here in seven days' time. Not before."

AS SHAN EMERGED from the forest into the mill pool glade, he saw that Gust was crouched miserably upon the roof of the house. He called the grim down to him. Gust settled fawningly beside him.

He seemed disturbed. For a few moments, Shan's heart stilled. Had Taropat done something to himself after all? He ran to the house, threw wide the door, expecting to find Taropat dead or drunk. But he was sitting beside the fire, his feet on the fender, reading. He looked up when Shan came in, and Shan could see he was trying to conceal his expression, perhaps smothering embarrassment, concern or urgency. "I've been to see Master Thremius," Shan said.

Taropat nodded. "Have you eaten?"

"Yes." Shan sat down on a chair beside the table, resting his chin in his hands. "I'm not going back to Holme," he said. "This is my home now. You've made it so."

Again, Taropat nodded. "I spoke hasty words. I did not think, for one moment, you'd heed them."

"Master Thremius is pleased with me now. He says he's going to teach me properly."

"Did he?"

Shan wrinkled his nose. "Well, in a way. He told me to return to him in seven days. What do I do in the meantime?"

Taropat shrugged. "That is up to you."

"I want to learn, though. I want to start now. Now you have told me your story, I feel there's a reason behind everything that's happened to me. I don't know if I can make a difference to anything, but if people don't try, nothing will ever change. I'm eager to try. I want knowledge and strength. I want to go from here one day and find the dark heart of Magravandias. I want to crush it."

Taropat smiled. "I'm glad you're enjoying yourself."

Shan got the impression that Taropat felt he had done whatever part he had to play, and was now passing responsibility to Thremius and Shan himself. Shan felt uncomfortable with this distance. "I have a different life now," he said. "It's bigger than it was. I have you to thank for that."

"Well, at least I have done some good."

Shan sighed. "I think you should lay Khaster to rest. He's far too much of a worrier. He's determined to see the worst in himself. He's better off dead."

Taropat's smile widened. "Sometimes, Khaster is a habit, that's all. I can assure you I'm now always fully aware of my own bizarre and unique magnificence."

"I want to learn from *you*," Shan said. "You brought me here. You saved me. If you push me away now, it's because of the past, of your own hurt."

"I'm not pushing you away. I'm just trying to read. Stop worrying."

There was silence for a while, but Shan could not stand it. He felt full of words. "Gust is upset," he said. "He won't come in."

Taropat glanced at him. "Gust will be fine. You should remember he is not human and sometimes our tumultuous emotions feel like fire to him." He went back to his book. "There's tea in the pot. Help yourself."

Shan drummed his fingers on the table. "I feel I should be doing something."

Taropat looked up at him again. "A good student can apply himself to his studies. He should not need wet-nursing all the way."

"Can I go into your workroom?"

"Of course. You know what not to touch by now."

It was the first time Shan had been into the room alone. He took a mug of tea with him and closed the door behind him. The long low chamber was dark and silent. Unseen presences seemed to cluster in the shadows. I am comfortable in here, Shan told himself sternly, peering nervously into the corners. I belong here. He walked the length of one of the worktables, his fingers trailing over the array of artifacts and books that lay there. His hand came to rest on a glossy dark object: the scry mede. It seemed peculiarly significant. Shan put down his mug and picked up the mede with both hands. Taropat had tried to teach him to use it, but on the occasions he had seen cloudy images in the glass, he thought he'd just imagined them, wished them to be there. Today, things were different. He carried the mede into the bare room curtained off to the side, where Taropat conducted his rituals. Perhaps Shan would be able to attend one of those rites now, learn the names of the gods that Taropat appealed to. Two lamps burned dimly on the altar. They were never allowed to die. Shan sat down in the middle of the circle painted on the wooden floor and placed the scry mede before him. The air smelled exotically of old incense and Shan's skin prickled as if emanations from past conjurings still crackled in the folds of the curtains.

"Great powers of the universe," he murmured. "Let me see. Let me see." He was leaning so close to the glass, his breath was clouding it. Yet he knew he should not wipe it with his hands. There was a terrible curiosity inside him. Khaster Leckery had fled the Magravandian camp in Cos, but what had happened afterward? Shan felt there was more to know, information that Taropat could not bear to contemplate. Tayven had said that should he be killed a great power would be released. Had it? "I have to know," Shan whispered. "Show me." He stared without blinking at the mede, until his eyes watered. His head felt tight and aching, as if held in a vise. He was concentrating too hard. It wasn't working.

Exasperated, Shan flung himself backward and lay on the floor, arms outflung. I must acquire these skills, he thought. I want that power. He closed his eyes, conscious of a throbbing ache behind them. Perhaps Thremius would give him the knowledge that would unlock the doors in his mind. He could feel the ability "to know" hovering inside him, yet he couldn't bring it out. Maybe he was too impatient. Yes, that was it. He sat up again, determined to try once more. For a moment, he saw his own face looking back at him from the polished surface, and then he realized it wasn't his own face at all. It was the face of a young man, squinting and peering, as if trying to look through a dirty window. He was very handsome, like a royal prince. Bayard? No, he didn't look at all how Shan imagined Bayard. There was no smirking cruelty to the face. It looked tired, confused, but not evil. Shan stared at it. Somewhere, was someone seeing him, perhaps in a mirror or a window? "Who are you?" Shan said aloud, unsure whether sound could cross the void that separated them.

The face did not alter for a few moments and then a strange expression crossed it; incredulity, shock and perhaps fear. Similarly, a shock coursed through Shan. He put the mede down hastily and it skidded across the floor, revealing only a dark surface once more. Shan's flesh crawled. He felt sick and disorientated, filled with an instinctive horror. He hadn't seen anything hideous, yet the image had affected him greatly. He knew who it had been as surely as if the young man had spoken to him. Tayven Hirandel. A phantom, perhaps hungry and vengeful. Shan stared at the mede for some minutes, hardly daring to move. He felt as if some other world might sense him and come pouring through the black glass. The atmosphere in the little room was charged and uncomfortable. He had to get out.

Shan got to his feet and ran through the curtains, fighting with the heavy fabric. Beyond, the workroom was too dark and watchful, yet he balked at explaining himself should he hurtle out of it back into the living area. Taropat would ask him what was wrong. He couldn't bear to tell him. Shan sat down on a stool and took up his mug of tea again, which he found was cold. His heart was racing. The face in the mede had been Tayven's, he was sure of it. He knew Tayven was dead, but the more he thought about it, the more convinced he became that the image had been of a living person. He just sensed it. But he had no real experience. How could he be sure? He might just be wishing Tayven was alive, because the alternative was more frightening. Shan was shivering uncontrollably. He felt he had seen something he hadn't been meant to see. How could he tell Taropat about this? It would seem like a crass attempt to prove himself, to show off. Taropat would be angry, scornful, perhaps hurt.

"Control yourself," Shan said aloud. His hands were clasped tightly before him. He closed his eyes, attempted to regulate his breathing. You must forget this. Do something else. Forget it until you see Nip again. After some minutes, he was able to open one of Taropat's books on herbalism. Nip had said to him that knowledge of the properties of plants was essential for a magus. He had learned a couple of dozen, now he would learn some more. He would draw them, repeat their names and attributes until the darkness in his mind was expelled. With shaking hands, he took up his own notebook and turned to a clean page. He would ignore the curtains to the ritual room that moved faintly in a breeze he could not feel.

Some hours later, Taropat opened the door and told Shan that dinner was nearly ready. He sauntered into the room and looked over Shan's shoulder. "Neat work," he said. "You're getting better at this."

Shan knew his work was precise, as he had applied his whole

concentration to it, not because of diligence, but because of fear. He swallowed with difficulty, hoping Taropat wouldn't sense his unease. The truth was his jaw was rigid with tension, and he was relieved beyond measure to have an excuse to leave the workroom, but Taropat must not become aware of this. Shan made an effort to smile. "I enjoy it," he said.

Taropat nodded. "Good. Later, I'll see how much you've learned."

After dinner, Taropat opened a bottle of wine and tested Shan on his knowledge. After a glass or two, Shan was tempted to confess what had happened in the workroom, but managed to restrain himself. He said nothing at all until the night before he was due to return to Master Thremius.

All week, he'd concentrated on the herbs. Their study required no psychic work. He was afraid of opening himself up in that way, sure that some image would come to him that he'd rather not see. He and Taropat were sitting in silence after dinner, Taropat by the hearth with his nose in a book as usual, and Shan at the table, writing in his notebook. He felt a strange shiver down his spine and looked up to find that Taropat was staring right at him. "What is it?" Shan asked.

Taropat pursed his lips. "I'm not sure. Perhaps you can tell me."

Shan frowned, although his mouth had gone dry. "I don't know."

Taropat closed his book slowly and smoothed its leather binding. "Well, I have been busy in the garden all week, but today went into the workroom."

Shan swallowed. He couldn't fill the pause, but shrugged.

"The energy in the ritual room is soured and I found the scry mede in there. Can you explain this?"

Shan blinked at the page before him. He knew his face and neck were crimson. "Oh, I tried to look into it the other day, but nothing happened."

"Why didn't you replace it? It was on the floor."

Shan shrugged again. "I forgot. I'm sorry."

There was a silence, then Taropat said, "You don't *have* to tell me what happened to you, Shan, but you must be careful. If you want to act alone, you must accept responsibility for the consequences, and realize I cannot help you with them. The scry mede is not a toy. It is a mirror of the universe, but it is also a portal. If you don't know what you're doing, you can let something through, even invite it in."

Again, a silence. Shan put down his pen, still staring at the page, then said hurriedly, "I looked into it, expecting nothing, then I saw a face looking back at me that was not my own. That was all. But there was a feeling that came with it. It was dark. I should have told you, I know, but I thought you'd be angry."

Taropat sighed. "Did you close down the room psychically after you'd had this experience? Did you seal it?"

Shan shook his head.

"Then you must go back and do it."

Shan looked up in alarm. "Now? Why? It's too late, isn't it?"

"Yes, probably, but you should still do it. It will be a good lesson."

Shan hesitated and then said, "Is there something in there? Do you know? Have you sensed it?"

"I sensed a discharge of negative energy. I could have dispelled it myself, but feel you should be responsible for doing this." His voice was mild, but Shan sensed the imperative beneath the tone. He got to his feet. "Come along, you've seen me do it many times when I've used the mede in there. You know what to do."

Awkwardly, Shan followed Taropat to the ritual room. He had not set foot in the place since the incident with the mede had occurred. The atmosphere had not improved. He could feel something seething in the shadows. Beneath Taropat's gaze, he performed a minor banishing ritual, then drew the sealing symbols in the air. At once, he felt lighter, less threatened. Taropat was right. He should have done this before. Why had he been so afraid? He had knowledge and that gave him power. He knew how to protect himself, yet fear had made him stupid.

Taropat patted his shoulder. "There. All is as it should be. Well done."

Shan felt giddy with relief. "It will never happen again, I promise," he said.

Taropat frowned. "Nonsense. You have achieved communion with the mede. That is an important step. You must continue, but do things properly from now on."

Shan's shoulders slumped. "I didn't like what I saw. I don't want to do it again."

Taropat shook his head. "Don't be ridiculous. There should be no room for fear in your head, boy. If you can't conquer that, you might as well give up now and resign yourself to tending my garden." He smiled. "Anyway, what was so bad about it? Will you tell me now?"

Shan looked away. "I felt I wasn't supposed to see it. It was like stumbling across a group of bandits by mistake and realizing that they'd seen me spying on them. I think . . . I think the face was Magravandian."

Taropat nodded, sucking his upper lip. "Hmm, that makes sense. The magi of the emperor are always snooping around. You will have intrigued them, no doubt."

Shan laughed shakily. He knew it hadn't been a Magravandian magus.

Taropat put his hand on Shan's shoulders and steered him out of the room. "Come along. A flute of good port should restore your spirits. Despite what you might think, and what you assume I think, you have done well."

Back in the warm kitchen, which was lit only by the light of the open stove, Taropat told stories about things he'd seen himself in the scry mede. Shan drank the fiery port, feeling it numb his body and mind. He laughed and grimaced at the right moments, yet the tales that normally intrigued him barely entered his consciousness. All the time, he was thinking about how he wanted to be honest with Taropat. He sensed the man knew only too well he was holding something back. Fear of the consequences held his tongue. He told himself he didn't want to hurt Taropat's feelings in any way, but another, more honest part of his mind knew only too well he was afraid of setting events in motion, which could not be contained, which would change everything. If Taropat thought there was a possibility Tayven still lived, he might want to do something about it there and then, and make Shan take part. I want to make a difference, Shan thought, but not yet. I'm not ready. He felt as if massing forces pressed against the membrane of reality, and it would take all his strength to keep them from breaking through.

10

THE REBELS OF COS

TAYVEN HIRANTEL HAD THOUGHT at first that the flash he saw through the trees was the shine of sunlight on water. He had been drawn to investigate. But the trees did not grow thinner, and neither did a pool reveal itself. What he found instead was a shard of glass lodged into the trunk of an ancient oak. The damaged bark had grown around it so that the glass had become a living mirror. Was this the object that had called to him secretly for so long? He'd dreamed of it, certainly, and that morning, the air had shimmered before his eyes, filled with a strange immanence. Tayven had felt compelled to wander deep into the forest alone. As he'd walked, images of the past had come back to him, images of his childhood, the time of innocence. Normally, he refused to look back in time, because his mind could not go further than what had happened to him in the Magravandian battle camp. But these memories were bearable. They had made him feel both melancholy and uplifted. He had no doubt that something was afoot. There was something to learn. And now, perhaps, he had found it. He thought that the shard of glass must have been placed in the tree by a sorcerer long ago, as part of some unfathomable ritual. Few people travelled through these primordial woods and, as far as Tayven could gather, no one naturally lived there. These were the cloud forests of the far wilderness of Cos, inaccessible and remote. Only rebels haunted the wild terrain, and over the years, they had become used to the rarefied air. Many of them had given birth to mystics.

Tayven hacked through the tall ferns and looked into the glass. He half expected to see the face of an aged magus or witch looking back at him, and was fully prepared for that, but what he saw was a younger version of himself. That was more shocking. It was the image of a Tayven who'd attracted the wrath of Prince Bayard. Tayven recoiled instinctively, his spine chilled by a breath of bitter memory. No idyllic childhood recollections now, but those of pain and fear. He uttered a low curse. For a brief moment, he saw terror in the face before him, and then it was gone. The glass was old and cloudy. It could not reflect reality.

For some minutes Tayven stood staring at the glass, calming himself. He believed that everything that happened in his life held a message and was strongly significant. What was the message here? He knew that he'd accepted the past, but he did not relish its return. Out here, he was safe from it, or so he'd thought. His life had begun again in Cos. He wanted to remember no other.

Some years before, he had been born again, to Princess Helayna, the woman who found him. She had been out with a patrol of her men, looking for survivors who might have crawled from the battle-field far below. She had not expected to find a Magravandian among the narrow paths that burrowed through the crags of the Rhye. For some time, she didn't know she had, because Tayven was insensible, incapable of communicating. Later, when he was whole again, she'd told him how, on that terrible morning, she'd thought she'd found one of her own people, violated and broken.

"Would you have killed me if you'd known the truth?" Tayven had asked her.

She hadn't answered. He knew it anyway. Helayna hated Magravandians.

The patrol had carried Tayven, along with other survivors, back to a hidden camp, high among the peaks of the Rhye. Tayven remembered opening his eyes for the first time, and how his vision had been filled with the image of Helayna's stern, hawklike face. She'd spoken to him in a foreign tongue, her tone harsh and guttural. He could not understand a word of it. Men had appeared around her. One of them had poked him gently with the butt of his spear. He hadn't been able to remember who he was, or where he was, or what had happened to him. He had simply come out of a darkness into the world, shorn of all the human faculties that stem from learning. He was primal instinct made flesh.

In one of the huts of the camp, where all the wounded were taken, Tayven found the most comfortable spot and curled up like a homeless cat. Cossic physicians attended to his hurts and it was only a few days later, when he muttered some words in Magravandian, that Helayna was summoned once more. She arrived, accompanied by two male officers, suspicion oozing from every one of them. Now, she spoke to Tayven in his own tongue. "Who are you? What were you doing on the crag path? What happened to you?"

Tayven knew that, during that first significant conversation, his beauty—his curse and his blessing—had probably contributed toward saving his life. "I don't know," he'd answered, honestly, to every question they put to him.

They spoke together afterward, and although Tayven's memory had recorded it for him, he wondered how he'd known what they'd said. They wouldn't have spoken in Magravandian. Yet he *had* known. Perhaps he remembered the feelings conjured by the words.

"It's clear to see what he is," one of Helayna's companions said. "Look at him. Shall we dispose of him?"

"No," said Helayna. "He may be useful."

"He's lost his mind."

"It could return."

Tayven lived in a cocoon of ignorance for several weeks, enjoying life at its most basic level. The other wounded men and women in the makeshift hospital—those who could talk—were fascinated by him. They began to teach him their language, and from those who knew Magravandian, he learned that he was privileged, because a princess had taken an interest in him. He learned she was a great rebel leader, but that meant little. He'd lost his image of the world. Every day, Helayna would come to question him, accompanied by her seeress, an old woman named Mab. They both tried to make him remember things, to no avail.

"Well, no one's looking for him, that's for sure," said Old Mab dryly.

"He's highborn," Helayna said. "Look at his hands. He's not a soldier."

"He's one of their playthings," Mab decided. "Perhaps he upset someone."

Helayna shook her head. "I'm not sure. It seems strange, finding him there, so soon after the battle. I wonder what's meant by it." She was not a conventionally beautiful woman. Her face was too hard. She wore her hair tied up on her head with rags, and affected the garb of a man. But there was something compelling about her; her presence, her confidence, her movements. It was easy to imagine her in splendid robes, gliding down a staircase into a hushed hall full of people, gazing down her nose at them. "What happened to you, boy?" she asked, "Who did this?" Clearly, she did not, for one moment, consider one of her own people might be responsible.

"I can't remember anything," Tayven said, adding, "only your face." Even in his confused condition, he knew how to please.

Then, one night, he woke up in darkness, full of recall. It had come back to him in a dream. He remembered the blows, the scorn, the sureness that death was imminent. He remembered who he was, and all his history. He remembered Bayard. Panicking, Tayven uttered strange guttural cries and attempted to escape from the hospital, disorientated, clawing at the walls in desperation. His fellow patients tried ineffectively to calm him down, but then Helayna came running, and she was able to constrain his flailing limbs. All he could do was scream in her face. She held him close. "You are safe," she said. "You are safe."

He did not tell her everything, because that was his way. He told what he knew she wanted to hear, things that would fire up her anger against the Magravandians. "They are beasts," she said. "Their own people aren't safe from them."

Tayven could not remember how he'd got onto the mountain path. He'd lost consciousness while still in Bayard's pavilion, but Helayna thought he must have been flung out onto the battlefield and left for dead. His will to survive must have enabled him to make the impossible crawl to find sanctuary. "You'd have died if I hadn't found you," she said.

He nodded. "I know."

"My brother will be with us again shortly," Helayna said. "He has been on a mission in the south. He will want to speak with you."

"What can I tell him? That Valraven Palindrake is invincible? I think he already knows that. I was a squire, nothing more. I don't know anything that could help you rout him."

"Palindrake is not invincible," Helayna said. "Whatever legends he's created around himself, he's still only a man."

She believed the Cossics could still win, if they could only kill Valraven. Tayven knew this was a delusion, but he was happy to live in the camp and become part of the rebel community. A quick student, he swiftly learned their language, to be able to think like they did. They weren't racist toward him, which surprised him. They didn't consider he might be part of an elaborate espionage plot, which certainly wouldn't be beyond the Magravandians. He mentioned this to Helayna, who only snorted. "I can see your soul," she said, "and it shines. It is not the soul of a spy."

So much for her perspicacity.

When Ashalan returned to the camp, he'd been badly wounded in the leg. Tayven, astute to possibilities that might enhance his position and make life more comfortable, accompanied Helayna on her visits to the exiled king, who was recuperating in his dwelling. Tayven was able to turn on his "shine" as Helayna referred to it, and quickly charmed Ashalan into submission. I am like a serpent, Tayven thought. I can hypnotize people. Almorante had told him this long ago, and had also taught him how to make the most of his talent.

It did not take Tayven long to realize that Ashalan was close to giving up. His wound took a long time to heal. He was exhausted. Helayna, ever the optimist, refused to be broken by the staggering defeat the Cossic forces had suffered at the Magravandians' hands. The same could not be said for Ashalan. He wasn't stupid. He knew that Valraven's army had cut down the flower of the Cossic resistance in that misty mountain valley. It would take a long time to recoup and by then more of Cos would be under Magravandian control. Within the rebellion itself were many factions, some of which had been infiltrated by Magravandian agents or seduced by promises of power from Almorante. Tayven knew this but didn't tell Ashalan or Helayna. His business, as he saw it, was to survive, and the rebel headquarters seemed fairly safe for now. He had no intention of returning to Magrast.

One night Tayven managed to engineer a visit to Ashalan without Helayna's presence, and seduced him. It was not much of a challenge. Ashalan, tired and hopeless, was sodden with romantic and melancholic thoughts. He spoke of an ancient legend, in which a Cossic king had taken as a lover a boy belonging to a conquered Mewtish emperor, which had caused all manner of unpleasantness. Tayven was impatient with this. He'd lost all his own romantic inclinations. He realized that he must help Ashalan recapture the man he'd once been. The rebels might not be able to win their war, but they could survive in the wilderness undetected, perhaps forever. For that, they needed strong leaders. Helayna was an inspiration to them, but they had a spiritual link to Ashalan. To the Cossics, he was the life of their land. If he withered and failed, so did they, and Tayven realized it was not in his personal interests for this to happen. He became Ashalan's inspiration, and used every ancient legend he could think of, and several that he made up, to help drag Ashalan out of his pit of despair. He saw the bloom come back into Ashalan's eyes. His body became straighter, his limp less pronounced.

Helayna was almost tearful in her gratitude for what Tayven did for her brother. "You have brought him back to us," she said. "It is your shine. You are so special." She was stroking his face as she did this.

I am actually hateful, Tayven thought. Whatever was good in me has been beaten out. I don't care about anything except myself.

One night, Ashalan questioned him in detail about his relationships in Magrast. All Tayven had told the Cossics about what Bayard had done to him was that the prince hated him because he was a favorite of Almorante's, but that night, perhaps because the moon was full and the air heady with the scent of cedar, Tayven shuddered and remembered Recolletine. "I loved a man named Khaster," he said.

"A Magravandian?" Ashalan asked, and for once Tayven could give him an answer he would like.

"No, Caradorean."

"Ah, Caradore," said Ashalan, sighing. "I went there once. It is the crown of the world. What was he like, your Khaster? What happened to him?"

"He was a melancholic dreamer who was broken into a thousand pieces by Magrast and her scheming princes," Tayven said curtly.

"Is he alive or dead?"

"I don't know. I hope he's dead, because I hate to think of what he's like if he lives." Tayven shook his head. "No, he can't live. Not after what happened."

"Tell me," Ashalan said.

Tayven did so, from Khaster's perspective.

Afterward, Ashalan frowned. "He was not how I'd expect a Caradorean to be, exactly."

"No, he wasn't. He'd already been mauled throughout his childhood by Valraven Palindrake, and later by the Dragon Lord's infamous sister, Pharinet. They destroyed him long before he came to me. The Khaster that should have been had disappeared deep inside him. I tried to bring him back . . ."

". . . As you did for me . . ."

"But it didn't work. I didn't have time."

Ashalan was silent for a moment, then said, "You will have your revenge, Tayven."

"I know," Tayven answered simply, but he also knew it would not be expedited by Ashalan or his Cossic forces. One day, Tayven would be given the opportunity to do it alone. He would not rest until he had Bayard begging for mercy at his feet. The prince would not die quickly. Tayven had already invented enough tortures to last considerable weeks.

Sometimes, he looked at himself and disliked what he saw, what he had become. Almorante's fey mystic was gone for good. He remembered how he was that time in Recolletine with Khaster and how it seemed now as if that boy had never lived. He'd believed he was clever enough to guide Khaster and himself through dangerous waters to safety, but he'd been careless, too confident. He still had his shine, but it was the radiance of a black sun now, full of poison.

Several years after Tayven joined the Cossics, a Mewtish man named Surekh found their hidden retreat. He astounded everyone with the information that he had been searching for Tayven, so Mab had been wrong after all. But Surekh was not employed by Almorante, Valraven, Bayard or any other faction Tayven would have expected. He was an agent of someone else, who was looking for Khaster too. Helayna wanted to kill the Mewt straight away, being traditionally suspicious of his race, but Ashalan, more measured, listened to what he had to say.

"I will not say you have friends," said Surekh, "but there are other powerful men in this world who oppose the empire. You need not expect an alliance from them, but you can trade information. This you will need when the world changes, when Leonid dies and his sons fight over the crown. Survive out here if you can and wait to see what happens. I ask for only one thing."

"And that is?" said Ashalan.

"Allow me to take Tayven Hirantel back to Mewt with me."

Tayven and Ashalan had exchanged a glance, and Tayven's heart sank, because he knew Ashalan was thinking of the old legends again, and how this circumstance had painful resonance with them. But Ashalan only smiled at him. "Do you want to go?"

Tayven paused, then said, "I've always wanted to visit Mewt."

"Then go," Ashalan said.

"It will be only for a short time," said Surekh. "My employer wishes to meet him, that's all. We will send funds back with him, which may help you."

"What use have I for funds out here?" Ashalan said, laughing.

"Not yet perhaps," said Surekh, "but circumstances change."

"I never refuse a gift," Ashalan said.

So Tayven travelled to Akahana, the capital of Mewt, and there met with the Magravandian governor of the city, Lord Maycarpe. They had met before, of course, in Magrast, but only briefly. Maycarpe wanted Tayven to find Khaster for him, but would not reveal why. Khaster's younger brother worked for Maycarpe, so perhaps it was just a personal favor.

"I want you as my agent," Maycarpe said. "Will you work for me?"

"Against my people?"

Maycarpe frowned. "What?"

"The Cossics."

"Great Madragore, no!" said Maycarpe. "I have no interest in them, pathetic remnants that they are. I want you on my side, Tayven. I have looked for you for a long time."

"Do you know what's going to happen? Is Leonid going to die soon?"

Maycarpe smiled. "I only know that certain of our aims are in accord."

"Will you tell Almorante you have seen me?"

Maycarpe shrugged. "I don't know. He comes here often. Do you want him to know?"

"I don't care," Tayven said. "He'd never find me. I won't return to Magrast."

Maycarpe narrowed his eyes. "I like the danger in you. It is an improvement."

"Useful to you, maybe."

"I admire survivors. It is why I want Khaster Leckery too."

"You are optimistic," Tayven said. "He was never much of a survivor. Why are you so interested in him?"

Maycarpe leaned forward in his seat. "Don't you know why? Didn't you sense it yourself?"

Tayven was silent for a moment. "I doubt you and I sense the same things."

Maycarpe made an expansive hand gesture. "Find him, Tayven."

WHEN TAYVEN SAW the image of his younger self in a piece of glass lodged into a tree, he had not long returned from a visit to Akahana. Before that, he'd been scouring the countryside of Cos, as he'd done many times before, for any evidence of Khaster. As usual, he'd had to report to Maycarpe he'd found nothing, but now, being presented with this unexpected phenomenon in the tree, he found himself thinking of Khaster again. He reached out and touched the clouded glass. "What are you trying to tell me?" he said aloud. "Are you reaching out through time, lost Tayven, to reach me?"

No answers came to him. Not then.

II

THE PATH OF THE STUDENT

SHAN PRESENTED HIMSELF at Master Thremius's abode at the appointed time. He looked forward to a day of revelations and surprises, conscious that becoming aware of Taropat's history had been an unusual form of initiation. But all he found at the old tree was Nip alone, dressed in travelling clothes, stout boots and a hooded cloak. She carried a tall staff. "I thought you weren't coming," she said. "I'm to take you to the lady."

"What lady?"

"She lives in the northern part of the forest. It's a bit of a hike."

"I thought Thremius was going to teach me now."

Nip raised her eyebrows. "Did you? The Lady's been waiting to meet you. Taropat has kept her away. Thremius must have argued hard with him to get him to agree to this."

Shan thought about these words. He'd never seen Taropat and Thremius together, but then he wasn't aware of all of Taropat's movements. "How do the magi communicate?" he asked. "Does Taropat come here?"

"Sometimes," Nip said, "but they have other methods too. They meet in dreams and in the voids beyond the world. Also, they like to get together from time to time in the real world, to get drunk and argue, but your presence has made Taropat's house off-limits. I've been to gatherings there, when there have been over twenty people in Taropat's kitchen, magi and apprentices alike."

"Why doesn't he want me to meet them?"

"More the other way around," Nip said. "He doesn't want your head filled with too many opposing views as yet." She thumped her staff against the ground. "Well, we'd better get going. We want to be there before the day is over."

Shan hesitated. "Will we be staying the night?"

Nip laughed. "I'm leaving you behind there," she said. "You'll have a new home for a while."

Shan was shocked by this. Why hadn't Taropat told him? He hoped his mentor knew about this plan. "I'm not sure about this," he said. "Taropat's mentioned nothing about it to me."

"There's nothing to worry about," Nip said. "You will enjoy the Lady's company, and what she'll teach you. It'll open up a whole new universe for you." With these words, she swung round in a practiced swirl of cloak and began to march toward one of the forest paths. Shan sighed, shook his head, then followed her.

They travelled a few paths Shan was already familiar with, then branched off into unknown territory, following the course of a narrow rushing stream. Nip said that the water flowed both ways at once, which Shan took to be a joke. When he looked over the banks, he saw the water roiled and curled around the many sharp rocks protruding from beneath its surface, which perhaps gave the illusion of a contradictory flow.

Shan had thought Nip's staff was for effect, to make her look more like a magus, but he soon appreciated its practical use. She used it efficiently to attack the thick undergrowth that in many places completely blocked the path. It didn't seem as if many people passed this way. The further they went into the forest, the denser it became. In the glades Shan now knew as home, the trees were tall and majestic, but here they were gnarled and hunched and spreading, stooping low to the ground like a gathering of malevolent hags. It didn't take much of an imagination to see faces in the flaking creases of bark. Spiny twigs reached out like pinching fingers. The leaves were a strange color too, being dark as if with blight. The early gold of autumn did not show here, and the air smelled of rotten hay. "This is a hinterland," Nip whispered, drawing close to Shan's side. "It is a place where spirits walk."

"Winter already seems to rule here," Shan murmured back.

Nip nodded. "Yes," she hissed. "In a way, it does."

Beneath their feet, the ground was littered with shavings of bark—a dry, spongy mass—similar to that found in a pine forest, but the trees around them were not pines. It was difficult to judge exactly what kind of trees they were.

As they walked, Nip pointed out rare fungi and plants to Shan, listing their properties. Shan only half listened to her words. It was clear their journey was nearly over, and he hadn't yet broached the subject of what he'd seen in Taropat's scry mede. He was afraid Nip might think he was making it up. Now, it seemed so unlikely the face he'd seen had been Tayven's. At best, Nip would scoff at him, tell him he'd been too influenced by Taropat's story. That was the most likely explanation anyway. It could have been anyone's face in the mede. Perhaps he'd wanted it to be Tayven's, for the same egotistic reasons he was afraid of being accused of.

The sinister trees dwindled out and were replaced by an almost impenetrable wall of rhododendron. It looked hundreds of years old, full of spidery, dusty tunnels and foliate caves. Shan could not discern a proper path, but Nip seemed to know the way. She wove confidently between the ancient trunks and tangled branches, knocking bloated spiders aside with a fearless hand. After only fifteen minutes or so, they emerged from this jungle onto the lip of a large valley clearing. Below, the valley was ringed by yellowing oaks. Within their circle of protection was a large house wreathed in ivy, surrounded by an immense garden. Some of it appeared functional, where vegetables and herbs were grown, but the majority of it was decorative, with walkways, arbors and grottoes. Yet other corners were wild and overgrown. "Here we are," said Nip. "Lady Sinaclara's domain."

There were no roads in or out of the clearing. The Lady must be self-sufficient. Shan imagined that few could find their way here.

Nip ran down the grassy bank and through the circle of oaks. Shan followed her. As they burst out of the trees onto a lawn hemmed by high hedges, a flock of black doves rose up in alarm. Their flight was strangely blurred. Beyond their clattering wings, Shan could see the turrets of the house, its watchful windows. He and Nip crossed the lawn and walked along a grassy avenue of trimmed hedges. The light was odd, like twilight, yet the sun had not yet sunk below the trees. The house was visible at the end of the walk, framed by ordered foliage. A terrace could be seen; behind it, long open window-doors led into the house. Shan saw a peculiar evanescent shape float out of them, swathed in transparent blue veils. Perhaps it was only a swatch of fabric caught on the wind. "What's that?" he asked.

"The Lady," Nip replied. "She knew we were coming."

Shan could see now that the shivering form was indeed the figure of a woman, dressed in blue. He'd expected an elderly lady, a female version of Thremius, but Sinaclara was young, or at least appeared so. As she drew nearer—and Shan could tell now that she was walking rather than gliding—he saw that her gown was embroidered with the eyes of a peacock tail and the bodice was adorned with feathers of the same bird.

"She is the pavoniata," Nip said softly, "priestess of the peacock angel."

The Lady came to a halt in front of them and held out her arms. "Nip," she said. "How good to see you. It's been too long. I forget myself sometimes, hidden away here in my domain." Her hair was the red of autumn, her eyes the blue of summer sea, her skin pallid as snow.

Nip hugged her briefly and then turned to introduce Shan. "This is the friend Thremius asked me to bring to you."

The women exchanged a glance, from which Shan could not help but feel excluded. "A new face is always welcome," said the Lady.

"His name is Shan," Nip said. "He is apprenticed to Taropat."

Sinaclara inclined her head. "Here is my home," she said. "Enter."

She led them through the open windows into a large, dark drawing room, where a fire burned hungrily in the hearth. The room was stuffed with antique furniture and artifacts and the air smelled of spicy incense. Huge statues of foreign gods pondered in niches, some of them grotesque and frightening.

Lady Sinaclara pulled on a rope by the hearth and a servant appeared almost at once, an ocher-skinned woman with slanting eyes and exotic dress. "Nana, our visitors have arrived," Sinaclara said.

"I will have tea brought in," said the woman, bowing her head, while delivering Shan a scorching glance.

"I hope you are hungry," said the Lady to Shan. "We rarely have guests, so when we do, we tend to smother them."

Shan smiled uneasily.

Until the refreshments arrived, the Lady talked about her garden. Nip responded with apparent interest, but Shan could not relax. He felt oppressed in that room, light-headed, as if a great unseen force pressed down upon him. He did not want to stay there without Nip.

The servant, Nana, reappeared, supervising a couple of younger girls who bore heavy trays. The tea consisted of an array of fiery foreign dishes, accompanied by an unidentifiable hot beverage that tasted of stale smoke. Shan could barely eat. The spices burned his mouth, the drink made him feel nauseous.

The Lady must have noticed his discomfort. "The flavors take some getting used to, I know," she said, "but persistence repays the palate. The food is Jessapurian. It is all we eat here, because every one of my staff comes from Jessapur. I guarantee that within a few days, you will learn to relish it."

Shan managed a weak smile, swallowing with difficulty. How long was he supposed to stay here? He would starve. He'd read of Jessapur in Taropat's books: a distant and frightening land of sorcerers and demons. "How many days will I be here?" he said awkwardly, aware of giving offense.

Nip reached out and squeezed his arm. "I'll come back for you the day after the winter solstice," she said.

"That's months away!" Shan exclaimed.

Both Sinaclara and Nip laughed.

"He doesn't want to be left alone with me," said the Lady. "Am I so frightening, Shan?"

"He is afraid of your kitchen," Nip said quickly, perhaps knowing Shan was incapable of a polite reply.

The Lady frowned in concern. "Oh, is it that bad? I can ask Nana to bring you some white bread, if you like."

Shan shook his head. "No, I'm fine. I just didn't know I was to stay here that long. It was a surprise."

"Shock, more like!" said the Lady, smiling. "I won't eat you, I promise."

Shan felt as if he were the butt of a private joke between the women. "I'm pleased to be here," he said stiffly. "I'm concerned only for Taropat being alone for so long."

"He was alone for a good while before you came to him," said the Lady. "Do you think you're that indispensable?"

Shan flushed. Why did she twist things around, make him feel stupid? "He has been . . . out of sorts recently, that's all."

The Lady snorted. "Taropat out of sorts? I'd like to see that!" She narrowed her eyes at Shan. "You mustn't miss him that much. It isn't good for you."

Shan's flush deepened. "I won't. I . . ."

She reached out to pat his knee. "Female company will inspire you."

Nip put down her plate, which was empty. "Well, I'd better head back."

The Lady frowned. "You don't have to leave, Nip. Stay here the night."

She shook her head. "Thank you, but I'd rather get home. I can travel swiftly by myself. It won't take that long."

"Well, if you're sure . . ."

Nip stood up and turned to Shan. "I'll see you soon," she said. "Good luck."

Shan wanted to throw down his plate, still full, and say that he was leaving with her, but he was afraid to. The feeling shamed him.

He knew about fear, what it could do to him, yet he could not banish
it. It reminded him, yet again, that knowledge without experience is
not enough.

Nip picked up her staff and sauntered out through the windows
onto the terrace. Shan watched her departure until he could no longer
see her. Why wouldn't she stay just for one night? Was she afraid of
this house? Sinaclara sat silently nearby. He knew that she was watching him. Eventually, he had no excuse to stare at the garden and had
to turn back. He found that the Lady was paying full attention to her
food. She didn't say anything, but continued to eat precisely and
slowly. The silence was unbearable. Was she annoyed with him? Shan
cleared his throat self-consciously. "Could I have some water, please?"

The Lady looked up. "If you want to. There's a vase of flowers
over there. Drink from that."

Shan stared at her, horrified.

Sinaclara laughed. "Joking," she said, and put down her plate.
"We'll get you some water from the kitchens. I want to give you a
tour of the house. This is going to be your home for a while. You
must begin familiarizing yourself with it." It seemed that in every
room, around every corner, a sinuous snaky Jessapurian lurked in the
shadows. Sinaclara greeted them all cheerfully. To Shan, they looked
like a society of necromancers, their fingernails stained with blood.
They gazed at him with suspicion and what he thought was malice.
It was as if they could see right into him, and what they saw there
they despised.

Sinaclara took him to a gallery on the second floor of the house
that was full of terrifying statues of Jessapurian deities, all sprouting
multiple limbs, clutching weapons, and multiple heads armed with
fangs and horns. "I lived for a long while in Jessapur," Sinaclara said,
patting the flank of a snarling black demon. "I've a great affection
for the place. I learned so much there." She folded her arms. "I've
lived in many places. Mewt was fascinating too."

"I've never been anywhere," Shan said inadequately, trying to
avoid the gaze of a particularly fearsome idol.

Sinaclara nodded. "Not yet, no, but I envy you, Shan. I envy the
fact that soon you will have your first sight of Mewt, of Jessapur and

other countries. That first experience cannot be repeated—the foreign scent of a place, the newness of its sunsets, dawns and twilights, the ambience of its nights, the perfume of its days, the secret knowledge that hangs in the very air waiting to be discovered or reveal itself."

"Will you take me to these places?" Shan said, wondering if this was why his visit was to be so protracted.

The Lady shook her head wistfully. "No." She made a clear effort to brighten. "Come, I've shown you the kitchens, the bedrooms, the parlors and the bestiaries. Now, I'll take you to the heart of this house."

The temple was on the ground floor. Arched windows were set into every wall, but high up, so you couldn't see out. The walls were lined by columns, between which were bowls of fire on tall pedestals. At the far end was a plain cube altar and in front of this a shallow fire pit. On a stool beside it sat a veiled woman, who occasionally replenished the flames with chips of sandalwood. The air was heady with the woody scent. Shan looked around himself, awed by the atmosphere of sacred power. There were no statues in the temple. But for the columns and the bowls of fire, the only decoration was the polished mosaic floor; a complicated design of stylized serpents and birds.

"Is this a Jessapurian temple?" Shan asked.

Sinaclara shook her head. "No. Come with me. I'll show you."

Beyond the altar, long curtains of indigo velvet screened off a hidden area. Sinaclara slipped between the drapes and Shan followed her. He uttered an involuntary gasp, his whole vision filled with what lay before him. There was another simple altar, but behind it, in a tall cavity in the wall was a statue of an immense winged man. The stone was painted to make the effigy more lifelike. He was naked but for the sweeping feathers of his peacock wings that curled around him like a cloak.

"Who is it?" Shan murmured.

"Azcaranoth, the peacock angel," Sinaclara said. "I am his priestess."

"He is so beautiful."

Sinaclara nodded. "Yes."

"Am I to learn his worship?" Shan asked.

Sinaclara smiled to herself. "No. I will teach you about the life force of the universe, and you will learn about yourself. You may see in this god before you the darkest aspects of mankind, the darkest aspects of you. He is merciless compassion and compassionless mercy. He is a force neither for good nor evil, but beyond both."

"That sounds worse than evil," Shan said, without thinking.

"Many have thought so," Sinaclara said. "Azcaranoth was born into an ancient race, the Elderahan, who were once the rulers of this world. In those days, humanity were little more than beasts of burden, who were used as slaves by the Elderahan. Azcaranoth was cast out from his people for giving humanity self-awareness and knowledge, so that they could evolve into something greater than what they were. Even though our race would not exist but for him, many stupid people still believe him to be the corruptor, the devil, if you like. But the Elderahan were too proud, and like many great races, they fell from power. Now, their diminished descendants hide from human eyes, mere shadows in the forest. You will know them as elden."

Shan shivered as he gazed up at the angel. "Looking up at him now, I don't feel he's left this world at all. Maybe the elden are stronger than they seem."

Sinaclara smiled. "Perhaps. I have paid a high price for knowing Azcaranoth, but the scars are not visible. Once, I lived in a great city and knew fame and riches. Now, I am here, in this wilderness paradise."

Shan wasn't quite sure what to say. "Some people might prefer it here. I would. I don't fancy cities."

Sinaclara smiled sadly. "It is certainly a beautiful place, but I am surrounded by the hinterland. I have looked through the pylons of the underworld of all religions and carry its essence with me always." She went to the statue and leaned over the altar to kiss its feet. Her hands caressed the tips of the wings. Shan had a feeling the statue could come to life, step down from its niche. Sinaclara could will it to be so. She was in love with the angel.

———

SHAN'S ROOM IN Sinaclara's house was far grander than the one he lived in at Taropat's. He had his own servant, a handsome Jessapurian boy, who woke him politely every morning with breakfast, and tidied his room when he wasn't there. Shan never learned his name. The boy might be called a servant, but Shan had the impression that in the great scheme of things he was far below this silent, dignified youth. Shan could not rid himself of the tendency to be grovellingly deferential in the other's presence, which he was sure must be annoying. He fantasized about being able to converse with the youth, perhaps spend happy hours with him in the garden discussing all that Sinaclara taught. The Jessapurian would admire Shan's incisive mind. Shan would be invited to spend evenings with all the other Jessapurians, and the adults would be astounded at his penetrating insights. It was a satisfying fantasy, but Shan knew it would never become reality.

Every day, the Lady met with Shan in her sitting room and instructed him in the wisdom of the great thinkers of the world. They took their meals in there, and sometimes their conversations continued till dawn, when Shan would drag himself to bed, dazed by all the things Sinaclara had said to him. His mind wrestled to assimilate all he learned, for sometimes the philosophers' pronouncements were contradictory.

"Is there any one truth?" Shan asked, more than once.

Sinaclara would always laugh. "If there is, we have yet to discover it, but real learning comes from the act of trying."

"I don't know which ones I agree with, though," Shan said. "I'll read one and think, 'yes, he's right,' then read another and think, 'no, she is.' It's all so confusing."

"When I first began, I chose the one I liked the most and agreed with them," Sinaclara said. "You can always change your mind later. The best part is when you understand enough to start picking apart the arguments of your favorite thinkers. Because, of course, every argument can be picked apart. It's the gift of language."

The old scholars were often colorful characters who appeared to have stepped from the pages of myth. "Consider Hotekh the Mewt," said Sinaclara. "He has been dead three thousand years. It is said he would go to the plaza in the center of Akahana, and stand there immobile for days at a time, neither eating nor sleeping, but entering a kind of trance. The youth of the city would gather round him—at first probably to taunt and jeer—but when old Hotekh came out of his trance, he would preach to them. He told wondrous tales of a magnificent and beautiful realm that existed beyond human senses, yet was around us all the time. Pure truth could be found there. Hotekh called this place the Kingdom of Intelligence, because it could only be experienced through the human mind's ability to reason and contemplate. He said that our visible, real world was but a sad reflection of this sublime kingdom, a shadow cast by the great divine light that shines there. This light he called the true sun. He said that it was brighter than any other sun imaginable, but that it did not hurt to look upon it."

"How did he know this?" Shan said. "Had he seen this realm with his own eyes?"

Sinaclara smiled, shook her head. "Not with his physical eyes, perhaps. Hotekh preached passionately about the importance and necessity of truth—of what he saw as goodness—and how we can only find this truth through the light of our own reason. For Hotekh, this was the soul itself." Sinaclara's face took on a dreamy expression. "If we can only step beyond our senses, break the chains of illusion, which creates and sustains our 'real' world, we could enter the Kingdom of Intelligence, and experience the sublime enlightenment to be found within its divine light. It's around us all the time, yet we can't perceive it. We are blind and deaf to it, through our own ignorance and limitations." She smiled. "I like to believe that Hotekh really did experience his Kingdom. He was a very wise man, and extremely honest. He died for his beliefs."

"He was persecuted for them?" Shan did not expect such a thing to happen in Mewt, where wisdom and knowledge were held in such high esteem.

Sinaclara nodded. "He was put to death for corrupting the youth of the city. It was thought the ideas he put into their heads were strange, and that the young people would no longer attend to their duties. It was true a great number of them became prone to meditating continually in their search for the Kingdom of Intelligence." Sinaclara shrugged. "Ironically, Hotekh had already claimed that the only way to enter the Kingdom was to surrender the physical body."

"So he claimed."

"So he claimed," agreed Sinaclara. "But the reason I've told you about him is because his teachings had such an influence on other thinkers for many centuries afterward. His work also has great relevance to workers of magic, who seek to transcend the mundane world. I like Hotekh's ideas. Think hard upon them, Shan. Are we not chained within this world by our senses, believing only what they can perceive? How do we know that is true reality? We might only be analyzing mere illusion, those shadows cast by the light of the Kingdom. People kill each other for what they believe in, what they think to be truth."

Shan considered this. "Perhaps Hotekh wanted to believe there was more because he couldn't bear the real world and all its horrors, and that's why he dreamed up the Kingdom."

Sinaclara nodded. "That's a good point. It was an argument vehemently taken up several centuries later up by a new breed of sages. A Magravandian magus, Ipsissimus Masooth, was the most eminent of them. His argument, however, was more political than spiritual. As you know, Magravandias is ruled by an emperor, who is believed to be an earthly incarnation of the god Madragore. A god, being greater than a man, could be said to be part of the larger power of the universe, therefore part of the Kingdom of Intelligence, which is greater than our world. You can see that Hotekh's beliefs actually legitimize men like the emperor. Can that be right? Can that be truth? The emperor's rule is oppression, a tyranny of religious fear. Masooth was brave enough to speak out against it and published a treatise of his theories. Nobody had dared to say anything like it before. He disputed the existence of any realm beyond the visible, and claimed that ideas such as the Kingdom were merely illusions created by our minds, and that *all* our impressions derive from our what our senses perceive. From these impressions come our ideas. It was, in fact, the exact opposite of what Hotekh preached. Masooth was denying the upper realms that traditionalists believed in, saying that we'd merely thought them up for our convenience, to uphold our dearly held ideas. There is no divine light, Masooth said. What we perceive with our senses is all there is. So how can we have a divine emperor? He was called to the Fire Chamber, where the councillors of the emperor sat in office. There he presented his arguments, and the debate went on for many weeks. Neither side could really prove their point beyond doubt. Masooth defied the councillors to come up with an idea they first had no impression of. What about a mountain of pure diamond? one of them said, no doubt thinking himself very clever. I have never seen it with my eyes, yet I can imagine it. Doesn't this idea come from the Kingdom of Intelligence? Masooth batted this aside as he would a fly. Rubbish, he said. You can think of diamonds and you can think of mountains, both of which you have seen before. It is merely a matter of association in your mind to link the two and thus come up with a diamond mountain.

"Eventually, the councillors became so exasperated, they exiled Masooth from Magrast and told him he would be put to death if he dared show his face there again."

"Hmm," Shan murmured. "It seems to me that a philosopher's life is perilous, perhaps even futile."

"Indeed," replied Sinaclara. "But their trials have borne fruit which we can now taste for ourselves. You have to decide what you believe in, Shan. Can you think of an idea without having had any experience of it? It's more difficult than you think. It's a question that has eluded the greatest minds since Masooth's courageous treatise." She pulled a sour face. "Personally, I don't like his ideas. They're too cut-and-dried and tediously staid. I don't like to think that nothing else exists in the universe except our own minds and their meager interpretations. The thought is frightening, don't you think?"

Shan was silent for a moment, inwardly agreeing with what Sinaclara said, yet he felt that he ought to argue, that she expected it of him. Eventually, he said, "You seem to be able to discuss it without fear."

Sinaclara smiled. "One of my greatest lessons was to understand that fear always takes shelter in belief, something those pathetic Fire Chamber councillors could obviously not accept."

Shan wrinkled up his nose in perplexity. "But what about the peacock angel? You still have beliefs, don't you?"

Sinaclara nodded thoughtfully. "Yes and no. Once you realize that your belief may be founded upon fear, fear of nothing, and of no purpose, then conflict ends, fear ends, belief ends and knowledge starts. If I have a belief it is in the life force of the universe, and Azcaranoth is merely one of many of its masks. That mask happens to suit me. I like it and work with it."

Shan thought it was rather more than that, but held his tongue, saying only, "Who taught you this lesson?"

"It was the Caradorean poet Almoretia Crow. Her most striking idea was that it is folly for us to think that we can have true knowledge of everything. She felt that all truth was relative. She was a tortured soul, who believed that all conflict arose from fear, a fear that leads people to justify their beliefs enough to kill and be killed. She wrote that the only way to conquer this terrible condition of the soul was simply to accept things for what they were. Almoretia proclaimed through her songs that the only way to accept this was to live as if there were nothing beyond this life, as if we were not created for a purpose. Essentially, she thought we were born from nothing and thus will return to nothing."

"But, if that is true, what are we to make of our lives then?" Shan asked.

"That is the beauty of her philosophy," Sinaclara said, "because, if our future is not preordained, if it is merely a big black nothing, then what we project into that nothing will be our purpose. And this can be anything which we ourselves affirm and more importantly, choose."

"It sounds difficult and lonely," Shan said.

"It is," Sinclara said. "That's the whole point, Shan. Almoretia's dirges spoke to me, even though I don't wholeheartedly agree with them. They tell of the great anguish of being abandoned to our own choices, of having no god who gives succor, purpose and answers, who can take responsibility for our life and all the choices and mistakes that we might make. And that anguish of responsibility, of being responsible for everything in our world, is the only misery of life. But joy and ecstasy can be found when we affirm our choices, *in the face of nothing*. I learned the hard way that if something bad happens because of a choice I make, then I must affirm it as if I *willed* it to happen, as if it had been my goal." She leaned toward him earnestly and her voice became a low hiss. "Every pit of misery, every instance of suffering, hardship and heart ache, *affirm it*, Shan, as your own, as your life, in the face of nothing."

Shan swallowed with difficulty, feeling as if she'd slapped him. Did she know about what had happened to him?

"If you can do this," Sinaclara said softly, "then you are what Almoretia termed a genuine man, a man of great strength, whom no other can crush or conquer. Do you understand what I am telling you? Do you?"

Shan's eyes felt hot. "I didn't make it happen," he said hoarsely. "I didn't."

Sinaclara regarded him with a fiery gaze. "Affirm it, Shan. Take it into yourself. Take strength from it."

He spoke hurriedly, gasping in a small voice, like a child. "I could have gone to the forest that day. We needed some kindling. I could have gone there. Then I wouldn't have been in the same place." He put his hands over his face. "Did I will it? Did I want it to happen? Oh great gods!"

"You wouldn't be here now if it hadn't happened," Sinaclara said, leaning back in her chair.

Shan was silent.

"You're alive, aren't you, and your experiences have made you the perfect companion for Taropat, because you understand some of what he's been through. The Shan that was would have lived and died an ignorant peasant. If I said to you now that I could alter time and send you back to your home the day before the Magravands came, would you do it? I'd let you go back with full knowledge of what will happen. You could make your escape, hide, even warn your people. Many of you could survive. But you will never have this. The knowledge you've gained will be forgotten. Taropat, Nip, Thremius, myself, all the people you will meet in the future, you'd never have known us and never will. You'd never make a difference, and still the Magravands would vanquish Breeland. Think on it, Shan. Think hard. If you had the choice now, would you go back and live that little life under the yoke of Madragore?'

Shan closed his eyes, shook his head. "No," he whispered, then uttered a groan. "How can I think that? My father . . . My aunt . . . *What does that make me?*"

"I can't send you back," Sinaclara said gently. "And no one's asking you to live through it again, are they? It's over, Shan. Accept it as a situation that merely is—or was. Go forward and walk in the light of the true sun."

Shan lay back exhausted in his chair. "Is this what Taropat had to do—with Khaster, I mean?"

"Oh yes," said Sinaclara. "I was there some of the time while he was doing it." She stood up and came to crouch beside his chair, reaching out to stroke his face. "Through all this, there is one constant, my Shan. Life itself. The great force that creates and sustains it. That is certainly not open to interpretation. Whether you accept that there are creator gods or not, we are alive and there is an energy that has given us this life. If we become fully aware of the life force, we can attain the power to change our surroundings and our destiny."

"How?" Shan asked.

Sinaclara pushed the hair back from his face. "Through magic of course. You must learn and remember that where your intention goes, so energy flows. Only life energy has the power to create and re-create. There is no other secret to it than that. The hard part is to learn how to direct your intention in harmony with your own life force."

Shan had already learned a lot from Nip about how a magician should be able to perceive and manipulate the essence of nature. He had also learned from her, and from Taropat, about the nature of fear and how awareness of it, and the subsequent freedom from its effects, was the first thing that set a magician apart from ordinary people. All that Sinaclara had told him expanded these concepts, but how could he live by them? Ideas were one thing, practice another.

Sinaclara stood up and went to pour them both a glass of fruit cordial. "The prophet Mipacanthus wrote that we are all part of the music of the universe," she said. "There is no division between us and any other mote of energy. We are beings of energy. We are the song."

Shan took the glass from her. He wasn't sure it felt real in his grasp anymore.

TIME PASSED STRANGELY in the house and garden of the pavoniata. Surely only a few weeks had passed, yet Shan felt as if he'd lived there for years and had years' worth of experience. He could see that he stood at the foot of a long, lonely road up the side of a dark mountain. He had dedicated himself to a particular path. Sinaclara had not spoken directly of how Shan might become the person Taropat had wanted him to be. With her, Shan's journeys had all been to the deepest corners of his own psyche, yet now he felt as if he'd been given weapons that might be effective against the might of the empire. He understood what motivated its leaders. He could see the great cloud of fear, shot with red and black, that was the god-form of Madragore, created by men, sustained by men. Sinaclara had given him hope. She had taught him how it might be possible to reshape the mask of the god. He felt his youth gave him freshness and clarity. Thremius had spoken of how he learned from the young. Shan felt he had all the experience he needed to go forth and change the world.

At night, he would lie awake in the starlight and plan the future. He saw himself smiting the Dragon Lord and the evil prince, Bayard, through the force of his will and his own goodness. He would lead armies under white banners. As to who would make up these armies, he had yet to decide, but surely Taropat had some idea. Shan thrummed with energy. He felt privileged. He felt strong.

One night, Shan awoke in darkness to find Sinaclara standing by his bed. She put a finger to her lips, then whispered, "Come."

He scrambled out of the blankets and put on a dressing gown, then followed her into the silent corridors of the house. She was barefoot, dressed only in a simple shift of dark blue, her hair unbound down her back. She took him to the temple, which was ablaze with the light of a thousand candles. The indigo curtains were drawn back to reveal Azcaranoth, resplendent above his altar. The temple was full of Jessapurians, who were humming a low song in harmony.

Sinaclara stood behind Shan before the angel and put her hands upon his shoulders. "Speak to him," she said, "for one day you might have need of his presence."

"What should I say?" Shan asked.

"What your heart feels," Sinaclara said. "Ask for his help in those matters that press upon you."

Shan stared up at the angel and thought, I do not want to ask for help. I want you to show me something. Show me the future.

He closed his eyes, willing an impression to come to him. All he could see was a dark king enthroned, surrounded by a lurid indigo light that hurt the eyes. This king held a sword in his hand. Suspended above his head, rather than resting upon it, was a tall crown that emitted a strong golden radiance. There was power in this man, but he seemed evil. Shan thought his face looked as if it was made of frozen lightning.

Is this a true king? Shan thought. Am I to conquer him? Or is it *my* king? Is he part of myself?

Then the image changed. He saw a mighty city of crystal, rearing up toward a sky of aching blue. He saw ethereal forms gliding in and out of the narrow towers. He heard their holy song. A city of angels. Azcaranoth's city. And in his head, he heard Sinaclara's voice. "This you will see with your eyes one day. Dream of it, my Shan. Learn its territory."

The image faded from his mind and he opened his eyes. He felt Sinaclara's hands upon his shoulders, heard her heavy breathing. He saw that the peacock wings of the angel had unfurled, revealing his perfect body. It was covered in scars.

12

RITES OF WINTER AND DEATH

IN THE GARDEN, leaves dripped from the trees and the chill breath of winter was immanent in the smoky mist of morning. Sinaclara said that a great festival was approaching, one that was far older than the nameless god Shan had known in childhood. "It is the time of dark and of cold," she said, "when the fields are unyielding with frost and life sleeps in the earth. During this time, the world dreams, and in her dreams, she relives the past. Images of the dead appear to those who are aware enough to perceive them."

"I know of this festival," Shan said. "In our village, we would put out saucers of blood and milk for the spirits. Girls would wear red ribbons in their hair and the lads red garters on their knees. On the night of the Grave, we'd build a bonfire on the green, and dance in a circle to keep the spirits at bay."

"These are old customs," said Sinaclara, "memories of older practices. In ancient times, the Night of the Grave was called Aya'even, which in the old tongue meant the feast of the dead. It is but one point on the great wheel of life, death and rebirth. Because of its associations with darkness and the dead, it has within it inherent hope, for without death, there cannot be life. This is why it is still celebrated by those who no longer remember its true meaning. The memory of that hope lives on."

On the eve of Aya'even, Sinaclara told Shan she would take him into the forest. "There you might meet Lord Aya himself, for now you have eyes to see."

Shan paused before saying, "And the spirits of the dead. Is it possible to see them on this night?"

Sinaclara eyed him for a moment, then nodded. "Yes, as creatures on the web of wyrd, it is our duty to lead stray spirits to their lord at that time."

"Is it possible to discover whether someone is yet in this world or the next?"

"It is possible," said Sinaclara.

They went into the forest just before dusk, which now came earlier in the day. The sun's descent painted the sky crimson and against it the branches of the trees looked black and stark. It was as if a great fire burned beyond the wilderness, as if the world burned. Tendrils of mist seeped through the trees like astral fingers, feeling for the living. Black crows made a cacophony high overhead, the sound of madness, and it seemed to Shan as if the whole forest rustled and quivered with unseen running things that twittered and clicked just below his hearing.

Sinaclara led them to the trunk of an ancient oak and here they sat down among the groping roots. The Lady had a leather satchel with her, which now she opened. She took from it a flask and two cups of hard stitched leather. Shan would not have been surprised to learn they'd been fashioned from the skin of a man. "What are we drinking?" he asked, knowing Sinaclara would offer him no ordinary brew.

She smiled and poured out two measures of a murky-looking fluid.

Shan told her about the day Gust had given him flowers to eat and how they had allowed him to see spirits, too many spirits, he recalled.

Still Sinaclara would offer no information about the contents of the cups, so Shan just drank his draught, expecting fire, expecting bitterness, but all he tasted was earth. The flavor lingered in his mouth. It wasn't pleasant. It tasted like grave dirt. Perhaps that was what it was.

Sinaclara sighed and leaned back against the pleated bark of the oak. Wood smoke combined with the early evening mist that rolled, catlike, around the toes of the trees. Shan sat in silence beside her. He guessed the draught he had taken had narcotic properties. He could feel his mind flexing, as if new channels of thought were opening up. He felt he had aged ten years in the brief time he had been with Taropat and Sinaclara. How could so much have been crammed into just a few months? The person he'd been before was dead. Death. Tonight was its night. He exhaled, and his own breath seemed to smell of wood smoke.

"It is Lord Aya's perfume, you know," Sinaclara said. Her legs were stuck out straight before her, her palms upon her thighs. "He is drenched in it."

Shan knew she meant the smoke. He said nothing.

With another sigh, the lady got to her feet and held out her hand to Shan. "Come, we must go to the celebration."

"With other people?" He'd thought this night was to be private.

"Of course," Sinaclara answered. "A festival is not a festival unless there is a crowd to witness it."

They walked along an avenue of rhododendron, until they reached that strange part of the forest that Nip had called a hinterland. Although Shan could see nothing, he was very much aware of the burgeoning life around him, not in the hunched trees particularly, which appeared to be already dormant, but in the shadows between them: rustlings, crackings, the sound of breath. The ground mist was thicker here, and the presence of wood smoke strong enough to make his eyes smart. Presently, Shan saw an amber glow through the trees ahead, and could hear a strangely hollow drumming sound. Sinaclara led him from the hinterland, through a circle of ancient oaks, into a clearing, which was dominated by an immense bonfire. Sparks gushed up into the air from it, flaming petals. The fire roared hungrily. The wood that comprised it must be very dry. Around the fire a group of figures gathered. Some were throwing twigs into the flames, while others danced, slowly and sinuously. Yet more stood in small huddles, sipping from wooden bowls. To the side, three swarthy yet beautiful young men sat beside a long hollow log, which they were beating with sticks, creating complicated rhythms. To dance, you'd have to choose which theme to follow. The drummers' hair hung in black rags over their chests, like headdresses of crow feathers. "Who are these people?" Shan asked.

Sinaclara let go of his hand. "Torozenti," she said. "Followers of the old way. They live nearby, in caves."

"In caves?"

Sinaclara shrugged. "They are very homely caves. They've been lived in for thousands of years. It's a tradition."

"Are they magicians, witches?"

Sinaclara laughed. "They harvest the forest, they make boats for the river. But they follow the old ways. Magic is in their blood."

By this time, the group had noticed newcomers were in their midst and approached them. They appeared disappointingly ordinary, not that different from the villagers of Holme. "The Lady, the Lady," they sang.

An elderly woman sailed forward and offered Sinaclara a wooden bowl. "Drink from the pot, Lady, drink."

Sinaclara inclined her head and did so. "Greetings, Ama Maya. I thank you." The woman did not offer the vessel to Shan. He found it strange that nobody commented on his presence. They were not curious about him at all. Neither did Sinaclara attempt to introduce him. But despite this, Shan did not feel uncomfortable.

Ignoring Shan, Sinaclara began to talk with the Torozenti. Their conversation seemed no more than gossip. Shan stood to the side, looking round. He was mesmerised by the drummers, and even more so by the feral-looking girls who stamped and swayed to the rhythm of the drums. They were like dryads, tree spirits, dancing on a carpet of golden oak leaves. Their hair was twigs and russet foliage, their skin the tawny cream of the great pale fungi that grew within the trunks of hollow trees. Women, he thought. Just the single word. He was sure he could smell their skin. Moss and loam and blood. If this is the night of death, why am I thinking of life? There was a sense of excitement in the air, collared with danger. The lithe movements of the young women hinted at contained frenzy. The furious colors of the flames behind them transformed them into shadowy, leaping elemental creatures, born of fire, of smoke.

Then, without Shan noticing the transition, all was quiet. The drummers sat glassy-eyed before their drums, panting silently. The dancing girls could not stop moving, but paced restlessly on soundless feet. Everyone else was forming a circle around the great fire. Sinaclara took Shan's hand and led him toward the flames. They were roaring furiously. Whole tree trunks cracked and spat in their midst. When Shan looked up at the sparks, he thought he saw twisting, leering creatures forming, decaying and reforming there, like exploding constellations.

Shan stood in the circle, conscious of the slinking females behind him, who circled the fire like lionesses, afraid of the heat, yet drawn to it.

The older woman, whom Sinaclara had called Ama Maya, stood some way to Shan's left. Now, she raised her arms to the sky, and for some moments stood in silent communion. Then she spoke. Her voice rang out, clearly audible over the hungry flames. "We meet here on the night of the dead, the festival of fire, the cremation. We are gathered to bear witness to the dance of the dead, and to acknowledge its master, Lord Aya, who is Lord of the Dance, the Angel of Death, King of the Brimstone Fire."

Everyone around the fire now raised their arms, and cried out wordlessly. The girls who haunted the perimeter of the circle hissed like serpents.

When Ama Maya spoke again, her voice was low and hoarse, yet Shan could still hear every word. "Behold, the smoky veil is around us. The mist of the land is the veil between the worlds. Close your eyes. Listen for his footsteps. This is the realm of the dead. Listen for every sound: the howling of the wind spirits, the cackle of wood goblins, the murmurs of tree spirits. The trees are talking to each other, and on this night we understand their language. These are the sounds of wyrd, the sounds hidden within every shadow, and locked into the darkness of nature, the forest of the night. Only on this night do we truly hear them, for the creatures of wyrd perceive the coming of the Master of Shadows, the Walker Upon the Autumn Leaves."

Ama Maya's voice was like the wind in the trees. Shan could no longer understand her. She no longer spoke words. Something else. He felt himself drifting. His hands had gone numb. Then there was only wind, no voice at all.

Shan was immediately alert. His eyes snapped open. He was alone. Everyone had crept away. He turned round quickly and it seemed that shadowy shapes loped off on all fours into the trees. There was utter darkness beyond the light of the fire, despite the moonlight raying down from the hard clear sky. The ground in the clearing was carpeted with a thick blanket of golden leaves, and tendrils of mist writhed over it. Shan's senses were acute. The frosty air in his nostrils was a rich banquet of the ripe smells of autumn; smoke and fruit and decay.

Where had everyone gone? Shan shivered. His ears strained to hear laughter, but there was none. His eyes strained to perceive movement in the trees, but there was none. Then, upon the path that led twisting into the darkness, Shan saw a tall figure. It was suddenly there, from nowhere. It had not approached in any conventional fashion. The figure seemed cloaked in dark mist and it was watching Shan intently. Shan stared back, his spine flexing with dread. The mist was clearing. He could see the figure was male, but not a man. His face was as pale as the fullest moon and his eyes burned like smoldering embers; the color of autumn's golden gown. His face was framed by a halo of flaming red hair, yet he did not have a mouth. Beneath his fierce eyes was only pale blankness. Shan felt as if all his courage turned to a thin fluid and ran down through his body, through every vein and artery, out through his feet and into the ground. He was witless with a gripping primordial horror. The Lord of Death had come for him. This was Lord Aya. He did not need a mouth to speak, for the dead do not speak. The trident he held was the symbol of his kingship over the spirit world, but he could take souls with it.

Shan looked around himself in panic. A more rational part of his mind, the part that Sinaclara had spent so much time educating, told him that what he was seeing must be a vision inspired by the strange drink he'd taken, or else a trick. He wanted to believe the figure ahead of him was one of the Torozenti in costume. But the cold primal horror in his heart could not be denied. His magical training told him that what he saw was a discarnate entity.

Shan backed toward the fire, perhaps unconsciously seeking its protection against denizens of the night. But the flames suddenly roared out as if in an attempt to engulf him. Shan uttered a startled cry and leapt to the side, yet wherever he ran the flames snatched out to tease, goad and direct him. The whole clearing had become a mass of dancing fire. He was trapped.

The dark figure on the path raised his trident and pointed it toward Shan. Surrounded by flames, Shan sank to his knees. There was nothing he could do, nothing. He put his hands over his eyes, sure Lord Aya was gliding toward him, ready to pierce his heart with the three points of death.

"Are you afraid, little man?"

The voice was not that of a dark lord, but a woman's. Soft, gentle, full of humor. Shan raised his head, wondering if Sinaclara had come back to him, but the woman bending down to him was a stranger. She was not tall, yet gave the impression of immense height, dressed in different shades of green, a gown of rags and tassels, woven with leaves. Her hair was russet red, confined by a coronet of tiny red apples and the dried pods of plants and her face was long with slanting eyes. Inhuman. She seemed to emit an invisible light that eclipsed the frightening vision on the path behind her. Her beauty was terrifying, because of its inhumanity, yet Shan did not feel afraid of her.

"Who are you?" he asked her.

The woman smiled, and the parting of her lips released a breath that smelled of fruit, of corn lying wet with dew in the fields beneath moonlight. "I am she who adheres to his light and walks behind him in the realm between the underworld and the earth. He walks in silence upon the carpet of autumn mist. I am the music for his dance of the dead, the wind that sings and savages, the wind that haunts the living and gathers the dead. I am the Swarm of Wyrd. He is the sun that shines by night."

Shan pressed his fingers briefly against his eyes. This could not be real. But when he lowered his hands once more the woman still leaned down to him, softly smiling. A luminous ether smoked off her skin, the essence of the season.

"This is your night," said the Swarm of Wyrd. "You have a task to complete."

She held out her hand and lifted Shan to his feet as if he was no heavier than thistledown. He could do nothing but comply. She put her hands on his shoulders and made him turn to face the fire. Tongues of flame licked out, touching his skin, yet he could not flinch away. The Swarm's grip was too firm.

"Gaze upon this element," she said. "You will carry some of the fire with you when you leave this place. For leave, you must. On this night, the dead walk. In the forest of the night, they who are lost on the earthly plane wander and grieve. Your task is to gather up these souls and deliver them to the hands of Lord Aya."

Shan shuddered. "Must I do this alone?"

The Swarm's fingers flexed against his shoulders. "All those who would understand the ways of wyrd must tread this path. You must strengthen the light within you, for once it burns brightly, it will illumine your way forever. There is already a tiny flame within your heart. The same flame burns within every human breast. Can you feel it? Can you see it with your inner eye?"

Shan swallowed with difficulty. Yes, he could feel it. A glow within him, a small flickering flame.

"This light," said the Swarm, "is your protection against any evil spirit that walks abroad this night. It is this light you must use to guide the lost and the lonely to their Lord, for the restless spirits will recognize it. You must see it glowing golden within you like a candle flame."

"How will I guide the spirits?" Shan glanced behind the Swarm and could still just perceive a shadowy outline with a flaming halo round its head, standing on the path to the forest.

The Swarm turned Shan to face her completely. "This is the realm of the dead, these woods around you. Can you see Lord Aya between the trees?" She closed her eyes and smiled. "He watches us silently. He is with us now." She opened her eyes and looked down at Shan. "Go to him. Follow him as he walks abroad in the night. Go wherever he leads you. Go where you must. Listen for the cries of the dead, the call of an empty house or a lonely church. What ghosts will you encounter? What hopeless soul will cling to you for help? Go into the night and show them the way."

"But how?"

"Say to them 'I am the light to guide you. Come with me.' You need not fear because Lord Aya is already with you."

Shan was sure it would not be so simple. The forest of the dead. Not just of flesh, but thoughts, dreams and hopes. He knew instinctively that he would face the darkest parts of himself out there in the night with only the fearsome Lord Aya for company.

The fire, which had seemed so savage and threatening, was now difficult for Shan to leave. Here was warmth and light. Out there was only darkness. He realized then that he was alone by the fire. The Swarm had vanished. Perhaps she had never really been there. On the path to the darkness, Lord Aya still stood tall and menacing. Now, he raised his trident once more and Shan knew he must follow.

As soon as he began to walk forward, the Lord of the Dead turned around in a cloud of inky cloak and began to stride away. Shan ran to catch up, but Lord Aya always remained the same distance ahead, only the brightness of his flaming hair indicating where he was between the trees.

Shan knew how vast the forest was, and how easy it would be to become lost in it. Yet even before he'd caught sight of anything that resembled a spirit, he came out of the trees and found himself on a hilltop, looking down at a moonlit valley, where a sleepy silver river ran. Villages and farms huddled around the banks of the river, while at a further distance from the water, Shan saw great old houses and churches. Lord Aya was walking down the slope ahead of him. Shan followed. He heard a sound and looked down, to see a face distorted by fear looking up at him from the earth. He stopped walking immediately, and two hands scrabbled up to reach for him, dripping crumbs of soil. Without thinking, Shan said, "I am the light to guide you. Come to me." He reached out to take hold of one of the insubstantial hands, intending to haul the spirit out of the ground, but there was no need. A thin, spiralling wisp of blue-white smoke streaked up past him and flew toward Lord Aya.

Spirits came to him, exuding from the trunks of trees, flying as vapor in the air. He could reach out, say the charmed words, and feel a great sense of relief and joy as the entity was released into Lord Aya's care. This was no trial; this was rewarding and comforting. The landscape slept in peace, while he, as a savior of the dead, walked like a wraith himself beneath the shadows of the trees.

Then down into the villages, padding along cobbled streets, calling ghosts from the dark windows, from the steeples of churches, from cracks in the walls. All the time, Aya walked ahead of him, his hair streaming sparks. There was nothing terrifying about the Lord of the Dead; he was a redeemer, compassion itself.

Shan walked to the end of one of the villages and realized he had lost sight of Lord Aya. Was his task now over? How would he find his way back to Lady Sinaclara? He heard a sound that seemed to come from a shadowed lych-gate nearby. It could have been a smothered human cry, or the call of an animal. A dark churchyard lay beyond the gate. Perhaps another shade lurked there, seeking solace. Shan went through the arch of the lych and found himself in a graveyard crowded with ancient yews. The church itself looked ruined, abandoned, and all the gravestones hung askew. In many places, sinister oblong holes in the ground, that appeared to derive from subsidence, made it look as if the dead had been fighting to escape their earthly resting places. If Shan could have imagined the most eerie churchyard in the world, this would be it. It was the archetype of all such places. He looked around himself, but could see no spirits anywhere. It seemed odd, for surely a location like this would be the natural habitat of ghosts.

The sound came again. Was it an animal? Shan ventured cautiously into an avenue of yews that led off to the left. No moonlight came down between the thick branches and sound was hushed. What

was that noise? Not a cry, something else. Shan looked round, saw
nothing, but he could hear it. A distant thudding rhythm. Hooves. A
horse was approaching. Swiftly. Closer and closer. Shan strained to
see something behind him, but there was nothing there. Even so, the
ground had begun to shake. It sounded as if the animal was almost
upon him. But there was nothing there.

Fear came then. Gut deep, animal fear. Shan began to run. The
bitter juice of terror filled his heart. He could not feel the candle flame
inside him anymore. He sensed that what was coming for him was
terrible beyond imagination. He was alone with it. Always had been.
That was the most terrifying thought.

Ahead of him, he saw an oblong of twilight, which perhaps meant
he was near to the end of the avenue, close to the graveyard wall.
He could leap over it, run back to the village, bang upon someone's
door for assistance if necessary. The pounding of the hooves was
deafening now. He could feel hot breath on his neck, smell its sickening rancid odor. He dared not look round. Not now.

He burst out into bright sunlight. For a moment, he was dazzled
and confused, then his sight cleared abruptly. He was in a cornfield.
The bright sheaves were trampled and muddied. Ahead of him, he
saw a dark blur of activity, which swiftly swam into focus.

Shan cried out in revulsion and horror. Men were there, their
trousers round their knees. Magravandian soldiers. Something twisted
in their midst, mewing relentlessly, desperately, like a tortured baby.
Himself.

The landscape rushed past him, gathering him up, and he was
back there, frozen in terror and pain, pleading for mercy, finding none.
Horses stamped around him, crushing poppies into blood. He could
hear the rasping breath of the men. They did not speak. Their eyes
were dead.

Had the last few months been a dream? Was he still there, trying
to escape a ghastly reality? Had Sinaclara sent him back after all?
Had he done something, said something to indicate he wanted that?
No, please no.

Shan called out for Taropat, for Nip, for Master Thremius, for

Sinaclara. They had to exist. He had to have met them. Everything was moving too fast. The Magravandians were blurs around him.

Abruptly, everything slowed down. Shan could no longer feel his body, what was being done to it. Behind the Magravandians, he could see his friends standing in a line. They gazed at him expressionlessly. He tried to cry out, but no sound would come.

The Magravandians threw Shan to the ground, their lust spent. He was unimportant now, used up, finished. They ignored him as they rearranged their clothing. Chatting amiably to one another, as old friends do, they remounted their horses and rode away.

Shan lay still, trying to breathe. He was deafened by a clamorous rhythmic thunder, which he realized was the beating of his own heart. He could still see the hazy outlines of Taropat, Nip, Master Thremius and Sinaclara, but they were fading. He reached out painfully with one hand, sure he was dying.

Hod, his father, stood with drooping shoulders before him, slowly shaking his head. He held his best hat in his hands, which he was wringing continually. He'd always worn that hat for funerals. Shan's aunt glided into view, her fingers pressed to her lips. She too was shaking her head, tears pulsing from her eyes. After, came Shan's mother, the apple woman, her face streaked with ashes, her mouth a dark cavern of despair. Shan felt they were judging him. He was responsible for what had happened to him. He had let it happen. He had not fought hard enough.

Then someone else stepped forward, a beautiful young man with pale hair. He stood at Shan's feet and said, "How old are you?"

Shan was compelled to answer. "Fifteen."

The young man shook his head, smiling in a grave, sad way. "No, you are not. You are not a child anymore. Remember it. You are seventeen now. You have been for some time."

Shan said, "I'm not. I'm dead."

Again, the young man shook his head. "You are full of life. You must stop punishing yourself. It is a needless indulgence. Physically, you were powerless at that time, but it is your choice entirely to remain a victim now. Affirm what happened. You should let it pass. It is over."

"Are you Tayven?" Shan asked. He found he could sit up, for his body was no longer chained by pain. Reality had shifted. The others had vanished.

"No, I am you."

Shan laughed and couldn't stop. If he did, he would scream until his throat bled.

"Get up," said the young man. "Get up, boy. Run." An expression of urgency had come into his eyes. It affected Shan immediately. He leapt to his feet. The cornfield was quiet around him, yet he sensed a terrible approach.

"Run! Run!"

He was stumbling, scrabbling, making for the trees behind him. There, he might hide from his pursuers. He might find sanctuary. There were hooves pounding behind him. He could not relive that again. He couldn't. Uttering a scream of defiance, Shan pushed himself forward and dived into the shadow of the forest. He fell, tumbled over, and found himself in moonlit darkness once more on a winding flat path through the trees. The galloping horses were still behind him, but it would be easier to run fast here. Shan's limbs felt so strong, he was sure he barely touched the ground. It was like flying, but no matter how fast he ran, the horses were getting closer. He could hear the yelping of hounds and the heraldic bleat of a hunting horn. The air was chill. His breath was steaming. His heart felt as if it was about to burst.

They came upon him in thunder. Grit and stones flew up from their pounding hooves. Many horses. And dogs. Shan reeled among their heavy hectic bodies, helpless in the tide of forward movement that flashed past him, gathered him up. He could feel the heat of the horses' sweat, smell it. Their nostrils were aflame, their eyes rolled. Foam flew from their straining flanks. Huge hounds wove past Shan's legs. He could no longer run, yet was carried along stumbling, falling, pushed up like a cork on water. One of the riders reached down with one hand and hauled Shan effortlessly up onto the saddle before him. Shan could not struggle. Who were these people? They were not Magravandians. The rider who held him looked more like the Swarm of Wyrd, perhaps an elden creature. His face was long, the eyes slanted. He wore a tall helm and his skin was the color of moonlight. He did not speak, and his smile was sly.

"Who are you?" Shan cried above the hubbub of hooves and hounds.

The rider only smiled wider and gestured: look around. Shan twisted in the saddle and saw that the company was led by a man who wore a crown of antlers. A voice, soft and low, whispered in Shan's mind. "We are the Wild Hunt of the elden. We follow our stag king, Araahn."

I am dreaming, Shan thought. I drank Sinaclara's draught and I'm unconscious somewhere, dreaming. That's it.

He felt at once more at ease. Then another voice sniggered in his mind. Dreaming, yes, perhaps. But what if you're trying to escape reality because of what's happening to you in the cornfield? Maybe you're going mad. Maybe those moments will go on for eternity and you'll try different dreams to tell you they're not. You never met Taropat. Sinaclara is a phantom. You're back there and the moment you stop dreaming, you'll be dead. There is nothing beyond this world. You know that. It's why you daren't stop dreaming. The nothingness is waiting, Shan. How strong are you to resist it?

Shan groaned from the depths of his soul and, closing his eyes, leaned back against the chest of the hunter behind him. He could feel the movement of the horse beneath him, hear the shrill cry of the horn, the yelp of the hounds. He would stay in this dream. He would cling to it.

Suddenly, the rider cried, "There!" and Shan was compelled to look up.

The eld was pointing ahead, his alien face animated with excitement. Shan peered beyond the hunt. Yes, he could see it now: a white flickering shape. A beautiful white hind bounded ahead of the riders. Don't catch her, Shan thought. Please don't. He could see that the hind's perfect flanks were stained with sweat. Her movement, though still light and graceful, seemed weary. They would be upon her soon. The dogs would tear out her throat.

A gap appeared in the trees ahead, framing a brilliant red light. Shan thought of fire, but then realized it was the sunset. The hunt

pounded toward it and presently, Shan saw that the forest ended at
the edge of a precipice. His throat closed up. They would all plummet
to their deaths. There was no way the horses could pull up now. The
dream must end. He could not hold on to it.

As the hind made that final, desperate leap, Shan screamed in
terror. He tried to pull himself away from the rider who held him,
but he wasn't strong enough. But the hind hadn't fallen. She was still
running, running across the sky. At the head of the hunt, the stag
king, Araahn, blew upon his horn and with a bunching of its powerful
muscles, his great horse leapt off the cliff after the hind. It too galloped
along an invisible road in the sky. The hunt poured after it.

The moment came when Shan's own mount took that leap. For
a split second, he saw land far below, cloaked in darkness. Then, with
a mighty bound, they were galloping miles above it, toward a bloody
sunset.

She's not fleeing the hunt, Shan thought. She's leading it. We are
flying toward the future.

A feeling spumed through Shan's body that he had no words to
describe. It was partly immense joy, freedom, exhilaration, understanding, but also far more than that, feelings beyond the human
emotional lexicon. He wanted to bask in this experience, live it forever. Perhaps the hunter behind him sensed that. Uttering a hoarse
cry, the eld suddenly pushed Shan away from him roughly. Helpless,
Shan shot into the air. He was falling, limbs flailing. He could not
cry out, nor even breathe, because the speed of his flight pushed the
breath from his lungs. It was a fall of a hundred years. The land
below did not appear to draw closer. Perhaps this was oblivion, what
death was like, an endless fall.

He was floating now, slowly, like a wisp of down. Twisting his
body, he looked up and saw the Wild Hunt were mere specks of
darkness now, silhouetted against the red sky. The sound of their
passing faded away, and Shan was a feather wafting to earth.

He landed gently, curled up into a ball, his arms over his face.
After some moments, he sat up and looked around. He was in a forest,
a bleak place devoid of all life. The trees were not merely black and
leafless, but appeared burned. The ground was covered in ashes. Shan

got to his feet. Was this another dream? Yet it felt so real. He could smell the acrid scent of damp embers. He could rub the ashes between his fingers, feel the grit of burned earth.

Shan began to walk through the forest. He wondered whether this was the same hinterland that surrounded Sinaclara's domain, a different representation of it. Occasionally, he saw birds, ragged carrion-eaters, feasting upon a banquet of blackened bones. It was as if a great battle had taken place there, a battle among the trees. The victors must have set fire to it because there were too many dead to bury.

Ahead, Shan saw a flash of dark green through the relentless black and gray and presently came upon a holly tree. It was the most beautiful thing he had ever seen; perfect, glossy berries of deepest red nestled among the waxy leaves. The tree reared toward the sky; aching color in a colorless realm. Shan went up to it, bent down to smell its green scent. He rubbed its flexible spined leaves between his fingers, squeezed its berries. He must carry some of this living thing with him through the land of the dead. Surely the tree would not mind. Reaching in among the foliage, scratching his wrists on the leaves, Shan plucked a few berry-clad twigs.

Dawn was coming. He could sense it. He must walk and walk, until his destination and his destiny was revealed to him. His fingers played with the holly branches, winding them into a circular wreath. A crown of life. All was silent, but for the snap of dry wood beneath his feet, and occasionally the coarse lamenting calls of the birds of death.

Shan could no longer gauge accurately the passage of time. Hours, or perhaps only minutes later, he came to a clearing. In its center stood a great ash tree, upon which the body of a man hung upside down.

A group of men and women in the ragged garb of shamans were circling the tree, chanting in an undertone. Shan approached them and touched one of the men on the shoulder. "Tell me, sir," he said. "Who hangs here?"

The shaman turned to him and pushed his ash-streaked face close to Shan's own. "It is the sacrificed king of the land. He surrenders his own life in eternity, so that the land may thrive. What you see before you, boy, is the tree of knowledge. As the divine king hangs there, he channels its knowledge for humankind. I and my brethren attend him in his torment, awaiting the wisdom that will spill from his lips."

"Wait with us," said another. "Dance with us."

Shan ducked his head. "I thank you." He noticed three women sitting on the ground near the base of the tree. They were dressed in dark cowled robes and their bodies swayed back and forth. Shan could not see their faces, but he could hear them weeping. They seemed different from the other shamans, less wild of aspect.

Shan approached them and asked them who they were.

One of them looked up. Her face, shadowed by her cowl, was so lined it seemed she was made of tree bark. "We are the Wyrd Sisters, who weave the fate of kings through the web of wyrd, and who wait to midwife the birth of a new king."

"So why do you weep?"

"We are weeping for the king."

Shan drew closer to the tree. As he did so, the eyes of the hanged man snapped open. Shan jumped in surprise, but could not look away from the king's gaze. His eyes were the deepest green.

"He has seen you," said one of the shamans. "Speak, boy, speak quickly."

Shan's head was utterly empty of important thoughts, and this was clearly a most significant moment. He spoke the first words that came into his mind, unsure of whether he should be uttering them or not. "I wish to be reborn, as you will be, as the sun will be."

The king continued to stare at him. No words came from his lips.

He is a king, but he has no crown, Shan thought, and was compelled to lean forward and press the holly wreath he had made onto the head of the king. He had to push hard to make it stick there. The sharp leaves caught into the king's hair, the points dug into his scalp, but he did not speak. At the same time, Shan felt suddenly inspired with words. They filled him like music. He had to let them out. "Great king, my soul has wandered in the forest of the dead. My heart is bleak and dark. Grant me the secret of rebirth. Help me to understand the divinity of self-sacrifice, so that new life may be brought to my soul and light to my heart. Great King, through the blood of your sacrifice, give me enlightenment."

The king still did not speak, but from his brow, where the holly crown had pricked him, a single shining drop of blood fell in slow motion to the ground. Shan saw it soak into the black earth, and moments later green shoots began to sprout up. Green vines burgeoned profusely up the tree, insanely swiftly, twisting around every branch, around the body of the king, until they appeared to be growing into his flesh, entwining every limb. He opened his mouth to speak the knowledge, and vines shot forth from his lips, whipping around his face.

Shan could not hear words. The sounds that emerged from the king were the cries of birds, the howl of the wind, the crash of the sea, the crackle of fire. Yet those sounds entered Shan's flesh like arrows of light. Understanding bloomed within him.

One of the Wyrd Sisters spoke again. "The head of the king is the seat of knowledge. And the vine symbolizes that knowledge given to others. In this foliate head before us lies the secret of every god and king. All gods are as one before us. All kings who acquired enlightenment through sacrifice and rose again. We celebrate that knowledge. The king and the land are one. We and the land are one."

Now, the first rays of the rising sun struck through the forest, and touched the Tree of Life. As the sun rose, all was suffused with a blinding white light. Foliage crept back around the tree. It had grown from the king and brought new life to the forest. The infant sun had been born to nourish that life. The forest was fertile and rich and green, filled with divine radiance, and as the light of the sun touched Shan's face, so his spirit was reborn with the life of new knowledge. Shan knew he had been walking in the forest of winter for a long time, but from that moment the days would grow longer and light would return to the land of his soul.

He flung back his head and closed his eyes, bathing in the light, taking its energy into his body. As it coursed through him, he felt cleansed and renewed. All the darkness of the past was cleared away, its shadows could not remain in the light of the new day. He felt full of energy and enthusiasm and hope. Anything was possible from this moment forward. He was capable of achieving his heart's desires. "I affirm it!" he cried.

13

THE DRAGON'S CLAW

S HAN OPENED HIS EYES and found himself standing in a forest clearing before the burned-out remains of an old fire. The Torozenti were nearby, Sinaclara with them. They were all watching him intently. What had happened? There was snow upon the ground and the air was so cold. It did not smell of smoke.

Sinaclara came to him and wrapped about him a cloak of purple wool. Ama Maya offered him a bowl, which was filled with a bloody fluid. Red wine, the blood of the vine, the blood of the king.

"Let us drink in celebration," said Ama Maya, "the blood of self-sacrifice. The solstice is passed, and from this day the nights grow shorter. From this time onward, let us not fear the web of our fate lest the knowledge that has been attained become worthless. And, in the coming year, let us all walk through the mystic forest of our spirit knowing that it will be forever green."

Shan drank from the cup, and then passed it to Sinaclara, who drank and passed it on. If this was the day after the winter solstice, six weeks had passed. How was that possible? A single night. A dream.

The drummers began to beat upon their drums, and the lithy girls came twisting out of the trees to dance in the birth of the sun.

Shan had tears on his face. He felt taller, wiser. Sinaclara put her hands upon his shoulders. He touched her face. He leaned toward her. He kissed her as a man.

FOR SIX WEEKS, Shan had been running wild in the forest, presumably under the influence of the fluid Sinaclara had given him at Aya'even. It seemed impossible. How had he fed himself? How had he survived the punishing cold? Yet there was no doubt that it was now winter. The oaks around the clearing, which last time he had seen them had been gowned in gold leaves, were now naked. There was a rime of snow upon the ground.

The Torozenti surrounded him. They crowned him with ivy and led him through the forest to their rock village. Shan stared up at the immense sandstone cliffs, which were full of hollows and caves: dwellings. A vast cave at ground level was the Torozenti's communal hall, and here a feast had been prepared on long tables. Once everyone was inside, a group of men pulled shut tall wooden doors. The company sat down to enjoy the feast, illumined only by narrow shafts of sunlight that came in through slits high up in the rock wall. Ama Maya, clearly high priestess of the Torozenti, directed Shan to a seat beside her, while Sinaclara sat on his other side. Shan felt dazed, incapable of speech. He drank some of the dark, heavy wine and it went instantly to his head.

Sinaclara laid a hand over one of his where it lay on the table. "This disorientation you feel—it will pass," she said.

He shook his head in bewilderment. "What happened to me? Was it a dream? How did it happen? It seemed like only a single night."

Sinaclara smiled at him. "It was a rite that took you from death to rebirth. Perhaps, for you, it was only a single night. I was not with you. I cannot say what happened to your physical body as your mind roamed the ether. All I can tell you is that we left you by the fire at Aya'even and returned at the appointed time."

"Was I still just standing there?"

"Yes. You were gazing at the ashes of the fire."

Shan ran his fingers over his face, found a light growth of beard there. He looked down at his clothes, saw they were filthy and torn. "I must have taken food and water. I'd be dead otherwise. I must have found shelter." He rubbed his face. "It doesn't make sense to me. I saw things, experienced things. It felt real, but it didn't involve finding food or shelter."

"You were on the web," Sinaclara said. "Time means nothing there, and neither do the routines of our reality."

"It was harrowing, and yet, at the beginning, it wasn't. Shall I tell you what I saw?"

"If you want to."

"Don't *you* want to know?"

"I am interested, but I respect your privacy."

Shan frowned. "One thing puzzles me more than anything else. I was told I was older than I am, and now I feel different. I don't feel like a boy anymore. Is that possible? Have I aged in some arcane manner while I've been away?"

Sinaclara paused, then said, "No, you haven't. But what you don't realize is that you've lived in the forest for a couple of years, not mere months as you thought."

"During the rite? That is even more inconceivable."

"No, Shan, not recently. I meant you've lived with Taropat for that time."

Shan shook his head. "It's only been months. It was always summertime, no winter, no fall. It's not possible."

Sinaclara squeezed his hand. "You didn't want time to pass. You hadn't faced your demons. You wanted to remain a child. Despite what people want to believe, time is not linear. There is no past point, future point or now point. It's just a cycle of flux and mutability."

Shan remembered the mornings he'd awoken feeling as if he'd slept far longer than eight hours. Had he slept the time away? There were too many questions.

Sinaclara squeezed his hand. "For now, enjoy the feast. It is in your honor. Later, we can talk about your experiences."

As if her words had been a signal, the drummers started up, and girls ran into the hall, wearing black and silver ribbons. They spun and stamped around the feasters, calling out in strange, ululating shrieks. Shan's wine cup was never empty. It seemed a strange time of day for such an event. Celebrations of this kind belonged to the night.

At midday, the doors to the hall were thrown wide and hard winter sunlight streamed in across the table. Everyone rose from their seats and crowded outside. Shan and Sinaclara were drawn along with them. Shan was conscious of a sense of new beginnings. The clear cold air was cleansing in his throat and nostrils. It was nourishing, promising new life. Sinaclara took his hand and they walked between two lines of Torozenti, away from the rock village. They followed a wide, yet rugged path that snaked upward between ancient cliffs. Overhead, wide-winged birds dipped and screamed, their cries echoed by the children that ran in and out of the lines of adults. After only a short walk, the path brought them to the shores of a mountain lake surrounded by cliffs, which Sinaclara said was called Doon Pond. In the center of the lake was an island, skirted by mist, even though the sun was high. Boats were drawn up onto the narrow beach and the Torozenti indicated that Shan should climb into one of them. He glanced inquiringly at Sinaclara, who inclined her head and gestured at the boat. "This is a taste of what is to come," she said. "There will be a time when you remember this place and recognize it as a mirror for the true seat of power."

Shan climbed into the boat and Sinaclara got in beside him, wetting her gown to the knees in the process. Then the Torozenti pushed the boat out onto the glassy surface.

"Row to the island," Sinaclara said, reclining against some sacks in the bottom of the vessel.

Shan picked up the oars and began to row. "Why are we going there?"

Sinaclara only smiled.

They rowed into the mist so that the shore was hidden from sight. Sound was muffled in that still winter world. All Shan could hear was the creak of the oars, their splash in the icy element.

"This mist isn't normal," Shan said.

"Some parts of the lake are hot," Sinaclara replied. "The phenomenon is entirely natural."

"Where's the island? I can't see anything." Shan looked behind them. All he could see was a dull white wall.

Sinaclara did not respond to these questions, but stood upright in the boat. "Stop rowing." Shan saw her breast rising and falling as she drew in long, slow breaths. Then, with a final sighing inhalation, she threw back her head and raised her arms. "King of the water, king of the deep, king of the heart, king of sleep, rise unto me, come unto me, bring forth the precious thing you guard, for you must give up your treasure. I command you, in the name of Azcaranoth, the star and your master."

All was silent. Sinaclara stood rigidly, her arms still raised. After some minutes, she sighed through her nose and muttered, "He guards his treasure too jealously."

Shan wondered what kind of king hid in isolation upon a tiny island in the middle of nowhere. Where was the island? Sinaclara could see it presumably, even though it was hidden from Shan's eyes. Perhaps she sensed it. She might have been here a thousand times before.

"Why are we here?" he asked.

Sinaclara glanced down at him. She would not speak. Shan felt a cold shiver of anger pass through him. Things had just happened to him since he'd met this woman. He had not instigated them, nor taken action. She had given him knowledge, yes, but she held all the cards. She had given him no forewarning or preparation concerning what had happened to him on Aya'even. "You must tell what we're doing and why. I have to know."

"Hush," said Sinaclara. "Look." Without taking her eyes from Shan, she lowered her arms and pointed at the water.

At first it seemed a man was walking toward them across the still surface, which Shan knew was impossible. That could only happen in dreams or visions. Then he realized that the figure was actually emerging vertically from the lake. He must have been swimming, but in full dress? His clothes were soaked, his hair a waterfall around his gaunt face.

"Lord of this land," said Sinaclara in barely more than a murmur. "Have we disturbed your cold sleep before the appointed time? It is bad of us, but essential. Come to me, King Morogant, bring me the Claw."

The figure hung motionless in the water before them. Shan swallowed with difficulty. If the man was wholly human, he must be mad. But from the way the hairs were prickling on his arms and neck, Shan sensed this was no mortal man.

"Do you doubt my judgment?" said Sinaclara.

King Morogant shook his head. "No, Lady." His voice sounded like the wind sighing through the high canopy of the forest. He fixed his eyes on Shan, and they were like starlight seen from the bottom of a pit. "Come to me, boy," he said.

"Enter the lake," Sinclara commanded in a soft but firm tone.

"Why?" Shan said. "Why should I?"

"Because the king of the deep has something to give to you. It is important."

"What? What has he to give to me?"

"Enter the water and find out."

"He is in doubt," said the king.

"Yes," said Sinclara, "but you know that is inevitable."

"He is afraid."

"No, not that."

"Why?" Shan said. "Why not that? I might be afraid. You cannot see inside me."

"No?" said Sinaclara.

Shan glared at her for a moment, then stood up and lumbered over the side of the boat into the water. He made sure the vessel rocked alarmingly and took satisfaction from the fact that Sinaclara stumbled, reaching out wildly to stop herself from falling into the lake.

Shan had imagined the lake was shallow, for the man stood waist high in it, but the moment he entered the water, he sank down into darkness. For a moment, he felt utter terror, believing Sinaclara had tricked him and entered into some dark covenant with the Torozenti to sacrifice him to the land. Then he was rising in a caul of bright bubbles. His head broke the surface and he saw King Morogant rearing over him. He was a giant, terrifying. From his neck, the king took a cord and lifted it over his head. A talisman depended from it. With one hand, he took hold of Shan's hair and lifted him bodily from the water. Shan cried out and struggled, but his strength was no match for the giant. Ignoring Shan's flailing limbs, the king slipped the cord over Shan's neck and then released him. Shan sank again immediately. He took in a lungful of water. Above him, he imagined Sinaclara was laughing at his ignorance, delighting in the game of perplexing him, and subjecting him to experiences she took for granted, yet knew were incomprehensible to others. Damn her, Shan thought. When he rose in the water again, coughing out icy fluid, he did not attempt to climb back into the boat, but struck out for the shore. He would not be her plaything. She could row herself back, or get the mad giant to do it.

SHAN WALKED OUT of the water, his ragged clothes icy and sodden around his body, which felt surprisingly warm. The Torozenti were waiting for him. A girl ran forward and offered him a wreath of ivy. He presumed he was to crown himself with this. Instead, he took the ring of foliage and placed it upon the girl's head, leaning forward to kiss her cheek. "It suits you better," he said and began to walk away from them.

"Wait," said the girl. "Return with us to the village. We have warm clothes for you, more food, more wine. There will be dancing . . ."

Shan raised a hand in salute but did not stop walking. "Enjoy your feast," he said. "A friend is waiting for me."

He could feel the Torozenti's perplexity behind him. Perhaps he wouldn't be able to find his way back to Sinaclara's house, but at that moment he didn't care. He thought only of his friend, Nip, who was always eager to tell him things, share her knowledge. She was the open book to Sinclara's triple-sealed parchment and she had promised she'd return for him at midwinter.

The path from the caves to the clearing where the rituals had taken place was wide and well defined, with no confusing turnings, so Shan was able to find his way back there quickly. He paused for a moment to stare at the damp ashes of the fire. He had learned much during his stay in this place, but the knowledge had come at a cost. He had learned pride.

A boy had walked this path to Aya'even, a man returned at midwinter. How had this happened? Tricksters, illusionists—whom could he trust? He knew none of these people, really, not even Nip. His life seemed to be a dream. He had always been who he was now; the past had not existed. Was this how Khaster Leckery had felt the day Taropat's essence entered his body? Shan shuddered. Could that mean an alien presence was inside him now? He did not feel so. His hand went to the talisman King Morogant had placed around his neck. It wasn't a natural claw, but carved from stone and covered in intricate designs. He felt no power in it. He knew then that the artifact itself was not the reward; it was the experience of attaining it that imparted knowledge and power. Yet Shan could feel none of it. After his sojourn in the forest of the night, the episode at the lake seemed inconsequential. He felt as drained as if he'd wept for days.

WHEN HE RETURNED to Sinaclara's house, Shan found she was there ahead of him, sitting by a small table on the terrace. He'd been able to find his way back fairly easily. He knew the forest now, as if he'd lived there all his life. The Lady was wrapped in a soft woollen shawl of peacock blue. Her hair appeared a little damp, and she sipped from a tall glass. A slim carafe, another glass, and a plate containing wafer-thin biscuits lay before her. Shan tensed when he saw her. Would she be angry that he'd left her? He drew in his breath resignedly and marched onto the terrace. Sinaclara smiled at him, apparently without irony.

"Did you fly back here on a broomstick?" he asked.

Sinaclara put down her glass carefully and wiped a biscuit crumb from her lips. "I know the quickest routes back from Doon Pond."

"I thought Nip would be here. Perhaps I'd better set off to meet her."

Sinaclara ignored this suggestion and regarded him thoughtfully for a moment. "Did you believe it would be easy? Nothing can be gained from the easy path. You already know this in your heart. We must talk. Sit down. Have a biscuit."

"I'm not sure what I've gained," Shan said, but sat down at the little table.

Sinaclara laughed and poured a measure from the carafe into the spare glass. "You speak from pique. You know very well what you've gained."

Shan lifted the talisman from his neck. "This? It is a pretty ornament, and no doubt very old. Or does your friend in the lake carve them himself to give to any hapless soul you deign to mystify in the name of learning?"

Sinaclara pushed the glass toward him. "There are three artifacts," she said. "They are old, and were constructed at a time when they were needed. Now, it might be said they are needed again. The men and women who crafted them put their own will and intention into the objects. They are like windows onto the past."

Shan sighed, picked up the glass, sipped. Birch sap wine. "Why would I need it? We are playing games out here in the wilderness of the world, while all manner of atrocities take place beyond our sanctuary. We cannot affect that. We are too caught up in dreams."

"You know that isn't true."

"Do I?"

Sinaclara leaned toward him so swiftly, Shan could not resist drawing back from her. "You are on a hard path, Shan. But remember you chose it."

"Taropat chose me."

Sinaclara shook her head. "Have you learned nothing? Perhaps you will fail, for simply making the choice does not guarantee success. Your responsibility is to learn, to become worthy of the task." One of her hands had curled into a fist upon her breast.

"Are you filled with hate?" Shan said. "Have you suffered at the hands of the empire?"

Sinaclara collected herself. "I see the future," she said. "I see the fork in it. One way will lead to a soulless world of greed and cold, spiritless thinking. The other is the way of the divine, where great kings and queens will lead their people forward full of wonder for the mystery of life."

"That is an ideal."

"Of course, but without ideals there is no hope."

"One man alone cannot change the world, nor one woman."

"No, but one can inspire many others. How do you think Leonid Malagash's ancestors took control?"

"I don't know. Tell me."

Sinaclara refilled both their glasses. "It happened at a time when Magravandias was nothing more than a hundred tiny realms governed by warring feudal lords. The great empire of the world was Mewtish then, and the divine sun kings of Akahana had brought prosperity to the eastern lands. Magravandias, or the Western Territories, as they were then known, were inhospitable, and although their mineral resources were of interest to Mewt, the empire had more accessible and fertile mines elsewhere. The Territories were largely ignored. There were no cities, and little culture. Barbarians roamed across the plains and through the mountains slaughtering one another. One tribe, the Malagashes, were more warlike and successful than most. Their leader, Casaban, though a great drunkard, was a charismatic character. There was something about his fearlessness and strength that heartened people, to the extent where other tribe leaders felt they could do with some of his magic. It is said that a meeting was called and Casaban Malagash rode to a sacred site in Magravandias and there met with the chieftains of six other tribes. Seven. A magical number. He offered them his help if they would swear fealty to him, be princes to his king. The chieftains were seduced by his persuasiveness. They agreed to his demands, and there undertook a ceremony. At this place, there were seven lakes and at each lake, a different lesson could be learned."

Shan drew in his breath to interrupt, but Sinaclara raised her hand to silence him. "Each chieftain allied himself to a different lake. They became the embodiment of the spiritual powers that resided in the landscape there. What they actually did was rediscover an ancient mystical landscape that had been set down millennia before by the descendants of Azcaranoth's people. Its power was dormant."

"I thought you said there was little culture, that the early Magravandians were barbarians. How did they possess the knowledge to reawaken the sites?"

"They acted in ignorance at first, but the experience they had at the lakes changed them. Casaban elected to take for himself the seventh lake."

Shan shook his head. "That's impossible. Taropat has told me about this place. It's Recolletine, isn't it? No one has been to the seventh lake. I know."

"Of course people have been there," Sinaclara said, "but there's no easy way to reach it. How do you think Casaban became emperor? He was wilder than the others. He did not trust them. He wanted their lands for his own. So, he took it upon himself to learn the lessons of all the lakes. Only in this way could he gain ascension to the seventh, and once he had done that, the others had no power over him. No one did."

"But how did he do that? Prince Almorante tried it. He couldn't. It's inaccessible."

Sinaclara leaned back in her chair. "The path is hidden, and once revealed, perilous. But Casaban had advisers. He was king, but he had also a mystic, a bard and a warrior around him. The mystic gave him the desire to learn, the bard gave him the spirit of freedom, and the warrior gave him might in battle. It was coincidence, perhaps, that four such men should meet in one lifetime, but their union was powerful. They shared a vision and they realized it. Casaban unified the Territories, and for many generations it was a nation to be reckoned with. Mewt respected it, and later so did Cos, but Casaban's descendants were more ambitious than he had been. They worshipped fire and the lessons of the lakes were lost. Still, the might of their chosen element seared the world and continues to do so."

Shan nodded thoughtfully. "I begin to see a picture," he said.

"Good."

Shan leaned forward earnestly. "The lessons of the lakes. Taropat said to me at the beginning that the weakest part of Magravandias would be its heart. That is where I must go. I must reach the seventh lake. I will use the Malagashes' own neglected power against them."

Sinaclara smiled. "You begin to see a picture," she said. "It is more complex, however, than you think." She took a drink. "Maybe one day you'll paint the rest for yourself."

Shan bristled. "What do you mean? Why tell me this if you don't mean I should go there?"

"Did I say that? Almorante has aspirations to power too, and he is no fool. Tatrini, the empress, wants it for her son, Bayard. She is no fool. Gastern is the rightful heir and he has the sacred blood of his father. They live in that land. They breathe its air, absorb its essence. They are powerful people, and they have knowledge. Do you really think you can best them there?"

"I don't understand you," Shan said bitterly. "It sounds as if you think the empire should continue."

"Unity should continue," Sinaclara said, "but with awareness."

"Then what is my task? What has all this been about?"

"Your task is to learn," Sinaclara said. "You have the dragon's claw, which is the symbol of the warrior. Now you must aspire to its aspect. You have walked the first path, and it seemed hard, but it was not. When you look back upon this time, you will appreciate that. When you see the full picture, you will look back and see how your time with me helped create the composition."

"Speak plainly to me. Am I to be what Taropat suggested I could be? Or am I merely to become someone like Thremius or yourself, proud of my knowledge, ascetic and isolated, scornful of everyone else?"

"You do not know me," Sinaclara said. "I am not scornful of you. I have a role, which I must play. That is all."

"But who decides that role? You enjoy it. You were bored before I came here. Teasing me has given you pleasure. You are like a cat with its prey."

"If that is your perception, I will not argue with you." She reached out and lifted the dragon's claw on its cord. Shan tensed. He could feel the warmth of her hand. Sinaclara ran her fingers over the intricate carvings. "With the Dragon's Claw, you have the key to the way of the warrior. The Dragon's Eye will give you the sight of the mystic, and the Dragon's Breath will bring the song of the heavens to your heart, which is the way of the bard. Then you may aspire to the crown of the king, the crown of silence, which is the harmony of all the elements."

"Another artifact?"

Sinaclara dropped the talisman. "Artifacts are only symbols. You cannot collect them like rare vases and hope to become more than you are. You have to learn the lessons beyond the symbols. Now, you have started. It is better to learn than to know."

"How can that be so? If you never accept you have knowledge, you will never act. There has to come a time when you know. And that is the time for change."

Sinaclara smiled. "You have started," she said. Sighing, she re-filled her glass once more. "Part of my fate is to be misread, to be mistrusted. I accept that."

"Fate? What would Almoretia Crow have to say about that?" Shan said, smiling.

Sinaclara shrugged. "I told you I didn't agree with everything she said. I never said I believed in her great nothingness. I just said that imagining it, and living your life as if that's all there is, makes existence more meaningful. Almoretia Crow was always depressed and wanted to inflict her grim view of life on the world. Despite that, she had a way with words, which I admire. Anyway, philosophers, for all their pondering, are not magicians. Someone who is both has a far clearer view of reality. For a start, they realize everything is unclear."

Shan laughed.

Sinaclara hesitated, then said, "Although I wasn't bored before you came here, your presence has brought a new and delicious flavor to my domain. I shall cherish it once you have left."

Shan felt slightly embarrassed. "I'm surprised to hear you say that."

"I know. I saw you come here, a frightened boy in a young man's body, and I have seen the man you should be start to bloom. I take satisfaction from that, even though I did not do that myself. I was merely the catalyst."

"Was I really lost in the woods for so long?"

She nodded. "Yes. But perhaps not in the time of this world. You went into the spirit of winter and attained rebirth at the Tree of Knowledge." She leaned toward him once more and reached out with her fingertips to touch his face gently. "Now I would show you springtime."

Shan's face burned at her touch. Her fingers traced softly down his neck, tugged at the cord about it. "More visions?"

She shook her head and stood up. "Come with me. It is cold out here."

They went into the house and Sinaclara closed the long windows behind them, drew the curtains. A fire burned in the great hearth and the air smelled of cooking fruit. Sinaclara's staff would be preparing her winter feast in the kitchens. She sat down upon the bear skin by the fire and took off her shawl. "Sit with me, Shan," she said.

He sat down beside her. She looked radiant in the light of the fire, her red hair catching the light and shining with its own soft flames. She took the pins from it and let it tumble down over her shoulders, as women who desired men to find them attractive had always done. Sinaclara was beautiful. Was he reading this correctly? She took one of his hands and rubbed it against her breasts. Yes, he had to be. "There has to be a first," she said huskily. "This is something I can teach you in plain language."

She taught him well, time and again: how to pleasure a woman thoroughly, how to prolong the act. He was hungry with a virgin's lust for new experience, she perhaps from long abstinence. The afternoon was waning when he took her for the last time. They had been wild in their passion, but now, in the twilight, and the sunset of the dying fire, he made love to her slowly, curiously. It seemed his mind shot out of his body and he was up on the ceiling looking down. She was a white star beneath him, his body pumping languorously. This feeling was true magic. Gods had given this to humanity as a holy gift. How was it possible to experience such exquisite sensation?

It was Sinaclara's first scream of repletion that brought him back to his flesh, and scream it was, like a vixen. She writhed beneath him, her red hair threshing around him, urging him to speed, but he wouldn't relent. He brought her to the point of release again and again. Her cries must have reached the farthest corners of the house.

And so it was, as he reared up on straight arms above her and roared out his own moment of ecstasy, that the door opened. His cry trailing off, Shan turned his head, expecting to see an outraged servant. But Nip stood at the threshhold, her face lit up with surprised amusement.

For a moment, there was silence. Sinaclara's hair was tangled over her face. She breathed hard and fast, her legs still flexing around Shan's back, her fingers curling and uncurling in the bear skin, clearly unaware of any intruder. Shan could only stare at Nip in astonishment.

She sauntered into the room. "Thought you were killing each other," she said. "Had to see. Sorry."

Shan pulled away from Sinaclara, hurriedly grabbing his clothes and struggling into them.

Sinaclara just sat up and said, "Hello, Nip. How are you?"

"Very well," Nip said, smirking.

Sinaclara reached for her clothes. "You must take some refreshment before you begin the journey home. Do you want anything, Shan?"

Shan could barely speak from embarrassment. He shrugged. "No, I don't think so."

"But it's a long journey. Even if you start off now, it will be midnight by the time you get home."

"It doesn't matter."

Sinaclara shrugged. "Well, it's up to you." She stood up and pulled the cord to summon Nana.

While Nip consumed some fiery Jessapurian food, Shan went to his room and collected up his few belongings. He stood for a moment in the middle of the carpet, his mind still reeling from what had happened downstairs. He realized he would miss this place and its mystifying mistress. He hoped she would visit Taropat's home now. He wanted to see her again. He wanted to touch her again.

Downstairs, Sinaclara did not indulge in any meaningful good-byes, but merely hugged Shan, kissed his cheek, and told him to take care of himself. It was as if nothing had happened between them.

"I can return," Shan said, "or you could visit Taropat again."

Sinaclara smiled. "We'll meet again," she said. "Now go."

Shan and Nip walked back through the forest in silence
for a while. Shan felt awkward, unsure of what Nip really felt about
what she had seen earlier. It was Nip who eventually broke the silence.
"You've grown into yourself. Not before time. We knew the Lady
would solve your problems."

"I solved my own dilemmas," he said.

Nip eyed him shrewdly. "What's that around your neck? A gift
from the Lady?"

"Yes," Shan answered shortly. If he had grown so much, why
did he now feel so edgy and defensive? He had looked forward to
meeting his friend again, but found he couldn't confide in her. The
journey was not an easy one. Shan wished he was making it alone.

By the time they reached Thremius's dwelling, it was well past
midnight. Above the trees the sky was clear and hard, lit by a million
stars and the swan light of the moon. Frost rimed the bare branches
that glistened in the starlight. Shan felt homesick, but for where? He
felt cleansed, yet also full of confusion. He felt inspired with poignant
hope by the stark beauty of the landscape, yet his heart felt insecure
and lonely. Life had seemed so simple before he'd made the journey
to Sinaclara. The Shan he'd been had lived in ignorance, but now that
blissful state was gone, and it would never return. He had taken a
fork in the road, and though it might lead to greater knowledge, it
was hard and cruel. Knowledge was a burden. It changed you into
an outsider.

Nip wanted Shan to speak to Master Thremius of his experiences,
but Shan demurred. He yearned only for Taropat's house by the mill
pool, hoping that peace of mind waited for him there. "Then I will
accompany you," Nip said.

Shan sensed she envisaged a few happy hours spent with Taropat
and his liquor supply, listening to Shan's adventures as he related
them to his mentor. "No," he said. "I'm tired. I'm just going to sleep
when I get home."

Nip looked crestfallen. "Is there anything wrong? You seemed fine earlier—more than fine!" She laughed, a bright sound that trailed off into awkward silence.

"I am fine, and thanks for the offer of company, but I need to think on my own for a while. I'll drop by in a day or so." He reached out and stroked her face, something the old Shan would never have dreamed of doing.

Nip reached for his hand. "I was worried for you," she said. "I've always seen your pain, Shan, smelled it even."

He nodded. "I know. You're my best friend, Nip. I'll see you soon."

He knew she watched him as he crossed the glade and entered the haunted dark of the forest beyond.

Relief flooded Shan's body when he saw the welcoming gleam of the windows of Taropat's house. He could hear the water churning in the pool and there was Gust crouched on the roof, as if he'd been waiting for Shan to return. The grim lifted his leathery wings and threw back his head to utter a mournful yet jubilant cry. He leapt gracefully into the air and swooped across the clearing to land by Shan's side. "I'm home," Shan said. He felt like weeping.

Taropat was where he always was at the fireside, his pipe in his mouth, a book open on his lap. He looked up as Shan came through the door. "Ah," he said, "I was wondering whether you'd return tonight. It's a long journey from the Lady's domain."

Shan dropped his bag onto the table. "I was eager to get home. Much has happened to me."

Taropat nodded. "You must be hungry. Sit down. I'll fetch you something."

Shan sat at the table and put his face in his hands. He could feel his heart beating in every fiber of his body. Now he was back, he wanted to feel as if the past few weeks had been a dream, but he couldn't. His own ghost sat at this table. If he looked up now, he felt sure he'd see a younger version of himself staring back at him, amazed. He became conscious of scrutiny and steeled himself to face the specter, but when he dropped his hands he saw only Taropat standing nearby, gazing at him in concern.

"I hope I haven't done you wrong," he said.

"What do you mean? Sending me to that strange witch?"

Taropat put a bowl of meat and gravy down before Shan, along with a plate of bread. "No, before that. I have tried to mold you, indoctrinate you. Perhaps I hadn't the right." He poured cold ale into a tankard and pushed it across the table.

Shan picked it up and gratefully took a swig. "And if you hadn't done that, I would still be in Holme, half a person. The Magravandians ruined my life before you became a part of it. We share that heritage. We are brothers in it."

Taropat sat down and folded his arms on the tabletop. "I would not dispute that. Yet I look at you now, and you seem bitter somehow, even though more whole. Your eyes have been opened and you will never close them again. In some ways, that is cruel."

"I want to be awake," Shan said. "Whatever you've done for me is necessary and ordained. I am sure of it."

"I suppose I must accept that. We are both on the web. We each have our part."

Shan ate in silence for a while. He knew Taropat would not ask questions but wait for the information to be offered. When he'd finished his dinner, Shan said, "A measure of your best port would be appreciated. I want to tell you what happened to me."

"My pleasure." Taropat got up.

There was a strained atmosphere between them, which Shan guessed must derive from the fact that he had changed so much. Perhaps Taropat was unsure how to treat him now.

Shan told the whole story, omitting no detail. Taropat listened in silence, smoking, and drinking the port. At the end of it, he said, "I didn't do enough for you. I was blind to the extent of the damage within you. I thought I'd healed you. It was a conceit."

"Don't be ridiculous. It was something I had to heal myself. You have done so much for me. More than enough."

Taropat pulled a wry face. "Yet I let you keep hiding, playing at being a child. Perhaps that was convenient for me. A young man is so much more difficult to control than a child. Also, it's possible I wanted to prolong the idyll. I enjoyed teaching you. I enjoyed your sense of wonder. Now, I feel some of that is destroyed by truth, by awareness."

"Some of it is, yet I feel there are far more wondrous things to discover. I will just look at them with wiser eyes."

Taropat smiled. "I mourn your damaged innocence, yet I can see we can be friends now, not just teacher and student."

Shan nodded. "That will please me. There's so much more you can teach me, though."

Taropat did not reply. His expression had become slightly guarded. Shan dismissed the feeling of alarm this inspired, the sense of ending. Lightly, he said, "The question is, where do I go from here? What should I apply myself to?" He lifted the talisman off his neck. "I have the Dragon's Claw and it seems to me that ultimately I must go to Recolletine." He hesitated, unsure of how Taropat would react to those words. "Would you agree?"

Taropat considered, then sighed. "I'm not convinced that the Seven Lakes and their supposed properties aren't just part of Sina-clara's wishful thinking. The Claw is a symbol, but because it once meant so much to so many, it has been invested with human intention. However, it is still just an artifact. You must guard against being infected with others' obsessions." He took a draw off his pipe. "I set you upon a certain road, which you have no choice now but to travel. Think only of yourself, your own development, not wild schemes for the future. You can't tell how you will change over the next few years, how your views of the world may change. Thremius and I have discussed the next stage of your training. You must go to Mewt."

Shan frowned. "Mewt? Why?"

"You have taken the first path, and the reward for it was the Claw. As the Lady pointed out, now you must earn it. The disciplines of the warrior will be of great use to you, in unexpected ways. Thremius has spoken to me about this. There is a man in Mewt who will train you. His name is General Tuya."

Shan could tell Taropat was not happy about this. "Mewt? Why? It will be crawling with Magravandians. The Mewtish queen herself is a willing vassal of the emperor."

222

Taropat nodded. "I know this. But Thremius trusts Tuya implicitly."

Shan shook his head. "It doesn't make sense. I will be vulnerable there. People will ask questions."

Taropat sighed. "General Tuya is used to receiving apprentices from various magical orders around the world. You would be seen as just another young acolyte searching for the way of light."

"Thremius seems to have taken a great interest in my future all of a sudden."

Taropat raised his hands expressively. "We can only assume Sinaclara has spoken well of you."

"Already?"

"They communicate regularly, but not in any conventional fashion."

Shan narrowed his eyes. "Does she communicate with you?"

"No. We had a . . . disagreement shortly after I came here."

Shan grinned. "Really? What happened?"

Taropat stuffed more tobacco into his pipe. "Thremius was here to greet me when I finally found my way to this house. It was just like coming home to an old friend. Taropat and Thremius go back a long way together. Sinaclara arrived shortly afterward along with several other magi and sorceresses of the forest. It was a homecoming party, and a happy time it was too! My new/old friends heard Khaster's story and it was a great unburdening for me. A release. Then the dear Lady came out with the remark that was destined to stand as a wall of ice between us for the foreseeable future." He paused.

"What?" Shan said, eager to know.

"You have heard this before, from Nip. Like her, Sinaclara believes in Valraven Palindrake."

"What do you mean, 'believes' in him?"

"She thinks I misjudged him."

Shan frowned. "How would *she* know?"

"As I've said before, the adepts of this region are like cells in a vast intelligent brain. They know much that ordinary folk don't. They might not interact with the outside world to any great degree, but they know everything that transpires in it. I am no different."

"But Palindrake is the Dragon Lord of the empire. He betrayed his country—and his friend."

"Such is the inference I made, but Sinaclara saw differently. We argued. We'd both had a lot to drink. She lectured me on the divine providence of kings and I railed back about betrayal and dissipation. I told her she did not know Palindrake, had never even met him. I've known him all my life, so I am better qualified to judge. I also told her that women tended to judge Palindrake on appearances. If he was ugly, no doubt they'd all think he was a monster. Sinaclara would not accept my view. She told me I should forgive him, seek him out, offer him my support. The idea was laughable. I dread to imagine how the night might have ended up if one of the other women hadn't intervened. Since then, I have refused to be in Sinaclara's company. She's misguided, arrogant and autocratic."

"Yet you let her have her way with me—in every sense.'

Taropat rubbed his eyes. "Whatever my opinion of her, she is very knowledgeable and powerful, and an excellent teacher. I was not prepared to let my prejudices affect your training."

"How unselfish of you! Yet you must have been worried she'd try to infect me with her beliefs. You've already virtually admitted it."

Taropat smiled wearily. "I wasn't that worried. Her beliefs are a dream, Shan, and I don't think you're foolish enough to be seduced by dreams. Maybe, in a different world, what she said might be true or at least worthy of consideration. Caradore is a special country, and the Palindrakes are a special family, but now they are tainted, and whatever hopeful future they had has been changed. I think Sinaclara identifies Valraven with her beloved peacock angel, and more than a touch of romance colors her convictions."

"You're undoubtedly right," Shan said. He sighed. "Still, I don't want to go to Mewt yet. Perhaps Thremius is right, and I should undertake this training, but I'm not yet ready. I feel there is more for me to learn here."

Taropat nodded. "I sympathize, but the fact is you must leave almost at once. There can be no delays in the process you've started."

"I could refuse to go."

"You won't, though! You know what I'm saying is right."

"But with Thremius? Can't you come with me?"

Taropat looked confused for a moment, then shook his head. "No, you misunderstand. Thremius won't be going with you."

"That's a relief. Just you and I then?"

"No, just you."

"But . . ." Shan shook his head. "I can't go alone. I don't know that country. I hardly know this one. It's such a long way. How will I support myself, find my way?"

"It will all be taken care of," Taropat said. "You will leave in three days' time."

"That soon? I can't!"

"It is time to face the world, Shan. You've learned all you can here."

"That's not true! I know hardly anything. I don't have the least measure of your knowledge and experience."

"You will learn more along the way. You have the tools. You are the journeyman. You must find the experience for yourself. I cannot give it to you."

"You are casting me out!"

"Yes," Taropat said quietly. "That is the way it must be."

Shan could see the pain in Taropat's expression. This did not come easily to him. That alone told Shan he was facing the inevitable.

14

PROPHECY OF THE CAT GODDESS

O N THE FEAST DAY of the cat goddess Purryah, Merlan Leckery ate a god. He was drunk at the time, and probably would have refused otherwise. His friend, the young Mewtish commander, Herupka, had egged him on, telling him he was infested with demons, who were sapping his strength. Merlan was convinced the weariness that had oppressed him for the past few days was only the effects of the oppressive heat that preceded the annual flood, but because Herupka was so insistent, gave in.

In Mewt, there were no discernible seasons. Once a year, the normally slow and lazy river Tahati burst its banks in a great flood that irrigated the land. On the day this began to happen, Purryah had a feast, which was necessarily rather an impromptu affair. It was said the inundation was caused by the weeping of forty river goddesses, who lived in caves in the uplands of Elatine, where the river was narrow and crashing and fierce. Mewt was a land where the gods outnumbered the populace. Why have only one river goddess when you could have forty? Any priest could make a god for you, on a scrap of parchment with some spit and a smudge of black ink. He

would name it for you and then it might act in your favor. If you
ate the god, or rather the parchment bearing his name, you might
have visions or be able to smite an enemy with a thought. You could
also banish demons who had procured temporary lodgings in your
body.

Merlan hadn't really taken it seriously. He had sat in the shade
in the outer court of Purryah's temple, while Herupka chattered to
the presiding priest in Mewtish. He felt light-headed, dreamy, and the
incense smoke came out of the temple in drifts, pouring like perfume
down his throat. Later, when the priest, appeased by money, brought
out the brown scrap and handed it to Merlan, he felt unnerved. He
didn't want to do it.

"Now," said Herupka, and Merlan thought about how the Mewts
secretly hated the Magravandians, and Herupka, under cover of
friendship, might have organized a poisoning. No one knew they were
there. His employer, Lord Maycarpe, was out in the desert. Merlan
had spoken to no one before they'd left. Still, the heat and scent of
the incense worked their own magic, and Merlan swallowed the scrap.
It seemed to melt in his mouth, perhaps made out of rice paper.

"You have taken Merytet into you," said the priest in Mewtish.

"Merytet?" Merlan felt as if he'd just taken a draught of a powerful narcotic philter and must now wait for its body-racking effects.

"A daughter of Purryah," Herupka said. "She will identify the
demon and cast it out."

What demon? thought Merlan, and then remembered a thousand
of them. Not supernatural beings from beyond the veil, but very real
ones: fears, anxieties. Sometimes, he felt privileged being part of Maycarpe's magical machine, but at other times, he felt like a fly caught
in the grease on the cogs, who would presently be ground up by the
inexorable, slowly turning metal. The Mewts were a very sensitive
race. Perhaps it was these fears that Herupka had identified.

Merlan knew that Valraven Palindrake had been to visit Maycarpe
at Queen Neferishu's palace. Merlan only found out about it by accident, on an occasion when Maycarpe had been absent from the city
and he'd had opportunity to nose through the papers in his employer's
office. There was a receipt from a Magravandian passenger vessel for

monies paid in respect of a private cabin aboard the *Lamia*. The vessel
had sailed from Caradore, where it was known Palindrake was spend-
ing some time with his family, directly to Mewt. There was no direct
indication the passenger had been the Dragon Lord, but Merlan just
knew it was. Why hadn't Maycarpe told him about it? He remembered
an occasion some weeks previously, which the receipt confirmed was
only a day after the vessel docked at Akahana, when Maycarpe had
gone to a reception at the palace without him. This was unusual,
because Merlan was generally included in every event of this kind.
Valraven had slipped into the city and slipped out again without causing even a ripple. It was absurd. If the Magravandian ex-pat matrons
had caught even the slightest whiff of his presence, there would have
been a frenzy of soirees, parties and excursions. Valraven was a celebrity. Everyone loved him. The fact that Maycarpe had excluded
him was one worry, but why had the Dragon Lord himself avoided
Merlan? The last time they had met had been at Caradore. Palindrake
was supposed to be a changed man now, with the knowledge of his
family's history revealed to him. He had found himself again, allegedly. Merlan had had a part to play in that drama. He had been present
when Valraven had stood upon the shore at Old Caradore and invoked the ancient sea dragons. For a few days after that, Palindrake
had been almost like a friend. Merlan had seen another side of the
man, relaxed and convivial. But the friendship had not been main-
tained thereafter. Merlan was afraid certain information had come to
light. Before Palindrake's arrival at Caradore, Merlan had conducted
a brief affair with the Dragon Lord's wife, Varencienne. Had she felt
compelled to confess this infidelity to her husband? Surely not. Yet
why had Palindrake avoided him? They'd parted as friends, and had
even spoken briefly together of Khaster, which hitherto had been a
taboo subject. Valraven had told Merlan something, a heartbreaking
fact. Even now, Merlan found it uncomfortable to think about. The
Dragon Lord had trusted him then.

The cabals of the Magravandian magi were terrifying, because it
was so easy to fall out of favor within them. If Valraven had spoken
badly of Merlan to Maycarpe, it could affect his position in Mewt. He
couldn't confront Maycarpe about it, because he'd have to admit pok-

ing around in his employer's private papers. So, he suffered, and wondered. The sweltering heat of the city seemed to reflect the tensions that ran in lines of power from Mewt right to Magravandias. If Leonid the emperor was a lion, his sons were wolves, and now their eyes shone in the dark, brilliant with hunger and ferocity. It couldn't go on like this. Something would happen. Everything would change, and when it did, Merlan very much wanted to be on the winning side.

"You feel it," Herupka said, breaking Merlan's reverie.

"If there are demons, they have human faces, my friend," he replied and stood up. For a moment, he felt dizzy and the hot air sizzled in his ears like the hiss of a cat. Behind them, the darkness of the inner temple was a cool haven. Merlan addressed the priest. "May I go within to pay my respects to the goddess?"

The priest eyed him for a moment, until Merlan reached for his money pouch. "A donation for the sacred animals of Purryah," he said.

The priest smiled slyly and bowed, his lean hand snaking out to take the coins from Merlan's fingers. Merlan did not feel their touch.

He went into the temple and immediately the breathing darkness claimed him. The air was alive with the music of cats, their cries, their purrs, for the temple was full of them. Strangely enough, it was rare a visitor caught sight of them, at least not here in the outer courts. Merlan went to the public shrine. Purryah, a golden cat-headed woman, stood majestically in drapes of coiling incense. She was surrounded by bowls of water in which cut petals floated. Lamps glimmered on the floor. Merlan feared the gods of Mewt. Maycarpe embraced them, invoked them, laid himself open to their subtle energies. Merlan was more cautious. He knew that Purryah might be a beautiful creature, who could trot toward you, purring, to accept caresses, but she was also the fierce, disdainful beast who could very well claw you once you reached down to stroke her. She was a cat, after all. Merlan suspected the petitions of her worshippers would merely bore her. You could not rely on a cat giving you attention when you were in the mood to desire it. "Well, my lady, will you speak to me?" Merlan said aloud.

At that moment, a priestess emerged from the shadows, her face set in an expression that portrayed well her feelings toward disrespectful Magravandians. She spoke quickly in a desert dialect so thick Merlan could not understand a word. He presumed this was the desired effect. "I have paid for this privilege," Merlan said in Mewtish. "I have taken the essence of Merytet."

The priestess continued to stare at him in a hard fashion for some moments, then said in strongly accented Magravandian, "She says someone will come for the Eye, and then you will learn something you dearly wish to be true. You will never be the one, not you. It's him, the other one."

Merlan stood very still. "Of whom does she speak, your reverence?"

The priestess shook her head. "That is all. You will know when the time comes. You can believe what you hear then."

Merlan frowned. "But what of demons?"

"There is only one. You know its name. It looks you in the face, yet you try to push past it to see beyond, to see something that isn't there."

"Explain this to me."

The priestess grimaced. "You must go now. You have heard."

Merlan reached for his money pouch, but the priestess only raised her hands and somehow glided back into the shadows until it seemed she had never been there at all. The shrine felt strangely empty now. Merlan shivered. Somewhere, perhaps far away, something of significance had just happened. He looked at the statue of the goddess. "Thank you, lady," he said, and left the shrine.

Outside, the heat hit him like burning fists. Herupka was waiting on the wall, lazy and smiling. "Did she speak?" he asked.

Merlan nodded. "In her fashion."

MERLAN'S HEAD WAS POUNDING by the time he entered the cool offices of the governor. As usual, Maycarpe was a vigilant presence beyond his open door. He called out Merlan's name as Merlan tried to steal past. "Here, boy!" he called.

Merlan went into the room.

"You're as red as an open wound," Maycarpe said. "Try to stay out of the sun. You should know by now that this time of year is not one when we pale-skinned interlopers can walk at ease in the treacherous labyrinth of this witch of cities."

"I went to Purryah's temple," Merlan said. "Herupka believes I am infested with demons."

"Oh," said Maycarpe, disinterestedly. "Well sluice yourself down, tidy yourself up. We have an appointment later."

Merlan rubbed his face. "Where?"

"The palace. Neferishu has had a surprise visitor."

"Who?" Merlan asked quickly.

"Prince Almorante."

"By Madragore, he kept that quiet. No fanfare? No warning?"

"He was in Elatine, attending the state funeral of Prince Nebunka, and decided to make a detour on his way home."

"Here, at this time of year? It's hardly tourist weather."

"Almorante, as you know, is never the tourist."

"What does he want?"

"I presume he wishes to whip us invisibly and make us dance on our toes. The winter was hard in Magrast, they say. Leonid has had a bad chest."

"Ah, I can virtually hear the flap of vulture wings atop the bed canopy."

"Nothing that serious, I'm sure, but Almorante will be here to assess loyalties, perhaps make promises. You never know."

Merlan wasn't sure whether Almorante knew Maycarpe's true face. He kept secret his occult activities, behaving always as the urbane and effete governor of this incomprehensible and inhospitable country, slightly bewildered by it all. But Almorante was astute. Surely, he saw through the mask? The mere fact he saw fit to visit Akahana and butter up the queen meant he must sense Maycarpe was more than he appeared. Mewt was a danger because it was slippery. There were no rebellions to put down, no apparent underground treachery to quell. The Mewts were perfect subjects, who had accepted their Magravandian conquerors philosophically, yet always there was the feeling that things were going on in private and one day the plan would be revealed. It would catch them all unawares. Should that ever happen, however, Merlan was sure Maycarpe would be part of it. He was thick with the Mewtish priests, almost one of them. A man of many masks.

THE PALACE OF the Sun lay a short distance outside the city, approached by a processional avenue lined with stone gods. The wide-flagged road sloped upward as the palace lay in the foothills of the Peaks of Silence, where certain temperamental goddesses lived, one of whom was a sister of Purryah. The great tiered halls of the queen's abode, approached by an enormous ramp, were made of pink granite. Seated statues of Purryah, over thirty feet tall, flanked either side of the main entrance, where the most handsome of Neferishu's guard stood to attention, their spears longer than the height of two men. Neferishu had only recently become queen, since the death of her far older brother eight months or so before. Mefer had always been a prince, never king, but Leonid, the emperor, had granted Neferishu the correct royal title upon her accession. Perhaps he felt she was less of a threat, being female. A rather shortsighted assumption.

Lord Maycarpe and Merlan approached the palace by carriage, but were obliged to alight at the foot of the ramp, as horses were not allowed on the polished stone. Climbing the ramp, it was possible to look down to either side and see the lower stories of the palace where the servants lived. Here too were the workshops and offices, whose functions ensured that the queen's life progressed in a manner of continuous luxury. Merlan thought about all the human dramas that must be enacted behind those ranks of narrow windows. So many people lived there.

Beyond the great pylons of the ceremonial entrance, the guests entered a beautiful courtyard filled with exotic plants and trees from all the hot countries of the world. They had all been chosen for their scents, which now combined in the sultry evening to excite the senses. Cushioned benches were arranged around the ornamental pools and fountains, and low tables had been set out, not yet laden with the banquet. Merlan loved visiting the palace. He knew that it had not

changed for thousands of years and that Neferishu was the youngest
in a dynasty that stretched right back to the days of Harakhte the
Great himself. There was a solid certainty about Mewtish tradition.
It seemed impervious to change, as if the gods had designed it millennia ago and, content with their work, saw nothing in it that needed
alteration. Other cultures might rush and stumble about, have revo-
lutions, build empires, die of plague, even, but Mewt continued at her
own pace, blessed by the otherworld. It bent its knee to conquerors,
yet miraculously remained untainted by their presence. And the conquerors, having secured the diamond of the world, saw no reason to
reshape its polished facets. For that, Merlan was thankful.

Courtiers in pleated linen glided around the courtyard, greeting
new arrivals, while exquisitely beautiful servants offered refreshment—
wine from the queen's acclaimed cellar. She was a connoisseur of
wines, and many a visitor from foreign climes had won her favor
merely by offering a rare addition to her collection. Neferishu was
not yet present in the garden, and neither was Almorante, but Merlan
recognized a few of the prince's closest aides mingling with the other
guests. There was a sense of excitement in the air, perhaps not wholly
connected with the presence of an imperial prince on Mewtish soil.

Senotep, the queen's vizier, noticed Lord Maycarpe's presence,
excused himself from a clutch of guests and came over. "Her majesty
is conducting a private gathering within," he said. "Your presence is
requested."

Merlan wondered whether he'd be left in the outer court, but
neither Maycarpe nor Senotep said anything as he followed them into
the palace itself. Lamps hung from the ceiling, burning scented oil.
Statues of Neferishu depicted as various goddesses clustered in every
alcove, as well as a few of her dead brother, Mefer, who had been
like a father to her. Senotep led them to a reception room nearby.
Merlan heard Neferishu's voice speaking, low and huskily, even before
the great doors were thrown open.

The Mewts were famed for their beauty, but the queen did not
conform to the usual slender template of perfection. She was a big
woman, in her early thirties, who carried herself like a goddess. Her
dense black hair, when unbound, fell to her thighs. Tonight, she wore

it plaited with golden thread, crowned with a wreath of fleshy purple flowers. Her voluptuous body was draped in cloth of gold and indigo and there was gold dust upon her eyelids. Her jewelry was scant, and in comparison with some of the other ladies present, she seemed underdressed for the occasion, but there was no doubt that the queen dominated the scene, both in splendor and presence. She turned to the door as it opened, and her face bloomed into a smile. "Darris!" she exclaimed, sailing over to kiss Maycarpe's cheek. "You are late."

Maycarpe bowed. "Apologies, your majesty."

In fact, they were not late at all. The queen eyed Merlan closely, an experience that always made Merlan's spine tingle. "And you have the lovely Master Leckery with you."

Merlan bowed to her. "Your majesty."

"Come, join the gathering," Neferishu said, slipping a hand through one of Maycarpe's elbows.

Merlan saw Prince Almorante sitting upon a couch, surrounded by Mewtish courtiers. It seemed most of his party were outside in the garden. He straightened up as Maycarpe approached. "Good to see you again, Darris. You look well."

"A deception," said Lord Maycarpe, bowing. "The climate here disagrees with my constitution. My poor frame is plagued by the season."

Neferishu laughed. "You should not believe him, Mante. Lord Maycarpe is almost a native now."

"You've been here long enough," said Almorante, grinning.

Maycarpe grimaced. "As a Magravandian, my body will never become inured to the rigors of the climate."

It was all an act, and everyone was aware of it, yet indulged the governor. It was one of the ways he made friends. He was such a character. While Maycarpe, the prince and the queen exchanged more bantering remarks, Merlan surveyed the gathering, wondering if there was anyone he wanted to talk to. A few of the Mewtish ladies caught his eye, and he made a mental note of which cliques to join later on, but then he found himself looking into the face of a young man who looked both shocked and bewildered. It was a face who clearly recognized him, yet Merlan had never seen this person before. For just the scantest of moments, and with a shiver of pure dread, he thought it was Tayven Hirantel. But no, this youth was younger, less bitter of countenance. Merlan looked away, slightly discomforted, and made to attach himself to a group of Mewts standing around the refreshment table. But then, the staring young man came right over to Merlan and touched his shoulder.

Merlan turned around, composing his face into an expression of mild annoyance. "Excuse me?" he said.

The young man ducked his head. "Excuse *me*, sir," he responded. "I don't wish to seem importunate, but I must ask you. Are you Merlan Leckery?"

Merlan nodded. "I am. What of it? Do I know you?"

The young man shook his head. "No, but . . . the resemblance is extraordinary. I knew it had to be you."

Merlan frowned. "What do you mean exactly?"

"Your brother. Your brother, Khaster. You look so much like him."

Merlan's flesh went momentarily hot, then cold. He helped himself to a sliver of smoked fish from the table. "That has been commented upon before. Are you in the prince's party?"

The young man shook his head. "No, no. I am at present a barely tolerated member of the household here."

That surprised Merlan. The youth didn't look the type to belong in the queen's palace. "May I ask in what capacity?"

"I am training under General Tuya. My master sent me here."

Merlan knew that many occult masters sent their apprentices to Tuya to be trained in certain mystical aspects of the martial arts. The general's apartments were in part of the palace complex, so that he could be close to the queen at all times. Training under him granted certain privileges, but it also meant this young man must be worthy of Tuya's attention. He didn't take just anybody as a student. Appearances could be deceptive. "You must be an ascetic, then," Merlan said.

The young man shrugged, pulled a wry face. "I wouldn't say that, exactly."

"Are you Magravandian?"

A pause, then, "Yes. My homeland is part of the empire."

"So, how did you know Khaster?" Merlan thought the young man wasn't old enough to have known his brother.

"It was a long time ago," he said. "I visited Magrast as a boy."

Merlan felt this might be a lie, but why? He smiled. "You must have a good memory."

"I didn't *know* Khaster," the young man said hurriedly. "I only saw him, but yes my memory is good."

"He must have made an impression, all the same," Merlan said. "Where did you see him exactly?"

"Oh, at some function or another. I was with my parents."

"What function?"

The young man's mouth had thinned to a pale line. Merlan could see he was discomforted. "It was a long time ago." He bowed his head. "I won't detain you."

He began to walk away, but Merlan said, "Wait. Who are you anyway?"

The young man hesitated for a moment, then said, "I am Shan."

Merlan knew then, instinctively, that he must get to know this person. Perhaps this was what Purryah had portended. "Please, there's no need to rush off. I won't plague you with questions. You clearly have your reasons for reticence. Try some of this fish. It's very good."

Shan smiled hesitantly, then began to heap a plate with food.

"Clearly, you have a good appetite," Merlan said.

Shan shrugged. "My usual fare is nowhere near as lavish as this."

"Whose is?" Merlan took a drink of wine. "How long have you been here in Akahana?"

"Only a couple of weeks. I wonder if I will ever get used to this heat."

"The answer is no." Merlan grinned. "Still, there are compensations. Where else in the world would so many beautiful women be gathered together in one room? Have you met the queen, personally, I mean?"

Shan nodded. "Oh yes. I am here tonight at her request. She comes to watch me training with Tuya. It is like being stalked by a lioness."

Merlan laughed. "I can imagine! It is said she has a taste for pale-skinned, fair-haired youths. As far as I know, only one has ever eluded her, so beware. But perhaps you don't need the warning."

"I am her humble servant," Shan said dryly. He hesitated. "Who eluded her?"

Merlan sensed a certain pointedness about this question, and, un-likely though it seemed, he guessed his new companion already knew the answer. "Someone called Tayven Hirantel. Perhaps you have heard of him."

Shan's face had colored. Could he be an erstwhile lover of Hir-antel's? "Yes, I have heard the name. Exactly when did Queen Ne-ferishu try to seduce him?"

Merlan was silent for a moment, as his mind made equations of all he had learned. Khaster, Tayven—where did this youth fit into the picture? "She never stops," he said carefully.

"Hirantel is here, in Akahana?"

"He may be. I don't always know. My employer, Maycarpe, has dealings with him."

"I thought he was dead."

"He was—for quite a while."

"What do you mean?"

"I think you already know. What is your connection with Hir-antel? Does it concern my brother?" Perhaps these questions would frighten Shan off. He looked pained in the extreme.

"It's nothing. Just gossip."

Merlan laughed. "You are not adept at subterfuge, my friend. Come, tell me. I will not be shocked."

"There's nothing shocking to tell. I just heard that Tayven Hir-antel died in Cos—about the same time as your brother."

"But it's well known what happened to Hirantel. Everybody knows. It seems strange you know only half the story." Merlan could tell Shan was wrestling with the dilemma of whether to flee before he betrayed himself entirely or stay in order to gather information. Merlan decided to be generous. "No matter. I have no right to pry."

"You're not. It's . . ."

But whatever Shan might have said was silenced. At that moment, one of Neferishu's handmaidens came up to summon both Merlan and Shan to the queen's side.

"Ah, Merlan, I see you have found Tuya's new protégé," Neferishu said. "Isn't he pretty?"

Merlan cleared his throat. "We have been getting acquainted, your majesty," he said.

"Good. Come and sit with us for a while. Soon, I will have to join the peasants in the garden, but first I wish to bask in the light of male beauty." She patted the couch for Shan to sit beside her. Over her head, Merlan grimaced at Lord Maycarpe, for they were both used to the queen's somewhat forthright manner, but instead of returning the grimace as usual, Maycarpe's gaze was fixed on Shan. Merlan had never seen such an expression on his employer's face: amazement and what looked like greed.

"Excuse me," Maycarpe said, never once looking up at Merlan, "but that is a most unusual talisman you have there, young man. May I see it?"

Shan looked up, appearing to be immediately wary. His right hand went to his throat, gripped the cord that circled it. "It was a gift," he said, rather unnecessarily. Merlan had not noticed the talisman, but Maycarpe's sharp eyes had spotted it at once.

"I would like to examine it," said Maycarpe. "I have an interest in antiquities, and that artifact appears to be quite old."

"I'm not sure it is," Shan said. "I think it's a copy of an old design."

"Nevertheless, would you . . . ?" Maycarpe held out his hand, waggled the fingers.

With clear reluctance, Shan took the talisman from about his head and handed it to Maycarpe.

Almorante, who had been lounging back, chatting to a couple of his entourage, now straightened slowly in his seat. "What is that, Darris?"

"Oh, a bauble," said Maycarpe, staring at the talisman in his outstretched palm, "a trinket from the past, but, as I said, I'm fascinated by such things." He handed the talisman back to Shan. "It is not a copy. You must make sure to keep it safe."

"I will." Shan put the cord back over his head, and tucked the talisman discreetly inside his shirt.

Merlan, observing the proceedings, noticed that Almorante was interested because Maycarpe was interested, but now, having noted the prince's attention to the matter, Maycarpe was feigning indifference. The talisman had looked like nothing more than an old stone carved into the shape of a claw and covered with ornamental markings. A thousand like it could be bought from curio stalls in markets throughout the empire. But it could not be ordinary, or perhaps the one who wore it gave it a certain uncanny shine. Of one thing Merlan was now convinced: Shan was more than he seemed, much more.

"More wine," said Neferishu, breaking the silence. She clapped her hands to summon a posse of servants.

Maycarpe gave Shan one last speculative glance, then turned his attention to Almorante. "The one thing I love about this land is the abundance of antiquities that seem to emerge from the sand wherever you tread. Have you an interest in history, your highness?"

Almorante ducked his head. "I appreciate lovely things, but then you find that the most significant of artifacts are usually plain and, at first sight, unremarkable."

Maycarpe nodded. "Hmm."

There was a silence, then Almorante said, "Talking of lovely things, I find that yet again, Tayven is not here when I visit. Are you keeping him from me, Darris?"

Maycarpe pulled a rueful face. "You are unkind, and know very well that your visit was impromptu. How could I have foreseen it?"

Almorante raised an eyebrow.

Maycarpe ignored the implication. "Tayven is not here. He is in Cos."

"I would like to speak to him and, out of deference for his experiences, have refrained from summoning him formally to Magrast, but it would gratify me if you could arrange a meeting. I will be returning to Mewt in a couple of months' time."

Maycarpe lifted his hands. "I will do what I can, but Hirantel is a law unto himself."

"He is a Magravandian subject," Almorante said quietly. "I don't want to exert my prerogative, but he must accept he cannot run from the past forever. I invested a great deal in him. No expense was spared in rescuing him from Cos."

"I have told him that," Maycarpe said, "but perhaps because it was actually *my* people who eventually unearthed him, he feels he was abandoned by the royal house. A wrong assumption, of course, but Tayven's experiences have changed him. He is a bitter man, even dangerous in his melancholy."

Inwardly, Merlan was as tense as a wire. He was surprised Almorante could discuss this so openly, when it was obvious why Tayven Hirantel avoided him. Almorante's own brother had been responsible for nearly killing him, yet Bayard had never been reprimanded, let alone punished, for his actions. Tayven knew this, and wanted nothing to do with any of the Malagashes now. Neither had he needed rescuing from Cos. He sometimes cooperated with Maycarpe, because in that he saw a way to avenge himself on those who wronged him. Tayven no longer regarded himself as Magravandian. He did not recognize Leonid as emperor, nor his sons as princes. Any meeting between Almorante and Tayven would be unwise at best. Merlan felt uncomfortable around Tayven for several reasons: his past associations with Khaster, the manner in which he'd been abused and the fact that he seemed dangerous and mad now. Tonight, even though he was not physically present, Tayven's spiritual presence was very much in evidence. Merlan could feel it, like a creature crouched in the dark, ready to leap out and hiss. He glanced at Shan. Yes, there was a connection there. Shan was lapping this up, trying to piece together the story behind the meager words.

There are no coincidences, Merlan thought. Something is happening.

Queen Neferishu clearly sensed the tension in the air, because she broke up the gathering and herded everyone outside into the garden. Almorante walked at the head of the party, the queen's arm linked through his. Maycarpe hung back. He addressed Shan in what Merlan knew was a deceptively careless tone. "I would like to invite you to the governor's palace," he said. "Please, indulge me, and arrange something with my assistant here. There is a matter we should discuss, to our mutual benefit." With these words, he sauntered after the royal party.

Merlan and Shan exchanged a glance. Merlan wondered whether he was looking at a potential ally or a threat, and sensed Shan felt the same. "Don't worry," he said. "Maycarpe will just want to try and buy your talisman off you."

"I can't sell it," Shan said. "It was a gift."

"I only said he'd try," Merlan said, smiling. "He's not a monster, Shan. It would stand you in good stead to be called an acquaintance of the governor. He won't take offense if you refuse his request, but if he likes you, it would undoubtedly make your stay in Akahana much more profitable for you."

"You don't know why I'm here."

"I thought you said you were in training."

"I am," Shan said, "but I'm not interested in climbing social ladders. That would make a travesty of my work."

"It's not that bad," Merlan said. "You might learn something. I think there are things you want to learn. Play the game. It's what I always advised my brother to do. Not that he ever took my advice."

Shan looked away. "All right. I'll come." He paused. "Will you do something for me?"

Merlan shrugged. "If I can. What?"

"I want to meet Tayven Hirantel."

Merlan laughed. "By Madragore, you too? What is this?"

"I have something to tell him. It's important."

Merlan rolled his eyes. "How in demand he is! I wish I could command such attention. Did he break your heart too?" Shan did not answer. He looked angry. Merlan considered he had perhaps been too forward. "Forgive me, that was rude. Still, I am not in contact with Hirantel, only Maycarpe is."

"I'm not an ex-lover," Shan said coldly. "This is more important than pique."

"As I said, I'm not in contact. It seems you might have to butter Maycarpe up more than you thought."

Shan gripped briefly the talisman round his neck, through his shirt. "When shall I come?"

"Come tomorrow. Strike quickly."

Shan nodded. "I will be there in the late afternoon."

15

THE STORY OF THE EYE

SHAN COULD NOT BEAR to go out into the garden, but slipped away through the shadowed corridors of the palace, to the small room he occupied in a corner of General Tuya's expansive quarters. There, he threw himself on the bed, his heart beating furiously, trying to compose his hectic mind for thought. He felt feverish, sick. He had been right. Tayven was not only alive, but had returned, in some manner, to the life he had known. He was not like Taropat, hidden away. The sketchy picture drawn by the scant words Shan had heard that night did not resemble the portrait Taropat had painted of a beautiful serene mystic. Dangerous? Bitter? What had happened to Tayven after Khaster had fled? How had he survived?

It had been agony being in Merlan's company, unable to tell him his brother was alive, but Taropat had made Shan swear to silence. "You will meet Merlan in Akahana," he'd said, "I have no doubt of it. Fate will make it so. He must not know about me. Do you understand? You never met Khaster Leckery, never heard his name. Your master is Taropat, and you must avoid even mentioning that to anyone but General Tuya."

Shan had pledged an oath, which already he'd partly betrayed. It felt wrong not to tell Merlan the truth. He'd been friendly, and seemed an open, pleasant man. It seemed so unfair to Khaster's family to keep silent. What of his mother, his sisters?

Shan turned onto his side. Why did he want to meet Tayven? Because Taropat did not swear you to silence with him, he thought. But what about the consequences? What if Almorante found out Khaster Leckery wasn't dead? Tell one person and Shan would risk the whole of Akahana knowing. And yet, because of what he'd seen in the scry mede, and the way he had felt, Shan was aware of a connection between himself and Tayven. They were part of the same pattern. In his guts, Shan was sure they had to meet. He ran his fingers over the Dragon's Claw, which now lay outside his shirt. The talisman was cool, even though Shan's flesh was not. Had Maycarpe recognized the artifact for what it was? Shan had been careless. He should have hidden it.

Stop it, Shan told himself. Fear is your only enemy. You know this. Give in to it, and these Magravandian monsters will overwhelm you. You must stay calm, centered. Your talisman is a gift from a woman who loved you once. She was your first lover. That story is true and it will suffice. You need not necessarily know how and where she acquired the artifact. Forget its significance. Think only of her.

When Shan had finally set foot on Mewtish soil, he had felt strong, confident and proud of himself. He had made the long, unknown journey with comparative ease, and had learned to enjoy his own company. Taropat had given him a generous amount of money, which meant he had been able to secure comfortable accommodation along the way and the best modes of transport.

Taropat had walked with him to the great road that skirted the edge of the forest, where Shan had taken a passenger coach south to the coast. A swift ship had carried him across the waves of the Ambree Sea to the Elatinian port of Udanke. As the *Mermasine* sailed with her stern to the dawn toward this unknown land, Shan had stood on deck, thinking about what Sinaclara had said to him about foreign travel. The sun laid its first rays upon the brass towers of Udanke's temples and Shan's flesh tingled. The air already smelled different.

At Udanke, Shan had quickly found a caravan bound for Mewt. By now, he felt quite the seasoned traveller and spent the long, often uncomfortable, journey across the Elatinian desert absorbing the ambience of the landscape. He employed his senses to the full, vowing never to forget each moment. After some weeks, the caravan reached the river port of Tahut, on the Mewtish border, where Shan secured passage on a felucca heading for Akahana further south. At Tahut, Mewtish and Elatinian cultures mingled, but it still seemed to Shan as if he had crossed an invisible mysterious border, into an ancient time. An immense statue of the fierce lioness goddess, Sekt, guarded the river to Akahana. The felucca was dwarfed by her presence. Passing beneath her gaze, Shan shivered. He could not help but feel that wondrous and terrifying experiences awaited him.

Akahana was dizzying, mainly because it seemed to be several different places at once. On the surface, it was all bustle and heat, yet Shan was immediately aware of a dark and inscrutable undercurrent— magic hanging in the air, as Sinaclara had foretold. It also seemed as if the ancient past was very close to the present and that it would be possible, either accidentally or otherwise, to slip between the two.

Shan found his way to the Sun Palace without much difficulty, and there presented the letters from Thremius and Taropat he'd carried all the way from Breeland. There had been little fuss, only a short wait before one of Tuya's aides came to fetch him from the gate. Shan had been led through the maze of the palace to Tuya's quarters and training yards. The general was almost exactly as Shan had imagined him: tall, aloof and with a mystifying Mewtish character, as if he continually guarded secrets. Tuya had been expecting his new student and, with cool politeness, installed Shan in comfortable accommodation with a servant to see to his needs and show him around. Shan was told his servant would escort him to the general the following morning, but until then he was free to explore the city and the areas of the palace that were not off limits to him. Everything had seemed easy. But, after only that one evening, Shan realized just how fully Akahana was riddled with Magravandians. What should he have expected? Still, it unnerved him. The Mewts were so friendly with their conquerors, and the palace seemed full of them. Shan could only see them as the enemy, and after only a few days felt he had to confide in his tutor about this.

Tuya listened in silence. Then he said, "We were conquerors once."

Shan looked up at him. "But. . . ."

"The empire of Mewt was larger than the Magravandians. We were the kings of the world."

"Then how can you accept these people here? How can you eat with them, talk with them?"

"It is their turn," Tuya said, "and not all Magravandians are slaughterers."

"I cannot accept what they've done."

"You must. It is part of what I'm trying to teach you."

"You're teaching me to fight."

"A fighter who cannot think and reason, a fighter who cannot have compassion, is weak," said Tuya.

"Must I love my enemies as I cut them down?"

"It helps," said Tuya.

After this, Shan found, strangely, that the sight of a pale Magravandian face no longer moved him to rage. If anything, he felt condescending toward them. They were so arrogant, and so blind. He applied himself to his training with discipline and passion.

While the general was a taciturn man, he was not cruel and gave praise where it was due. Shan, so far, had worked well under him. He discovered that the first principle of fighting was to know your own body, to feel the subtle play of energy in its muscles and sinews. He was learning to hear the silence within so that he could function like a machine, yet with grace and swiftness. So far, he hadn't touched a weapon, but the training had opened him up to himself. When fear came now, he found it easier to control.

"A warrior must know fear better than fear knows itself," Tuya said.

Shan did not feel afraid now, but confused. He wanted to do the right thing. Everything that happened to him in Akahana would be part of his training, preordained and meaningful. He must be alert for signs and signals. He must interpret them correctly, act accordingly. First, he would visit the Magravandian governor.

MAYCARPE'S PALACE, WHICH COMPRISED an enormous suite of offices and sumptuous apartments for himself, his staff and guests, dominated the main square of the city, close to the Harakteion, where the greatest of Mewt's emperors was entombed. The governmental building was comparatively new, yet had been constructed in the ancient Mewtish style. Just beyond the soaring portal was a reception booth, where a clerk in Magravandian livery sat in charge of an immense guest book. Shan wrote his name within it, scanning the lines above for anyone that he might know. He was looking for Tayven's name, of course, but it was not there.

The receptionist guided Shan to a dark, cool room a short way into the building, and here Lord Maycarpe and Merlan Leckery were waiting for him. Shan suspected that Merlan had made sure he was present, perhaps to shield Shan from his employer's persuasions concerning the talisman. Shan had considered leaving the artifact in his rooms, but as he feared constantly that it would be stolen, eventually decided he must keep it with him. Maycarpe might even consider he'd leave it behind and send someone to search his rooms while he was absent.

Maycarpe was polite and welcoming, offering refreshment and asking intelligent questions about Shan's training. But Shan was not deceived. This was just the preamble. He refused alcoholic drinks and accepted only fruit cordial. Merlan didn't say much, but his eyes were watchful.

Eventually, Maycarpe clearly decided the time for small talk was over. "You must know why you're here," he said.

Shan put down his glass, said nothing, but kept his gaze steady on the governor's face.

Maycarpe did not appear disconcerted by the lack of response. "Where did you acquire the talisman you showed me last night?"

"A woman gave it to me. We were close for a time."

Maycarpe nodded thoughtfully. "Why did she give to you?"

Shan shrugged. "It was just a love gift. Something to remember her by."

Maycarpe stared at Shan piercingly, but Shan refused to shift his gaze. He must betray nothing. "Why are you so interested in it?"

Maycarpe tapped his lips with steepled fingers. "I am trying to tell myself you speak in ignorance, yet my instincts, which believe me are preternaturally sharp, insist otherwise. I think you know exactly what that artifact is, young man." Shan opened his mouth to protest, but Maycarpe raised a hand and continued. "Oh, you do not trust me and why should you? You see me as the enemy, don't you?"

Now, Shan had to lower his eyes.

"I am not your enemy," Maycarpe said quietly. "You should consider that I perhaps want the same things that you do."

Shan glanced up sharply. "That is unlikely."

"You should not make inferences until you have gathered all the information," Maycarpe said. "That is the Dragon's Claw, isn't it? Such an artifact would not find its way into the keeping of someone less than worthy. Who sent you, Shan? Who is your mentor?"

Shan shook his head. "I cannot speak. I have been schooled by mystics who insist on privacy. They are not part of the world—your world."

"But will you at least admit I'm right about the talisman?"

"What is the Dragon's Claw?" Merlan asked.

Maycarpe looked up at him. "It is a symbol of rank, a very ancient one, given to the champion of the divine king."

Merlan frowned. "A Mewtish king? The artifact does not look Mewtish."

Maycarpe shook his head. "No, this was a kingdom that thrived long before Harakhte's armies carried the Mewtish banners across the world. It was not an empire, as such. In those days, the king was the spiritual life of the land. He could be crowned or sacrificed as his priests saw fit. Different days, they were. This kingdom lay in the heart of what is now Magravandias. It was called Ivirian, which is an ancient word for truth."

"How did you recognize the artifact?" Shan asked.

Maycarpe laughed. "First, by its appearance, which is documented in certain Mewtish magical scrolls, secondly by the life force and history I felt within it when I touched it, and thirdly by your reaction to my interest, which you sought and failed to conceal."

Shan felt himself grow hot. "I can't deny what you've said."

"I'm glad you've given up the pretence," Maycarpe said. "It astounded me to see the Claw here in Akahana at this particular time. I had to speak with you about it."

"What significance does the talisman have?" Merlan asked.

"Its significance now?" Maycarpe paused, stuck out his jaw, stroked his throat. "At times of change, artifacts of this nature have more power than you'd imagine. We invest them with that power because they are symbols. Men will follow symbols, you know. They are masks for the life essence of the universe, just as the faces of gods are."

"Times of change?" Shan said, frowning. "What is changing?" For just a moment, he imagined that something had already happened without him being aware of it; another hero had infiltrated the empire. He was too late.

"The wheel of life never stops turning. You both know this. Have I not taught you, Merlan?" Maycarpe glanced at Shan. "And your own mentor will have told you the same. Leonid is a golden king, who has brought a certain amount of unity to the world. His Dragon Lord has humbled Cos, which is no mean feat. Before Magravandias, Cos was the leader of the world, just as righteous and autocratic as Magravandias is now. Ask the Mewts. They'll tell you, for they forget nothing. Cos has had its day, even though its rebels believe otherwise. Before Cos, it was Mewt, and the sun king Harakhte butchered his way to power in the name of light. Does that surprise you? Did you not think that a Mewtish empire would surely have made the world a spiritual haven, its peoples enlightened? Think again. In the not so distant future, Leonid will be succeeded by one of his sons. Who will this be? Gastern, the rightful heir? Almorante, the clever one? Or Bayard, lily of the empress? As a servant of Leonid, whom should I support?"

"The victor," Merlan answered dryly.

Maycarpe smiled. "But who will that be?"

Shan was shocked by this conversation. He knew, from Taropat's account, how things were in Magrast and the subtle play for power enacted there, but he was surprised a man like Maycarpe would speak so openly to a stranger. Perhaps he was trying to draw Shan out, get him to betray the fact that some people thought someone other than a Malagash should sit upon the divine throne. He cleared his throat. "Most people think that Almorante will be the one."

Maycarpe nodded. "That's where I'd put my money too."

Merlan snorted in derision. "Tell that to Tatrini."

"She is a driven woman," Maycarpe said, shaking his head. "Her love rules her heart. She means well, I'm sure. But if the empire Leonid has built is to survive, other aspects need to be taken into consideration." He held out a hand to Shan. "Give me your talisman for a moment."

Shan took the cord from his neck and handed the artifact over. As before, he felt uneasy seeing it in Maycarpe's hands.

Maycarpe held it up before his face. "The Dragon's Claw," he murmured, "badge of the warrior. The dragon is the spirit of the world, inherent in every living thing, and even in inanimate objects. Its claw is deadly. It can rake out the eyes of a nation, sunder its heart."

"How can it do that?" Shan asked.

Maycarpe glanced down at him. "The power of its legend can band men together, make them bigger than they are as individuals. It also has a spiritual energy. If someone such as Valraven Palindrake were to wear this talisman, he would not only be invincible but more than human."

"Is that who you want it for?" Merlan asked, a little sharply.

Shan uttered an outraged curse. "Palindrake? No!"

Maycarpe handed the talisman back to him. "The Claw is not for Valraven." He sighed theatrically. "We are all part of the Great Work, and it is our task to further the evolution of the human spirit. Sometimes, people resist essential changes, because they are uncomfortable. We, as magi, know better."

He is flattering me, Shan thought. He knows nothing about

me, yet now calls me a magus, includes me in the Great Work. I must be wary.

"Come with me, both of you," Maycarpe said.

Shan glanced at Merlan, who shrugged. Together they followed Lord Maycarpe from the room.

He took them deep into the palace, to his own private apartments. Here, he left them in his sitting room, which smelled of musty, over-ripe fruit, and presently reappeared carrying an ebony box. This he set down upon a table. "The body of the dragon is sundered," he said, "its parts scattered. Great Foy, the dragon queen of Caradore, lies in deathlike sleep beneath the ocean. The fire drakes writhe and spit in the hearts of the Magravandian army. The basilisks of the earth element have fled into the deepest caverns of the world, and are remembered only by strange, isolated tribes. In ages past, the cockatrices of the air were combined with the elements of Foy, and are therefore dormant also. All these fabulous beasts are masks of the universe. They should be made whole, one thing. A man may be strong as an ox, but his brain might be damaged. He could not be king. A man could have a great brain, but be weak as a kitten. He could not be king. A man could be clever and strong, but have no wisdom. No king. He might have all of those things, but no spirituality, no aware-ness of the unseen, which makes a true king. All the elements must be in balance to make the king. Do you understand?"

"Such a man could not exist," Merlan said. "If he did, he would not be a man, because humans are imperfect."

"Even the greatest of divine kings are allowed their flaws," May-carpe said. "I'm not talking about perfection, but balance. I have studied the concept of divine providence all my life."

"I understand about the dragon and the king," Shan said. He went to Maycarpe's side. "There are other artifacts, aren't there, other symbols?"

Maycarpe smiled slowly. "Oh, you're an eager one. Look at you. Fancy yourself as king, do you?"

Shan did not respond to this jibe. He remembered what Sinaclara had told him. "Aren't there?"

Maycarpe put both his hands on either side of the ebony box and lifted the lid. Within lay an article wrapped in dull purple silk. "Take it out," Maycarpe said to Merlan.

Merlan did so. He unwrapped the silk to reveal a spherical object that looked as if it was made of dark red glass. In its heart, a red spark glowed.

"What is it?" Maycarpe asked. "Guess, Merlan. What part of the dragon is this?"

Merlan was silent for only a moment. "Its eye," he said, words that were echoed in Shan's mind.

"Good, good," breathed Maycarpe. "But you would have been a fool not to have guessed it."

"How did you get it?" Merlan asked. "How long have you had it?"

"Oh, a long time," Maycarpe answered. "As to how I acquired it, that is a story I have never told."

"Was it given to you, as the Claw was given to me?" Shan asked.

Maycarpe shook his head. "Oh no. I had to rescue this artifact from my own people. If you would hear the story, you must swear an oath never to speak of it."

"Gladly," said Merlan.

"Good, then bear your arm."

"What?"

"It has to be a blood oath," said Maycarpe, "otherwise it can be broken. By your blood sacrifice you must swear to the gods you will never speak of this matter to anyone. Should you do so, the gods will take you."

"It seems extreme, Darris," Merlan said. "Is the knowledge you'd give us so terrible?"

"I committed a kind of treason," Maycarpe said. "I like my privileges, Merlan. I wouldn't want to put them in jeopardy. Any of the sons of Leonid would do more than kill to get their hands on these artifacts. You must swear."

"I will do so," said Shan. He rolled up his sleeve, presented the pale skin of his forearm.

Maycarpe went to a tall cabinet in the room, and opened it. Within could be glimpsed all manner of strange paraphernalia. Maycarpe took a ceremonial dagger from one of the shelves and handed this to Shan. Its edge was incredibly sharp, like a surgeon's knife. Shan guessed it had been used for many sacrifices. He could barely feel the kiss of its blade against his skin.

Merlan watched inscrutably as Shan cut his flesh and spoke the oath. Maycarpe collected some of Shan's blood in a bone cup. Then he turned to his assistant. "Well, Merlan, will you make the pledge or leave this room?"

Sighing, Merlan rolled up his sleeve. "Give me the blade," he said to Shan.

After Merlan had dripped his blood into the cup, Maycarpe did likewise. "Don't look surprised. Why should I ask you to undertake an oath that I would not? I swear I will not reveal to anyone, other than those who are part of this, that either of you know about these artifacts."

Once the sacrifice was completed, Maycarpe covered the cup with black silk and replaced it, along with the dagger, in the cabinet. "Now, sit down, both of you," he said. "I will tell you the story of the Dragon's Eye.

"Four millennia ago, after Ivirian fell, the artifacts, which had been created by the wisest magi of the land, were dispersed. Some of them have resurfaced from time to time, and done their work for men, but never all together. The Eye was found by Harakhte himself, near the beginning of his reign. He found it in an Elatinian shrine to Challis Hespereth, who is a very ancient goddess, venerated mainly now in Cos. The Eye lay in the mouth of a priestess who was found dead, by her own hand, before the altar. No doubt she feared the appetites of the conquering army, and through her death hoped both to escape rape and to take the Eye with her to the grave. It is said that Harakhte saw it shining through her cheek, and thus investigated the corpse. More likely it fell from her lips when the body was hoisted outside for disposal. In any event, Harakhte became its owner. From surviving priests, he learned the legend of its power. Whoever had the Eye had the sight of the dragon. They could see etheric matter with their own eyes, such as the glow of footsteps after someone has walked away. Only serpents have this faculty naturally in our world. The Eye also bestows wisdom. By the right person, someone who is attuned to it, it can be used for distant viewing, like a crystal ball."

"Like a scry mede," Shan interrupted.

"Yes," said Maycarpe. "Like that. It is said Harakhte used it to spy upon those who resisted him. But the Eye was not enough to guarantee his eternal kingship. He foresaw his own death within it, on the morning before the king of Cos killed him in battle. Thus, the Eye fell into the hands of the Cossics. But they could not use it. Harakhte had been empathic with the artifact, but the new emperor, King Alofel, was not. He simply installed the Eye in the state museum in his own capital, where it was displayed only as a curio, still stained with Harakhte's blood. The Dragon's Claw would have been more use to Cos, as it would have resonated more with the character of the king, but of course, they did not have it.

"For generations, the Eye lay in the museum, and was then transferred to a storeroom, to make way for what the Cossics considered to be more important exhibits. I went to Cos as a young man, to study in the library at Tarnax. At that time, Leonid had made no incursion onto Cossic soil, and relations between the two empires were cordial, if wary. I knew that situation would inevitably change, but for a time, I was able to learn from the Cossic scholars. I came across the Eye by accident, and recognized it for what it was, because my mentor in Magrast had spoken to me of it. Once I held it in my hand, I knew for sure. I could *feel* it. The dragon artifacts were legends, magician's tools that lived only in ancient stories, yet here one was, the Eye once held by Harakhte himself. I could not believe it. The curators of the museum knew it as the Dragon's Eye, but did not believe it was anything more than an ornament. They considered themselves rational men, and the ancient Mewts to have been riddled with superstition. I knew the Eye should not be left in the museum, because I feared it would eventually fall into the hands of the Malagashes. The fire priests are more astute than the Cossic scholars. They would know exactly what the object was, and probably already knew of its existence. I had little doubt that once Cos fell to Magravandias, as it was clearly fated to do, the priesthood would come searching for the Eye. I was faithful to the crown, but knew in my heart, this must not happen. I loved Leonid as my emperor, but for all that he called himself sun king, I knew he was not, not in the eyes of the universe. In his hands, or rather in the hands of his magi, the artifact would be misused, as Harakhte had misused it. But how could I take the Eye? It was regarded only as a curious antiquity, but the Cossics would not just give it to me. If I made inquiries about it, they would wonder why I wanted it. It might make them reconsider their opinions, especially once Leonid began to make his assault on their country. So, I made certain preparations. I found myself a jeweller in the darkest corners of the city, and had him fashion me a copy of the Eye. He had no idea what he was making, for he'd never visited the museum. Once I had this facsimile, I hid it in my quarters, to await the right time to use it.

"A few months later the news came that Magravandias had taken the capital of Verna, a country owned by Cos. I would have to leave immediately. The city was thrown into turmoil, and my Cossic friends were most concerned for my safety. Magravandians were leaving the country all around me, in panic, and we knew that perhaps within the hour, the king of Cos would send his guards to round up anyone that remained. I did not wish to be a prisoner of war, but neither could I leave without the Eye. To cut a rather long story short, I went to the museum, and there, taking the greatest risk of discovery, made the exchange. I fled with the Eye, pursued by a band of soldiers, but my horse was swift. I made the border, running into a troupe of Magravandian soldiers, who happily chased off my pursuers. The Eye has been in my keeping ever since."

"What an adventurer you were!" Merlan exclaimed, his voice colored by awe.

Maycarpe shrugged. "It had to be done." He took up the Eye from where it lay on the table and wrapped it up once more in the silk. "But it is not mine. I am just its guardian."

"Whose is it?" Shan asked.

"It belongs to the magus of the divine king," Maycarpe said, "but there is no magus, and no king. Not yet."

"Can there be?" Shan asked, getting up.

"Oh yes, with blood, with tears, with pain, there can be."

"You talk of more than one artifact," Merlan said. "How many more are there?"

Maycarpe glanced at Shan. "Tell him."

"My teacher said there were three, but then named four," Shan said. "The Dragon's Breath is linked to the Eye and the Claw, but there is another, which is perhaps more powerful or different than the others: the Crown."

"That's correct," Maycarpe said, "but whether these artifacts are actual objects or simply spiritual concepts, I am not sure. The Dragon's Breath, surely, must be knowledge, but as for the last one, the Crown, who can say? I feel it might simply be divine kingship itself."

"The Dragon's Crown," said Shan. He could see it in his mind, shining in darkness.

"It is actually called the Crown of Silence," Maycarpe said.

"Yes, I know," Shan replied. "The woman who helped me get the Claw told me."

"Why 'silence'?" Merlan asked.

"Because it symbolizes the attainment of total awareness," Maycarpe said, "oneness with creation, and that is the silence within."

"It is also a real crown," Shan said. "I'm sure of it."

He became aware both Maycarpe and Merlan were staring at him speculatively.

"So," said Maycarpe, "I have given you my story. Now, trust me enough to give me yours."

Shan hesitated. Should he speak? Should he tell the truth, or make up a story? These were Magravandians, at least Maycarpe was. And yet he had spoken candidly. It seemed Maycarpe was not that different from Thremius and Taropat. He was first and foremost a magus, devoted to the Great Work. In the event, Shan opted to tell the partial truth. He spoke of the ravage of Holme, but in order to back up his story to Merlan of how he'd once seen Khaster in Magrast, he claimed to be the son of Sir Rupert, of fairly noble blood, and added a few years to his age. He explained how when the Magravandians came, and slaughtered his family, a great magician had rescued him from the ruins of his home, making the situation sound more circumstantial than it had been in reality. He spoke of how this magician had needed an apprentice and had taken Shan under his wing. "I was trained by this magician and some of his colleagues," Shan said. "The culmination of that training was a kind of spiritual initiation. After it, a learned woman took me to a lake high in the mountains of Breeland and there I received the Claw from a king who came out of the water. Following this, I was sent here to train under General Tuya, for a true magus must be skilled in all disciplines."

"But why were you given the Claw, Shan?" Maycarpe said. "What does this coven of magi want from you? You can be sure they want something. Are you aware of it? Speak truly."

"I think they want what you want. They want to prepare for change."

"They seek to make a king of you, don't they," Maycarpe said quietly. "Perhaps your family's blood has some relevance in this. Bloodlines are very important in such matters."

"No," Shan answered hurriedly. He'd said too much, he was putting himself in danger. "It's not that. There is no king. You said so."

"Then you are the warrior," Maycarpe said. "I wonder who they believe their king to be?"

"They have not said. That is the truth."

"I believe you," Maycarpe said. "You are just a pawn to them. They will keep you in ignorance, for in knowledge lies power. They will keep you in check."

"You do not know them," Shan said bitterly. "You cannot make these judgements."

"You have given us no names," Merlan said. "Who are these people?"

"Their names would mean nothing to you," Shan answered. "They hide from the world."

Maycarpe laughed. "Oh, sweet boy! How innocent you are! I do not need names. One, at least, is Master Thremius. Am I right?"

Shan's mouth dropped open. "Well . . ."

"It is. I know of the Bree magi. I have corresponded with Thremius in the past."

Surely, this was impossible. Taropat and his friends were opposed to Magravandias, Taropat in particular. But then, that was probably Khaster's influence. The old Taropat might not have cared one way or the other. "You guessed correctly," Shan said.

"I know now it is folly to ask you for the Claw," Maycarpe said, "and in fact I see that it is safe in your keeping. You are meant to have it."

"What about the Eye?" Shan asked cautiously.

Maycarpe ran his fingers over the ebony box. "Oh, that is not yours, Shan. I know you want it, but it is not for the warrior. It belongs to the mystic."

"Do you know who that is?" Merlan asked coolly, arms folded.

Maycarpe nodded, spoke softly. "Oh yes."

"Who?"

Maycarpe went back to the cabinet and from it took a leather pouch. Was this another artifact? He took from the pouch a ring, and seemed about to pass it to Merlan, but then pressed it into Shan's right hand. "The owner of this ring is the one," he said.

Shan looked at the piece of jewelry. It was a signet ring of some kind.

"Tayven Hirantel gave that to me," Maycarpe said.

Involuntarily, Shan's fingers closed over the ring like steel.

"Is it his?" Merlan asked sharply.

"Give it to him," Maycarpe said to Shan.

Shan did so. Merlan turned the object over a few times in his fingers, then uttered a cry, throwing the ring down on the table as if it had burned him. "It is impossible! You mock me!"

"I assure you I do not."

"But what is the meaning of this? Are you trying to tell me I'm the one? Is that it?"

Maycarpe shrugged. "It may be a mantle you have to assume."

"What is it?" Shan asked. "Is the ring yours, Merlan?"

"No," Merlan said coldly. "It is Khaster's."

16

ARROW FROM THE DARKNESS

TAYVEN HIRANTEL LAY on his stomach on a narrow cliff ledge, looking through a telescope down at a Magravandian camp in the valley below. He was spying on Valraven Palindrake, aware how dangerous it was to get so close to the Dragon Lord, but unable to resist it. He did not fear capture, punishment or torture, even though if anyone could catch him in this familiar terrain, it would be Valraven Palindrake.

Through the exaggerated focus of the telescope, Tayven could see minutely the polished Magravand horses tethered at their hay nets. He could see the soldiers sitting around, attending to their weapons or gossiping.

And there was Palindrake himself, stepping out of his pavilion into the morning, lifting his chin to sniff the air, like a predator.

How do you make me feel, Dragon Lord? Tayven wondered. I look down upon you now, and know I could release an arrow, spit out a dart, fire a gun. But I could not kill you. The arrow, the dart, the bullet, they would take another target. Someone else would die for you, without even realizing it. I want to hate you, yet I can't.

There is something more to you than what you show, something I don't know.

Tayven knew that Valraven and his elite guard were here in the mountains seeking Ashalan. Intelligence had informed the rebels that the empress Tatrini wished to speak with him. It did not take a genius to work out why. She was going to offer him some sweetmeats from her table. She would offer him a deal such as that enjoyed by Neferishu in Mewt. In return, he must pledge support to Prince Bayard. That was the empress's secret agenda, but the official line was that she was simply helping to make peace in Cos, use a woman's touch to expedite her husband's work. An ambassador for harmony, she would calm the ruffled tempers of the belligerent males. She would bring Ashalan to Magrast in a huge calvacade and entertain him to tea. She would find him a royal woman to marry and give back to him his palace in Tarnax. When he sat upon the throne there, the empress's hand would forever be laid upon his shoulder, lightly but firmly.

Tayven did not really know which way Ashalan would jump. It was extremely unlikely he could win back his throne by force. Perhaps compromise was the only way. The erstwhile king of Cos had no allies left that had the might, or even the inclination, to take on the Magravandian empire.

Ashalan was being cautious. He could have made contact with the Magravands at any time, since Palindrake's elite company had penetrated these high, lonely crags, but perhaps he feared being won over too easily. Capitulation would cause a rift among the resistance, but Tayven knew in his heart that eventually Ashalan would meet with the Dragon Lord. It was only a matter of time. Helayna, however, would never give up the fight. If Ashalan yielded to Palindrake, she and her supporters would melt away into the Cossic Mountains, into legend. Tayven knew how fond Ashalan was of his sister, and that he would not want to lose her. He would be torn. But if he did elect to cooperate with the empress, Tayven had already decided that he would remain in Cos with Helayna. Ashalan would grieve over him, but Tayven's feelings for the exiled king were not strong enough for him to brave returning to Magrast. He could not face his family.

Also, Bayard would not relish his return and would no doubt do his best to get rid of Tayven again. Even if Tayven took Almorante's stance and made it known he had forgotten the past, he could not stomach seeing Bayard become emperor. If that should happen, Tayven's sole task in life would be to assassinate him. Tayven felt the familiar red tide of anger swell up within him. It wasn't good to have such thoughts. It wasted energy. He was here, safe in Cos, and Bayard was thousands of miles away in Magrast.

Tayven was about to put away his telescope, when Valraven turned and seemed to look right up at him. That was impossible, of course, but a shudder passed up Tayven's spine. He knew he was drawn to the Dragon Lord, but it was not a sexual feeling, nor even one of admiration or affection. It was beyond words. In his mind, it resembled a billowing cloud with dark edges. What was hidden within it? Valraven stood tall and still, his black hair gleaming in the clear sunlight. He looked like a proud stallion, eyes wild. Tayven had no doubt he could sense scrutiny. Would he send some of his Mewtish trackers up into the crags in an attempt to flush the spy out? If he did, they would fail.

Tayven heard a low, chirring sound and recognized it as a signal from his friend, Gallina. She must have come looking for him for a reason. He crawled carefully back into the spiky shrubs that surrounded the ledge, emerging onto a high cliff path that overlooked a deep canyon, one of the roads through the mountains. Gallina was hunched down upon the path below, a slender elfin creature, her long bow slung over her shoulder. She and Tayven had become close over the years, mainly because they shared the faculty of appearing delicate and fey while being at the same time deadly.

Before Tayven even reached her, Gallina said, "Two things will happen. One is that Ashalan will meet at sundown with the Dragon Lord."

"Already?" Tayven had not expected it to happen so quickly, and yet why had he been drawn to spy on Palindrake this morning? Tayven never ignored omens. He jumped down beside his friend. "Ashalan could be betrayed. This might be a trick."

Gallina pulled a sour face and stood up. "He has made up his mind. His arguments are persuasive. He doesn't think it's a trick."

"No, I don't suppose it is," Tayven said. "What's the other news?"

"You've been summoned to Akahana."

Tayven sighed. "Why?"

"Maycarpe has sent for you, that's all. We are not told why, but we can guess. He will be curious about what is happening here."

Tayven shook his head. "I take it Ashalan has already made contact with the Magravands, then?"

Gallina nodded. "Yes, while you were here watching them. He sent Mentril and Thayne to intercept some of Palindrake's Mewtish scouts. They named the time for the meeting. We assume Palindrake will accept it."

Tayven uttered a caustic laugh. "It was fortunate for Ashalan I came out here, then. He wouldn't have wanted me around when he gave the order."

"No, I doubt he would."

"And Helayna?"

Gallina shrugged. "He waited until she left camp to go hunting. She'll be back soon, so she'll hear soon enough. No doubt she'll insist on being present at any treaty meeting."

"I will go to Akahana now," Tayven said. He was assailed by an instant and overwhelming uneasiness. He had to get away.

Gallina regarded him speculatively. "You should wait. Go tomorrow. You'll have more to trade then."

"I can't be at the meeting, Lina. Palindrake must not see me."

She stuck out her lip, considered. "I understand your feelings. Still, you will hear about it afterwards from Ashalan." She paused. "What are you afraid of? You're never afraid. That worries me."

"I feel a hurricane coming," Tayven said. "I want to take cover."

"Should I?"

Tayven glanced at his friend. He knew she looked upon him as her oracle and didn't want to mislead her. "I think this is personal. See what happens at the meeting."

OVER THE YEARS, as Magravandian trackers had continued to hunt them down, the Cossic resistance had moved their encampment higher into the peaks of the Rhye. Many small settlements were hidden among the isolated crags. Ashalan's latest headquarters was an eyrie of twigs and flapping leather. Dwellings of woven branches were connected by high walkways of rope and boards. From a distance, it looked like the nesting ground of the great dragon vultures that haunted the air above the peaks.

Gallina uttered the calls to alert invisible guards to their approach, but there was no discernible movement among the rocks as they climbed the treacherous trackways to the camp. Old Mab was waiting for them outside her dwelling. She was drinking tea with a suave Mewt, who was dressed in black suede from head to foot—Surekh, Maycarpe's messenger.

"You must speak to Ashalan, Tayven," Mab said, the moment she laid eyes on him. "This meeting with Palindrake is unwise."

Tayven bent to help himself to some tea from her pot, which was brewing on an open fire at her feet. "So, what's his excuse for it?"

The old woman grimaced. "Concern for his people, so he says. You and I both know he's tired of fighting."

Not just tired, but disabled. The wound Ashalan had received in his leg had never healed properly. He was still lame, and the mountainous terrain was often difficult for him. Tayven had noticed the limp was becoming more pronounced, and it was now beyond his capabilities to lift Ashalan's spirits. He knew the exiled king believed he had lost his power, his vitality, even his inherent kingship. This day had been presaged for months.

"He'll return to Cos and leave Helayna to the rest of it," Mab said. "He thinks his days are done."

"Maybe they are," Tayven said.

Surekh spoke for the first time. "This could be the catalyst you need to find the way to reach and murder Bayard, Tayven. It might be convenient to be able to slip between Tarnax and the mountain encampments."

"You know too much," Tayven said coldly.

Surekh raised an eyebrow. "Providing, of course, Ashalan doesn't betray the whereabouts of those who don't share his particular vision of peace."

"Palindrake might demand that as part of the deal," Gallina said. "We might all be in peril."

"Helayna would never allow that," Mab said. "She is our only hope."

"You don't fancy returning to Tarnax, then?" Tayven said to her, smiling. "Don't you yearn for a comfortable house with doors to lock and a soft bed to climb into?"

Mab made a disparaging sound. "Helayna's back. You'd better go and arbitrate. No one else can."

Tayven found Helayna in her brother's dwelling, berating him. He could hear her raised voice from over a hundred yards away. A group of her men sat on the ground outside, silent in their eavesdropping. When Tayven presented himself at the doorway, she turned on him. "Did you know about this?"

Tayven glanced at Ashalan. He looked weary, defeated. He was no longer a leader in the sense Helayna wanted him to be. "I've just heard," Tayven said. He addressed Ashalan. "Do you know what you're doing?" It was a rhetorical question.

"We cannot play at being free in this way," Ashalan said, rubbing his face. "We are deluding ourselves. We are not free and no longer an irritant to the Magravands. They have driven us too high, too far away."

"Two years ago, you would die rather than admit defeat," Helayna said. She was eight years younger than Ashalan. She had more stamina and her zeal would endure for longer. "There are still thousands of us, hidden in the mountains. We are still a force to be reckoned with."

"Split, divided," said Ashalan. "Fragmented. We are no longer an army but isolated communities. Children who have been born out here are nearly adults. It is different now."

"We have chosen this life. None of us want to return to the city and live beneath the countenance of Madragore."

"I'm sure that won't be compulsory," Ashalan said. "We should simply accept what is, and ally ourselves to the greater power."

Helayna threw up her arms and roared. "I can't believe you! I won't accept this. I won't!"

"Maycarpe has summoned me," Tayven said.

Ashalan turned his attention to him, clearly grateful for the change of subject. "He will want to hear the outcome of this."

"Yes."

"Be careful. He's one of them. Slippery and self-serving."

Helayna uttered an explosive snort. "The people you would bend your knee to. You coward!"

Ashalan ignored his sister. "Carry word to Akahana. Tell Maycarpe I will go to Magrast."

"I'm sure he'll think this the best thing you could do," Tayven said.

"What do you think?"

Tayven shrugged. "What is best for you is not best for me. I have been given succor among your people. I have re-created myself. I cannot return to Magrast. Perhaps your place is on the center stage, but mine will be forever in the shadows. We must each do what is right for the future."

Ashalan smiled sadly. "Do you share Helayna's view? Do you think we should continue to fight?"

Tayven shook his head. "I haven't said that. It is not my place to judge. I only know what's right for me."

"Oh, for Challis' sake!" Helayna cried. "Tell him he's a fool, Tayven. He will lose me and he will lose you, all to become Leonid's lapdog and live a quiet life. Where's the victory in that? It is the easy way out, but the wrong one. If we continue to stand against the Magravands, eventually others will join us."

"We have lost more allies than we've gained," Ashalan said. "Wake up, Helayna. It's over."

"For me, never!" Helayna said. "We owe it to our parents, to our people, to keep fighting. The Magravands cannot best us in this terrain. They know that. They cannot win by force, so they attempt seduction.

You are mad to fall for it." She leaned over her brother. "Can't you see that they need you? Why else would all this be happening? They have never won Cos. They merely keep it in check. They have never routed us. We're always ahead of them. While our movement lives, Cos has a kind of freedom. The Magravands cannot relax here, nor let down their guard. If you returned to Tarnax, everyone would see it as the heart of our country being broken."

"I can do no good for Cos out here," Ashalan said. "Times are changing. The empire is unstable. I need to be in Tarnax. Maycarpe is our ally. He will help us."

"Maycarpe thinks only of himself. You said so."

"Perhaps so, but in his selfishness, he gathers allies." Steel came into his voice, and for a moment, Tayven could see a ghost of the man Ashalan had once been. "You are right. Two years ago, I would have died rather than admit defeat. But I can do no more out here, hiding among the crags, my body ravaged by pain. I am no longer fit for this life. Why can't you accept this? In Tarnax, my health will improve. If Tatrini has created a chamber of leaders, I must be among them. It makes sense. I am no longer a warrior, Helayna, but I can be a politician. I can still work for our people. Two years ago, I wouldn't have been given the option."

"Then do it alone," Helayna said in a low, cold voice. "I cannot condone it."

"Will you attend the meeting with Palindrake?"

She expelled a contemptuous snort. "If I do, it will be only to fire an arrow through his heart."

Ashalan glanced at Tayven, who shrugged. "I won't be there, Ash. I'm sorry. I can't."

"Then I will do it alone," Ashalan answered. "I know you each have your reasons for abandoning me, but I don't hold them against you."

"Pompous prig!" Helayna cried and marched out of room.

"Tay?" Ashalan murmured.

"She feels things strongly," Tayven said. "She's hurt, because she fears she's losing you. Maybe she is."

"Am I losing you?"

"I think you're doing what's best for you," Tayven said guard-edly.

THE DRAGON LORD had been asked to visit the Cossic en-campment an hour before sundown. Ashalan's most trusted scouts, Men-tril and Thayne, would meet him some distance from the camp. Whether Palindrake would agree to be blindfolded for the journey, Tayven could not guess. Somehow, he doubted it.

Shortly before the Dragon Lord was due to arrive, Tayven climbed one of the high blackwood trees at the edge of the encamp-ment. He crawled out along one of the thick branches that overhung a drop of several hundred feet. He wondered what it would be if he was the sort of person who would consider throwing himself down into the green abyss below. Death had never been an option for him. That was something Almorante had been so wrong about. He pushed the thought from his mind. He didn't want to think of past associa-tions. Palindrake was different. Tayven had never really known him in Magrast. Now, as he sprawled along the thick tree limb, soaking up the last heat of the day, he thought about what Maycarpe believed, or wanted, Valraven Palindrake to be. Did the Dragon Lord know that some people thought he could be a rival to the warring Malagash princes? And, if so, did he share that dream? Tayven wasn't sure what he thought about the matter himself. He had to admit most of what he knew about Valraven Palindrake came from the legends that had risen up about him, and most of those were probably extremely exaggerated, if not entirely untrue. He'd had very little firsthand ex-perience with the man. In Magrast, Tayven had been little more than Almorante's concubine, far beneath Palindrake's notice. Still, it was tempting to believe the Dragon Lord could eventually take over from the Malagashes. To Tayven, he was the better of two evils. At present, there was no other potential emperor lurking in the wings, not that Tayven knew about.

The sun sank down behind the mountains, casting a strange pink glow over the landscape. Tayven extended his senses and fancied he could hear the jangle of harness, the clop of hooves upon the gravelly track far below. He heard the chirring calls of his comrades, passing messages back and forth from hidden crags. Tayven looked down and saw a strange tusked face looking back at him from the branches of a lower tree. A Magravandian fetch? He cast a symbol of greeting down to it, and the creature disappeared in a flash. Tayven laughed softly. He felt aflame, full of a sense of imminence, and climbed farther up the tree, into the thick dark foliage, to a place where he could watch the camp below. A fire had been lit and already Ashalan's most trusted staff were seated around it, speaking quietly but urgently. Rings flashed in the firelight as they gestured at one another. Ashalan was not there and neither was Helayna or her clique of close allies. Would she shun the meeting or insist on being present to cause trouble? It was impossible to judge.

Valraven Palindrake came alone. He rode his fine black horse into the camp, accompanied only by Mentril and Thayne. He was not blindfolded. Once he'd dismounted, and was standing haughtily, ignoring the men around the fire, Ashalan came out of his dwelling. He had dressed well, but his limp was apparent as he made his way slowly to the Dragon Lord.

Tayven's heart convulsed. He knew Ashalan was a good man who was trying to salvage something useable from ashes. He *would* be of more use to his people back in Tarnax. Helayna was blinded by her passions, her prejudices.

Tayven heard a strange swishing sound and then a sharp thunk. An arrow. It had hissed out of the darkness and struck the earth near Palindrake's feet. The Dragon Lord ignored it, and nobody else seemed even to notice it, as if a glamour had been cast upon them. Tayven squinted into the twilight. Helayna must have been responsible? Where was she? Did she really intend to try and kill the Dragon Lord or had that just been a warning? Palindrake appeared neither vulnerable nor uneasy. Fire another shot, Tayven thought, and one of our own people will take it through the heart.

Palindrake bowed. "I am pleased we are having this meeting, my lord."

Ashalan sat down upon a chair that had been placed in readiness for him. "Inevitable," he said. "Please sit."

Palindrake glanced at another empty chair set nearby and after a slight pause sat down in it. As he did so, he looked up at the black-wood tree and Tayven's whole body shuddered.

The meeting was hardly exciting fare and progressed exactly as Tayven has envisaged. Tatrini was the power behind the peace campaign and, yes, Ashalan was invited to Magrast to partake of her hospitality. There, he would meet with Leonid and the tempting offers would be made. It seemed too good to be true. Helayna was right about one thing: Ashalan clearly was quite important to the Malagashes. His was the bloodline of the great King Alofel, who'd once bested Mewt. He would make a charismatic ally, whose cooperation would show the world just how powerful Magravandias had become. In return for Ashalan's fealty, and the surrender of his troops' arms, certain Cossic prisoners would be released and land would be restored to those Cossic nobility in exile who were prepared to follow Ashalan's lead.

The only difficult moment came when Valraven Palindrake said, "You can, of course, guarantee that all your people in the Rhye will lay down their arms and follow your orders?"

Ashalan hesitated.

"If they do not," Palindrake continued smoothly, "Leonid will order me to root them out. And I will, eventually. Their safety cannot be guaranteed. I hope you understand this."

"I understand your words," Ashalan said.

"Princess Helayna?" Palindrake murmured politely. "Does she understand?"

She will come forward now, Tayven thought. She will insult him, cause a scene. Yet there was only silence, but for the crackling of the fire and the uneasy movements of the Cossics around it.

"I am doing what I think is best for my people," Ashalan said. "I will not go back on my word. But you and I both know I cannot speak for everyone. Opinion is divided. It is beyond my control."

Palindrake inclined his head. "I understand the difficulty of your position, but if you have any care for the dissenters, you will use your royal powers of persuasion to make them see sense."

"One man's sense is not another's," Ashalan said. "All I can give you is myself and those who are loyal to me."

Palindrake nodded thoughtfully. "I too have a headstrong sister," he said. "For all the problems she presents, I would not want her to be any other way."

Still, Helayna did not show herself. Tayven imagined her in hiding close by, feeling much as he did now, wrestling with conflicting feelings concerning Valraven Palindrake. He knew Helayna well, and guessed that part of her could not help but admire the man who came alone to an enemy camp, who did not flinch as an arrow hit the dirt at his feet. Part of her would want to join Ashalan now, share the feast that was due to follow, but her principles would not allow her to give in.

"I will escort you personally to Magrast," Palindrake said to Ashalan. "You will, of course, be permitted a retinue. It would be best if Princess Helayna was part of it."

Old Mab brought out the feast then, casting caustic glances at the Dragon Lord. Was this how it was to end, so bloodlessly? Tayven slithered back along his branch. He felt he should seek Helayna out, that she would need his company. He felt slightly disorientated.

With barely a rustle of leaves, Tayven dropped to the ground and slunk off into the darkness. Where would she be? He skirted the camp, heading for the cave in which Helayna had made her home. He sensed she was alone. Such was Palindrake's power that her companions would have made themselves scarce. Talk and bluster was one thing, action in the face of Palindrake himself another. Tayven jumped with the ease and precision of a cat onto a ledge above him. His senses did not alert him to anything being amiss. Therefore, when someone grabbed hold of him, pinning his arms to his sides from behind, he was taken completely by surprise.

"Are you one of her creatures, Tayven? Was it you that fired the arrow?"

Valraven Palindrake. Tayven knew fear then, gut deep, primal

270   ⸺ Storm Constantine ⸺

fear. He didn't want to feel it, sought to control it, but it controlled him. He couldn't even struggle. "No," he gasped.

Palindrake released him. "By Madragore, I've sensed your presence in these mountains for months," he said. "I never believed you were dead. Then we learned for sure you weren't. I'd wondered when we'd run into each other. You went to the people you were working with, didn't you?"

"No," Tayven answered, rubbing his arms. He felt cold, as if a ghost had passed through him. "I never saw them again. Another faction. Small. Not part of Ashalan's movement. Helayna found me after Bayard had done his work. She saved my life."

"How fortuitous. Maycarpe hasn't kept your confidence, you know. He told Almorante you were alive."

"I wasn't important back in Magrast, and I'm not now," Tayven said. "I'm just an exile, like Ashalan. I have discarded the past. Why speak to me now? What do you want?" He could barely see Palindrake in the darkness. The Dragon Lord seemed part of it.

"You don't deceive me," Palindrake said. "I *know* you, Tayven. I was stupid not to realize it before."

"What do you mean?"

For a moment, the Dragon Lord seemed almost human. "It would have been wrong of me to prevent what happened. I hope you understand that."

Tayven frowned. "I don't know what you mean. You were never part of my life. You never will be. I'll disappear again. It's not that difficult."

Palindrake smiled grimly. "Easy to disappear, difficult to remain visible. You are nearly a ghost, Tayven." He paused. "I will tell you something. It is of great importance."

"I want to hear nothing about the past, nothing!" Tayven snapped.

"Not your past. Mine."

"I do not want it in my keeping."

Palindrake was silent for a moment, then made an emphatic gesture, from which Tayven couldn't prevent himself flinching away. "I am not who you think I am. Whatever you've said to your new king, you are mistaken. You have been changed by events beyond your control. You are not alone. The man who led the army in Cos when you were with Khaster is not the one before you now. It is important you know this, for the future."

"Why tell me this?" Tayven asked.

"An instinct," Palindrake said, and then shook his head. "You may run from life, Tayven, but it is hunting you, and it will find you. Have no doubt of it. And when it does, you will remember this conversation." He paused. "I can see it in your eyes. You know the truth in your heart already. Are you man enough to accept it?"

Palindrake took a step backward and it seemed that shadows closed around him like a cloak. "If you're Helayna's friend, stop her making a grave mistake," he said. "One day, I hope we shall all bear the truth. Together. All of us."

Tayven opened his mouth to speak, but Palindrake had already gone. Tayven realized he was shivering. What had just happened? It seemed as if the Dragon Lord had never actually been there.

17

FACE FROM THE SCRY MEDE

QUEEN NEFERISHU SENT for Shan daily, once his work with Tuya was finished, but would never keep him longer than an hour or so. She made jokes about desiring him, but never actually initiated anything. Perhaps she was waiting for him to do so. They were never alone together anyway. "You are a little mystery," she would say, narrowing her cat's eyes at him.

Shan was wary of her and mistrusted her. She entertained the Dragon Lord in her private apartments. To Shan, she betrayed her own people constantly, because she loved comfort. But perhaps that was not the whole story.

Shan was sometimes amazed at the way his life had changed. Only a few short years before, he'd been nothing more than a peasant, thinking only of goats and harvest. Now, he disdained the seductions of a queen, and lived in a royal palace. What would his father think of this, and his aunt? Had his mother ever foreseen it, if only slightly? Is this fortune? Shan wondered. He should feel lucky, perhaps, and not take it all for granted. But he had to admit he felt at home in Akahana, mixing with Maycarpe and the court. He had a right to be there, perhaps a divine right. He was no longer a peasant boy, but a young man who mixed with royalty. He had learned how to act like a nobleman, as a son of Sir Rupert would act. His past did not exist. No one knew about it, anyway. They'd never find him out.

At night Shan would think about all that Maycarpe and Sinaclara had told him. Who was the right king and could it ever be himself? He could fantasize about it easily, but was sensible enough to realize the reality was far-fetched. Someone would one day take Leonid's place and Shan would dearly love that to be someone other than a Malagash. Now, his life seemed to be on hold. Secrets had been revealed to him, but nothing had actually happened. He wrestled daily with the knowledge that he kept from Merlan about his brother. One day, surely, that would have to come out. He missed Taropat and wondered how he was getting on, alone in the forest of Breeland. Shan considered writing to him about Tayven, but felt that was a piece of news he had to deliver personally. He didn't want Taropat to be alone when he found out.

One afternoon, General Tuya had business outside the city and Shan was left to his own devices. He decided to meditate in one of the gardens and was sitting in silent contemplation when he was disturbed by a handmaiden of Neferishu's. "The queen desires your presence," she said.

Shan wondered then whether the general's absence had been arranged.

The queen received him alone in her water garden, where she sat in a boat, eating chunks of fruit. The garden was inundated owing to the fact the great river was in flood. "Tonight," she said, "A reception will take place here at the palace, which I wish you to attend."

He bowed. "It will be my pleasure." The message could have been delivered by hand.

"Now, you may talk to me. We've never had a chance to before, so I have made it happen." She gestured for him to join her in the boat and when he had settled himself carefully against some cushions, said, "I wish to know about you. What is your full name."

"Shan. The honorable Shan Sathe."

The queen examined him. "Tell me of your origins."

He shrugged. "It is hardly interesting, your majesty. I was the son of a Bree nobleman, Sir Rupert, who was killed during a Magravandian attack on our community. Despite my blood, I had what you might call a very humble beginning."

"Then why are you here in Akahana now?"

Shan felt the queen's interest was more than simple curiosity. He spoke with care. "After the Magravandians came, I needed a place to hide for a while. A magician took me as an apprentice. It is through him that I am here."

"That is interesting. Tell me about the magician. Tell me what he taught you."

The queen's gaze was fixed, compelling. Shan could imagine a man's will being swept away beneath it. "I was taught how to read the portents in coincidence. I learned about the secret properties of plants and trees. I learned about the dance of life, the essence that permeates everything. I learned how to shield myself from the emanations of others."

Neferishu recoiled only slightly. "Emanations? What are these?"

"The emanations are comprised of the same essence that causes life to be. Every living person is full of it. It is the wellspring of their emotions, their thoughts. Sometimes, we need to guard ourselves against the feelings and thoughts of others."

Neferishu looked thoughtful. Clearly, she did not regard this as something that would pertain to her own predictions. "That is true. Can you teach me this technique?"

Shan paused. "I am not a master, only a student, your majesty. I have neither the knowledge nor experience to teach others."

"That's what the teachers say," the queen said. "I expect it's to keep you humble. I've been on at Darris for years to show me some of his trickery, but he always squirms away somehow. Not you, Shan. I feel you could teach me adequately. I have a desire to know more about magic, the magic of the western world. It is different to ours."

"I would have said Mewtish magic was superior," Shan said.

Neferishu shrugged. "It is different," she said, "that is all. Anyone who says their own particular knowledge is the best of all is a fool, and can learn nothing. They will end their days in ignorance, when they could have known so much."

Shan nodded. "Yes, that's very true."

"The Mewtish priests know everything," Neferishu said. "They have studied the secrets of every corner of the world. They keep it all in a hidden library, deep beneath the desert sands. They will not teach me. They will not teach anyone but their own. It is how they keep their knowledge exclusive. I am a queen, and they bow to me, but they will not give me the means to become as powerful as they are."

A glimmering of light came into Shan's mind then. He knew for sure now that this interview was about rather more than seduction. "Many students must have come to General Tuya from overseas across the years. Have you spoken to none of them before?"

Neferishu pulled a sour face. "Yes. Most of them are dour creatures, ascetics. You are not. I would like to meet your teacher, I think. Is he handsome or old and withered?"

"Handsome," said Shan, "at least one of them is. I have three mentors. Another is an old man, as you described, while the third is a woman, both strange and beautiful."

"You are lucky," said Neferishu.

Shan could tell she meant it.

"The world is in flux," said the queen. "Everyone with a smattering of esoteric knowledge can feel it. The wisest are now making preparations. I consider myself wise. I must modernize my weaponry."

"Surely you're safe," said Shan. "You have many allies, the emperor among them, or so I'm told. Whatever happens to the world, Mewt is sacrosanct. It is the spiritual heart of the planet. I've been told this many times."

"Leonid will not be emperor forever. He is temperate. Whoever follows him may not be."

"I feel sure that no one on this earth would violate Mewt," said Shan. "If I were emperor, I would cherish it above all other countries."

"If *you* were emperor?" said Neferishu with music in her voice. She laughed. "Let us speak frankly. If Almorante succeeds, he will bleed Mewt dry of knowledge. He will find the hidden library, of this I have no doubt, and blood may be spilled because of it. He has no respect for our traditions, only thirst for knowledge. The same applies to Bayard, except I feel he will also want to sit upon the sun throne of this country. He may even force me to marry him. Ugh, what a thought! As for Gastern, he is blind to every god but Madragore, and will seek to impose the religion of fire more stringently about the world. None of these possibilities appeal to me, but I know there are others. I can feel them. Cabals of magi discuss them and the vibrations of those conversations make my skin prickle. Could this refer to the emanations you told me about?"

"Most certainly," said Shan.

"I want you to trust me," Neferishu said softly. "I have many friends, Shan, and I know they will seek to protect me, but the one thing that would give me the most protection of all, they will never give to me. I want you to tell me what you know. You do know things, I can feel it. Who does Lord Maycarpe wish to see succeed Leonid, for example?"

"I am not sure," Shan answered. "All he says to me is that he will give his loyalty to whoever wins the fight."

"They all say that," Neferishu said bitterly, "but I don't believe it. I'm not sure I believe you, now."

"I speak the truth," Shan said. "You have my word, your majesty."

"Then Maycarpe is lying to you too," Neferishu said. "Perhaps you should delve for the truth yourself."

The queen's voice reverberated through Shan's head as he walked back to his own room in the palace. He could not hear words, only the sound, a soft shushing like the water against the boards of her little boat in the garden. The world was a web of secrets, an immense web, populated by innumerable scuttling spiders. The spiders were small, but somewhere, Shan felt sure, there was a big spider who could remove all the others if it wanted to. Thremius and Taropat had sent him here to learn martial arts, yet he felt that was only a small facet of the knowledge that flowed to him. He had climbed a delicate thread onto the web, a spiderling. Maycarpe had noticed him, and so had Neferishu. Perhaps this was dangerous. He was still unclear about what Maycarpe intended for the future. He had plans, and Shan was sure the magus wanted him to be part of them. Unfortunately, Maycarpe kept silent on the matter, deftly deflecting direct questions.

In his room, Shan found a note from Merlan: "Are you going to the reception at the palace tonight? If you're not, contact Maycarpe the instant you get this, and make sure he takes you with him. You will see why later."

Shan put down the note. Golden afternoon sunlight made a pattern of squares on his rug. The city seemed so quiet, dozing in the heat. Yet somewhere, threads were being pulled. He could feel it within him, small, secret tugs. He thought of Taropat then and wondered whether, tonight, he would break his vow and tell Merlan everything.

NEFERISHU'S SOIREE WAS HELD in the Court of Cats, which was an area of the palace where the goddess Purryah had allegedly appeared to one of the queen's ancestors. Tall slim statues of seated felines flanked the court, interspersed with palm trees whose delicate foliage fluttered in the warm evening breeze. A pool in the center seethed with huge, whiskered catfish. The roof, of glass, could be winched open, which now it was. Awnings had been erected around the sides of the court and here Neferishu's servants had laid out a sumptuous supper of river fruits, plump crawfish in sauce, slivers of exquisite smoked fish, roasted water weed tubers peppered with tart aromatic nuts and glazed with honey.

Shan arrived five minutes late to be sure at least some other people were there before him. On entering the court, Shan saw Neferishu reclining on a couch near the pool, surrounded by a coterie of men. No other women appeared to be present. Music was played softly by three musicians seated among the cat statues. Maycarpe was there and Merlan, General Tuya and several of Neferishu's closest advisers. It seemed to be an intimate gathering. The only stranger Shan saw was a young man seated near to the queen, sitting upright, rather defensively, on the edge of his couch.

"Ah Shan!" exclaimed Neferishu, noticing his approach. "You are the last to arrive."

The young man on the couch looked up then, and Shan saw a jolt of recognition in his eyes. It took a moment for it to be returned. Shan felt himself grow hot.

"A reunion," Merlan said smoothly. "Here is Tayven, Shan, who you were so anxious to meet again."

"We haven't met," Shan said quickly. It was one of those moments when he wished he had the power to make himself vanish. Merlan had set this up.

"I think we have," Tayven said. "Your face is familiar."

"A long time ago perhaps," Shan answered, trying to think of a way to change the situation.

Neferishu appeared to be highly entertained by the undercurrents flowing through her courtyard. She drew up her knees and patted the couch beside her. "Come, sit here, Shan. I have a most unusual wine to open tonight. It comes from far Shinkemya, where they brew all their liquors from the bodies of lizards and snakes."

Shan sat down next to the queen, and everyone waited in respectful silence while her steward set about serving the wine, in which the flaking corpse of a fire lizard floated.

Neferishu took the first sip. "It looks dreadful, I agree, but the taste is unparalleled. Come, everyone, try it."

Rather gingerly, the company of men took tentative sips from their glasses, an act followed by surprised expressions of delight.

"A strange fire," said Maycarpe, holding up the glass to the light. "I taste spices, but no hint of rot, for which I am relieved."

Neferishu laughed. "Not all the vintages are so fine. It is a risk you take, every time you open a flagon. Isn't it, Tuya?"

The general grimaced. "On some occasions, I have tasted the grave rather than heaven."

"So, now we are all gathered and have whetted our palates," said the queen. She turned a lascivious glance upon Tayven Hirantel. "So, tell us your news, beautiful one. We know there have been developments in Cos."

Tayven shrugged. "It will hardly come as a surprise. Ashalan has signed a treaty with Palindrake. He will return to Tarnax and resume his place upon the Cossic throne, as a vassal of Magravandias."

Maycarpe shook his head. "Strange. I had a romantic thought that the dethroned royalty of Cos would never bend their necks to the sword of the Dragon Lord."

"Not all of them have. Princess Helayna remains intransigent." Tayven drained his glass of lizard wine.

"And what of you?" Maycarpe asked carefully. "Will you go to Tarnax with Ashalan or remain with Helayna?"

"I cannot go to Tarnax. My only course is to remain in the wilderness with the princess, but there seems little point to it now. Her continued defiance is only a gesture. Palindrake won't even bother to flush her out. He has Ashalan. He has Cos."

Maycarpe tapped his lips with steepled fingers. "An interesting development."

"An inevitable development," Tayven said. "Palindrake always wins, one way or another. It was only a matter of time."

"You would be more effective in Tarnax than in the mountains," Maycarpe said.

Tayven stared at him with some hostility. "No. I had one task to do for you, a task no one could ever complete. Other than that, I have kept you informed of developments in Cos. I have done enough."

"Yet you are here, now. Interesting."

"The encampment is crawling with Magravandians. Helayna has vanished. I needed to get away."

Shan noticed that Tayven's fists were clenched in his lap. It seemed Neferishu was well aware of the tension too. "Indeed you did need to get away!" she said. "And where better to come than here?" She flapped a hand at Maycarpe. "You mustn't bully him, Darris. Let him enjoy this evening in convivial company. You'll have plenty of time to talk politics tomorrow. Come, more wine."

Tayven's presence had only just begun to sink into Shan's mind. For months, he'd wondered about meeting him, now he was here. Taropat's description of a fey, spiritual being seemed extremely misguided. Tayven appeared to be prickly and difficult, and his face was harder than Shan had thought it would be. Clearly, his experiences in Cos had marked him. Shan could not imagine how he could ever broach the subject of what he'd seen in the scry mede, never mind the whereabouts of Taropat. He suspected that Tayven would harbor bitter memories of Khaster.

As the evening wore on, the lizard wine ensured that conversation flowed more easily. Neferishu held both Shan and Tayven in her net, and kept their attention upon her. She was on form that night, abrim with witticisms that couldn't help but lift any awkward mood. Tayven remained somewhat terse, yet polite. Occasionally, Shan caught him looking at him speculatively.

Neferishu excused herself from the company and glided into the palace, and for some moments, Shan and Tayven were left alone.

"I know you," Tayven said in a low, almost vicious voice. "Whom do you serve? Almorante? Bayard?"

"No one," Shan said. "I am from Breeland."

"Maycarpe, Leckery, they wanted us meet. This is a plot. I am not stupid. They want me to return to Magravandias, stir up the wasps."

"That may be true, but I'm not part of it," Shan said. He paused. "Do you remember where you know me from?"

Tayven drew back a little. "Why did you want to meet me? Have you been tracking me? It is a waste of time. I could disappear now in an instant if I wished to."

"I haven't been tracking you. I have seen you before, only we have not met." He paused again. "We have a mutual friend."

"The only friends I have are in Cos."

Shan didn't respond to that. This was neither the time nor the place to reveal anything. "Perhaps we could talk at some point." He wasn't yet sure whether he should reveal what he knew or not, but the wine had loosened his tongue. A cool detached part of him was aware of this.

"I don't think you will say anything I want to hear," Tayven said. "You should be aware I distance myself from all connivings."

"What I have to say has nothing to do with anything like that."

"You are Maycarpe's protégé. It must have."

"I am not his protégé. I was sent to Akahana to train under

General Tuya. Maycarpe took a liking to me, that's all. I'm not a friend of Magravandias, but I'm playing the game here. It's as simple as that. We have to talk."

Shan became aware of a looming presence and turned round. Maycarpe was standing behind him. "This is urgent talk," he said. "Do you two know each other?"

"Yes," said Tayven.

"No," said Shan.

"Some confusion over your relationship, it seems," Maycarpe said.

"We met once, but we don't know one another," Shan said, aware he had to deflect Maycarpe's interest. "After that meeting, I was eager to make Tayven's acquaintance again." He risked a rather flirtatious smile. Tayven raised an ironic eyebrow.

"I see," said Maycarpe. "Puppy love! You must have been very young indeed."

"Some people make an impression upon you, whatever age you are," Shan said. "From just one meeting, you can carry them with you for the rest of your life."

"How poetic!" Maycarpe said, and laughed. "I wish I had met such a soul." He was clearly bored by what he thought was romance rather than intrigue, and drifted away.

Tayven shook his head. "What was that about?"

"He must not know our connection," Shan said. "My mentor's privacy depends on it."

"What is our connection, then?"

"Not here. It is too dangerous."

"I have to admit, I'm now intrigued. We will speak later, as you desire."

Shan had noticed that Merlan avoided him that night. Perhaps he was uncomfortable around Tayven. From what Shan had been able to observe, Merlan hadn't even looked in their direction. Now, Shan tried to catch his eye, judge his mood.

Tayven said, "Why do you look at him in that way? Are you accomplices?"

Shan turned back. "No, he's just a friend. But he's keeping out of the way tonight. I suspect it's because of you."

"Probably. I have an unreasonable hatred of him."

"Why's that?"

"He's alive," Tayven said coldly.

Neferishu sashayed back to her seat, and sat between them. "You look like conspirators," she said. "Give your attention to me, now. I demand it!"

From anyone else, it might have sounded arrogant and spoiled, but from Neferishu, it was a joke. His inhibitions lowered by the wine, Shan was suddenly overwhelmed with a feeling of warmth for her. He leaned toward her and kissed her cheek. "I am privileged to know you, your majesty," he said. "Please indulge my importunity."

Neferishu laughed delightedly. "Excellent!" she said. "Now, Tayven, if you would only succumb to the same impulsiveness as Shan, my life would be complete."

Tayven ducked his head. "You know I admire you greatly."

Neferishu rolled her eyes. "Really! You are a tease. You break my heart."

She was still laughing, but Shan sensed, deep within, that she spoke the truth.

Later, she and Shan were left alone for some minutes and Neferishu said wistfully, "This party is for him. He comes here too seldom. I expect that now Ashalan has caved in to the Magravandians, he'll come even more infrequently, if at all." She sighed.

"He spoke earlier of a quandary over what to do now," Shan said. "Perhaps you could persuade him to remain here in Akahana. Offer him a position in your staff."

"Tried it," Neferishu said. "He wouldn't bite. He knows that Almorante and Palindrake come here often."

Shan saw Tayven walking back toward them. "He can't run from the world forever."

"Yes he can," Neferishu said. "That is the tragedy of it."

Tayven did not sit down beside the queen again, but merely bowed. "I must take my leave, your majesty. The journey today has tired me."

"You are staying with Lord Maycarpe?" Neferishu inquired.

"In the governmental buildings, yes."

She smiled, her voice betraying no hint of her true feelings. "You must visit me tomorrow. I too would like to hear about the meeting between Valraven and the Cossics."

Tayven returned her smile with apparent ease. "It will be my pleasure. I'll welcome an escape from Maycarpe's oppression."

"Good," said Neferishu. "Early evening then. You may take dinner with me. I will send my litter for you."

Shan stood up, concerned his opportunity for a private talk with Tayven wouldn't happen. But Tayven smiled at him slyly. "Perhaps you would walk with me, Shan."

Shan did not hesitate. "Yes. If you like."

Neferishu made a wordless sound of resigned disappointment and flopped back into her cushions. "You are Magravandian. I should have guessed."

Tayven took Shan's arm. "Shall we go?"

Once outside the court, having passed through a gauntlet of knowing, surprised and gloating eyes, Tayven dropped Shan's arm. "They are off the scent. So, tell me then."

"I can't. Not just like that. It's too important."

Tayven nodded thoughtfully and pointed at Shan with an accusing finger. "Shall I tell you how I know you? I saw you in a magical mirror. Your face. Laugh if you like, but it is true."

"I know," Shan said. "I saw your face too once, but in a scry mede."

Tayven stopped walking. "What is this?"

"There is a connection between us, but I'm not sure what you'll think of it."

"Try me."

"My mentor," Shan said. "He knew you."

"A Magravandian? Who?"

Shan struggled for words, sure Tayven wouldn't believe him. Shaking his head, he walked away and Tayven came after him.

"You must speak. What is this?"

"I heard a story," Shan said. "A tragic story. It affected me. I went into my mentor's workroom and there picked up a scry mede. When I looked into it, I saw a face looking back at me. I always knew it was you. Because of the story. It was your story, you see. That's what I was told."

"Who told it to you?"

"A man named Taropat," Shan said.

Tayven frowned. "It means nothing to me."

"It wouldn't. How can I explain? Taropat, I think, has lived for many hundreds of years. At least, his consciousness has. He takes a new body when one wears out. The body he has now he acquired some years ago, in Cos."

Tayven's eyes narrowed. "Go on."

"He doesn't eclipse the personality that comes with the body but somehow melds with it, so that his host retains all their memories, quirks and preferences. This body, Tayven . . . by the gods, this is difficult!"

Tayven took hold of Shan's arms, gripped them painfully. "Tell me!"

"Khaster," Shan said. "It is Khaster."

There was a moment's silence, then Tayven exclaimed, "What! That is obscene. I won't believe it!" He pushed Shan away. "You think you can get to me with a story like that? What kind of person are you? Whom do you serve?"

"It is the truth," Shan said. "I know it sounds incredible, but it isn't. Khaster lives, Tayven. He lives in Breeland, but he is now Taropat."

"You lie! I won't hear more of this. I should slit your throat for your effrontery."

Tayven made to walk away swiftly, but Shan caught hold of his right arm. "No. You must listen. I was nothing other than a Bree peasant until Taropat changed my life. He rescued me, he trained me. Eventually, he told me his story. I can tell it to you now. No one but Khaster would have known the details I've learned. I know about how you met in the Sink, your holiday at Recolletine, everything."

Tayven paused. "Khaster failed me," he said, "as I failed him. It was all a hideous mess. It should be forgotten. I don't believe he lives. If you have any compassion, you'll let him remain dead for me."

"Compassion does not come into it. I was trained to speak only truth. I will not lie. The moment I saw your face in the scry mede I knew that one day I would be here telling you these things. It was inevitable."

Tayven put his hands against his face, ground the heels of them into his eyes. He groaned. "Inevitable. Always. Nothing in this world is ever finished." He lowered his hands. "Does Maycarpe know of this?"

Shan shook his head. "I've told no one, not even Merlan, because Taropat bade me to remain silent on the matter. He named Maycarpe and Merlan in particular. But he did not mention you. He thinks you're dead too."

Tayven appeared calmer now. "Maycarpe wants Khaster, you know," he said. "Some years ago, he sought me out and told me he thought Khaster had survived. I tried to find him, but there was no trace. I believed Maycarpe to be mistaken."

"Come to my quarters," Shan said. "I will tell you the whole story."

LATER, ONCE TAYVEN HAD left, Shan lay upon his bed, unable to sleep. He felt unburdened, but also uneasy, as if he'd released a monster into the world that could not be stopped. It was the same feeling he'd had that day when he'd seen Tayven's face in the mede. He realized his first thoughts about Tayven's feelings for Khaster had been wrong. There was no bitterness there at all. Once the information had sunk in, it seemed that Tayven was glad to hear Khaster was alive, more than glad. This worried Shan, because it was not something he'd expected. It diminished his control over the situation, for now Tayven might act independently. Shan had revealed too much. A man like Tayven, trained as a tracker, might be able to penetrate the forest of Bree and find the tall, narrow house. And what would happen then? Still, it was too late to worry now. The damage had been done.

He had to know, Shan told himself, blinking at starlight. He had a right to.

18

A COMPANY OF WORTHY MEN

THE FOLLOWING AFTERNOON, Shan received an invitation to visit Lord Maycarpe. Merlan met him at the door. "Did you get what you wanted?" he asked.

Shan regarded him thoughtfully. "If you're referring to Tayven Hirantel, I said what I had to say, yes."

"He will tell Maycarpe everything you said to him," Merlan said. "I hope you're prepared for that."

Shan shrugged. "I have nothing to hide. It was a personal matter."

Merlan glanced at him shrewdly. "You don't believe me, do you? Ah well, you'll soon find out."

Shan thought that Merlan was merely being spiteful because of his own opinions of Tayven. But the moment he walked into Maycarpe's office and saw Tayven sitting there, apparently completely at ease with the governor, Shan thought he might have to revise his opinion.

Maycarpe looked up. "Ah, Shan, you are here. Good. Now we may begin."

"Begin what?" Shan asked. He gave Tayven a pointed look; he merely pulled a rueful face and raised his hands.

"Work in which we are all fascinated and involved," Maycarpe said. "We have who we need now. This is why I sent for Tayven. It has nothing to do with what the Dragon Lord is getting up to in Cos. That is a trifle. It does not concern us."

Shan frowned. "I'm all ears."

"Then sit down, make yourself comfortable. My servant is preparing us a beverage."

Shan gave Tayven another pointed glance. Had he told Maycarpe anything?

Merlan would not sit but leaned against the blackwood dresser, his arms folded. His expression was grim.

After the drinks had arrived and the servant had departed, Maycarpe said, "Which of you knows where your little company has to go now?"

"I wasn't aware we were a 'little company,' " said Merlan dourly. "What do you mean?"

Maycarpe sighed theatrically. "What have we been talking about recently, Merlan? Really! Is your memory so short?"

Shan realized at once what Maycarpe meant. The warrior, the mystic, the bard. This was how he saw the three of them—the companions of the true king. "Magravandias," Shan said. "Recolletine. You want us to go to the seven lakes."

Maycarpe seemed surprised, if not disappointed, Shan had curtailed his game. He nodded. "Yes, that is my thought."

"I will never set foot in that country again," Tayven said, "and neither do I wish to become involved in any of your schemes."

"You are already involved," Maycarpe said, with uncharacteristic harshness. "Get used to it. You were involved from the day Almorante took you there, and bungled through the initiations in his hamfisted, uninformed way. He has no patience or discipline to undertake the rigors of true magical training. He looks for the easy way."

"I'm not interested in your opinions of Almorante," Tayven said. "Whatever happened to me there was a long time ago. I'm not the same person." He paused. "Why do you want us to go there any-way?"

"He seeks to make a magical company of us," Merlan said coldly. "A brotherhood of worthy men." He laughed. "Very likely."

"For what reason?" Tayven asked.

"The lakes quest should be undertaken in the correct manner," Maycarpe said, "then you'll have a chance of attaining the Crown."

"The Crown? It cannot be done," Tayven said. "It is a dream, and powerful as an idea only because it is not real."

"You don't believe that," Maycarpe said smoothly. "That is only your bitterness talking. You try so hard to extinguish the light in yourself, but it is a fruitless task. This surly exterior you present is merely a conceit. You are who you are, Tayven. I'm not impressed by the dramatics."

Shan shifted uncomfortably in his seat. "I hardly think you have the right to say that."

"Save your pity," Maycarpe said. "Tayven is tougher than you might believe. He knows what I'm saying is right. Don't you, Tay-ven?"

"I will not return to Recolletine, not for anyone."

"You are very proud," Maycarpe said. "You think you're the only person fit to wield that power in this cruel and uncertain world. You regard yourself as its guardian, its protector, but you're not. You are its initiate, one of them. You cannot shirk that responsibility."

"There's little point to this," Tayven said. "What good would the Crown do us if we had it? Who is fit to wear it? No one. Not in this world, this time. It belongs to a more enlightened age. It should stay there and exist only in our reality as a legend."

"Shan thinks he's fit to wear it," Maycarpe said.

"I don't!" Shan exclaimed.

Tayven shook his head. "This is just another of your games, Maycarpe. I won't play."

"We already have two of the dragon artifacts," Maycarpe said. "The third I believe is to be found at the lakes. I want you to retrieve it, Tayven, and more. I want you to reach the seventh lake, attain the Crown. I know you can."

"But why should I?"

"Because it is your destiny. You began the quest, but were too young and guided by fools. The universe does not blame you for your failure. You may try again."

Tayven grimaced. "It has all left me. My innocence and idealism were shattered." He glanced at Merlan. "What has *he* got to do with this?"

"He must assume the mantle left cold on the battlefield by his brother."

"What?"

"Some years ago, I asked you to find Khaster Leckery, for his name came to me often. I believe now I was slightly mistaken. Merlan, undamaged, whole and healthy, is the Leckery who must become the mystic of the brotherhood. He will wield the Eye of the Dragon."

Tayven laughed. "That is the most ridiculous thing I've ever heard. You might as well give the role to Queen Neferishu."

"Harsh," said Maycarpe, raising a hand to silence Merlan's outraged response. "And somewhat prejudiced."

"Khaster is the only one who should take that role," Tayven said. "I began to prime him for it, years ago. I would have succeeded too, given more time. It is a farce to pass that responsibility to his younger brother. It would not work. The idea is as slapdash as any of Almorante's schemes."

"But Khaster is dead," Maycarpe said, "or if he isn't, he might as well be. We have no choice. The only other option is not to try at all, and that is unthinkable."

Tayven shook his head. "No. I won't cooperate. That is my final word. Shan is just a boy and Merlan Leckery is unsuitable. I would be embarrassed to join such a company."

"And I cannot stand the company of such a self-righteous, rude and opinionated prig," said Merlan, with some levity in his voice. "His insults are too outrageous to annoy me. I look at him and see someone whose present charisma is the result only of past privileges. Even now, he shares the bed of an exiled king to give himself kudos. Who will be the next rung on your ladder, Hirantel?"

Tayven gave Merlan a beatific smile. "Perhaps Neferishu. She has been patient. It should be rewarded."

"You disgust me!" Merlan said.

"Stop it!" Maycarpe said. "You're behaving like schoolboys. Look at Shan. He, of all you, has the most dignity."

"I was thinking," Shan said.

A tense silence came into the room. Shan looked about him. Maycarpe's expression was guarded, Tayven's bland, while Merlan looked alert and curious. Shan could see right through them all. He laughed softly and shook his head. "I see. Was all this necessary? Why didn't you just ask me outright?"

"What do you mean?" Merlan asked.

"They don't want you to be part of this company, Merlan. There's someone else they have in mind. They seek to trick me into helping them, because they believe they can play upon my own desires. They know the quest cannot take place without this person, and they think I'm eager to start on it, that I want to be king." He leaned forward in his seat. "All I want is what is best for everyone." He turned to Merlan. "You were right. Tayven told Maycarpe everything I said to him." He addressed Tayven. "You've disappointed me."

Tayven shrugged and Maycarpe said, "You speak in ignorance. A true magus understands that he has to dance on both sides of the coin. Utter goodness is as bad as pure evil."

"I have my mentor as you have yours," Tayven said.

"He taught you well then."

Tayven nodded. "Yes."

Merlan expelled an incredulous snort. "All this time, I believed the act. You played it well, Tayven."

"Thank you."

"Khaster is alive," Shan said. "This is what I told him last night, Merlan. I'm sorry. I wish I hadn't."

The color drained from Merlan's face. "You knew this?" He shook his head, apparently speechless. The others in the room watched him carefully, until Merlan punched one hand against the other. "You told him, not me? You're as bad as he is."

"No," Shan said. "I was bidden to keep silent. I had to respect that, no matter how much grief it caused me."

"You knew it would come out sometime while you were here," Maycarpe said. "Don't deny it."

"Of course. I was considering speaking to Merlan about it, but not this way."

"Where is he?" Merlan said. "How do you know about him?"

"He is my mentor," Shan said. "He is now called Taropat. He lives in Breeland."

"Will he come here, if you send for him?" Merlan asked.

"Khaster wouldn't," Shan said, "but I suspect that Taropat might."

"I must go to him," Merlan said. "At once."

"No, Tayven must go to him," Maycarpe said. "The past must be resolved before the future can take root in the present."

"I think that would be a great shock to Taropat," Shan said. "It might be better if I returned home and spoke to him. He might come back with me."

"We need that shock value," Maycarpe said.

"You don't know him," Shan said. "You don't know how much the past still hurts him. I've learned his ways. I think I know how to handle him." He risked an invention. "Also, if Tayven set foot in the forest of Breeland, Taropat would know about it. He'd hide. Tayven would never find him. The other magi would probably play with Tayven for years, send him in circles, or into strange worlds. I just know it wouldn't work."

"Then we must improve the odds," Maycarpe said. "Use our magic."

"No magic would work in Breeland," Shan said. "The magi are too strong. They aren't fools."

"It depends on the nature of the magic," Maycarpe said. "Glamours and efforts of the mind would not work, I agree. I would advocate manipulating fate, improving the odds of chance in our favor." He gestured at Tayven. "What do you think? Will you go to Breeland if the conditions are right?"

"Yes," said Tayven. "It is my fault Khaster ended up the way he did."

"He thinks that of you," Shan said.

Tayven shook his head. "No. I was always more than he believed I was. Bayard had my measure far more accurately than Khaster ever did."

"Were you really working with the Cossics to get Bayard murdered?" Shan asked.

"Of course. Why else would I go to that godforsaken place?"

"Then I can't let you back into Taropat's life. I will die before I reveal his exact whereabouts to you."

"Don't be stupid, Shan," Maycarpe said. "Despite appearances, Tayven was fond of Khaster Leckery. He had two reasons to be in Cos. He just can't admit to it, because such emotion doesn't conform to his current image. As I said, he danced on both sides of the coin; master of intrigue and cunning and devoted lover to a damaged man."

"Almorante should have kept him out of Cos," Tayven said. "He could have done so, easily. Khaster was there as my companion, my cover, rather than the other way around. I could have done more. I could have persuaded Almorante to keep Khaster by him in Magrast. That is where my guilt lies."

"Do you intend to unburden yourself of this to him?" Shan said. "Make your guilt his pain?"

"No. I will show him I am alive, that's all. I will show him I bear no grudge. I will persuade him to come to Akahana." Tayven turned to Maycarpe. "How do we improve the odds of this happening?"

Maycarpe said nothing but turned in his seat to pick something up from the table beside him. He held out his hand to reveal a die. "We use the weapons of chance," he said. "We will invoke the cosmic joker, the fool. Taropat, or Khaster, is already in Breeland, and the way he will react to Tayven's appearance is already set. It exists, if you like, as if it is a single card in a pack of reactions that have been previously shuffled. We cannot read his mind, even if we can make good guesses. The top card has already been chosen by fate and lies facedown before us, so the random factor lies within ourselves. Our chances of guessing the top card of a shuffled deck are not very good, so we must build up the random force to make fate work in our favor."

"This is how Taropat found me," Shan said. "He used a die at every crossroads until he came to Holme."

"Then you understand what we're doing," said Maycarpe.

"You're losing me," Merlan said. "What do you mean?"

"Tayven will be guided by the fool," Maycarpe said. "This die will be his compass and his map. By the time he reaches Khaster, he will know the top card, trust me. And fate will ensure he reaches his goal. It will start here, now. We will decide upon six options for what Tayven must do next today."

"I'm going to have dinner with Queen Neferishu," Tayven said. "That is already decided."

Maycarpe shook his head. "Not exactly. I choose that if you roll the number one, you will neglect your appointment, and face whatever consequences arise. Shan, you choose for number two."

"I choose that you will be half an hour late."

"Merlan?" Maycarpe said. "Number three?"

Merlan shrugged. "I choose that he must insult the queen in some way."

"Be more specific," Maycarpe said.

Merlan smiled. "He must tell her she is ugly."

Shan laughed. "He can't do that! That's cruel—and patently untrue."

"This is the game of chance," Maycarpe said. "The option has been chosen." He frowned. "I choose that number four means he will do nothing but enjoy a pleasant evening with a delightful lady."

"Number five," said Shan, "means he must go to the palace barefoot."

Merlan laughed again. "And finally, number six means he must sleep with the queen and tell her he loves her."

Tayven glared at Merlan. "You have a one in six chance of finding my hands round your neck."

"But this is the game," Maycarpe said, clearly enjoying himself. "Now, throw the die, Tayven. Give yourself to chance."

Tayven sighed, then took the die from Maycarpe. "I must be mad," he said, and blew into his clenched fist, where the die lay concealed. Then he threw and everyone leaned forward to see the result.

Tayven closed his eyes. "Dear gods."

"You played," said Maycarpe, "you must go with it. Build up the random force in your favor."

Merlan shrugged. "It was a one in six chance."

"Can you do it?" Shan asked.

Tayven stared at him without speaking.

"Of course he can," Maycarpe said. "Despite his preferences, he is still a man. Of all the options, six was destined to be the most difficult. But the prize is great, and will not come easily. Learn this lesson well. It will be your guide in Magravandias when the time comes."

19

RETURN OF THE GHOST

TAYVEN MET THE TRAVELLING fortune-teller in the forecourt of an inn at the Bree port of Fishpaw, where he had paid for a room for the night. Her colorful clothes had attracted his attention, and also the fact that she was playing idly with a pair of dice, sitting alone at a table, with a gray cat coiled around her neck. Tayven, always alert for signs, asked if he might join her for dinner. She agreed, told him her name was Serena, and at once tried to get him to give her money for a reading. Amused, Tayven did so. As the landlord of the inn served their evening meal, Serena set out a tattered set of divining cards upon the beer-stained table.

"You are on a momentous journey," she told him.

Tayven smiled, said nothing. Anybody staying at this inn would probably be on a journey.

"You play with fate," Serena said. The cat on her shoulder appeared to study the cards with great concentration.

"Who doesn't?" Tayven responded and began to eat.

"No, you really do," Serena said sternly. She had a robust build and looked as if she could break a man's neck with ease.

"Yes, I really do," Tayven said, enjoying himself.

Serena laid out more cards. "So many broken hearts," she said, shaking her head.

Tayven sighed, raised his hands expressively, fork waving. "Such is my curse."

"One day it might catch up with you," said Serena darkly. "I think your trouble is you don't know how deeply other people feel. Is this because you can't feel that deeply yourself, or because you are conditioned to think that others are interested only in your beauty? I can see that you doubt others' feelings. You believe yourself to be unloved. In effect, you hate the very people who want to love you."

Tayven fought with rising discomfort at these words. "So what is my future?"

Serena laid out three more cards. "You will meet a tall dark man and come into money."

Tayven laughed. "That bad? Tell me what you really saw."

"That *is* what I really saw," said Serena scooping up the cards. The cat jumped from her shoulder and began to help itself to her dinner.

Serena had hired a wagon, which she was going to drive across Breeland to a fair farther west. Her journey would take her through the Forest of Bree. Tayven offered her more money for a ride, which she accepted.

Two days later, they were deep in the watchful forest, where summer was a humid breath between the ancient trunks. Serena had uncovered the wagon so that her clothes and bedding could be aired. Tayven lay among the blankets, throwing his die onto an upturned saucepan, watched by the inscrutable gray cat, who seemed to regard him with derision. He was throwing an unusual amount of sixes, which to him now signified not only the most powerful of actions, but also the most difficult. He laughed and joked with Serena, but inside he was numb. Each moment brought him closer to Taropat. How would he face this stranger he'd once known? What, really, was there to say? Khaster had been potentially useful to Almorante, but when that usefulness disappeared, Almorante simply started looking elsewhere. Now, someone had use for Khaster again. Lord Maycarpe.

And to coax Khaster into cooperating required a deception. Some things he must not yet know, for both Tayven and Maycarpe knew that the truth would send Khaster further into hiding. *Am I any better than Pharinet?* Tayven wondered, but still knew he'd do what he'd set out to do. He remembered Valraven Palindrake telling him he would remember their conversation in Cos, and he did. It replayed itself through his mind to the rhythm of the falling die.

Serena clucked to the oxen that drew the wagon and began to sing in an out-of-tune voice. Occasionally, she'd turn and flash her unnaturally white teeth at her passenger. Tayven found it increasingly difficult to return her smiles. He could no longer quantify his feelings, perhaps because they were focused entirely on the throw of the die. *One, I am afraid; two, I am excited; three, I am nervous. . . .* In truth he could feel none of those things. He was aware only of a serpent biting its own tail; a circle completed.

Serena halted the wagon at a crossroads, where five paths divided like the arms of a star and disappeared into a gloom, speared by rays of sunlight. "I go this way," she said, pointing to the path ahead. "Which way are you going?"

"Give me a moment," Tayven said. Five paths, six choices. One of them would mean staying where he was, sitting at the center of the crossroads. He could not contemplate going back. The die roll was two; a path to the right. "I get off here," Tayven said, and jumped down from the wagon, pulling his backpack after.

"Be careful," Serena said to him and clucked to the oxen once more.

Tayven watched the wagon trundle away from him into gold-shot shadow. He hoisted his backpack higher onto his shoulder. Down this path, if fortune was truly on his side, he would find the man he'd known as Khaster Leckery. He could throw the die now to determine how Khaster might react to their reunion, but ultimately, at this final stage, Tayven wanted to leave some aspects to true chance. Neferishu had advised him to do that. Tayven smiled. He had judged the queen wrongly. When he'd gone to dine with her that night, he'd got drunk too quickly, able to think only about what the die had predicted. He wanted to get it over with as soon as possible, and had crudely groped for the queen's hand across the table, while uttering inane yet lascivious remarks. Neferishu guessed what was on his mind, but fortunately did not divine the true reason. She believed he was only trying to please her. "You know I love you, Tayven," she said. "But I don't want your pity. If you can't come to me with equal feeling, then you mustn't come at all."

He'd felt humbled by her honesty. "I have forgotten how to be human," he said, and drank more wine. He realized he felt nauseous.

Neferishu shook her head at him, bemused. She led him from the table to a couch and there held him close against her body. "I have dreamed of this so often," she murmured.

Tayven, to his horror, found he was weeping. Neferishu soothed him, stroked his hair. She didn't press him to speak, but somehow the words came tumbling out. It felt like vomiting. He would speak until he was retching on dry words. Even in his stupor, he retained enough control not to say anything Maycarpe would want kept back, but he could talk about Khaster, about Cos, about his journey to come. He said that he would use a die to find the man he'd once known.

"There must come a time," Neferishu said, kissing his forehead, "when the die stays in your pocket. Remember that. If you find him."

Tayven felt completely comfortable nestled against her. This was what love must be like, to feel so safe. Had he ever really known that? Just before he fell asleep in her arms, Tayven said, "I love you, Neferishu."

THE GLADE WAS exactly as Tayven had imagined it from Shan's detailed description. There was the waterwheel, turning slowly, and the great oaks that surrounded the crooked narrow house like a fortress. There was the yellow horse, tethered by a long rope, cropping the startling emerald lawn around the mill pool. Skeins of perfumed smoke drifted in the still hot air. A few birds called, but their songs were languid, as if everything drowsed in the summer afternoon. Tayven paused at the edge of the glade. He felt like an interloper now, someone who would shatter the peace of this idyll, bring the past, and all its traumas, crashing back. It was the only time he'd felt tempted to turn around, return to Akahana, and tell the others his journey had been unsuccessful. What right had he to be here, like some black-winged, doom-bearing angel? Khaster had found a life; it had been given to him. He had found some kind of peace.

A man came out of the house, and before Tayven could melt back into the greenery, he knew he'd been seen. He froze. This was undeniably Khaster before him, older, yes, and his hair had receded a little, but other than that, there appeared to be little change. The expression on his face was not that of shock, nor even recognition. He looked faintly puzzled, a little irritated. Tayven did not, could not, move. This was not Khaster, he told himself. This was Taropat. He must remember that.

Taropat was carrying a large wicker basket, which appeared to be full of vegetable scraps. This he placed down carefully on the ground and began to walk purposefully toward the forest. When he was only a few feet from Tayven, he performed strange and complicated gestures with his hands and uttered a few words in an unknown language. Perhaps it was a curse. Tayven still did nothing. Taropat screwed up his face in vexation, and performed the gestures again. Then he made a dismissive gesture. "Stay then, it means nothing to me." He walked back toward the house.

"Khas!" Tayven called, involuntarily.

Taropat froze, and for some seconds did not look round.

"Khas," Tayven said again, in a lower voice.

Taropat turned. "What *are* you?" he hissed.

Tayven lowered his backpack to the ground. "It's me," he said. "Tayven Hirantel. Do you remember?"

Unexpectedly, Taropat laughed. "What do you want this time?"

Tayven raised his hands. "Nothing. That is . . ." He was lost for words. Not even the die could have predicted this reaction. He couldn't have thought of it as an option.

Taropat folded his arms and nodded appreciatively. "Yes, you've got it well. The aging, the suggestion of travel. Convincing. I'm impressed. Now tell me what you want."

"Shan told me you were here," Tayven said. "We met in Akahana."

Taropat raised his eyebrows. "Why continue this? Why not get to the point? Show me your true self if you dare."

"This is my true self," Tayven said.

"Ah yes, a ghost. I see. Some might be convinced by that. But wouldn't a ghost resemble a person's appearance at the time they died?"

"I'm not a ghost. I'm not dead. Like you, I survived what happened in Cos. You are more of a ghost than I am." Tayven took a step forward. "Listen to me, Khas, Taropat. I was taken from the Magravandian camp as good as dead. Bayard's people left me in the wilderness, where I could have died, but the Cossic resistance found me. I have lived with them ever since. A man named Lord Maycarpe, who is your brother's employer, sent Mewtish trackers to find me— and you—but was successful in that they only found me. I have spoken recently to Merlan, and to Shan. That is why I'm here, now."

Taropat turned away abruptly. "If you lie, go now, and there will be no retribution. If you lie and continue in this, I will destroy you, as you know I can. If you speak the truth . . ." He shook his head. "That could not be possible."

"I speak the truth. Look at me, and tell me I'm lying."

Taropat turned to him again, stared with narrow eyes. "The elden of this place seek constantly to deceive me. They are tricksters. When I first came here, they plucked an image from my mind, and have used it to torment me. I have seen you here a thousand times."

"No, you haven't. Look at me. Do I truly resemble what any spirit could mimic? Like you, I'm older. I've changed. Elden know nothing of the human heart. Their illusions have no real substance." he held out his hand. "Touch me now and tell me I'm not real."

Taropat hesitated, then reached out and briefly squeezed Tayven's fingers. He smothered a laugh with his hands that turned almost to a sob. "I'm dreaming," she said.

"No." Tayven lifted his luggage once more. "Take me into your house. Shan has told me about it. I want to see it. I'm hungry. Give me food. Then we can talk. We have much to discuss."

Inside, the house was dark and cool, and smelled pungently of herbs. A gargoyle-faced grim sat eating coal atop the stove. Tayven

sat at the table, while Taropat prepared a meal. Now, he felt disorientated and light-headed. It seemed inconceivable he was in Khaster's presence again. This man looked like Khaster, yet in many ways
he was entirely dissimilar. If anything, this was what Khaster should
always have been; tougher, more humorous.

Taropat chopped salad at the table. "I should have known the
consequences of sending Shan to Akahana would be more shattering
than we imagined," he said. "I made him swear not to tell Merlan of
my existence, but apparently he has broken that vow."

"Not exactly. He told only me. I was the one that spread the
news, if you like. Shan was not responsible for it. He did tell Merlan
eventually, but only because he had no choice. You brother would
have found out from Maycarpe, otherwise."

Taropat sighed. "I suppose this means I'll have to move on now.
Once this news gets back to Magrast, someone will come looking for
me. I know that."

"It won't get back," Tayven said, helping himself to some slivers
of onion. "Not from Maycarpe. Merlan will keep silent also."

"How thoughtful of them. Why? What do they want from me?
I can only assume their silence has a price.'

Tayven shrugged. "I won't deny it. There is work afoot. I too
am involved in it, somewhat against my will. Almorante knows I'm
alive, but so far I've managed to avoid him. Did you know Valraven
Palindrake has, at last, coaxed King Ashalan from hiding? He will be
at Magrast by now, being cosseted by the empress and sized up for a
suitable bride. Cos has finally fallen, Khas." He shook his head.

Taropat continued to chop the salad, and for some moments said
nothing. Then he sighed. "I feel as if I should play a role, be fractious
and demand my continued privacy. But that is a lie. Whatever I said
a moment ago about moving on, I've always known that one day I'd
have to go back to reality, make my mark. Taropat gave me the
means to make a difference—his knowledge. Some part of me has
always craved the opportunity to use it."

Tayven laughed uneasily. "This seems too easy! Won't you put
up a fight? I did, if only for show."

Taropat shook his head. "No. The day I took Shan from the

ruins of his home was the first step toward involving myself in the world again. This day was inevitable." He looked up and smiled. "But I'm glad fate has given me the gift of seeing you alive and well. That I did not expect."

"I wondered whether you'd be pleased to see me or not. I was your nemesis, you know, despite everything else."

"Oh, I know that, Tayven. I put my newfound talents to good use when I first came here. You were never what I thought you were, but if anything, I respected you more for it. Still, the picture I got was incomplete. One thing I could never be totally sure of. In Cos, were you working with the resistance to assassinate Bayard?"

"Not with Ashalan's people, but another faction, yes."

"What a pity you failed."

"That is an understatement. I wasn't careful enough. Neither were my colleagues. You and I paid the price for it."

Taropat nodded. "But look at us now." He pointed at Tayven with the chopping knife. "Would you rather be who you were? I wouldn't. For me, suffering has brought riches." He lowered the knife and stared out through the window. "Sometimes, I dream of Caradore and my life there, and when I wake, I know it could have been perfection. But here, in Breeland, I have found a peace I could never have found at home. I have true friends here, who have helped to heal me. Shan was the final medicine. When I watched him walk away from here, a great sense of tranquillity settled over me. I sensed I had to rest, and enjoy every moment, because a time would shortly come when I would have to leave here. Life would become difficult again for a while, but I knew I'd have the strength to face it." He shook his head, smiling. "I'd never have thought the universe would send you back to me first, the evidence of you, the proof that things can turn out well. Seeing you alive assures me that darkness doesn't always win."

"Perhaps I was always part of the darkness," Tayven said.

"Not to me," Taropat replied curtly. "But that is the past. We are both different now."

"You, very much so."

Taropat arranged the salad on plates with meat, cheese and bread,

"What is your motive?" Taropat asked.

Tayven grinned. "Revenge, but not just that. I like to think I have more noble ideals too, such as a desire for justice and fairness. Yours?"

Taropat paused, frowned. "If I am honest, I want to prove myself to others. Like you, I feel the Malagashes should be wiped from history, but most of all, I see Pharinet's face, her surprise and shock. I want to free Caradore, and for all of them there to know I was involved."

"Valraven Palindrake?"

Taropat uttered a low growl. "I want him discredited. I want him to return to Caradore. Let him lord it over the Palindrake lands, but with everyone knowing who and what he is."

"So will that involve both he and Pharinet being stripped naked, shaved, and driven through the streets with whips?"

Taropat laughed. "Now, there's a pleasant thought." He adopted a serious expression. "Totally inappropriate for an enlightened soul, of course."

"Dance on both sides of the coin," Tayven said dryly. "It's the only way." He paused. "Do you still want to be king of Caradore?"

Taropat screwed up his face, and for a moment a strange expression crossed it. Tayven knew that the words to follow it would not be the total truth. "No," Taropat said. "At the end of it, if I can, I want to return here and grow old, until it's time for Taropat to find a new body."

"What about the ones before you?" Tayven asked. "Are they still part of him, of you, or didn't they survive the transition to the next incarnation?"

"If they exist within me, they are only whispers," Taropat said. "Khaster isn't immortal, only Taropat is."

"It must be strange. I'd like you to describe it to me in detail."

"I will. When do you want to return to Akahana?"

"Shortly. But not immediately. We should talk more first."

After they'd eaten, they sat before the stove, and Tayven told Taropat all that had happened to him since they'd last seen one another. In return, Taropat described his own life's events. "So much has happened," Tayven said. "We could never have guessed it."

"I'm glad we didn't," Taropat said. "Forewarning would not have helped us."

Tayven wrapped his arms around his raised knees. "I can remember that terrible night quite well, and yet it does not seem as if it happened to me. I was out of my body somewhere, removed from the experience."

Taropat hesitated, then said, "How much has it affected you?"

Tayven shrugged. "A lot, I suppose."

Taropat stuffed tobacco into his pipe. "It affected me greatly too. Since then, I have been isolated in an emotional sense. No one has come near. Has it been much the same for you?"

Tayven looked away. "No, not in that sense."

"You must be resilient."

"I told you—I don't feel it happened to me. Also, I refuse to let Bayard affect me that strongly. One day, I will kill him, my hate is that deep, but I'll continue to live my life as normal."

"Do you have anyone now?"

"I did. It was Ashalan."

Taropat laughed. "Always the best, the highest."

Tayven shrugged. "Coincidence. He's gone to the Magravandians now. We've said our good-byes."

"I pity him."

"There's no need. We weren't that close. It was just convenience."

Taropat said nothing, but Tayven imagined he was thinking, *as with most of your relationships.* "It wasn't that way with us," Tayven said.

"I know," Taropat said, as if to soothe him. "Look, it's getting late. You can have Shan's bed. It might be a little damp, but I can prepare you a hot stone."

"If that's what you want," said Tayven, aware of the steel in his voice.

"You are too impetuous," Taropat said. "That's another change in you. You cannot expect us to carry on from where we left off. We are strangers now."

"And will we always be so?"

Taropat hesitated. "I can't answer that," he said. "I think it's inappropriate even to think about it just yet."

TAYVEN AWOKE LATE, to the sound of women's voices singing outside. He got out of bed and went to the ivy-shrouded window. Below, Taropat was stripped to the waist, chopping wood, his hair tied back at his neck. Tayven experienced a brief twitch of grief. He felt he'd let Khaster go somehow, as if he'd finished their relationship voluntarily and it had been a terrible mistake. He had put the mark of death on their friendship the moment they'd set foot in Cos.

Taropat put down his ax and straightened up to greet two females who were walking into the glade: a red-haired woman and a boyish girl. Forest witches?

Tayven dressed himself and went downstairs. By this time, Taropat had installed his guests at the kitchen table and was serving them breakfast. The aroma of sizzling bacon and freshly cooked bread made Tayven ravenous.

"Since when did you become such a good cook?" he asked lightly as he entered the room.

"A hobby of my predecessor," Taropat replied. "I have the time to do it now."

"And does so splendidly," said the red-haired woman. "You must be Tayven Hirantel."

"Yes."

"This is Sinaclara," Taropat said. He indicated the girl. "And this is Nip. Perhaps Shan told you about them."

"He did." Tayven gave Sinaclara a significant glance, but she did not react.

"News travels fast in the forest," she said. "I wanted to meet you."

"How's Shan?" Nip asked.

"He's fine," Tayven answered. "Quite the gentleman of the court. From what he told me of himself, I imagine he's changed a lot since he left here."

"He was given a firm foundation," Sinaclara said.

Quite soon, it became clear to Tayven that Sinaclara was there for rather more than social reasons, while Nip had only tagged along because she wanted to hear about Shan. Taropat was polite yet guarded, clearly waiting, and on the alert, for Sinaclara's true business to be revealed. After they had finished eating, during which the conversation was spikily tense, Sinaclara lost no time in coming to the point. "What will you do now, Taropat? Tayven is here for a reason, of course, and Shan will have sent him."

Tayven fully expected Taropat to evade the answer, but he spoke openly. "We are going to Recolletine in Magravandias."

"Good," said Sinaclara. "I'm glad events are moving along. You will seek the Crown there, naturally."

"We shall endeavor to complete the seven lakes quest and see what happens," Taropat said. "As to whether mythical artifacts are involved or not, we'll have to see."

"It is not a myth, Taropat," said Sinaclara firmly. "The Crown is real and will be bestowed upon the right person."

"The king," said Taropat. "And who is king?"

For the first time, Sinaclara hesitated. "There will be one," she said.

"I've a feeling you already know who it is," Tayven said, looking her directly in the eye. "Or at least have your own hopes in the matter."

Sinaclara shrugged. "It is not important, as yet. Tell me what has happened in Cos. I have heard rumors, picked up images."

Tayven related what he knew.

"This is wonderful news," Sinaclara said.

Tayven and Taropat exchanged a glance, and Taropat shook his head slightly to indicate he had no idea why she'd think that.

"Really?" Tayven said. "Most people think otherwise."

"But it shows the Dragon Lord is becoming what he should be," she said. "The events in Caradore worked."

"What events?" Taropat asked sharply.

"Your brother knows," Sinaclara said, "but has obviously been bound to silence. That is for the best. He would probably tell you about it, Taropat, if you asked him."

"What events?" Taropat repeated.

"Valraven went back to Old Caradore," Sinaclara said. "He woke the Dragon Queen. In some part, his heritage had been restored to him."

"That is impossible," Taropat said.

"It happened," Sinaclara said. "The empress Tatrini instigated it. She has her own plans for the future."

"Why haven't you told me of this before?" Taropat demanded. "How long have you known?"

"A short while," she said. "I haven't had time to come over and speak with you personally about it."

"What are the implications?"

"It is perhaps the first move in a great change. Caradore is precious to the empire and has been kept in chains too long. Now, a few of those chains have been loosened. Valraven waits, as do we all, for the time to act."

"This is not good news," Taropat said. "He will not want what any of us want. I'd prefer to have him merely as a component of Leonid's military. It will not help us if Palindrake acts independently. He is a slur upon his family's heritage."

"He is married to Leonid's daughter," Sinaclara said. "Perhaps this helps you work out the connections."

"Does he know of the Crown? If he does, he'll want it."

"I don't think so," Sinaclara said.

"Then we must act quickly," Tayven said. He felt as if Sinaclara had kicked him in the face. The information she'd revealed suddenly made sense of many things, not least his own feelings since meeting the Dragon Lord in Cos. Palindrake *had* changed, then.

"Didn't you know any of this?" Taropat asked, glancing at Tayven speculatively.

"I heard in Akahana that he married Princess Varencienne a few years ago," Tayven answered as lightly as he could. "It was a political marriage, I believe. At the time, it seemed of little consequence."

"It is of consequence," Sinaclara said. "I have no doubt the empress arranged it."

Taropat shook his head, smiling grimly. "So, he married again. I wonder what his lovely sister thinks of that. The princess must be a feisty creature to survive the wedding."

"Quite," said Sinaclara. "As she's her mother's daughter, I imagine she has her own agenda too." She leaned forward over the table. "You must secure the Crown as soon as you can. When you have it, bring it to me."

"Why?" Taropat asked.

"Because, one day, I shall crown the true king," she answered simply. "It is my destiny."

There was a moment's silence.

"Anyway," Sinaclara continued. "It must be safely hidden and where better than here in Breeland. I will be its custodian until the correct time. The forest itself will hide and protect the Crown."

"That makes sense," Taropat said, a remark that surprised Tayven.

"I am relieved you agree," Sinaclara said dryly. "Now, I wish to speak to you concerning a private matter." She glanced at Tayven and Nip. "Would you excuse us?"

Outside, Tayven asked the girl. "What's all that about?"

She merely rolled her eyes. "Don't ask. They'll probably never tell us. It's just their way." She paused, then said, "I miss Shan. Don't suppose I'll ever see him again."

"You don't know that," Tayven said. "I never thought I'd see . . . Taropat again either."

Nip gazed at him shrewdly. "Shan told me about you."

He grimaced. "A common feature of my life."

"You look a bit like him."

"I've been told."

"Fancy a walk?"

"Might as well." They went together into the forest. Shan had lived here, in close proximity to Taropat every day. Tayven felt a barb in his heart. Jealousy.

Later, after the women had gone, Tayven said to Taropat, "What did you talk about?"

Taropat shrugged. "She had advice about our quest, that's all. She likes to interfere."

"Do you trust her? Shan told me of your difficulties with her."

"Whatever my personal feelings, she is part of the web," Taropat said. "And therefore part of all that we do. Before we leave, I must also speak to Thremius. What I have heard today worries me."

"If we have the Crown, be it knowledge, power or physical artifact, we will have the upper hand," Tayven said.

"Mmm," murmured Taropat. "I am concerned about Palindrake, though. The thought of having to compete with him for the artifact is not a happy one. I don't want a confrontation."

"Oh, don't worry," Tayven said airily. "Palindrake is ultimately nothing, a lackey to the empire. Tatrini is playing with him, trying to woo him away from Gastern. If he falls for that, he's more stupid than I thought." He did not believe a word of what he'd said.

"Even the strongest of men can be rendered witless and stupid when a particularly luscious carrot is dangled before them," Taropat said grimly, "namely the carrot of power, or the promise of it."

"Perhaps, although despite my feelings toward Palindrake, I always thought him above such shenanigans."

Taropat glanced at him sharply. "Don't try to find anything good in that man. Remember, he could have saved you in Cos. He is a monster, Bayard's creature."

Tayven sighed. "Who can tell what really takes place in a human mind or heart? We shouldn't even bother trying to guess, but just get on with what we have to do."

Taropat became very still for a moment, then he spoke. "We are doing the right thing. I can feel it. We can make a difference."

"After all this time, we've reached a place," Tayven said, "a strange and wondrous place. It began in the Sink of Magrast, the lowest of places, the primordial slime. We have evolved out of it."

"But we must guard against arrogance, against pride."

"Such things, in moderation, can be strengths. They give courage and spirit."

"They can be weaknesses too. Remember, it was you who told me to dance on both sides of the coin."

MERLAN WAS WALKING by the Temple of Purryah in the early evening, and was compelled to enter the outer shrine. The wind had changed direction, and blew warm and scented from the sea. It was bringing something to Akahana, Something important. Merlan's heart was filled with a strange melancholy; the sunset itself moved him to tears. Image, thoughts and emotions from the past pressed down upon him, making him face things he'd buried deep. He had to escape the heaviness in the air and the temple promised a tranquil sanctuary.

There were no priestesses in the shrine, so Merlan knelt before the cult statue of the goddess, his mind too full of thoughts to form a coherent petition. He knew that his brother had arrived in Akahana. Had he and Tayven resumed their relationship? He dreaded meeting Khaster, or Taropat as he was now called, yet at the same time he yearned for it. Maycarpe had trained him well, and he knew, as well as Tayven did, how to survive in the supple, duplicitous web of cabals that was a network around the world. Yet he had knowledge that not even Tayven had. Maycarpe would never let Tayven know he wanted Valraven Palindrake to be king of Magravandias. Now, Shan would balk against such a suggestion and as for Taropat, his reaction was not difficult to guess. And there was more: knowledge that Merlan had believed he'd take to his grave, for only one person should know it, a person he'd believed to be dead. Palindrake had confessed it to Merlan, perhaps to absolve himself, perhaps to justify himself, but whatever the reason he'd made it clear he wanted no one but Merlan to know it—ever. Merlan didn't know why, but he'd sworn an oath. Yet if he revealed this knowledge, wouldn't it change the way Tayven and Taropat felt about the Dragon Lord? Wouldn't it sway them toward Maycarpe's designs? If it had been anyone else but Palindrake,

Merlan would have revealed what he knew, but he was afraid of the Dragon Lord, sure in his heart that the moment he spoke the truth Valraven would know.

He cast a few grains of incense into a bowl of smoldering charcoals at the feet of the goddess. "Purryah, let your daughter Merytet stand beside me. Guide my tongue, guide my heart." He clasped his hands together and pressed them against his forehead. A rushing sound started up in his ears that resolved itself into the music of many cats purring. His whole body ached with knowledge. He felt he should write to his mother and sisters to tell them Khaster lived, yet if he did that, they would want to see Khaster, and Merlan sensed that was not possible. Was it better to let them continue to believe he was dead? When he saw Khaster again, he wanted to tell him about Pharinet, how she had suffered, how she had been used by the Malagashes. Yet would Pharinet want Khaster to know that? He wanted to tell Khaster about Varencienne, how her marriage to Valraven was loveless, and that she was obsessed by a man she believed to be dead, how Khaster had been her guiding spirit through all that had transpired in Caradore following her wedding. Varencienne, of all of them, would want to know Khaster lived. In Merlan's opinion, she was the only Malagash fit to wield power in the future. The urge to contact her now was overwhelmingly great, not just to be a bearer of news she wanted to hear, but to have an excuse to maintain contact. Merlan had not seen her since the empress Tatrini had persuaded them all to go to Old Caradore and reawaken the Dragon Queen. He'd not dared to return home, even though his mother's plaintive letters tore at his heart.

"Purryah, you told me my brother would return," Merlan murmured, his body rocking upon his heels. "You spoke truly to me. Speak to me now, for I need your guidance."

But for the hum in his ears, the temple was silent. No priestess melted out of the shadows to whisper wisdom to him. Yet, despite this, Merlan did not feel he was alone. An idea came to him, and he was unsure of the motivation behind it. He must not let Khaster go to Magravandias without him. Maycarpe might have his perfect trinity, but Merlan felt there was some unseen factor the governor hadn't thought of. Merlan might not have an archetypal role in what was to come, but he had a purpose. He would insist on his place.

"Thank you," he murmured and got to his feet. On the way from the temple, he made a generous donation to the priest by the door. The old man offered no thanks. His face remained expressionless.

By the time Merlan reached the governmental building, he already knew what he'd find there. Sure enough, a group of people were waiting for him in Maycarpe's sitting room. "We wondered where you'd got to," Maycarpe said, but Merlan did not respond. He was staring at the man sitting across the room, a man who now got to his feet.

"I knew you'd be here," Merlan said, with difficulty. "I have visited the temple of Purryah. She's become something of a goddess of mine."

"Merlan," said the man, a single word full of feeling.

"Khas." Merlan crossed the room and embraced his brother. "I dared not believe it, yet I knew it to be true."

"You must know that in many respects your brother is dead. I am Taropat, Merlan. That is the name you must call me by."

Merlan drew away. "Say what you like. I know what my eyes behold, what my heart feels."

Taropat smiled. "As you will. You look well, brother. You have fulfilled all that potential that smoldered in Magrast."

"I don't know about that," Merlan said. "But I enjoy living here. I have learned much."

"So it would seem." Taropat sat down and gestured for Merlan to sit beside him. It was only then that Merlan became fully aware that Tayven and Shan were also present. Tayven's face was hard, yet Shan had clearly been moved by the Leckery reunion. Even Maycarpe was smiling benignly.

"So the cat goddess spoke to you again," Maycarpe said.

"Not exactly," Merlan answered. "I just sensed that Khas was here." He turned to his brother. "Sorry. Calling you by a different name will take some getting used to."

Taropat shrugged. "Just remember in public, that's all."

"Is this to remain a secret forever?" Merlan asked. "What of our family?"

"I'm not sure," Taropat replied. "My only concern at present is to undertake the quest of the seven lakes. Once this is all resolved, I will make decisions concerning the family."

"I wish I could send at least some word to our mother, let her know even a partial truth."

"She would never keep it to herself, you know she wouldn't."

Merlan nodded. "Still, it seems cruel to keep her in the dark. She's never stopped grieving for you."

"She has to be shielded from certain truths," Taropat said. "Let her keep her dream."

Merlan could not help glancing at Tayven Hirantel. "You are right," he said. He turned to Maycarpe. "Even though you have your trinity now, I want to go with them to Recolletine."

"I am relieved to hear it," Maycarpe said. "The fact is, I need you to go."

Merlan was puzzled, having expected an argument. "Why?"

"As assistant to the governor in Mewt, you can move freely through Magravandian territory. I will furnish you with the relevant papers and seals. The others will pose as your servant and guards."

"You won't have to take part in the actual quest," Tayven said.

"I'm just as capable as you are of visiting ancient sites and meditating there," Merlan said coldly. "It's not that difficult."

"There may be unexpected results," Maycarpe said.

"You trained me," Merlan reminded him.

20

LAKE OF THE RED KNIGHT

THE COMPANY ARRIVED in Magravandias to the soaring
splendors of the terrain in high summer. Shan was awed by the
grandeur of the great roads, with their crennellated guard stations and
the avenues of high poles from which enormous banners flapped, bearing the firedrake crest of the Malagashes.

Merlan, equipped with diplomatic documents, was able to lead the
party across every boundary, every border. They rode the king's
highway to the northwest, Taropat posing as Merlan's clerk, while
Tayven and Shan took the role of security escort. Shan could tell that
both Taropat and Tayven were jittery to be back on Magravandian
soil. What memories this return must evoke in them. As the road
began to climb into the mountains, it skirted the city of Magrast by
twenty or so miles. Looking down, Shan saw its huge, sprawling bulk
below them, the spiky towers of the alchemists' quarter, the great
domes and minarets of Madragore's cathedral. Merlan pointed out the
royal palace, clearly visible in its vast cradle of parkland. "That is
where Varencienne grew up," he said. "The princess, Leonid's only
daughter."

"Now mistress of Caradore," said Taropat with some bitterness. "It's a travesty!"

Shan noticed that Merlan colored a little. "You shouldn't judge her. You don't know her. She's a singular person, different from her kin."

Taropat gave his brother a shrewd glance. "And which part of the body speaks through you now, Merlan?"

"My heart," Merlan answered smoothly. "I know Varencienne quite well. She has done much to heal the hurts of Caradore."

Perhaps that remark was a little pointed. Shan winced inwardly, while Taropat merely looked away. He didn't want to hear it. He wanted Caradore, and all her people, to hurt for eternity.

A day later they had reached the foothills of the mountains. The holiday lodges of noble families were concealed among the huge and ancient trees, their tiered peaked roofs visible through the foliage like enormous widows' caps. Shan had never seen such beautiful scenery. Breeland was green and lush, with spreading fields and haunted forests, but nothing matched the fierce splendor of the raw mountain crags of Magravandias. The greens here were acidic, aching. Water gushed from precipices all around and the air rang with the eerie, mournful cries of wide-winged carrion birds high above. The area seemed to have been designed as a playground for the gods. Natural rock formations looked like ancient temples, while ancient temples looked like natural rock. The wind had made sculptures of the cliffs, which were a warren of caves and precipitous walkways. Shan saw a narrow bridge of rock spanning a great chasm, and Tayven told him it was not man-made. "It was used as a place of worship and sacrifice in antiquity," he said. "People were thrown from it to the sharp scree below. You can still find bones there and artifacts, jewelry and the like."

There was so much to explore. Shan felt the child rise in his soul. He wanted to investigate every feature he saw, but there was no time. This was not a holiday.

The group took lodgings in sheep farms along the way, and after two days were on the road to the lakes. Tayven and Taropat became more jittery, for the group would have to pass very close to Almorante's retreat. Tayven professed he was uneasy because it was possible Almorante might be in residence, but privately Shan wondered whether his jumpiness was caused more by the recollection of what had happened there. As the journey progressed, he'd noticed a sharpness between Taropat and Tayven, emanating mainly from Tayven. He'd mentioned it to Merlan, who'd said, "It's obvious why. Khas won't touch him. Hirantel feels slighted. He needs to be admired and wanted. I'm glad Khas has seen the light."

"He's not Khaster anymore," Shan couldn't help saying. "He's Taropat. You should remember that, Merlan."

"Whatever you say, and whatever happened, he's still my brother," Merlan answered. "He hasn't changed that much."

Shan thought this might be wishful thinking on Merlan's part. Altogether, they were not a convivial company. Shan felt he'd lost the closeness he'd enjoyed with his mentor, because the others were there. Merlan seemed to go out of his way to please his brother, and was almost obsequious, which Shan could tell irritated Taropat, who wanted to be treated as a renowned magus, not as Khaster, the weak Caradorean. Tayven had immersed himself in a waspish gloom, constantly sniping at Taropat and being openly rude to Merlan, who cheerfully encouraged him, obviously taking pleasure in Tayven's discomfort. Shan could feel no purpose behind what they were doing. They were just going through the motions. Surely they should have more of a bond than this? How could they undertake a spiritual quest together? The fire and zeal that Maycarpe had kindled within them at Akahana seemed to have faded away. Shan could not mention it, because he felt the others would simply turn on him. The past lay between them; a stagnant flood of unspoken words and unexpressed feelings.

The first lake, Anterity, lay in full view of Almorante's residence, which perched on the hillside above it. The group had left their horses at a farm some miles to the east, and had made the last stage of the journey on foot. They anticipated that horses would not be able to reach the seventh lake, and their presence made the group more visible. Near Anterity, Tayven went on a scouting foray and reported he could see no sign that the residence was occupied, other than by the couple who looked after it for the prince. Still, it might be seen as suspicious if they were spotted camping out near the lake, as Anterity was part of the estate. They decided to make camp in the woods nearby and would venture out to the lake after sundown.

By the time they'd finished erecting their tents and preparing a meal, it was late afternoon. Taropat sat before their campfire, turning the Dragon's Eye in his hands, making it glitter with red sparks in the flickering light. Maycarpe had thought they would need to use the artifacts during the quest, and had handed the Eye over to Taropat with somber ceremony. "Every site of this nature has a physical guardian," Taropat said, "as well as a spiritual guardian." He looked directly at Tayven. "Did Almorante contact the guardians when you first came here?"

Tayven shrugged. "He didn't attempt to contact any physical guardians, nor spiritual ones, in particular. It was a different system, in which the lakes have particular elemental attributes. Almorante petitioned the elementals of each site to impart its essence to me. He spoke a lot of words, which I think he got out of a book."

"As I thought," said Taropat dryly. "He only skimmed the surface. Our first task is to discover the physical guardian of the site, for only they can direct us to the spirit form. From them, we can learn the lesson of the lake."

"I've never heard of that," Tayven said. "Surely, we have only to concentrate on the aspect of the lake, what it represents? If there is a spirit guardian out there, it will come to us. I'm not sure about there being physical guardians. Who would that be for Anterity? The housekeeper and her husband? Almorante himself?"

"Anterity's attribute is that of the red ray," Taropat said. "It stands for will and drive, for physical strength. We will have to find someone who typifies those things. They might not even know their function. They will live or work in the area, almost be part of the landscape itself."

"Won't this be difficult at night?" Merlan said. "They might not be wandering around after dark."

Taropat smiled patiently. "We have to trust in synchronicity," he said. "Haven't you done that rather a lot already?"

Merlan looked away.

"I have waited for this day a long time," Taropat said softly, and Shan knew he was not referring to himself as Khaster. He shivered involuntarily. Taropat's tone had suggested, or revealed, far more than he knew. It was as if he had known that one day he'd return to Recolletine. A wave of paranoia swept through Shan's body. Could it have been more than coincidence that he'd been sent to Mewt and had there met up with Merlan, Maycarpe and Tayven? Was it possible that the magical training he'd had through Taropat had led always to this point? Shan glanced at Taropat who sat easily in the firelight, gazing meditatively at the artifact in his hands. Should I trust this man at all? Shan wondered. Has he used me all along? I don't know him, not really.

It was clear that Taropat knew a lot about the lakes, yet in the story he'd told of his life as Khaster, it was clear that then he'd known nothing. So he must have researched it since. Why? Had Sinaclara given him the information? He also seemed quite aware of the power of the Dragon's Eye, an artifact he appeared to have had no knowledge of before. It was possible, of course, that this was knowledge bequeathed by the original Taropat, but still Shan felt uneasy.

I must watch him, he thought, watch him carefully.

The sunset that night was extraordinarily bloody, the sky daubed with a hectic palate of crimsons and scarlets, while the sun itself was a bloated red globe, too heavy to hang in the sky. Shan saw this as an omen for what was to come. His mouth felt dry and he was aware of a slight queasiness in his stomach. If he really was the warrior of the company, then, of all the lakes, Anterity was the most important to him. Red was the color of the warrior, the color of war itself.

A single light burned in a ground-floor window of Almorante's lodge, but otherwise the landscape felt empty of human presences. Shan was acutely aware of the immensity of the mountains around them. The land seemed to thrum with energy, as if it was barely contained by the huge forests, ancient rock and undulating hillsides. Perhaps what they planned to do that night would unleash that slumbering power.

Once it was truly dark, the group emerged from their hiding

place. As soon as they left the cover of the trees, they could hear the faint hissing and bubbling that was Anterity's hot springs.

"There's no one here," Tayven said, rubbing his arms. "There was never anyone here."

Taropat did not reply. He went to stand at the edge of the lake, where the mud was red and sucking. Toads croaked softly but could not be seen.

Shan glanced up at the Retreat and shivered. The past seemed close that night. Perhaps, in the upper rooms, ghosts walked. Taropat must feel something, whatever he'd become or learned. Yet he seemed detached, totally in control of himself. Shan considered that Taropat was becoming more like Lord Maycarpe, which perhaps was due to his handling the Dragon's Eye. But was anyone else sharing these doubts? Shan was still wary of Tayven, but perhaps Taropat's own brother could shed some light on the situation. Shan edged close to him and spoke in a whisper. "Merlan, is it possible Maycarpe has been in touch with Taropat for some time without you knowing?"

Merlan glanced at him sharply and hissed, "No! What makes you think that?"

Shan shrugged, murmured, "I don't know. I just get the impression our quest here has been under consideration for a long time."

Merlan frowned. "I don't understand what you're getting at."

"Taropat knows so much about what we're supposed to do. Did he have time in Akahana to be so thoroughly taught in the subject?"

Merlan looked slightly uncomfortable. He considered for a while, then whispered, "No, it's not possible. If Maycarpe knew my brother was alive, he'd have told me."

Privately, Shan wondered about that.

Taropat's voice summoned them back to the task ahead. "Close your eyes, all of you," he said. "Forget the building above us, for whoever is there will not, cannot, see us. You must apply yourselves totally to what we must do."

Shan closed his eyes and, rather than being immersed immediately in an inner landscape, as he was used to, became more aware of their physical surroundings. Now, they were vulnerable. Anything could creep up to them undetected.

"We must conjure the spiritual landscape of Anterity," Taropat said. "We need no invocations for this, no words. Imagine the lake as you last saw it, steam rising from it to the stars. You can smell sulphur. See the rocks rearing up from the water, the spears of reeds. Now, I want you to imagine it all turning to metal. The reeds are twisted spars of rusty iron. The lake is mercury, the rocks are impenetrable lead. Everything is hot and tinged with red. Concentrate on this image."

Shan found it easy to visualize this scene. It was almost as if this was the way the landscape wished to be viewed. The island in the middle of the lake was a forest of rusting metal rods, contorted and twisted, encrusted with strange mineral growths. He felt that someone was watching him from there.

After only a few minutes, Taropat bid them all open their eyes again. The landscape appeared slightly different to Shan now, as if a phantom of the imagined scene was laid over it. Taropat stared at the island, his eyes narrow.

"There is no one here," Tayven said again. "This is not the right way."

Taropat ignored him and set off along the lake shore. Merlan and Shan exchanged a glance and then followed him. Uttering another disparaging remark, Tayven went after them.

A thick forest of thorny shrubs and trees obscured the left bank of the lake, but there were animal trails through them, which if you didn't mind being tugged at by thorns could be carefully negotiated. Taropat strode into the scrub with apparent determination. He moved through the spiky branches with ease, while his companions constantly had to untangle themselves. After only a few minutes, Shan's hands and face were smarting from a dozen scratches. "What is the point of this?" Tayven hissed to Shan. "He doesn't know what he's doing."

Like Taropat, Shan thought it best to ignore Tayven's comments. Perhaps it was part of Tayven's role in the group to be the dissenter, the doubter. Although Shan himself had doubts, they were certainly not about Taropat's ability to guide them. On the contrary, Taropat seemed almost too adept at that. Shan wished he had the courage, like Tayven, to voice his suspicions. If this cowardice haunted his heart, how could he ever hope to be a true warrior?

Merlan was ahead of Shan, but now he paused, his head to one side. "What's that noise?" Taropat had disappeared around a bend in the narrow path.

Shan and Tayven stopped walking. Shan heard a rhythmic low ringing sound, as of metal being beaten. He shook his head. "It sounds like a hammer," he said. "A smith's hammer."

They continued along the path and presently emerged into a small clearing. Here, there was a rough shed with a lean-to, where a furnace roared. Before it, as Shan had guessed, a big man stood beating a metal bar with a hammer.

"This was not here before," Tayven said. "I'm sure it wasn't."

"How could you tell?" Merlan asked. "Did you explore all these woods before? This place must be fairly hidden from view."

"I would have heard it," Tayven said. "Surely?"

Taropat stood with folded arms, watching the smith at work. The big man did not cease his labor or even look up. He exuded an air of wishing to be left alone. Wouldn't he think it strange, if not sinister, four men coming upon him at night? Yet he gave no sign of being discomforted. Shan imagined he was thinking that if he ignored the interlopers for long enough, they'd just go away. The noise of the hammer was deafening. Shan's head became filled with it, until he could hardly bear it. He wanted to hit something. The sound made him angry. The sight of the smith's hostile face made him angry. Here was a man who forged weapons for the empire. He had to. Didn't he live and work on Almorante's land? Perhaps he had even fashioned the weapons that had killed the villagers of Holme. A spurt of rage flowed through Shan's heart. I would like to kill that man, he thought, and the intention to take revenge was as strong and focused as the flames of the forge fire. As quickly as it came, the rage subsided, but the intensity of the feeling shocked Shan. It must be the influence of the spirit of Anterity. He must not let such feelings take hold of him, otherwise he would be no better than the Magravandians themselves.

Eventually the smith ceased his work long enough to wipe sweat from his brow, and in the silence Taropat said, "Sir, may I speak with you?"

The smith looked directly at him and grunted in a surly manner.

"We are investigating the seven lakes and their legends," Taropat said, clearly taking the grunt for assent. "You may be able to help us, seeing as you live and work so close to Anterity. I am prepared to pay for any information you may give us."

The smith continued to examine Taropat for some moments, then cast his eyes over the others. "This is Prince Almorante's land," he said at last.

"We are aware of that, as we are known to his highness," Taropat said. "I have stayed here before in the Retreat. It is a beautiful spot."

"Strange time to be doing your investigating," said the smith and beat at the anvil a few more times, during which Taropat could not reply, for he would not be heard.

When he was able, Taropat said, "I could say it is a strange time for a man to be working at his forge. Like you, we see all times of day as equally useful for both labor and investigation. We get more of a feel of the landscape at night."

"It comes into itself at night," said the smith.

Taropat took his purse from his belt and shook out what to Shan looked like an inordinately generous amount of coins, which he offered to the smith. "For your time," said Taropat. "What can you tell us of Lake Anterity?"

"Like all places of great age, there are many legends," said the smith, taking the coins and stuffing them into a pocket of his leather apron. "Some of them were invented solely to scare children, others are older."

"It is the older ones we are interested in," said Taropat.

The smith nodded and bade his visitors be seated on the ground. He himself sat on a great round stone near the forge fire. He folded his thick arms and began: "It is said that in olden days, there was a forge on the island, where a fire lizard crafted weapons. These swords and spears were magical, and whoever bore them would kill any foe who attacked him, or indeed anyone he wanted to attack. But the weapons came dear. The lizard would name high prices for its wares, such as a man's firstborn son, or his left hand, or an eye.

"One day, a knight came to the island and the lizard asked him for the soul of his girl-wife. The knight thought this was too high a price, but he had come to the lizard because he was threatened by a very powerful enemy. The knight was in sore need of a magical fire sword to defeat his foe. He was responsible for the people who worked his land and knew he had a duty to defeat the enemy. So, after some minutes of troubled thought, he agreed to the lizard's price and stood watching as the creature made the weapon. It was a beautiful sword, shining like the setting sun with blood red rays. The lizard held it out, pommel first, to the knight and said, 'Now, my lord, you must make the oath of payment.' The knight took the sword and held it in his hand. He could feel its power coursing up his arm. He thought of his enemy and smiled. Then he thought of his beautiful girl-wife, and with a great cry, swung the weapon and lopped off the lizard's head.

"Losing no time, the knight took the lizard's head to a sorcerer, who encased it in magical ice for him. So the lizard was no more.

"Before he went away to deal with his enemy, the knight hid the head away in a high room in his castle, which he secured with seven locked doors and seven staircases. His wife he bade keep away from that part of the castle, but she was a curious girl and could not resist finding out what her husband guarded so carefully. After the knight and his company had ridden out to quash the enemy, the girl crept into the forbidden area. She used pins from her pale hair to pick the locks and stole up the staircases. At the top, she came upon a bare room, where, within a niche in the wall, she came upon the block of ice. Her beauty was so great that the ice melted at once and the lizard head spoke to her. It begged her to return it to the island of Anterity, and that if she did so, it would grant her never-fading beauty. The girl agreed readily, and took up the lizard's head, which she hid beneath her shawl. She scurried out to the stables and demanded her horse be made ready for her. Then, she rode madly away, toward the north.

"Once back at the island, the lizard head asked to be placed next to its body, which still lay beside its forge. At once, the head and body rejoined, and the lizard was whole. It turned to the girl and licked her with its long hot tongue. It turned her soft flesh to metal, preserving her youthful beauty for eternity. But she could not speak, nor move. She was a statue of iron.

"The knight returned from his battle victorious to find both his wife and the lizard head gone. He rushed to the lake, but there were no boats to cross. He could see his wife standing on the edge of the island, still as death. Crying out in horror, he attempted to wade and swim through the lake to save her, but his armor was too heavy and he drowned. Some say he can still be seen on certain nights. His armor was stained red by the waters of the lake."

There was a moment's silence once the smith finished speaking. Perhaps unnerved by the apparent lack of response, he said, "That is one legend of many. Do you want more?"

Taropat shook his head. "That was the one we wished to hear." He stood up. "May we go to the island?"

"There are no boats save mine," said the smith. "You may use it, gladly, but I must warn you it is considered bad luck to walk the ground there. The lizard is wary of visitors now, and justifiably so. If you believe in such nonsense, of course."

"We are fully prepared for the risks," said Taropat. "And we intend to respect the lizard's domain, whether he still haunts it or not."

"I can see that," said the smith curtly and jerked his head to the left. "The boat's moored under that twiggy willow. Help yourself."

Once they were in the boat, Taropat took up the oars. "You see," he said to Tayven, with a hint of smugness. "We found the guardian. Now we are on our way to visit the spirit of the place, which appears to be a salamander."

Tayven nodded, his mouth pulled into a grudging smile. "Your methods are odd, but I admit that if Anterity should have a guardian, a smith would be the ideal archetype for it. I'll keep an open mind about the rest."

"Did Almorante know none of this?" Merlan asked. "Surely these legends are widely known?"

"When Almorante attempted his invocations here, he used the elemental correspondence system rather than that of the color rays," Tayven said. "He's too much the product of the empire's dogma. To him, this was the lake of metal, rather than fire. But, as denizens of the forge, he did address the elemental beings of fire, which of course are salamanders. So the smith's story does make sense. I've just never heard it before. Part of me believes it didn't actually exist before tonight."

"He might well have made up the story just to take my money," said Taropat, "but that really doesn't matter. We have to trust in coincidence. That legend, real or not, was the first thing the smith told us and it fits neatly into our task."

While the others discussed the smith and his story, Shan stared at the island. He closed his eyes briefly and an image came to him of a Red Knight standing on the shore, leaning on a flaming sword. He opened his eyes quickly, but the island was dark and empty. Was the red knight an aspect of himself? The knight of the legend had learned, bitterly, that might was not enough, yet what more than might did Shan have? He had been trained magically to a degree, but it had been made clear to him that his was not the role of the mystic. He was aware of the beat of blood in his veins, the anger that simmered beneath the surface. There was no Red Knight. The smith had made the story up to part gullible Taropat from his money. If the lesson of Anterity was connected with fire and war, why didn't they just set fire to Almorante's retreat? That would be both a magical act, in that it would reflect their true intentions, and also an act of defiance.

"We shouldn't go to the island," he said quietly.

The silence that followed this statement made him realize he could not have spoken as softly as he'd intended.

"What is it, Shan?" Taropat asked, the oars motionless in his hands.

Shan shook his head. "We should take action. There's nothing to be gained from quiet meditation. We should burn the Retreat."

He noticed Taropat exchange a glance with Merlan, who shrugged. "We are not here to commit arson but to undergo a spiritual quest," Taropat said, "attractive though the idea of arson may be."

Shan found himself on his feet. His body was acting beyond his volition. "Go back!" he cried. "Row to the shore. We must avenge the death of Holme! The warmonger should be gutted with his own creations!"

"Sit down," Taropat said calmly. "You are rocking the boat."

A part of Shan could only watch with dismal horror as another, alien part of himself lunged toward Taropat, intent on causing pain.

"Enough!" Taropat yelled before Shan touched him. "Get a grip of yourself, Shan."

Shan froze.

"It's Anterity," Tayven murmured. "It's affecting him."

"No excuse," Taropat declared. "Shan, you are no longer a fretful child. Act your age. If you don't, I might as well throw you overboard and leave you to drown in the lake. What you're feeling now is nothing compared with what is to come. Remember the warrior is useless if he is ruled by his base emotions."

Shan's anger subsided and he felt the heat of embarrassment rise up his face. "I'm sorry," he said, shaking his head. "Something . . . something happened . . ."

"You were weak," Taropat snapped. "Have you learned nothing from me?"

"Don't be harsh on him," Tayven said. "It's obvious Anterity would affect Shan the most. Also, he has a point about the smith. He probably does make weapons for Almorante."

"Almorante did not sack Holme," Taropat said. "Shan knows that. He's just being stupid."

Tayven shook his head, but did not pursue the argument. Shan sat with lowered head, filled with shame. He was filled with conflicting thoughts and feelings. Some part of him still trusted Taropat, but at that moment he could only think of Sinaclara. He thought he'd failed her in some way. Yet, if she was here, she'd have been aware, as Tayven was, of the hurt that still lingered inside him over the loss of his family. Taropat wouldn't even consider that. Sympathy was beyond him.

Between them, the company pulled the boat onto the shore of the island. It seemed that nobody had trodden there for many years.

Birds nesting in the undergrowth woke up and uttered eerie cries as the party intruded into their domain, but there were no lizards to be seen. Taropat led them to the center of the island, and here they found a cube of uncorroded metal, about a foot square, set into the ground. "Is this all that remains of the salamander's forge, I wonder?" murmured Taropat.

Shan shivered. He felt that their presence was unwelcome to the guardian of the site, but that his personal presence was especially so, and not just to the guardian.

"We must make a gift to the guardian," Taropat said. "Tayven, your knife, if you please. The only fitting boon here is blood."

Merlan grinned grimly at Shan. "Remember the last time, at Maycarpe's?"

"The beginning of it all," Shan replied, then paused and added, "or was it?" He forced himself to look at Taropat, who stared back blandly and took the knife from Tayven.

As Taropat cut himself and let the blood drip onto the metal cube, he intoned, "Guardian of Anterity, we come to you in trust and peace. Accept our offerings and give to us the knowledge of this site." He passed the knife to Tayven, who made the offerings and then passed the blade to Shan.

Shan stared at the knife for a moment, fully aware of what he must do. He saw himself applying the blade to his forearm, the blood dripping down. But then, another image came to him. Before he was fully aware of his actions, he had torn open the front of his shirt and slashed his own chest, a gash some six inches long. When he realized what he'd done, he uttered a groaning sob. Tayven and Merlan looked on in astonishment, but Taropat only raised a hand and shook his head, clearly to stem any remarks.

"Give the knife to Merlan, Shan," he said.

Shan was close to weeping. What was happening to him? It was as if some war spirit of the site possessed him and he was too disorientated to take control of it.

Once Merlan had made the offering, Taropat said, "Now, we must meditate. Invite the guardian to you and ask for his knowledge."

As he composed himself cross-legged in the circle of his companions, Shan felt as if his spirit was leaving his body. Reality was fraying all around him. He closed his eyes and became acutely conscious of the sting of the wound on his chest. The Red Knight stood just beyond their circle, leaning on the flaming sword. The knight neither spoke nor moved, and his face was hidden by his helm, which was fashioned in the semblance of a firedrake. The sword exuded a thick smoke, which eventually obscured the image of the man. Gradually, it condensed into the form of a tall, yet stooped quasi-human lizard. Like the smith beside the lake, it wore a long leather apron, and in its taloned scaly fingers it held a hammer. The creature fixed Shan with one of its blazing yellow eyes and its tongue flicked out, black, and dripping a steaming ichor. In his mind, Shan spoke to this vision. He tried to show it his heart, his true intention. He was not like the Red Knight. He was willing to pay the price to conquer *his* enemies. The lizard hissed and held out his hands, as if to offer something. The hammer it held had transformed into a flaming brand. Almost immediately, Shan's body was filled with a zinging sensation, which made him gasp aloud. He was the Red Knight, clad in burning armor. He was rampaging across a field of slaughter striking out with a sword that dripped gore. Magravandian soldiers fell into the bloody mud around him. He hacked off limbs, severed heads, all the while screaming with rage and lust. In his head rang the distant memories of the screams of the people of Holme. He had become their voice: a single shriek of vengeance. Then, in an instant, all went calm. He found himself back on the island, standing before a forge, where the lizard smith worked at the bellows. "Boy, you must temper the discord within you," it hissed. "For if you do not, you can never be the true warrior and overcome those who would be the master race. Resentment and vengeance makes nothing but slaves."

Shan dropped to his knees before the lizard. His body was still encased in the red armor and it was colored by blood, not rust. "Give me the lesson of the lake," he said. "Help me, wise one."

The lizard pulled a sword from the forge fire. Its blade glowed like a living ruby. Then, with a hiss, the creature sprang forward. Shan saw the sword swooping toward him, then his vision reeled as if he was flying through the air. The sky spun around him. He saw the trees upside down, the lake below. There was the island, where a headless body lay beside the forge. He uttered a scream of terror, then again everything became still. The armor lying below by the forge was empty. There was no body in it. He did not possess a corporeal form now. All that remained was his essence, the will to triumph and overcome the injustice of the Magravandian empire, without anger or bitterness, but with courage, affirmation and action. He remembered the visions he'd experienced after the festival of Aya'even. Affirm, Sinaclara had told him, and now he could.

He was kneeling naked before the lizard smith. The lizard held out a flaming brand to him and he took it. Its fire filled his mind.

Shan could not help but open his eyes and saw his companions staring at him in the clear starlight.

"Speak," said Taropat. "What happened?"

"You've been out for some minutes," Merlan said. "Are you all right?"

Shan nodded. "Yes. Some minutes, you say? It felt like seconds. I saw the knight, and then the salamander came to me." He told them all he'd seen. "I have the knowledge now. It's incredible. I feel it. Did we all experience that?"

"No," said Taropat. "The guardian chose only to communicate with you. What did you feel?"

"The lesson of Anterity is that I have a body, but I am not my body. Strength of will is not physical but also mental. Anterity is drive and determination. I think the flaming brand symbolizes Anterity's attribute. The fire is the will, the will to overcome, not to conquer and repeat the cycle of hatred. We shall only triumph if we affirm our own suffering as our responsibility. We will triumph once we can take action and relinquish reaction."

"Correct," said Taropat smiling. "You have learned well, Shan. Through you, we all have the essence of Anterity within us now. Each of the lakes will have a different message, and it may be that only one of us will connect with the individual influences directly." He stood up. "We must get back to our camp now and sleep. The first part of the quest is over."

When they returned to the mainland, they found that the smith had shut up his forge, which stood dark and empty. It looked as if no one had worked there for years, and they left the area quickly.

Back at their camp, Merlan revived their small fire and set about making them some tea. Taropat took out his pipe and settled himself on the ground, contemplating the forest canopy.

"So now you are truly the warrior," Tayven said to Shan.

Shan shrugged. "I'm sure it requires more than that," he said. "I feel as if I've been given a small piece of knowledge, which I have yet to actually practice. Perhaps it will help me fulfill my ultimate potential."

"So speaks the magician's apprentice," Tayven said light-heartedly. "You must also learn not to take everything so seriously." He clasped his knees. "Helayna should come here. I'm sure it would replenish her fire. She favors the aspect of the female warrior."

"She sounds like a fascinating woman," said Shan.

"She is. I hope she's faring well now Ashalan has deserted her. She'll hide her feelings, but I'm sure the way he caved in cut her to the quick."

"Was Ashalan right to do what he did?"

Tayven wrinkled up his nose. "He knew he could no longer fulfill the role he'd started out with. He'd become physically weak, but his mind is still acute and agile. No doubt the role he's now chosen for himself is the best one. No one yet knows which way the cards will fall when Leonid goes."

"Is that imminent, do you think?"

"Not if nature had anything to do with it, I'm sure. But we can all feel the flexing of the dragons' bones. Change is in the air. Who knows what form that will take?"

"Part of it is us here, now," said Taropat, who had apparently been paying attention to their conversation. "The Claw of the dragon is ready to strike, the Eye to see." He turned to Tayven. "What is the shortest time, in your opinion, that we could take to visit all the sites?"

"We could visit the first six in a couple of days," Tayven replied, "if we really pushed ourselves, but it would exhaust us. As for the seventh, who can tell? We don't even know if it's really there. Why?"

"Eat and sleep well tonight, and make the most of it. We must fast for the next couple of days. We must not rest."

"Is that a mandatory aspect of our quest or something you thought up yourself?" Tayven asked.

"You should know," Taropat said stiffly, "that physical deprivation heightens awareness. I'm sure all of you can appreciate how this will be useful."

"Won't we need all our strength for the journey, though?" Shan said. "Going without food or sleep will weaken us."

"You will be surprised what reserves of strength you can find," Taropat answered.

JUST BEFORE DAWN, they struck camp and made haste past Lake Anterity toward their next destination. Looking up, Shan saw the housekeeper of the retreat pegging out washing in the pearly twilight. She must have been up all night. Great sails of sheeting hung listlessly from the ranks of lines, for there was no wind. Perhaps the big wash indicated Almorante was coming to stay at his lodge for a while. Shan shuddered. Coincidence would make it so.

It took only an hour to reach the next lake, Oolarn. This, Taropat explained, was the lake of the orange ray, concerned wholly with knowledge, facts and logic, the inquiring mind. "Almorante had it all wrong," he said. "He tried to fit the lakes into the framework of the ancient Magravandian belief system, but really they conform to a more eastern system. I have investigated the subject thoroughly and there's little doubt in my mind that Jessapurian and Mewtish mystics shared their knowledge with early Magravandian mages. In fact, you could say that the whole western system developed from that union."

"The lakes could conform to both systems," Tayven said. "The elemental correspondences work as well."

"But it is not the whole story," Taropat argued, with emphatic hand gestures. "All other correspondences spring from the color energy of each site."

"Are you saying that all the work I did is irrelevant then?" Tayven snapped. "You knew nothing about these sites the last time we came here."

"I don't dismiss your work," Taropat said. "I just know there's more to it than you or Almorante saw."

"Stop bickering," Merlan said. "Look, there is Oolarn."

They had emerged from a forest path into another open hilly area. The lake was larger than Anterity and its placid surface swarmed with water birds. It was cupped on two sides by bare crags tufted with birds' nests. The area was far from being desolate and unpopulated. A small village was situated close to the lake and a network of wooden jetties spread out into it. Boats bobbed alongside them.

"This is the air site," Tayven told Shan and Merlan. "Here, Almorante invoked the sylphs, the air spirits."

"An aspect of mercurial orange," Taropat said.

Shan was feeling extremely hungry by now, but Taropat insisted they should only drink water. "For this to work to best effect, we need to be in an altered state of consciousness," he said. "The physical deprivation will open our minds to possibilities that might otherwise remain hidden."

"He means we will be hallucinating with exhaustion and starvation by the time we drag ourselves to the sixth lake," Tayven said dryly.

"Do you still disagree with this?" Taropat said.

Tayven shook his head. "No, I can see the sense of it. I just hope we're all up to it, that's all."

"Is everyone else comfortable with this procedure?"

Merlan and Shan exchanged a glance, then gave their assent. Shan felt they had little choice in the matter.

"Now, before we go any further, we must conjure the mystical landscape of Oolarn," Taropat said. "Sit down, all of you. Close your eyes. Breathe deep."

They sat down in a field of feathery grasses that swept down to the lakeside. The visualized scenery was in fact not that different from the reality. Taropat described high, windswept crags, where the air was in constant motion. Tall narrow temples were surrounded by mist and winged bird-people swept from pinnacle to pinnacle. Strangely,

Shan found vaguely erotic images coming to him. He visualized beautiful swooping women, with feathered breasts and yellow, predator's eyes. The image aroused him. When he opened his eyes, he almost expected still to see winged women skimming the surface of the lake and felt slightly guilty for his lascivious thoughts. He wondered whether the lake would have special significance for someone else in the group, as Anterity had done for him, but no one seemed to have picked up anything of significance. Shan did not mention his bird women. No doubt Taropat would scold him for being base and immature, and remind him that, as the warrior of the group, he was supposed to represent the epitome of chivalric valor.

As they walked toward the village, Merlan said, "Who, of all these people, will be the physical guardian of this site? Do you think they have some kind of leader we could approach?"

"It need not be so obvious a person," Taropat said. He glanced at Shan. "Shan, first words that come into your head. A person. Who?"

"Bird woman," blurted Shan, before he could stop himself.

"Bird woman?" said Merlan.

"That's what we must look out for, then," said Taropat.

They ventured into the village, where the smell of baking bread and cooking fish hung tantalizingly on the air. Shan's stomach growled. In the center of the village was a small square, dominated by the rough carving of a woman with wings. "There she is!" Shan said, pointing.

"An angel," Merlan said.

Taropat shook his head. "No, I don't think so. It will be some kind of local spirit or goddess."

"If that's the physical guardian, we'll have trouble communicating," Tayven said.

Taropat laughed and strode forward, the others following. On the far side of the monument, an old woman was hunched on the ground. Her back was weighed down by an astounding cargo: an immense wicker basket that towered over her head. It was filled with twittering, fluttering birds. Strange metallic instruments hung from the basket. Some of them appeared to be only scraps of rubbish, while others looked like astronomical tools or instruments of measurement. A tangle of nets hung from the woman's skirts.

"Here is our bird woman," Taropat said.

The old woman looked up at them, one eye screwed tightly shut. "Who are you?" she demanded. "Why are you looking at me?"

"We were admiring your merchandise," Taropat said.

"Well why didn't you say so?" the woman retorted. "Do you want a birdie? They're good and cheap. Put one in a cage for your lady love, or roast it on a spit."

"I'll pay for a bird or two," said Taropat, opening his purse.

"Wise man indeed," said the bird woman. "One for spitting, one for singing. That will be ten sickins."

"We are scholars," Taropat said, counting out the coins, "studying all the ancient myths of the lakes and their alchemy. I expect you know many stories about Oolarn. Can you tell us the greatest legend of the lake?"

The old woman uttered an outraged snort. "Stories? Stories? Do you think I'm a fire-sitter, then, with nothing better to do? I've been up since yesterday netting flitters. Stories indeed."

"So you know none?" said Taropat.

"I know everything there is to know about this place," said the old woman. "The people are numbskulls, too superstitious. They won't go out after dark for fear of the Pecker. Afraid he'll get them, see, peck through their eyes. I don't pay attention to rubbish like that. I've walked the shores of Oolarn and scrabbled through her mountains all my life. I've stayed on the cliffs at night. I watch everything, know everything. Never seen a Pecker."

"The Pecker," said Taropat, "is that a bird spirit?"

"No, of course he isn't. He's a rat or a dog, isn't he! Fool! What'd you think?"

Shan could see that Taropat was having difficulty restraining his amusement, although it was tinged with impatience. "Where is he reputed to roam, madam? Is there any particular area seen as his domain?"

"Have you no eyes to see?" snapped the bird woman, shaking

an arm in the direction of the cliffs behind her. All the birds in her cage began to cheep and flutter in agitation. "See that big tree up there? That's where they say he lives. It's a white tree. They say it's sacred. It used to be black but the woodpecker pecked it white. That's what they say. His name is Grotbeak."

"Thank you," said Taropat, "you've been most helpful." He began to walk away, but the old woman screeched after him.

"You've not taken your birds, mister. Are you so crazed as to throw your money away?"

"Keep the birds," Taropat said. "Sell them again. Accept it as a gift."

"Mooncalf!" spat the woman. "You want to visit old Grotbeak without a gift? Are you mad?" With astonishingly quick and contorted movements, she reached up behind her head with both hands, opened a small gate in the cage and plucked out a pair of birds with soft gray plumage and orange eyes. These she deftly packed into one of her nets and handed them to Taropat.

"I thought you said you didn't believe in Pecker," he said, smiling.

"I don't," said the woman, "but I respect him. Only a fool wouldn't. You have a beautiful face, mister. I'd hate to think of it pecked away."

Taropat bowed. "You flatter me with your concern, madam."

The old woman fixed the group with a beady stare. "Don't let your precious birds fly away before the job is done," she said. "Fear will lend them wings, you know. Soothe them as you use them, eh?"

"We shall bear your advice in mind," Taropat said and gestured for the others to follow him from the square.

Once they reached the sacred tree, they found it was indeed white, as if at some time all its bark had been peeled away. Its leaves were leathery and grayish green. Taropat bid everyone sit around it. "No blood here," he said, "we have the gift already." He opened the net and shook out the birds so that they swooped drunkenly up into the branches of the tree, uttering high-pitched screams. "Accept our gift, Grotbeak," he said. "Grant us the knowledge of Oolarn."

As before, the group sat and mediated for ten minutes or so, then
Taropat called them back to normal consciousness. "Well?" he said.
"Who has anything to report?"

"I saw him," said Merlan. "A strange creature, a bird man with
a human face but for a great yellow beak. He had no hair on his head
but a woodpecker's crest."

"I saw that too!" Shan interrupted. "Well, very similar, sort of."
He neglected to mention the harem of bare-breasted bird women who
had accompanied his vision of Grotbeak. "I had the same sensation
as before too; a sort of tingling, as if something entered me. The
lesson isn't so direct and clear as at Anterity, but I feel Oolarn's lesson
has to do with knowledge, the path of learning."

"When I saw Grotbeak," Tayven said, "he looked similar to how
Merlan and Shan described him, but I picked up a sort of amphibious
aspect to him too. He had a quiver over his shoulder, but it didn't
contain arrows that could wound. I sensed that if he should shoot me,
I would receive wisdom. Once he saw I understood this, he fired an
arrow, which hit me between the eyes. Then I knew that there is no
end to knowledge, and to believe you can know all is folly."

"What about you, Taropat?" Shan asked.

Taropat shrugged. "Grotbeak attempted to attack me, peck out
my eyes. Fortunately, I remembered the Eye of the Dragon and held
it out to him. It pacified him and he filled me with an orange light."
He glanced at Merlan. "I think you have more to say. What is it?"

Merlan shook his head. He looked uncomfortable. "Nothing really. Nothing useful, I'm sure. I just got the feeling that academic
knowledge amounts to nothing. It hasn't done the world any good,
or brought understanding where it is direly needed." He sighed. "The
feelings this inspired in me weren't at all positive. I felt like a selfish
ascetic, whose deluded wisdom has served only to expand my ego
and self-satisfaction."

There was a silence, then Taropat said briskly. "You were faced
with the pure form of your own soul, which resonates strongly with
the orange ray. Your esteem has just taken a knock, that's all."

These words didn't appear to comfort Merlan. Shan couldn't think
of anything to say.

"I shouldn't worry," Tayven said. "The lesson of Oolarn is to accept it is better to learn than to know. Essentially, we are in ignorance. In my vision, I realized how proud I was to believe I had great knowledge, but in effect I know nothing, I am nothing. We can only go forward from this point."

Taropat nodded. "For me, the lesson of Oolarn was the experience of the passion of the red ray tempered by the wisdom of yellow. Now, we must move to the next lake quickly. We should attempt to fit in four sites today. Do you think that's possible, Tayven?"

He nodded. "Yes, possible. I feel our grip on reality will be somewhat tenuous by tonight though."

Shan was surprised that Taropat didn't seem more concerned about his brother. It was clear to Shan that Merlan had been affected greatly by the feelings he'd experienced. Surely they should discuss what had happened more deeply before they continued? But Taropat was already on his feet, arranging his backpack on his shoulders. Shan was also concerned that Taropat had related his own experiences of Oolarn in such a matter-of-fact way. Shan suspected it hadn't affected him that deeply, which seemed strange. Surely Taropat possessed a stronger orange ray aspect than any of the others? Shan thought that he might have used the Eye to prevent the guardian, and thus the knowledge, from penetrating his own heart. Perhaps he placed no importance on the lessons of the lake at all, especially with regard for himself. Shan was again assailed by waves of suspicious paranoia. It was almost as if Taropat was just herding them around to go through the motions. He didn't want self-knowledge from the quest, but in that case, what *did* he want? Shan wanted to air these thoughts to Tayven and Merlan urgently, but how could he get them alone? Uneasiness coursed through him like a fever. He felt torn. Something was wrong and it should be addressed, but what if he was mistaken? Perhaps his doubt was part of the lesson of the quest, and he should cast it away, fix his sights on the goal. The Crown would not be won by a faint heart.

As Shan stood up, he felt slightly dizzy. He also noticed that Merlan had to lean against the tree for some moments. "These meditations seem so simple," he said, "yet I feel they have more impact upon us than we know."

"We are tapping into the energy of these sites," Taropat said. "It flows right into us. The task should not be easy, for then it would be worthless. There must be a cost for the knowledge you gain."

"Yes," said Tayven lightly, yet acidly, "but who is setting the price?" He went to help Shan stand up, ignoring Merlan, who was in more serious need.

Shan had to steel himself not to shake Tayven off. There were too many tensions and undercurrents. No harmony. If he spoke to anyone about his doubts, it would be Merlan, not Tayven.

21

LIONS AND WYRD CHARMERS

THE THIRD LAKE was called Ninatala, which Taropat said
represented the yellow ray of wisdom.

As they trampled the steep narrow path toward it, Tayven said,
"Almorante saw the third lake as fire. It might seem odd because most
people associate fire with the color red, but in Almorante's system,
Ninatala symbolizes the fire of the sun, the yellow, life-giving fire."

"Red fire and white fire have always been regarded as the magical
flames invoked by magi," Taropat said. "Orange fire is that of the
hearth, the stove. Yellow fire is life itself."

Shan was feeling slightly light-headed and uncertain on his feet
and he sensed Merlan felt the same, although both shrank from com-
plaining out loud. The air seemed thin, which perhaps contributed to
the feeling of weakness. Shan knew he was no feeble, pampered creature. He had survived for weeks in the Forest of the Night, yet after
only a few hours of deprivation, he felt dizzy and tired. He could
only assume the meditations themselves were having a subtle effect
upon him. Tayven and Taropat seemed unaffected. If anything, as the
journey progressed, they appeared to become stronger, more alert.

The group squeezed between a narrow opening in the rock and found themselves on a wide flat plain with the placid expanse of Ninatala before them. Ahead, beyond the lake, green, forested hills rose gently upward, and beyond them the smoky smudges of higher mountains could be seen. Shan turned around and shaded his eyes to survey the scene below, which they'd left behind. The panorama of forests and green hills seemed strangely symmetrical, as if it was some kind of landscaped royal parkland. Sunlight fanned down in broad rays through silver clouds, like the arms of a god, reaching benevolently to bless the earth.

"Beautiful, isn't it?" Taropat said, coming to stand beside his apprentice. "What you're looking at is the landscape of the sun king, the golden lion of the yellow ray. I already sense the sacred beast of this site, and doubt we'll discover anything to contradict that."

"It feels royal," Shan said. "It looks as if someone designed it, yet at the same time it's so wild and untamed."

Taropat laughed. "Many great thinkers have meditated upon that. Adragore the Lame said that because we can observe this wondrous order in the natural world, it proves the existence of gods, divine presences who created such order. He was contradicted by Countess Katarina of Molt, who rather stuffily suggested that if order could be observed in the natural world, it was purely the result of nature's random tendencies. She said that only a deluded fool would take this proof of the existence of divine beings. She accused Adragore of anthropomorphizing the gods."

"You sound like Sinaclara," Shan said, laughing. "But in what way do we make gods like men?"

"She meant that if we attribute the obvious order we perceive in the world to the actions of a god, what we are really doing is attributing our own mental processes and reasoning to that god. She argued that gods, if they existed at all, could not possess any human attributes, otherwise they'd hardly be divine."

"Do you believe that?"

Taropat grinned. "I think her argument was ridiculous. Any priest or sage will tell you that. However, I do believe that the gods cannot exist without us. It is a symbiotic relationship."

Shan was flooded with a warm feeling of tranquillity, which extended toward Taropat. He was himself again. This was how it should be, the close relationship between apprentice and master. The learning, the wonder of it.

Taropat smiled. "This place represents wisdom, but also the yellow ray of divine kingship. It is something we must be aware of if we are to succeed here."

Tayven muscled in between them. "Why is that?" he said. "Surely the Crown itself is more important than the king?"

Taropat moved away a short distance. "This site represents the ideal of when the Crown is manifest into the world. It can be regarded as the divine made physical. If we are to pull the Crown from the etheric realms into reality, then it is vital we succeed here above all other sites."

Tayven made a scornful sound. "That may be so for you, but I can't help thinking that the concept of divine kingship has been the scourge and misery of every empire that's existed. We should be moving away from that, surely?"

Taropat's expression became a pinched mask. "If you knew anything of worth, you would realize that all the divine kings, who have failed to fulfil their potential, have not undergone a quest of the soul such as this."

Tayven nodded slowly, his expression sly. "Ah, so now it becomes clear. You see yourself in that role, don't you? You remember what Almorante once said to you about Caradore, how he'd give it to you. You want to be king, to be emperor! And for this, the rest of us are being dragged behind, starving and exhausted."

Taropat stared at Tayven with an expression that bordered on the purest hatred. He said nothing.

"Don't be absurd, Tayven," Merlan said. "My brother has no desire to be king. Like the rest of us, he merely wants an end to Magravandian oppression."

"And there's quite a lot of that around here at the moment," Tayven snapped.

Taropat took a step toward him, and Tayven backed away. "If you remember, dear Tayven, it was not my idea to come on this quest

at all. Cast your mind back. Recall. *You* came looking for me. You
needed me."

Tayven snorted in contempt, even though Taropat was right.
"That may be so, but that doesn't mean I have to condone the way
you're conducting this show. You haven't let any of us have a say.
If it doesn't come from your balls, you just don't want to know, do
you? You have to be in control. It's that old fear, Khaster. Remember
it. You'd never let me fuck you, would you?"

There was a stunned silence. Shan thought he would die with
embarrassment. Tayven had gone too far. Taropat's face was a red
mask of indignation. Surely, Merlan would go for him? Merlan lifted
an arm, but Taropat acted first. He leapt forward and seized Tayven
by the hair. Shan was sure he could hear Tayven's roots ripping as
Taropat lifted him from the ground with inhuman strength. Tayven
kicked out, uttering a cry of surprise and pain. Taropat thrust his face
so close to Tayven's, Shan thought he was going to take a bite out
of it. "You grubby little whore!" Taropat roared. "You think to question me? Your kind has done nothing but breed corruption in royalty.
I should have let Bayard have his way with you that night in the
Soak. We might all be better off now!"

"Stop this," Shan yelled. "Just stop it!" He tried to wrench Taropat's grip away from Tayven's hair. Taropat turned on him and
snarled, no longer the wise and thoughtful mentor of a few moments
before. Merlan just stood uselessly to the side, as if dazed, his hand
still half raised.

"Taropat, no," Shan managed to say calmly, although he was
afraid of this inhuman rage before him. "This is not the way. Think
of our quest. Please."

Taropat stared at him for a few moments, then dropped Tayven
to the ground. He walked away from them, his hands wound with
long pale strands of hair.

Shan stood awkwardly over Tayven, who sat loose-limbed at his
feet, his face in his hands. "Tayven," he said, glancing to Merlan for
support, finding nothing but confusion. "He didn't mean that. This is
all getting out of hand." Tayven said nothing. His shoulders shook.
Sighing, Shan leaned down to pull Tayven to his feet.

Tayven wrenched himself away and turned savagely on his defender. "You stay out of this. I don't need your pity. The truth is, you wanted Khaster to fuck you too, or maybe he already has."

"What?" Shan was too shocked to remonstrate further. He glanced at Merlan, who shook his head.

"You're pathetic," Tayven snarled. "You're living in a fantasy. Son of a nobleman, are you? I think not. I know what you are, Shan. Taropat told me how he found you."

Shan stared at Tayven in horror.

"Yes, it's the truth, isn't it? You're just a peasant boy. Still, he trained you well. It doesn't surprise me. Khaster wouldn't want some rough little serf in his bed."

"How can you say these things?" Shan said. "What kind of creature are you?"

"I never lie about myself though, do I?" Tayven said, sneering. "My blood is noble, and I warm the beds of princes. You can never have what's mine."

"I don't want it," Shan said.

"You want noble blood, though, don't you?"

"For Madragore's sake, stop it," said Merlan wearily. "Do you want to destroy this quest?"

Tayven got to his feet. "Like I destroyed your brother? Is that what you mean?"

Merlan rubbed his face and rolled his eyes. "Oh, for the love of the flame! You're so selfish and vain. You are not the center of this, and it's certainly not about sex. Is that all you think about? If so, why are you here? Just grow up."

Before Shan could do anything to prevent it, Tayven flew at Merlan, who reeled backward to the ground. Tayven fell upon him, his clawed hands gripping Merlan's throat. He slammed Merlan's head against the unyielding earth. Shan leapt forward and hit Tayven in the face, so hard he had to let go of Merlan. Merlan scrabbled away, holding his throat, coughing. Tayven's body went limp. He lay down, curled up, in the crushed grass. The only sound was that of panting breath. Shan felt dazed, as if this wasn't really happening. "What's happening to us?" he cried. "This quest is not about *any* of us and what we want."

He heard Taropat say softly, "Oh, but it is, Shan, it is."

Shan turned round to question this, but there was no sign of Taropat. He'd vanished.

They waited in numb silence for hours for Taropat to return, but as dusk drew in Shan knew he would have to take control and suggested they make camp. Tayven and Merlan were both in a bad state. Merlan shivered uncontrollably, while Tayven continued to lie listlessly on the ground. Shan went off in search of food, despite Taropat's directive they should not eat, and found some small hard apples in a wild lakeside orchard. As he gathered them, he realized the others would never regard him in the same way again. He'd been revealed for what he was: a peasant. Shame stung his heart. Still, despite his humble origins, he at least was in control of himself. That should count for something.

Returning to his companions, he ordered them to eat, and perhaps the steel of the warrior was in his voice, for both Tayven and Merlan obeyed him. This scant nourishment seemed to revive them somewhat, and presently Merlan cooperated with Shan to build a fire at a campsite Shan had chosen in the shelter of an oak grove nearby. Shan found himself being short and defensive with Merlan, which eventually prompted the other to speak.

"It doesn't matter what Tayven said about your origins. You are who you are, Shan. Look at you now. Without you, we'd be helpless. I can understand why you enacted that little deception in Akahana. How else could you have retained credibility at court? It must have been terrifying. Anyway, noble blood counts for nothing. Tayven has it, and he's half the man you are."

"Thank you," Shan said.

Merlan smiled sadly. "It needed to be said."

As they huddled around the chuckling flames, the energy for words expelled, an atmosphere of reproach, embarrassment and regret poisoned the air between them. Shan's mind was reeling so strongly with fear and uncertainty, he was sure the fruits of his training had abandoned him. He had never seen Taropat that angry before. He had seen a man he had never suspected existed. Perhaps the old personality of Khaster had been evoked too heavily by the presence of his former lover, Tayven. And yet, both Merlan and Tayven had led Shan to believe that Khaster had been a mild and passive character. Shan now regretted not having voiced his doubts and suspicions earlier. They might have avoided that sickening and needless confrontation. Still, Tayven had clearly been harboring similar doubts, which perhaps meant Shan's worries had some firm foundation. Was it possible that, through some secret liaison, Maycarpe and Taropat had set this whole quest up? But what was their shared agenda? Who did they want to be king? The same person? Shan's head ached with these questions, but he no longer wanted to discuss them with the others. He had to believe that they would accomplish their aim, despite their differences. One thing was sure in Shan's mind: it was not a good omen that they had lost a day. Perhaps that was not all they had lost.

The morning dawned with what seemed like inappropriately jubilant birdsong and a moist breeze that promised rain. Shan, already awake and stiff with cold, watched Merlan and Tayven rouse from sleep. Merlan sat up and rubbed his face. He smiled tentatively at Tayven, who was probing his tender scalp with careful fingers. Tayven did not smile back, but neither did he react with anger. Shan thought they looked like kidnapped children, bewildered, empty of tears now, and resigned to their fate, hardly daring to hope that their parents would find and save them. During the night, Shan had slept fitfully, plagued by unsettling fragments of dreams. At one point, he had awoken to feel the strong presence of a bright and benevolent figure standing over him. He remembered being overwhelmed with warmth and certainty. A faint and distant sound, like the song of a beautiful siren, had pierced his senses. He had called out Sinaclara's name, but the sensation had vanished. Shan tried to recall the sound. He was sure it had been a voice calling. Now, breathing in the fresh sharp air, he felt calmer somehow, as if the ghost of this experience still lingered around him, instilling a sense of renewed vigor and comfort.

"He never respected me," Tayven muttered.

"What did you say?" Merlan asked.

"I wanted Khaster to respect me. He just used me as pretty comfort."

"Perhaps it would have been different if you'd respected yourself first," Merlan said gently.

Tayven shook his head, sighed, then looked up at Shan. "I'm sorry for what I said. It was unforgivable."

Shan shrugged. He had to agree and was not yet capable of uttering forgiveness.

Tayven laughed tentatively and rubbed his jaw. "You must have enjoyed throwing that punch. I don't blame you. I deserved it."

"You did," Shan said, "but let's forget it. We were all in a strange mood."

"You weren't," Merlan said. "Of all of us, you were the most sensible, for which we should be thankful."

"I shouldn't have attacked you like that," Tayven said to Merlan.

"It wasn't pleasant," Merlan agreed, "but I'm prepared to forget it."

But what about Taropat? Shan wondered. He was the cause of Tayven's frustrated anger, as much, perhaps, as Tayven was the cause of his.

After a meager breakfast of more hard apples, they struck camp and walked back toward the lake. They found Taropat at the spot where he had vanished, sitting cross-legged on the grass, gazing out at the divine landscape of Ninatala. He greeted them brightly as if nothing had happened.

"Ah, there you are! I trust high spirits are out of the way and you are ready for some work."

"High spirits?" said Shan, aghast.

"Where have you been?" Merlan snapped. "I was worried sick."

"There's no need to worry about me," Taropat said. "This landscape is food for my soul." He inhaled deeply.

Shan glanced covertly at Tayven, who was gazing at Taropat with tired eyes full of longing.

"We've slept and eaten," Shan said.

Taropat did not seem to object. "Probably for the best, under the circumstances," he said coolly. "We should expect some strange manifestations of emotion. It is part of a cleansing process."

It hadn't felt like cleansing, but perhaps Taropat knew best. Shan wasn't sure what he thought anymore.

"We should affirm that we are all in accord now," Taropat said. "We must forget our differences, see the harsh words for what they are."

"What are they?" Merlan asked coldly.

"Expressions of negative energy," Taropat replied. "It's like letting poison out of a wound."

Shan glanced at Merlan, whom he knew shared his thoughts that so much anger and resentment could not be conveniently brushed away as if nothing had happened. The argument hadn't resolved anything. It had just dragged old resentments to the surface. It should be discussed, but Shan couldn't imagine that happening.

"Then we must say we are in accord," Merlan said. "Are you all right about that, Tayven?"

Tayven just nodded, hugging himself, as if he was very cold.

"Good," said Taropat. "We should put petty human drives behind us. Just look at this place. It thrums with power."

His mood and enthusiasm were infectious. Shan dared to think that perhaps Taropat had been right about the fight. He went to sit beside his mentor and Taropat smiled at him. Behind them, the lake itself was a long, sickle-shaped body of water, which to Shan suggested a lunar aspect. He voiced this thought aloud, but Taropat, apparently back to his usual self, pulled a sour face and shook his head.

"No, the sickle represents the weapon used to cut the throat of the sun king at harvest time." He pointed at a wide, flat rock at the edge of the water. "We should conduct our meditation there."

Obediently, the group went to the rock and sat down. At Taropat's suggestion, they all took a drink from their water bottles. Taropat took one of Merlan's hands and one of Tayven's in his own and gently squeezed them. He was trying to put the previous night's events behind them. Merlan still appeared dazed and Tayven was clearly confused with emotion, but it seemed that a quiet unity had settled over them all. This prompted Shan to wonder whether a supernatural force was at work, and how long it would last. He suspected that Taropat found the emotional displays extremely inconvenient. He couldn't be bothered with dealing with their cause.

Ninatala was surrounded by shivering birch trees, whose branches drooped toward the water, heavy with swags of delicate leaves. As the sun rose higher, the light seemed golden, conjuring a rich array of green hues from the lawnlike sward of the plain and the foliage of the trees.

Taropat bid them all close their eyes to summon the spiritual landscape as before. "Everything you look upon shines with its own radiance, as if made of light," he said. "But it does not hurt your eyes to gaze upon it."

Shan felt a great sense of tranquillity drift over him. He was bathed in the etheric light of the landscape and felt it restored his strength. The air was so quiet, not even the twitter of a bird disturbed the sacred silence. A low rumbling sound began to purr in his mind, growing louder and louder. He pictured the lion guardian walking toward them. It was a mountain lion with a golden pelt and blazing yellow eyes. Shan could perceive the details of the beast with startling clarity; the black rim to its eyes and mouth, the soft white fur on its chin, the dark pink of its nose leather. The creature stood beside them, right by Tayven, who was sitting erect, cross-legged with his head thrown back, eyes closed. Shan's visualization was so vivid, it was as if his eyes were open. The lion opened its mouth wide and emitted a loud roar.

Shan jumped and opened his eyes. The roar had not been part of the meditation. The first thing he saw was an immense, incontrovertibly real, mountain lion standing right beside Tayven. Everyone else had opened their eyes as well. Merlan's mouth hung open in shock. Tayven flinched in fear, but Taropat reached out calmly and took hold of his arm.

"Remain still," Taropat murmured. "Don't be afraid."

Shan could not tear his eyes away from the lion's gaze. It looked at each of them in turn and moments seemed to stretch into an eternity. He had never seen such a beautiful, perfect creature, full of the potential for destruction, yet standing there beside them with easy grace, staring into their eyes as if judging their souls.

Then, the moment was broken. A high yodelling song echoed out across the plain. At once, the lion sprang away, loped to the edge of the hill behind them and disappeared over the crest.

For a few moments, no one moved. Shan felt stunned and disorientated by the experience and sensed the others felt the same.

"That was clearly the spirit guardian," Tayven said, and then raised his arm to point. "So is this the physical aspect?" Shan felt slightly uneasy at Tayven's restored humor. Had Taropat's simple hand-squeezing gesture prompted it? If so, he felt Tayven was deluding himself.

A young, clean-shaven man was walking toward them, dressed in the garb of a monk. His hood was thrown back and long dark hair curled over his shoulders. He carried a shepherd's crook and was accompanied by a small flock of sheep. He must have uttered the cry that scared the lion away.

It took some minutes for the shepherd to reach them, but when he did so, he bowed. The sheep began immediately to graze.

"Who are you, lords?" said the shepherd. "Has the Golden One brought you to me?"

"We are travellers," Taropat replied, "on the spiritual quest of the lakes."

The shepherd nodded eagerly. "Yes, yes. I see. You are blessed. He came to you."

"The lion is the spiritual guardian of this site, then, as I thought," Taropat said. He smiled. "Our meditation here seems rather cockeyed. I had thought we would meet the physical guardian first."

The shepherd laughed. "The Golden One can be a trickster. I am Ereven, the guardian of this site, as my father was before me, and his father before him. My family has been here for many generations. Come with me. I will take you to the shrine, where you may refresh yourselves with the holy waters."

The shrine was hidden amid a thick grove of mature birches at the far end of the lake. As they walked toward it, Shan noticed that

Merlan looked pale. Neither would he speak. Tayven too was silent, but his expression was rapt, as if he were contemplating some beatific thoughts. Taropat, as usual, seemed unaffected by what they'd experienced and talked to Ereven without reserve. "The guardians of Anterity and Oolarn seem almost unaware of their function, while you are clearly aware of it."

"That is the nature of this site," Ereven said. "Awareness. The further you progress along your path, you will find the guardians to be more aware of their function. In some ways, Ninatala is the midpoint, the site of reflection and refreshment. Some say that Uspelter has that function, being the fourth of seven, but I don't agree. The energies of the green lake can be capricious and deluding, whereas here at Ninatala all is clear and pure and holy."

"Do you get many people coming here on the quest?" Shan asked.

Ereven shook his head. "Not many. And most who do come here seeking truth don't know how to look for it. They want easy answers. I see them sprawling around the lakeside, stuffing themselves with food and wine, when any half-baked mystic knows you should fast on the quest. I never approach them, because they don't even know the sites have physical guardians. They will learn little, if anything at all. It is clear you and your companions are true seekers, because the Golden One chose to appear to you. I have never seen that happen before to strangers."

"Do you see him often, then?"

"Yes, usually as no more than a flash of gold among the trees. At the turn of each season, he takes a beast from my flock, but no more than that. It is a covenant between him and my family."

The shrine was a small, single-story stone building with a flat roof of wooden beams and clumps of grass, too haphazard to be called thatch. Within was a narrow bench before a plain cube altar, which was draped with an ancient golden cloth, embroidered with gold wire. Yellow candles burned upon the altar, but otherwise the place was unadorned. Even the floor was of packed dirt rather than flagstones or boards. The group sat squashed together on the bench while Ereven spoke a few prayers. Then he took them outside again, to the back

of the shrine, where a spring came out of a rock that had been fashioned into the face of a lion. A metal cup on a chain was attached to
the stone. "Drink," Ereven told them. "Refresh yourselves."

Taropat gestured for Merlan to drink first.

"How far do you plan to travel today?" Ereven asked.

"I want to reach the fifth lake by tonight," Taropat said.

"A hard schedule, but the best way," Ereven replied. "The fifth
lake should of course be visited after dark, but many would end their
journey here today, soak up the atmosphere." Ereven, of course, had
no knowledge of the delay they'd already experienced.

"We intend to push ourselves to the limit," Taropat said.

Ereven nodded, glancing at Merlan. "Well, I'll leave you to your
meditations now. Take as much of the water as you need, and of
course, make use of the shrine should you want to. I wish you luck
upon your journey and may the blessings of the Golden One go with
you."

After Ereven had left, Merlan slumped down on the ground beside
the spring. His skin looked waxy, slightly damp. Shan knelt beside
him. "What's the matter, Merlan? Is it the climb, the air, the lack of
food?"

Merlan shook his head, rubbed his face. "I don't know. I feel
odd, that's all. During the visualization at the lake side, I felt as if all
my senses were heightened acutely. I could smell so intensely, it made
me feel nauseous. Every sound hurt my ears. I could hear the grass
and the trees growing. The feeling hasn't left me."

Tayven knelt on Merlan's other side and touched his arm. "Me
too," he said. "I feel dizzy with it." He looked up at Taropat. "This
is the lesson of Ninatala. Heightened awareness. I can sense every
person in the world, every creature, however small. I don't think we
need to perform a further meditation. The guardians came to us directly. We've got what we came for."

Taropat nodded. "I would agree. How about you, Shan? What
did you pick up?"

Shan shrugged awkwardly. "Well, nothing like that exactly. I just
felt refreshed and strengthened. I still feel it."

Taropat smiled. "But that's it! The warrior derives strength from the king."

"Yes," Shan said. "I feel him here, don't you? He's all around. He really exists somewhere." Within myself? he wondered silently.

The others contemplated his words in silence for some moments, then Tayven said, "I can't believe how different the experience of the lakes is this time. We never met guardians before, but now I can see how it works." He sighed. "Although I hate to admit it, I suspect Almorante and I were like the visitors Ereven described to us before."

"You should be grateful," Taropat said. "You are experiencing the lakes properly for the first time, as we are." He turned to his brother. "We should drink more of the water, then press on. Can you manage it, Merlan?"

Merlan nodded. "Just give me a few moments to rest."

Shan and Tayven persuaded Taropat that they should wait half an hour or so, until Merlan felt some of his strength had returned. Then, they began the long walk across the plain to the hills beyond. The slopes were thickly forested with deciduous trees, again mainly birch and oak. Streams made waterfalls amid the lush foliage and the air was filled with birdsong. The group spied a small silver-furred fox, which they followed upward, believing it to be some kind of guide. To Shan, the woods seemed a place of great mystery, very similar in ambience to the forest of Bree. Merlan said that he felt much better there, more relaxed yet alert.

"This is the essential landscape of the green ray, the color of the heart," Taropat, said. "As you rightly interpreted, Shan, it shares many qualities with my home in Bree."

"Then perhaps we should be on the alert for trickster elden," Tayven said, rather curtly.

Taropat gave him a sharp glance, but said nothing.

Uspelter was a deep pool, cupped by fern-laced rock faces. A waterfall crashed into its far end, gauzed with ephemeral rainbows. On either side of the falls, water had carved smooth channels in the stone, creating natural slides. A troupe of otters played fearlessly in the dappled sunlight, slithering down the stone into the lake. The group stood on the edge of the rock opposite the waterfall, looking down into the crystal-clear depths. The sun seemed to reach even the darkest corners of the lake, creating a shifting underwater world. "This is the most beautiful place," Shan said. "It's perfect. I can't imagine how we could visualize the spiritual aspect. Surely, this is already it?"

"Not all of it," Taropat said. "We should still do the meditation and see what occurs."

The group settled themselves on the rocks and drank from their flasks. Then Taropat led them into the visualization. "Concentrate on the color green. See the trees, plants and moss glowing with their own life force. Feel the power of the water as it crashes into the lake. Feel the joy of the creatures as they gambol in the foam."

Shan breathed deeply, and it seemed to him that the air itself smelled green. He could remain happily in that idyllic spot forever. It was like an enchantment, lulling the senses, a fairy snare to steal time away from careless humans. He heard laughter too, female laughter, and thought of the glimpses he had caught in Bree of strange forest women, who had led him on a dance among the trees.

When he opened his eyes and looked down, Shan saw a pale shape floating in the water like a star. It was a water woman, her dark hair spread out like tangled weed. She was looking up at them, paddling the water with lazy arms and legs, unashamedly naked. Was she elden?

The others had opened their eyes and were also peering down at the girl, as if wondering whether she was about to disappear. Taropat stood up and waved to her, making no concessions to her modesty, whether she possessed it or not. She waved in return and turned onto her stomach to swim back across the lake toward the waterfall. Here, she emerged from her element amid some concealing ferns. Taropat began climbing down to the narrow shore, and after exchanging glances the others followed. "If this is the guardian, we are in luck," Merlan said lightly. "How about it, Shan?"

Shan laughed. "Beats the surly smith, the mad bird woman and the saintly shepherd!"

"This is an aspect of Uspelter's energy," Tayven said. "Be careful. She may not be what she seems."

The girl had emerged from the ferns, now clad in a diaphanous green shift dress that eddied around her slim pale ankles. With both hands, she wrung out her hair, which was twisted over one shoulder. "Good day to you, gentlemen," she said.

She could be no ordinary woman, Shan thought, because no ordinary woman could possibly feel so at ease in the presence of four strange men who had just watched her swimming naked in the lake. She could be mad, or more than that. She could be elden.

"Good day to you, my lady," Taropat said, bowing gallantly. "My companions and I are on the lakes quest. You must be an aspect of Uspelter made flesh."

The girl laughed in a free and unself-conscious manner. "Perhaps I am. I am Niree, charmer for these waters."

"Are you the guardian?" Shan asked.

Niree's face creased into a slight frown. "Why should these waters need a human to guard them? The opposite is true. The waters protect us." She pointed behind her. "Spelt—my village—is near here. I am the charmer appointed by our clan mother to talk with the wyrd-folk here."

"A true fairy charmer," Taropat said.

Niree smiled. "That's right. If you want to meet the guardians, that's easy enough if you can be patient and still. They play here every day."

"Elden?" asked Shan.

"No, they are not guardians," Niree said. "The otter tribe are. They are hiding themselves now, because they don't know you."

"Then we shall sit quietly and wait to make their acquaintance," Taropat said.

Niree laughed again and shook her head. "That won't work. You must enter the water, as they do, and play as they do. Once they realize you are not aggressive and stiff-minded, they will come forth again." She sat down on a wide, sun-warmed rock. "Strip off your clothes and dive in. I'll sit here and offer encouragement. The otter people know me and will be more inclined to trust you, if I'm here."

"You display an inordinate amount of trust," Merlan said. "What would your clan mother think of you encouraging four male strangers to strip naked before you?"

Niree merely rolled her eyes. "It is part of my work to offer help to pilgrims. Am I supposed to be afraid of you? At Uspelter, it is a mistake to rely upon physical strength. This is the lake of the heart, of love. No harm may be done here. Should anyone attempt it, the wyrd-folk would come out of the trees and rocks and take away their senses. The otter queen, Lileeka, would come out of the falls and chase the wicked people away."

It was obvious Niree believed in these protectors utterly, but Shan still thought she was reckless, if not a little stupid, to trust strangers so readily.

Taropat began to undress himself. "The otter queen, Lileeka," he said. "What form does she take?"

Niree hugged her knees, apparently not at all curious about the bodies being revealed before her. "She comes in many different forms. She is a nature goddess. Sometimes, she looks almost human. In the lake, you may ask questions of her and she may appear to you. But you have to offer a sacrifice."

"What boons does Lileeka like?" Taropat said.

"From men, the seed of life," Niree said, and waved a dismissive hand at their alarmed expressions. "Don't worry. You won't pollute the waters. This is the cauldron of fertility. Women bathe here at the blood time to ask Lileeka to help them conceive. Young men come here on the night before they take a woman in love. If Lileeka likes the gift, she grants great prowess to a man."

"What if she doesn't?" Shan couldn't help asking.

Niree grinned. "The flower droops, of course. Come now, throw away your cares with your clothes. Don't be shy. Taste the waters of love and freedom."

The lake was exhilaratingly cold. Shan dived in and swam to the bottom. His skin was dappled with moving sunlight and small dark fishes darted around him. Waving weeds caressed his skin. He imagined he swam in the womb of the earth, where all creation takes place. Was this the lesson of Uspelter, to be reborn from fear and conflict?

Shan broke the surface and saw his companions floating beside him. Every one of them had on his face an expression of incredulity. A place like this should not exist in such a cruel world. To find it there was to have hope restored.

On the steep banks, Niree played with her hair and sang a wordless song in a clear high voice, staring up into the trees that surrounded the lake. Shan observed her minutely. He had never met such a serene and uninhibited woman, but then his experience of women was not great. Niree seemed to embody the essence of freedom. She must have sensed him looking at her for she shifted her gaze toward him with a smile. She waved, stood up and removed her dress, before diving gracefully into the water. Shan's heart stilled.

For some moments, Niree did not resurface. Shan glanced at his friends, but they seemed oblivious. He did not fear for Niree, for she was clearly a water creature, but where had she gone? Then he felt cool hands upon his legs and Niree slithered up his body. She was like an otter, sleek and supple. With a low throaty purr, she put her hands upon his shoulders and kissed his mouth. Shan just found the wits to respond when she pulled away from him. "You looked so beautiful in the water," she said. "I had to join you." The moment was stillness itself. Shan could hear music in the spray of the falls, hear it in the rainbow light. This was magic.

Niree smiled, and called to Shan's companions. "What are you doing, floating about? Play, all of you! Be young. Be free. Go into the falls, climb the rocks, slide down the water chutes." She splashed water over Merlan. "Are you so dour?"

Merlan's arms slammed down against the surface. "No!"

Niree yelped in pleasure. "That's it. Play."

"First down the chute, then," Tayven said and began to swim toward the falls.

Taropat lingered behind, his expression thoughtful. "Yes, this playfulness is obviously the way to invoke the spirit of the place. We should perform these ritual actions in the correct way."

Niree snorted. "You are mad. Don't think. Just enjoy yourself. When you're drunk on the pleasure of it, make your sacrifice."

Shan had a feeling Taropat would find it hard to enjoy himself spontaneously in such a manner, especially as Tayven was there.

"He wears armor over his heart," Niree said as Taropat swam away. "But the waters may heal him."

"I hope so," Shan said. "He is my mentor, a great man, but he's suffered great hurt and he knows how to inflict it too."

"A perfectly balanced, wise and sane man could not experience the lakes properly," Niree said. "If he already knew every lesson, what could be gained from coming here?" She smiled and pulled away from him, back-paddling toward the falls. "Come, have fun with me."

This was true intoxication. Shan lost all sense of time, as he played in the waters. One by one, the otter tribe reappeared, and Shan found himself sliding down a smooth rock channel to the lake surrounded by their wet bodies. The otters carried him beneath the surface, weaving around him. He felt he might swoon away. The weeds fluttered slowly around him, drawing him down. Then Niree was pressed against his body. She took his face in her hands and kissed him languorously, wrapping her legs around his waist, arousing him instantly. She guided him into her and they hung, pulsing, in the light-filled water. Shan no longer felt he needed to breathe air. He could survive beneath the water forever, surrounded by the veil of Niree's hair, enclosed by her body. Still joined, she led them upward, and their heads broke the surface. Shan took in a lungful of air and it tasted like the rarest of wines. Blearily, he saw Merlan pleasuring himself nearby, lying on his back in the water. While over by the falls, showered in spray and light, Taropat held Tayven in his embrace. This must be a fairy enchantment: heady, sensuous, far removed from the ascetic purity of Ninatala. "Now," Niree breathed, and squeezed Shan hard. Pleasure cascaded through his body and he saw, just for a moment, an immense female figure suspended in the water before them, her arms outstretched. She was part otter, part human, her teeth sharp in her mouth, which grinned in delight. "See, it is Lileeka," Niree murmured, close to his ear. "She blesses us."

A great stillness descended over the lake. Shan floated in the water, with Niree beside him, both staring up at the clear sky through the overhanging trees. Shan felt as if his heart would burst with emotion. He felt like weeping and laughing hysterically.

Niree reached for his hand and murmured. "Uspelter is the home of sensuous abandon. Here, you may relearn how to be free like a child and to experience feeling without fear."

"You are priestess of these waters," Shan said. "A witch, a nymph. Have we spent a thousand years here? Has the world moved on without us?"

She laughed softly. "No, don't be fearful. You should know I don't become this intimate with everyone who comes here. But then most of them are wrinkled old men and pious women, who take it all too seriously. I can sometimes teach them to play, but rarely how to love. That, they must learn for themselves." She ran a hand over Shan's chest. "You, however, are a scarcity. I could not let such a tasty morsel pass through my domain without knowing him this way."

Shan hesitated, then couldn't resist asking, "Do you have a lover, Niree?"

She replied without pause. "I have several. Many men want me, because of what I am. I choose who I desire."

"Will it always be that way?" Shan said. "Will you ever settle down with one man, one day? What about children?"

"Our people do not marry," she said. "It is against our beliefs. Marriage seems a selfish thing to us. But one day, yes, I will have children. I want a daughter to take my place here. That's my little bit of selfishness. I don't want another woman's child to have this privilege." She smiled. "I can tell you this because you're a stranger. I will never see you again." With these words, she swam to the water's edge and climbed out, flinging her wet hair over one shoulder.

Shan followed her. He found Merlan lying flat out on the rock, his eyes closed, his mouth set into a smile. He no longer seemed at all debilitated. Shan poked him and he opened his eyes and smiled. "If only all spiritual lessons were like this," he said. "You, however, seemed to have been the chosen one here."

Niree nudged him with her foot. "Don't be jealous, sir. I'm quite sure Lileeka made your self-love delightful."

"It was a singular experience," Merlan said. "I saw her in the water, more animal than human. She swam around me, chittering with laughter."

"I'm not the chosen one," Shan said soberly. "Not exactly. Where are Taropat and Tayven?"

Merlan half sat up and twisted around. He glanced back at Shan, an eyebrow raised. "Healing waters?"

"It would seem so. We'll have to wait for them. Oh, for a good meal now!"

"I don't believe in abstinence," Niree said. "Everyone who makes it this far on the quest is always obsessed with it. It seems a needless martydom. Come back to Spelt with me. I'm due to dine with my father tonight. He is an excellent cook and would be happy for you to join us."

"Now, you are certainly the temptress," Shan said. "Much as we'd love to, we can't. We've made a promise to one another to abstain from food, and we've already broken it once. Now we should stick to it. Also, Taropat wants us to reach the fifth lake by tonight."

"Please yourself," Niree said. She stood up and wriggled back into her dress. "Well, I must go or I will be late for dinner." She leaned down and kissed both Merlan and Shan on the mouth. "It was a pleasure meeting you. Good luck on your journey. I'll promise you these will be the last pleasurable moments you'll have for a while."

With a careless wave, she climbed nimbly up to one of the rock paths and disappeared, before Shan could even utter a good-bye.

"Was she real?" Merlan said.

Shan exhaled slowly. "Very much so. Come on, we'd better dress."

"I don't feel that hungry now," Merlan said as he pulled on his trousers. "It's strange, almost as if my body has moved beyond it."

"I hope I soon share your enlightenment," Shan said dryly. "At the moment, I could eat a rock."

Merlan and Shan dozed beside the lake for a while, until they were awoken by voices. Shan opened his eyes and saw that the shadows had lengthened considerably. It was late afternoon. Tayven and Taropat stood over them. "Sleeping?" Taropat said, although his tone was light. "You are weak creatures, easily seduced."

"We dropped off waiting for you," Shan said. "Therefore, it has to be your fault."

"We had some talking to do," Tayven said.

"Is that what it was?" Merlan remarked.

"Of all of us, Uspelter's lesson was for me particularly," Taropat said. "It was a lesson I should have been courageous enough to learn years ago."

"And have you learned it now?" Shan asked.

He smiled reflectively. "Perhaps."

22

IN THE DARK OF THE WEIR

THE PLAYFUL MOOD OF Uspelter stayed with them as they journeyed to the fifth lake, Malarena. Twilight fell as they climbed a wide path between ranks of lofty evergreens. Softly, a different atmosphere insinuated itself among the group: tension. The jokes ceased, and all that could be heard was labored breathing from the steep climb. They appeared to be walking into a waiting darkness; the forest clustered thickly at the crest of the path. Hunger now gnawed at Shan's stomach, and even Merlan, who earlier had professed to have conquered his pangs, complained of feeling starved.

"Yes, we feel weaker," Taropat said, "for we've used a lot of energy, but our minds have entered into an altered state now. We are more open to noncorporeal influences."

Tayven, who was leading the group, suddenly halted in his steps. "Is that music?"

"It sounds like wind chimes," Shan said, "wooden chimes."

"I can hear water too," Merlan said.

"We are close," Tayven answered. His face looked strangely pale in the twilight. "The next two lakes are trials. We should be prepared for it."

At the top of the incline the path levelled out. The woodland around them was dusty, the trees surrounded by bracken, both this year's lush growth and the last year's rusty remains.

"This isn't the landscape I expected to find here," Merlan said. "It's so bleak. Surely, the blue ray is that of creativity, even emotion."

"It is," Taropat answered, "but here the waters will be turbulent."

As they approached Malarena, they found that many of the trees had been hung with long wooden chimes that clunked and tocked in the breeze. "Perhaps the guardian put them there," Shan said, "or pilgrims. Could that be the offering to Malarena?"

"I doubt it," Taropat said.

"Almorante and I didn't give offerings at all before," Tayven said.

"So what did happen here, then?" Merlan asked.

Tayven shrugged. "The same as with the other lakes. Almorante invoked the water spirits. He asked for the essence of Malarena to enter into me."

"You must have felt something," Shan said.

Tayven nodded. "Yes, I felt the atmosphere here to be very dark. It is not joyous emotion like the earth site of Uspelter."

They emerged from the trees by the lakeside. Malarena was surrounded by tall bulrushes. Its surface appeared calm, but they could hear the rushing of a weir to the left. Rotting jetties poked out into the lake, but the only boats they saw were dilapidated, half sunk in the water.

"It feels so desolate," Shan said. "Dank. I don't feel the presence of anyone near."

"Neither do I," Taropat said softly. He walked round the lake and stood staring down into the weir. The others remained where they were, close to the forest path.

"I don't relish a night here," Merlan said. "I can imagine being taken in our sleep by hideous ghouls."

"That's the next site," Tayven said gloomily. "Rubezal, the lake of spirit."

"Isn't spirit the last lake, the seventh?" Shan said.

"No, Pancanara has no element specifically. It is the combination of all other elements."

"Why should emotion and spirit be so bad?" Shan asked. "I'd have thought that the further we travelled, the more spiritual the sites would become."

"We are human," Tayven answered shortly, "the deeper within ourselves we travel, the darker the experience. What we are seeking is transformation."

"You must be feeling pleased with yourself about the transformation at the last site," Merlan said.

Tayven lifted his upper lip into a sneer. "You are crude," he said. "Have you no care for your brother? Uspelter gave him a kind of peace, an understanding of his fears. We didn't rush off into the undergrowth to rut like savages. If you must know, all that happened was that we went somewhere to talk, as I told you."

"But the offering to the lake," Shan said, as curious as he felt Merlan was. "Didn't you make one?"

"Yes, but it was a spontaneous reaction to the emanations of pure love and joy that the lake imparts. We didn't create it together like you and Niree did."

"Right," said Merlan dryly. He rolled his eyes at Shan. "If you want to put a spiritual gloss on it, that's your prerogative."

"Funny, I thought we were here for spiritual reasons," Tayven said. "Clearly, we have different motives for this trip."

"Your motive is obvious," Merlan snapped.

Shan was wondering whether he should intervene to prevent another argument, when Taropat hurried back to them. "Look over there," he said in a low urgent voice, "on the other side of the lake. Can you see anything, or am I just picking up an etheric image?"

The others all looked in the direction Taropat had indicated. At first Shan saw nothing, then he perceived a tall still figure in black, or was it just a dead tree?

"There seems to be someone standing there," Merlan said, "but I can't be sure."

"A hooded figure," Tayven said.

"I don't feel that's the physical guardian," Shan said. "Do you, Taropat?"

Taropat shook his head slowly. "I don't know. Whatever, or whoever, it is, they appear to be watching us."

"Shall we just perform the opening meditation as normal?" Tayven said. "If that *is* the guardian, perhaps they will approach us when they feel reassured we're genuine seekers."

Taropat nodded. "I was about to suggest that."

The spiritual landscape of Malarena was, like that of Uspelter, very similar to its actual form. Taropat described a brooding calm, beneath which great turbulence churned. "The lake is not just what we perceive with our eyes," he said. "We must extend our senses beneath its surface, see the great activity that is taking place there. It is a metaphor for human emotion: chaos and muddy uncertainty. In the darkness are specks of sparkling blue radiance, which are creative thoughts coming into being, directed down from the indigo ray of Rubezal."

Shan felt oppressed by the imagery he saw. Around the lake, shadowy figures moved among the trees like predators. He was relieved to open his eyes and find no physical manifestations before him as at Ninatala.

"The hooded figure hasn't moved," Shan said. "It must be a tree or an hallucination."

But even as he spoke, the hooded creature or individual lifted one arm and pointed directly at them.

"I don't like the look of that," Merlan said.

The figure drew back its arm and appeared to fling something toward them. A dark blot shot from its hand or the sleeve of its robe. Halfway across the lake this missile extended wide ragged wings and uttered a loud caw. The group was forced to duck as an immense raven swooped upon them. They felt the wind of its passing, but it did not attack.

"What in Madragore's name was that all about?" Merlan snapped.

"It's gone to the weir," Taropat said.

The bird had alighted upon a rotten tree stump that poked out of the water. It stood with its head to one side, regarding them through an unblinking yellow eye.

Taropat stared back at the raven, tapping his lips with one forefinger. Then, he made an emphatic gesture. "Yes, I think I understand. This is an extension of Uspelter, the same but different. Here too, we must immerse ourselves in the water of the soul, but it will be no playful, joyful exercise. We must jump into the weir in the dark. We must put our trust and our faith in fate."

"That would be very dangerous," Shan said cautiously. "We have no idea what's down there. Our limbs could get tangled in weeds, and what about the underwater currents? We could drown."

"That's the risk," Taropat said. "That's the lesson. The overcoming of the fear of death."

"We don't know that," Merlan said. "We haven't exactly met a guardian yet. Perhaps we should wait."

Taropat shook his head. "The guardian stands on the opposite shore. He has given us the message. The spiritual guardian is the raven, who now waits for us to act. The offering here is ourselves. We must give ourselves to the waters and trust we will survive."

"He's right," Tayven said. "Perhaps the reason Almorante failed here is because he'd never think of doing anything so reckless."

"Isn't starving us enough?" Merlan said, with what sounded like forced humor. "Do we have to drown as well?"

Taropat ignored the remark. "It is not yet fully dark. We should wait until it is before we attempt the trial. Drink from the flasks we filled at Uspelter. We'll need that energy to sustain us."

Darkness came quickly. The sky was clear and blistered with stars, and the moon rose full and round above the forest. A wan spectral light illuminated the scene, turning the surface of the lake to milky pearl.

Taropat stood up and began to undress himself. "We must do this in our own time," he said, "We must be on our own."

"I have a strong desire to run back down through the forest," Merlan muttered to Shan. "I hope Tayven was right to back up Taropat's idea."

"He has become Taropat for you now, then," Shan murmured back.

Merlan only shook his head, as if in perplexity. "Khaster would never, in all of eternity, have suggested a thing such as this!" He paused, then stood up. "Well, might as well get it over with. I hope we're all destined to finish this quest alive."

The four of them stood naked and vulnerable at the water's edge. Shan could already sense the powerful churning current beneath the surface. From where he stood, he could see nothing but blackness beneath. The moonlight could not fight through the thick branches of the trees to illuminate the waters of the weir. Taropat was breathing slowly and deeply, as if summoning strength and courage. When would he find it and jump? Shan had already decided to wait for someone else to dive in before he did so himself. He was hoping that the sight of that would free his body of the rigor that gripped it. It wasn't just physical fear, but a gut-deep instinct that what he was about to do was dangerous in more than just the obvious ways. Overcome it, he told himself, but still his feet were rooted to the spot. He felt like a lamb at the door of the butcher's shed, smelling blood and death, aware of gore-streaked metal in the ocher gloom. He glanced at Merlan, who looked back at him, his face expressionless. Tayven was frowning in concentration, while Taropat stood straight and tall, his eyes screwed shut. No one could do it.

We can't fail, Shan thought. I am the warrior. I must be their mettle and their courage. We can't fail.

Shan closed his eyes, took a deep breath and uttered an ear-splitting scream. Then, without thinking he jumped into the water. It engulfed him in icy cold and immediately he felt himself being dragged down. As Tayven had predicted, strong weeds whipped at his legs; the muscular tentacles would bind him until he drowned. Something buffeted him painfully in the side, which he realized was someone else's kicking limb. His body bumped off submerged detritus that could have been fallen trees or boulders. It happened too quickly to tell. Sharp objects cut into his flesh. The boiling currents threw him against every obstacle. He was afraid his bones would break. All he could see was swirling blackness, utter chaos. Rise! he told himself.

Reach for the air. It was like trying to pull himself out of chains. He would die. Involuntarily, he gripped the Dragon's Claw, which still hung around his neck, and willed it to give him the strength of the warrior.

A voice whispered through his mind: Sinaclara's. "It is within you, not the artifact. Energy flows where intention goes. Remember it. Remember it and focus."

Yes, that was the way. Clear the mind. Concentrate. With great effort, Shan visualized pushing the primal fear from his mind. It was an obscuring cloud that must be banished. He concentrated his physical energy into his solar plexus, forcing all of his will into the thought of rising to the surface. This, he fed with the energy of his will. He clove the water with his arms. His legs kicked against the current. His were the limbs of a god, unstoppable. As if pushed from beneath, his body arrowed upward. He had conquered the fear. He was free.

Shan broke the surface, gasping for air, and swam quickly, painfully, to the bank, where he pulled himself out of the water. His whole body was tingling, and for some moments, he could only lie facedown on the cold earth, breathing heavily. Then he forced himself to sit up. Where were the others? He called their names, but the surface of the weir was still. He got shakily to his feet, wondering whether he had the strength to dive back in and find them, but then a head broke the surface, followed by another. Tayven and Taropat swam toward him, bearing Merlan between them.

"Is he all right?" Shan called.

Tayven clambered out slowly, shaking so much he could barely control his limbs. Taropat had a deep gash on his forehead, which was bleeding heavily. "I think Merlan took a knock to the head," he said. "Help us, Shan."

Shan took hold of Merlan's arms and dragged him onto the bank. He was relieved to hear him groan, but what would they do if Merlan was badly injured? How could they continue? Taropat dragged himself out of the water, wiped his face of blood.

"Are *you* all right?" Shan asked.

Taropat nodded. "It's not much. What about Merlan?"

Tayven squatted down and ran his hands over Merlan's limbs,

then carefully examined his body. "Don't think there's anything bro-ken," he said. "There are no open wounds on his head."

"One of his hands is curled up," Shan said. "He's got something. Take it, Tay."

Tayven prised open the fingers of Merlan's left hand. A spherical object rolled out onto the ground.

"The Eye," Taropat said.

"Did you give it to him?" Tayven asked.

Taropat shook his head. "No."

"Why did he take it?" Shan said.

"Let's trust we'll be able to ask him later," Taropat said, picking up the Dragon's Eye. "Cover him with a blanket, Tayven. Quickly."

"As quick as I can," Tayven said, somewhat shortly. He clearly still felt weak himself, but went slowly to their luggage.

"What we did was madness!" Shan said to Taropat.

Taropat touched the wound on his forehead gingerly, winced. "We had to do it, Shan. You know that."

"I hope so."

"Merlan will be fine, I'm sure."

"He'd better be, otherwise we're turning back now, aren't we!"

Shan got to his feet. He felt invigorated now, full of energy. At his feet, Merlan had curled up on his side. "What did you see down there?" Shan said to Taropat.

Taropat shook his head. "Darkness," he said. "Impenetrable dark-ness. I had prepared myself for so much more—terrible visions—but there was only a void. For a while, I was Khaster again, and I was prepared to face whatever would be shown to me, but Malarena's lesson is not focused upon me."

"Tayven?"

"I don't know." Taropat placed a hand on his brother's shoulder. "Who knows what Merlan saw?"

Tayven came back with the blanket and they carried Merlan to a more comfortable spot nearby, a carpet of spongy moss beneath the trees. Merlan's eyes were open and he turned his head slowly from side to side. Tayven gave him some water and he swallowed.

"Can you speak?" Shan said. "Merlan, can you hear us?"

Merlan blinked, but said nothing. Taropat took one of his brother's hands and Merlan's fingers curled around his own. They were all so intent on their companion, they did not hear someone approaching, until a voice above them said, "May I assist you, sirs?"

The hooded figure they had seen on the other side of the lake now stood over them. He was swathed in a long dark robe, and his face was bony and ivory pale beneath his hood.

"That would be generous of you," Taropat said. "We went into the weir, as you probably saw. It looks as if Merlan here took a knock beneath the water."

The hooded man did not appear to think their actions were unusual. "Allow me to examine him," he said. "I'm adept at treating the wounds incurred in these waters."

The others moved aside so the man could squat down. "Many don't survive," he said, as he lifted Merlan's eyelids. "You should consider yourselves lucky." He examined Merlan thoroughly. "Hmm, nothing too serious. The injuries are not physical. He is in shock. All he needs is sleep. I have a posset I can give him to help his condition."

"You are the guardian of this site?" Taropat said.

The man looked up at him. "I am Nordren," he said. "Many years ago, as a young man, I undertook the quest of the lakes seeking enlightenment. When I reached Malarena, I could find no trace of a physical guardian. As I wandered the shore, I came upon a shack, in which I found the body of a man, long dead. The raven came to me and landed on my shoulder. I knew then I was destined never to complete the quest. Here I stayed, as a guide for others. That was my destiny."

"Have you ever entered the weir?" Shan asked.

Nordren shook his head. "I cannot. Should I do so, I could move on to Rubezal, and that is not my fate." He stood up. "Carry your friend to my dwelling. It is basic, but has floor space for guests who are not too particular."

Taropat hesitated. "We plan to take as little sleep as possible."

"Your aims are noble," Nordren said, "and I can tell from your breath you haven't eaten properly for some time. However, fasting is one thing, sleep deprivation another. If you do not rest for some hours tonight, you will never fulfill your quest. Rubezal is the hardest lesson of all."

"Has anyone completed the quest?" Shan asked. "Has anyone reached Pancanara?"

Nordren smiled grimly. "None have returned to say, but I'll tell you this. Some have perished here at Malarena. Others, who have stayed on the path this far, never understand the true lesson of the lake, or else realize it and cannot face it, turn back. Those that pass on may fail at Rubezal. You will see their bones there. I'm not even sure Pancanara exists. I think that once you have received the knowledge of Rubezal, Pancanara comes into being within you. I am sure it is a spiritual concept. Now, dress yourselves. Let's get your ailing friend to warmth."

As they walked back to Nordren's dwelling, carrying the semiconscious Merlan between them, Shan asked the guardian, "Would you have let us drown if we'd been unable to get out of the weir?"

"It is your decision to undertake the quest," Nordren answered. "If you emerge from the waters, I offer assistance. That is the way."

Nordren's dwelling was actually more comfortable than he described it. He was not so much of an ascetic as he appeared, for he had done many things to make his abode homely. Matting of woven reeds covered the floor, constructed from leaves of different colors that formed a complicated pattern. The scrubbed wooden table was decorated with an earthenware jug containing iris and bulrush, while against one wall was a surprisingly large bed with a thick mattress and quilt. Several oil lamps cast a warm, comforting glow around the single, spacious room. Curtains were drawn against the night, and cushions filled with rush down were piled in a corner. "Make your bed from those pillows," Nordren said. "You will find them more than adequate."

Tayven and Shan laid Merlan down on three cushions that seemed to curl around his body like comforting arms. Nordren offered them a blanket. Merlan appeared to be sleeping normally now.

"One small beverage won't break your fast," Nordren said and put a kettle onto his stove. "I brew a drink from nuts and herbs. It's very pure and will refresh you. It will also lend your friend a revival."

He took off his cloak to reveal a shiny, bald head that looked like polished ivory. His age was impossible to determine, for although his face was not deeply lined, he had an air of great maturity.

"Will Merlan be all right?" Shan asked. "Can he still travel?"

Nordren nodded. "He is in shock and should be kept warm. No doubt he'll have strange tales to tell of his experience when he wakes, but I have no fear for him."

"We're grateful for your help and will of course recompense you," Taropat said.

Nordren made a dismissive gesture with one hand. "No need. I want for nothing. As I told you, it is my function to aid seekers here. Tomorrow, I will take you across the lake in my boat to the path to Rubezal. It is far quicker than negotiating the track beside the water, for in some places it is now almost impassable, and you have to make a detour into the forest."

He gave Tayven, Taropat and Shan measures of his nut drink, served in metal mugs. While they drank, Nordren knelt beside Merlan and managed to get him to sip from a bowl. Then, exhausted, the group arranged themselves on the plump soft cushions for sleep, and Nordren climbed into his great bed.

Shan lay awake for over an hour, as one by one his companions began to snore softly. He noticed that Tayven slept in Taropat's arms, so their relationship must have been rekindled in some respects, no matter what Tayven had said. Just as he was drifting off to sleep, Merlan stirred beside him and uttered a few distressed whimpers. Shan put a hand upon his brow. "Hush, it's all right."

Merlan opened his eyes, which glittered in the glow of the one remaining lit lamp. "I saw it," he whispered. "Shan, it was in my grasp. I saw the Crown. I reached for it, but then something hideous, terrible, devouring came. It stirred the waters to mud and the Crown was lost. The beast had me in its jaws, but Taropat got me away. I have failed you."

Shan squeezed Merlan's shoulder briefly. "A hallucination, that's all. You're safe now. Sleep."

Merlan sighed. "I'm alive," he said and closed his eyes. Shan turned away onto his side.

23

BREATH OF THE SERPENT

SUNLIGHT COMING THROUGH Nordren's curtains woke Tayven very early. Taropat's arms were still curled around him. He pulled away carefully and found that Merlan was already awake, sitting on a chair by the window, staring out at the lake through the narrow gap between the curtains. His color appeared normal, and apart from the bewildered expression on his face, he seemed to have suffered no ill effects from the previous night's events.

Tayven went over to him and touched his arm. "Merlan," he said softly. "I'd like to speak with you. Let's go outside."

Merlan nodded and got to his feet without wincing, which Tayven took as another good sign. Taropat and Shan were still asleep, but Nordren's bed was empty.

Outside, the air was chill and fresh. "The landscape here looks different by daylight," Tayven said, "less sinister."

Merlan nodded glumly. "That is probably why, traditionally, seekers are supposed to visit the place after dark.

"It feels like autumn though, doesn't it? Strange. The smell of the air is wrong for summer and the colors are muted."

Merlan made no comment. Tayven examined him for some moments. Perhaps he was not as unaffected as he first appeared. Tayven drew a breath and said, "I need to speak with you about a personal matter."

He sensed that Merlan's body stiffened slightly. "What about?"

"Well, you're Taropat's brother, and I know you don't hold a high opinion of me. After what's happened over the past couple of days, I don't want you to think I intend Taropat harm."

Merlan turned his head and stared at Tayven unblinkingly for some moments. Then he said, "I don't think that. I just think it would be better if you left him be. Let the past stay in the past. He turned to you once because his wife shattered his hopes, his confidence and his dreams. I can't see the benefit of rekindling that time."

"It isn't like that. I know I carry a reputation, Merlan, and sometimes I joke about it, but essentially it isn't me. I don't know what's happening with Taropat and me, and suspect it's just an ephemeral aspect of our being here, but if anything will cause him distress, I'm sure it would be your disapproval. Whatever happens to us on this quest, we should just accept it and deal with the consequences later. I can sense, just as you can, that Taropat is still fragile, for all he's changed. Inside, a lot of Khaster remains."

"What did you talk about yesterday?"

Tayven sighed. "The quest mainly. He also talked about Shan, and how he feels the world should change. It wasn't that personal really."

Merlan was again silent for a few moments, then said, "We should guard against ourselves, our own hearts and minds. We are venturing into the unknown territory deep within and that which we churn up with the mud will be terrible." There was a hollow prophetic ring to his voice. "I'm also concerned that Taropat seems to be leaving his own mud untouched."

"What do you mean?"

Merlan sighed. "I hope I'm wrong, but I have to speak of it. Haven't you noticed how Taropat hasn't gone through any personal experiences yet? And what about the way he behaved after our fight? I think it's odd that he acted as if nothing had happened. We have to consider that he might not be as stable as we'd like to think. Now that you're close to him again, you should keep an eye on him. I get the feeling that beneath his unruffled exterior, there's something waiting to explode. We saw a small part of that yesterday."

Tayven considered these words. How could he dispute them? He'd taken great comfort from the scant moments of Taropat's physical embrace, but he could not hide from the fact that Taropat was an entirely different creature from Khaster. "I will be alert for signals," he said.

"Do you love him still?" Merlan asked.

Tayven hesitated. "I'm not sure what I love. That's the trouble."

Merlan nodded. "I can understand that."

There was a short silence, then Tayven said, "What happened to you last night? Why did you take the Dragon's Eye?"

Merlan frowned as if he could barely remember. "I saw the Eye lying among Taropat's clothes, and even though I knew I shouldn't, I had to pick it up, take it with me into the water."

"What did you see with it down there?"

Merlan rubbed his face. "I thought I was dying. The weeds sucked me down and my lungs filled with water. Then I saw something shining in the darkness. It was the Crown, symbol of the greatest majesty. I reached for it, could feel its warmth. I knew that if I could only touch it, even briefly, our quest would be blessed. I did not expect to rise from the water holding it in my hands. I knew that I was only seeing it in my mind, but its secret was there."

"What secret?" Tayven asked.

"The one we must know in order to attain the real Crown. I understood the immense importance of the artifact, how its peace-bringing properties would bring power to the king, and therefore his subjects and the land itself. For just a few moments, the Crown was before me, as real as you or I." He shook his head, screwing up his eyes. "But then, for some reason I became uncertain about everything, I doubted it was really there. It all started to feel very wrong, a terrible fear shot through me. I reached out for the Crown, but before I could touch it, a terrible chthonic beast rose up from the depths and enclosed me in thorny tentacles. It taunted me, putting thoughts into my head.

It had shown me the Crown, because it knew I could never possess it. None of us can. Does the Crown exist in reality?" He shrugged. "Who knows? All I know is that we can never complete our quest, Tayven. I saw us all in a bleak and dismal landscape, separated, wandering desperate, blind. I saw the bones of men all around us. What awaits us at Rubezal is more horrifying than we can imagine. It is extinction of the soul."

"I don't believe that," Tayven said carefully. "What happened to you was a test, Merlan. You saw the Crown, which is the symbol of our success, and you confronted your fear. Don't give in to it. You survived. You conquered the weir. The Crown may not be in your grasp, but at least you saw it. You know it exists, if only in your mind."

"What of it?" Merlan said bitterly. "I am afraid now. Wasn't the lesson supposed to be the overcoming of fear? I haven't felt that, I haven't learned it. All I learned is that our quest is folly. We are deluding ourselves, seeking legends, seeking dreams, like little boys lost in a fantasy. Here, in this rarefied air, we can forget about the horrors of the battlefield, the exquisite cruelty of the court. This place and its dreams have no bearing on such foul human constructions. But we are human and the lakes cannot help us. We are flawed."

"I know more about the horrors of the battlefield than you do," Tayven said. "And I also know that what we're doing here is right. Maycarpe is right. In your heart, I believe you know that too." He paused, then said carefully, "You and I are uneasy confederates, but you know we share a secret. You beheld the Crown. You know who should wear it."

Merlan stared at him for a few moments. "I know what Maycarpe thinks, and perhaps you share his vision, although somehow I find that difficult to believe."

"Do you share it?"

Merlan shrugged. "I did for a short time, but now I think that we are grasping at straws, looking for the most likely candidate. Perhaps the true king is not known to us yet. He may be yet to be born."

Tayven nodded. "You may be right. I think our minds should remain open. But don't give up, Merlan. We're so close to success."

Merlan shook his head, his mouth a grim bloodless line. "What did you see, Tayven? What did Taropat and Shan see? I'll tell you. Nothing. For you it was a test of physical danger, but you were wrong. Now, you are not prepared for what will follow."

TAYVEN SAID NOTHING to Taropat or Shan about his conversation with Merlan. Nordren returned to his dwelling and brewed them more of his restorative beverage, then took them to his boat and rowed them across the lake. The early-morning sunlight had disappeared behind thick cloud, which was gradually descending over the mountains in a suffocating shroud. Sound was muted and the thick slap of the oars against the water made it sound as if they travelled through mud.

As he worked powerfully at the oars, Nordren offered them advice on how to approach Rubezal. "Markers have been left, but you have to recognize them," he said. "It all gets very bleak up there, believe me."

"I thought you hadn't been there," Shan said.

"I haven't and I wouldn't, but I've been told," Nordren replied. "Some have returned from there with hollow eyes. They said that the atmosphere of the place drove them away. It broke their spirits and took their minds."

Tayven glanced at Merlan, who made no comment. How could they approach this site if one of their party had lost heart? Tayven knew it should be brought out into the open, but perhaps Merlan didn't want to speak in front of Nordren.

They disembarked where a narrow path snaked off between a thick forest of twisted thorn trees. "Perhaps we'll see you on the way back," Taropat said lightly to Nordren.

Nordren only smiled. "Good luck."

The group watched as the guardian's boat glided back into the mist. "Well, there's no point in delaying," Taropat said briskly. "Is everyone ready?"

"Yes," said Shan.

Tayven nodded, glanced at Merlan, then said, "How about you?"

Merlan looked back at him. "Whatever I say will have no effect."

"What do you mean?" Taropat asked.

"Tell him," Tayven said.

Merlan shook his head.

"Tay?" Taropat said. "What is this?"

"Merlan saw something beneath the waters of the weir last night. He saw the Crown, but he also saw us fail in our quest."

"It was fear," Taropat said. "We knew that would happen."

"You don't know anything," Merlan said in a dull voice.

"Then why don't you tell us?" Taropat said, halfway between sweet and sharp.

"You want the truth? I think we should turn back. There's no reason to continue."

There was a moment's silence, broken by Shan. "Turn back? Ridiculous. We experienced Malarena. We passed through. We're truly on our way now."

"Merlan thinks otherwise," Tayven said.

"Do you agree with him?" Taropat asked.

Tayven shook his head. "No, but I think he should speak, be heard."

"He saw monsters in the weir," Shan said. "It was his own fear. He had to conquer it, as we did."

"I saw our folly!" Merlan cried. "Our folly at going against the might of Magravandias. The wrath of the empire lurked there, the dark heart of every king who's been corrupted and has caused pain, suffering and oppression. *That* was the monster." He screwed up his eyes, shook his head. "These lakes are owned by an ancient race of demons, who have a great hatred and jealousy of humankind. They spawn fear and the lust for power within any man or woman who has the will to conquer. The journey lulls the senses, seduces, and it's only here, at Malarena, when the claws are bared. Fools have swallowed up the delusion by then. They think they're experiencing spiritual truths. But it's not that. The lakes are the world's vengeance on man."

"An interesting premise," Taropat said dryly.

"Perhaps Merlan should wait for us here," Shan said.

"There is no coming back," Merlan said. "That's what you don't understand. Nordren knows it. I could see it in his face."

"We all go on together or not at all," Taropat said. "Is that what you want, Merlan, for us to turn back now and never know whether we could have attained the Crown? Never know whether the real demon was the pernicious fear of failure?"

"I know what I saw," Merlan said. "The Crown, if it exists, is beyond our reach. We are not worthy of it. I will continue, because I have trodden the path of no return. I can't go back, but now I know the truth and I can't pretend otherwise."

Taropat sighed. "You have to fight this. Otherwise, you will be a weak link."

"He should not come," Shan said. "He played his part, which was to get us into Magravandias. It is you, Tayven and I who form the trinity. Merlan does not have to be with us. He *can* turn back."

"It will blight his life," Taropat said bitterly. "You know it will." He put his hands on his brother's shoulders. "Merlan, you are strong. You had a bad experience last night because you knocked your head and you've barely eaten or slept. Be with us. Remember hope. You were always so positive, so much stronger than I was."

Merlan pushed Taropat's hands away. "I'm with you, brother. I'll not desert you. I have no choice."

"We will succeed," Taropat said. "I know it. We've come this far. We were meant to come."

Tayven could feel Taropat's conviction, but knew it wasn't even touching Merlan. "Rubezal will be difficult, we know that," he said. "We were prepared for it. Remember, I've been there before, and I returned to tell the tale. The lakes are what you make them. Last time I was here, I was with Almorante, who didn't know what he was doing. Now, we do. I came here unarmed before, and if there was any evil influence present, surely it would have had me them."

Merlan glanced at Tayven sourly. "It's already had you, Tayven. You were nearly destroyed by what Magravandias stands for."

"But he wasn't destroyed," Taropat said. "Look, he stands here now, still strong, a shining light who has overcome his suffering."

Tayven winced inwardly, averted his eyes. Was that really how Taropat saw him?

Taropat shouldered his backpack. "We can't waste any more time. Let's get started."

Tayven felt the discussion was far from finished but already Shan and Taropat were a few yards ahead on the trail. Tayven touched Merlan's arm. "I know what you saw. Believe me, I of all people accept what you're saying, but my gut instincts tell me we should go on. At least accept you *might* be wrong."

Merlan said nothing, but followed the others up the path.

THE TRAIL TWISTED and turned, seeming to loop in on itself to make the journey longer. It rose steeply for a couple of miles, then abruptly plummeted into a valley of thick thorn, where Tayven almost expected to see dead princes impaled on the clawed branches. There was a musty smell to the air, and a pervading mist made it impossible to see far ahead. It really was as if they were walking into the unknown, another realm, a hinterland.

"Are you sure this is the right way?" Shan said. "We've been going downwards for half an hour now. Rubezal is higher than Malarena."

"The path tricks us," Merlan said.

Taropat threw his brother a caustic glance, but ignored the remark. "According to Nordren, we have to pass through the valley of thorns to reach the quickest trail to Rubezal. Which way did you and Almorante come before?" he asked Tayven.

"Not this way. We had trackers from the Magravandian army with us. They cut a path through the thorn forest that skirts the northern shore of Malarena. We took a straight route, but I don't think we could follow it now. I have a nose for direction, but not to the same degree our guides did then."

"We're going miles out of our way, I'm sure of it," Shan said. "Do you think Nordren lied to us?"

"We've seen the signs," Taropat said. "The crossed twigs at the wayside, the reed ribbons on the trees."

"Twigs fall from trees and accidentally cross," Merlan said. "Reed ribbons fall from the nests of birds."

"Merlan, shut up," Taropat said. "Tayven, what do you think? You know this landscape best of all of us."

"Well, we're heading roughly in the right direction, but I agree with Shan that this does seem a tortuous route. Once we've crossed the valley, I think we should bear east. There are no landmarks I recognize here."

The valley floor was a swamp of shallow lakes, spongy grasses and sucking mud. Tayven stepped on a tuffet of sedge, which promptly capsized, causing him to plunge a foot into the bog. He lost his boot pulling himself out and found that a group of dirty white leeches had attached themselves to his leg. Shan pulled them off, while Tayven's stomach churned. He had lived in a wilderness for years, and was used to dealing with the worst of parasites, but here there was something distinctly repellent about the wildlife. Amphibians they caught sight of looked diseased, being blotchy and scabrous, and all the birds that watched them from the weirdly desiccated foliage had patchily bald heads, as if their feathers had fallen out through sickness.

The path out of the valley was littered with sharp stones, which soon made short work of the cloth Tayven had wrapped around his bootless foot. The places where the leeches had attached themselves itched abominably. "I've lost all sense of time," Tayven said. "Is it afternoon yet?"

"I would tell you if I could," Taropat answered, "but the last time I took my watch out, I noticed it had stopped. That was at eleven. It seems hours ago, but I can't be sure."

"I don't relish reaching Rubezal after dark," Tayven said.

Merlan uttered a hollow chilling laugh.

"Use the Eye," Shan said to Taropat. "Perhaps you can see something in it."

Taropat shook his head. "It's not a compass, Shan. We have to find our own way."

They entered a high narrow chasm, where only a few stringy shrubs grew from the gray rock, but then the path turned a corner and a vast expanse of water and swamp lay before them. Trees grew around it and from within it—immense stately willows pouring their foliate hair into the water. Their leaves were yellow rather than green and their barks were hung with garlands of creepers and moss. The sky above was colorless and heavy, while the waters themselves looked black like oil. There were no water birds present, but bedraggled crows roosted in the willows.

"Rubezal," Tayven said, "we're here."

"Makes Malarena look like an idyll," Shan said, putting down his backpack.

Merlan slumped to the ground and sat with raised knees, his hands pressed against his eyes.

"Nothing like a show of morale," Taropat muttered, taking out his water flask.

"This is the lake of inspiration," Tayven said, glancing at Merlan. Shan snorted. "Really?"

"Yes. You can see it if you try. It's a matter of perception. Here, ideas are born from the cauldron of the dark mother. It is the lake of spirit, but also of self-delusion."

"What do you mean?" Shan asked.

"All self-delusions will confront you here. You'll either overcome them or fail in the quest."

"Is that what happened to Almorante?" Taropat inquired rather acidly.

Tayven did not reply directly. For a few moments, he stared into the inky water. "I remember that being overcome by the dark beauty of this place felt . . . *strange*. I'm sure Almorante felt it too."

Taropat nodded. "If you half close your eyes, the place does have a strange beauty," he said.

Tayven walked to the water's edge. "Here, the water is black and fecund," he said. "The secret to Pancanara lies hidden here. I . . ." He paused. "We couldn't find it before." He turned back to the others, gazing particularly at Merlan. "We shouldn't be afraid, for if we are it is only fear of the unknown, of the occult and mysterious. We should embrace it, let go enough to be prepared for anything."

"Sounds like you're glad to be back," Taropat said.

"It is right this time," Tayven answered. "Shall we perform the first meditation now?"

Taropat nodded and sat down, while Merlan and Shan did likewise.

"We really are going into the unknown," Taropat said softly. "What lies beyond here? Pancanara, success? What are the alternatives?" He fell silent, and the only sound was the soft lisp of the wind among the sedges and the occasional caw of a crow. "See the landscape of Rubezal in your mind," Taropat murmured. "The mist, the reeds, the trees, the marsh, the still tracts of water. Overhead, great vultures are circling in the empty sky, but silently. As we peer into the fog, we see shapes protruding from the water. Gradually, we realize they are corpses, some in armor, their skeletal arms still holding swords aloft. Others are mere shapeless masses of rags. These are the ones who failed here." He paused a moment and then said in a loud voice, "We call upon the guardian of Rubezal. We are seekers in truth. We call upon you. Come to us. Reveal to us the guardian of this place."

In his mind, Tayven saw shadowy shapes emerging from the mist. They were seekers who had come to this place before them: knights, mystics, priests, priestesses, witches and shamans. The eyes of some were dead, empty, while others were only skeletal corpses, and had no eyes at all. Were these sad wraiths the guardians of Rubezal? The last time he'd been there, Tayven had visualized a very different aspect of the lake. It had been the realm of the crone, stirring ideas in her black pot. She had spoken to him while he'd been in trance, but there was no sign of her now. What had she said before? "You are brother to the king." He had taken that to mean his relationship with Almorante, and that it was a prophecy Almorante would one day take the throne of Magrast. Almorante had liked that, suddenly convinced that their quest was over and they'd been given the information he had been seeking all along. Tayven hadn't thought otherwise at the time, but now in retrospect he wondered whether Taropat was right. Had Almorante failed to overcome his deepest illusion about himself? But his last visit hadn't been like this. Perhaps their meditation had been too simple and the true spiritual aspects of the site had remained in hiding.

Tayven heard a sound. Vultures? He opened his eyes. No, not the caw of birds. It was human laughter. He saw a ragged figure capering about nearby. He could not tell whether it was male or female. Its hair was a mess of tangles and twigs, its clothes mere rags tied together to create a weird fluttering robe. It carried a tall twisted staff and its feet were bound with flaking scraps of hide and fur.

Tayven glanced at Taropat and saw that his eyes were also open. Merlan's head was drooping toward his chest, his hair falling over his face, while Shan's face was screwed up in concentration.

"Open your eyes, all of you," Taropat said in a low voice.

Merlan did not raise his head.

The strange figure hopped toward them in an odd, crablike manner. It turned its head from side to side like a bird. Tayven saw that its matted hair was pinioned with stiff black and white feathers. From the scrawny naked chest revealed by the rents in its robes, it was still not clear whether this was a man or a woman. Its age was also indeterminate.

Taropat stood up. "Are you the guardian of this site?"

The figure cackled and brandished its staff in Taropat's direction. "You can't breathe, can you? Want to breathe."

"We seek the knowledge of Rubezal," said Taropat patiently. "Tell us your name."

The figure ceased laughing and tramped through the marsh toward them. "They all want knowledge," it said. "That's why they come. I watch them. I'm Goodgog. What have you got for me?"

"We have coins," Taropat said. "Will you help us?"

"We'll have to see," Goodgog replied, somewhat loftily. "Isn't my choice. The serpent will decide. Then it might let you breathe. It's been waiting a long time. Give me a coin."

Taropat took out his purse and offered a bronze sickin to the guardian. It wrinkled up its face. "Not that. I only eat gold, or maybe silver."

"I don't have gold," Taropat said, "but I do have silver." He offered the guardian another coin.

The guardian took it, sniffed it, then swallowed it. "Good," it said. "That's better. Clears the sight, silver does." It then peered at Taropat's companions. "What pretty creatures. Are they for the serpent?"

"We are all here to seek knowledge," Taropat said.

"Oh," answered Goodgog in some disappointment. "Better drowned. More pretty then."

"The serpent is the spirit of this place?" Taropat said. "What shall we offer it?"

"Not your place to decide," answered the guardian. "It takes what it wants, your life or your soul or your sanity. I like to watch."

"Hmm," said Taropat. "We intend to pass on from this place with all those attributes intact."

"Then you must fight him," said Goodgog. "But when you do he'll take the form most likely to squash you flat. That is the way."

"If we vanquish the serpent, may we pass to Pancanara?" Taropat asked.

The mad creature laughed. "If you vanquish the serpent, I'll take you there myself, otherwise I'll feast on your bones. It's all one to me."

"The lake exists, then?" Shan said. "It's a physical place?"

"Why are you here?" Goodgog snapped. "Because there is no seventh lake?" The guardian uttered a snort of derision. "Course it exists. No one goes there though. No one passes beyond Rubezal, not since the days of the great king. I wasn't here then, but the place remembers."

"Have you been there?" Tayven asked.

"I know the path," said Goodgog. "That's enough."

"But you haven't actually seen it."

The guardian shook its staff in Tayven's face. "Shut up, boy! What do you know? You'll be dead in a moment. The serpent'll have you. He likes tender flesh. I like to watch."

"What must we do to invoke the serpent?" Taropat said.

"Invoke him?" Again the guardian laughed. "He's already here. Walk out into the marsh a short way and invite him to eat you. He'll be up from the depths soon enough."

Tayven glanced at Merlan. He did not think Merlan would be strong enough to confront the spirit of Rubezal.

Taropat clearly had no such considerations. "On your feet, Merlan," he said. "We're nearly there now."

"Taropat," Tayven said softly, shaking his head significantly.

"What?" said Taropat.

"He can't."

"Why not? He got this far."

"It's up to Merlan," Shan said. "Only he can decide."

Merlan raised his head. His expression was utterly without hope. "I will go to the serpent," he said.

"Merlan, no!" Tayven snapped. "You'll have to fight for your life, your sanity. Can you do that?"

"Do I want to?" Merlan said.

Tayven raised his hands in exasperation. "Taropat, this is a travesty. We can't do this. Would you sacrifice your brother to the lake?"

The moment he said these words a tense stillness fell between them. Taropat said nothing. Tayven shook his head. "No!"

"He's not destined to die," Taropat said. "I'm sure of it."

"Death might be the least of his worries," Tayven said.

Merlan stood up. "I will do it. I can't go back."

Tayven put his hands upon Merlan's arms. "You don't have to do this. You are not one of the three. You've fulfilled your task already."

Merlan smiled sadly. "I made myself part of this. I am prepared to face whatever comes."

"Then I'll be with you," Tayven said. "I will be with you in the dark. I am the light, remember."

"Touching," Taropat said. "He is more me than I ever was, isn't he, Tayven?"

"Khaster would never have come this far," Tayven replied.

Taropat shrugged. "Well, let's get this over with."

The guardian accompanied them to a small island of stiff sharp swamp grass. It watched them compose themselves on the damp ground with a disturbingly greedy relish. Mist was thickening over the water, making ghosts of the trees. "The serpent has the Dragon's Breath," said the guardian. "Guards it. Is that what you've come for?"

"The third artifact," Shan said to Taropat, who nodded.

"Only the true bard may wield it," said the guardian.

Taropat turned to Tayven. "Do you understand what this means?"

Tayven nodded glumly. "This is my site. I should have known."

"It is a great responsibility," Taropat said. "We do not yet know whether the Breath is a real artifact or not, but its lesson must pass to you here." He turned back to Goodgog. "You recognize us for what we are, don't you?"

The guardian put its head to one side, stared at Taropat with an unexpected sanity. "I see what I see. Tides are missed, sometimes. Human failing. You can only try." With these words, the guardian flapped a dismissive hand at them and splashed away through the bog.

"This must be taken as a good sign," Taropat said. "Is everyone ready?"

"As we'll ever be," said Shan.

"If that's possible," said Merlan.

Tayven swallowed hard, his heart beating fast. He nodded.

As Taropat began the meditation, Tayven found it very difficult to close his eyes and relinquish control. Something told him he didn't have to.

"See in your mind's eye the spiritual landscape of Rubezal," Taropat said. "The guardian will come to us. Go to him pure in heart. Think only of the Crown. Show that our intentions are pure."

The mist was now so thick, Tayven's companions were mere shadows beside him. An instinct compelled him to stand up. Surely the group had been sitting close together? He could not see them at all now, and when he walked around a few paces, he still could not find them. He was alone. He heard, in the distance, a peal of lunatic laughter. Overhead, a vulture screamed.

"Come to me, then," Tayven said aloud. "I'm ready."

The scene before him was utterly still. He could see only a few feet in front of him. "Merlan," Tayven said, then louder. "Merlan? Where are you? Find me. Hear my voice."

There was only silence.

Carefully, Tayven ventured forward. Water rose about his ankles, seeped into the welts on his leg where the leeches had bitten him. "Merlan!" He couldn't fail a friend, and despite their differences he was sure that was what they had become. Perhaps there was some truth in the implication Taropat had made. Merlan had taken Khaster's place in Tayven's mind. He was the weak and vulnerable one now, and Tayven felt he must help him, as he couldn't have helped before.

He heard a hiss in the fog ahead of him and began to splash toward it more quickly, only to fall forward. The ground disappeared beneath him. He sank beneath the dark waters only to rise swiftly. Now he swam. The mist cleared a little and he saw another low island ahead, ringed by stunted leafless tress that grew out of the water, their bare branches hung with tatters of withered vines. Something moved there, slowly.

Tayven pulled himself out of the lake, grasping the warty roots of the black trees. Another hiss echoed through the thinning mist. The serpent. Tayven crept forward, his hand reaching instinctively for the dagger that hung at his hip. The air was incredibly cold and the mist of his breath seemed only to thicken the fog around him. He needed clarity. He needed warmth.

Tayven pushed through a tangle of drooping branches and found himself in a mud-floored clearing. Moisture dripped from the tortured limbs of the trees and the air smelled fetid. Something writhed in the mud: a mass of thick slimy coils streaked with filth. The serpent. Here it was. Immense and full of guile. Ragged fins along its flanks suggested it was an amphibious beast. Its head, which rose hissing as Tayven approached, was that of an ugly fish. Tayven froze. The serpent's head reared higher and higher. Its eyes were acid yellow, fixing him with a flat gaze.

"Come to me." Tayven's fingers closed about the knife, although in his heart he sensed this weapon would be of little benefit in any fight to come.

The serpent shook itself, and its image wavered. Tentacles rose from it, which presently Tayven realized were arms. The serpent had acquired a semi-human appearance. To the waist, it had the form of a beautiful boy, which melded into flexing coils. The creature's limbs wove upon the air in a cruel dance. It smiled, showing sharp teeth, and a narrow forked tongue flickered out. "Come to you?" it lisped. "Why should I? What have you got that I desire?" It cupped its childlike face with its hands. "Not your beauty, for am I not as beautiful as you?"

"You have something I desire, demon," Tayven hissed. "The Dragon's Breath. I am the bard to the king. It is mine by right. Give it to me."

The serpent cackled. "If you are really the bard, then you'd know that song of the king is one only of truth."

"I know it," Tayven said. "I am here before you."

The serpent chuckled again, a hideous chitinous noise that sounded like the clashing of a thousand beetle wings. "But you *have* lied, lovely bard. You have lied to your comrades, haven't you? You knew what you wanted for yourself all along. Not the Crown of Silence, that's for sure, because silence does not flatter a bard."

"I have not lied," Tayven said. "Look into my heart and you will see the truth."

The serpent's slit eyes widened in mock horror. "Don't you know that when a bard lies he commits murder? He murders truth, and from the lips of the king's bard, that kills a part of the world. If, indeed, you are the one you claim to be."

A deathly cold stole through Tayven's body, paralyzing his flesh. He tried to speak but found that his tongue, even his breath, had frozen in his mouth.

The serpent lunged toward him, drew back. "If you come for me, I will bite and kill you with my poison. Your poison, evil child."

Dread folded over Tayven like a tide of stinking slime. Dread was the breath of the serpent. The creature ran its hand down its smooth flanks. "A mirror in a tree," it said. At once, its face transformed into a reflection of Tayven's own. "Such shallow pride, such vanity. Perhaps you have everything I desire after all."

Tayven felt consciousness begin to slip away. He could not breathe. The fetid air burned his mouth and throat like sulfurous gas.

He must hang on. He must keep his senses, his wits. This was the lesson of the lake.

"Ahhh," breathed the serpent, "to be desired by princes and kings. I am you, Tayven. I am the snake inside your pretty skin that bit them and poisoned their hearts."

Tayven managed to take a breath, though his throat burned. "No," he gasped. "You lie."

"Khasterrrrr." The serpent whistled the name. The sound of it vibrated the ground beneath Tayven's feet. "I seduced him with my beauty and pretty songs," said the serpent. "He came to my arms and lay there willingly. I was his destruction. But for me, he would now be sitting at Almorante's side, companion to the king."

"Almorante is not king," Tayven spluttered. "He never will be. You lie."

"I do lie, because I am you," admitted the serpent, "Your pretty songs were nothing but lies and now, because of you, your friends will perish here. I will devour them for their false trust in your deceit. Why don't you sing for me while I feast, lovely bard? I like a pretty tune."

"You are an illusion," Tayven said. "I deny you."

"You cannot deny yourself, for are you not a master of illusions? You are many things. Remember them."

Tayven found himself unable to look away from the face of the serpent, a hideous caricature of his own features, attenuated and sly.

"Look well, bard, and judge yourself to be an illusion." The image of the beast shivered again, and another torso appeared along-side the first, rising from the same body. This aspect had six arms, all of which held weapons. Its face was twisted into a brutal sneer. "I can kill Khaster in any manner you choose," it said. "The blade or the dart, or a cup of poison. Which will it be?"

Then another body squeezed out of the squirming coils, lunging forward to breathe in Tayven's face. It was an old man, with long straggling hair and rheumy eyes, which were rimmed with thick, flak-ing makeup. "I was lovely once," it said. "My face has now betrayed me. Can you believe it? Now I am a twisted and withered flower condemned to sit before a mirror for eternity. The torment of lost beauty is no illusion, Tayven, neither is the fear of it that eats at your belly."

Another body sprang forth, and another, beseeching him, threatening him. Tayven's mind whirled in confusion. Each of these disgusting manifestations was an aspect of himself. His self-revulsion was made flesh before him, hungry for his energy, a forest of undulating forms that surrounded him completely. He felt as if the life was being sucked from his body.

"You cannot deny me," said the serpent, "because I am everywhere and everyone. I am all that is ignoble within you."

Tayven had sunk to his knees in the mud. A rank dismal rain fell from the oppressive sky. All was lost. No hope. Everything was his fault. He had turned the damaged Khaster into the emotionless Taropat. He was a being of cold vanity, an empty spiritless whore who led greater men astray for his own gratification. He closed his eyes, feeling the serpent forms closing in upon him. Khaster was dead, his heart ripped out. The quest was over. Tayven did not believe in the Crown strongly enough. He hadn't believed when it could have counted, when it had mattered. The world was a vile place, and evil influences within it corrupted everything that had the potential to be great. Valraven Palindrake. At one time, he could have been the man to be king. Maycarpe's secret hope was that the Dragon Lord still was the one. Palindrake knows me, Tayven thought. In Cos, he saw into my heart. He is my king. There is no doubt. Whatever he was, whatever he is, he is still more than any of us. Isn't it our duty to guide him, to be his knights against the dark influence of the Malagashes? Isn't that why we're here? If we were strong enough. If we believed enough. He expelled a groan and pressed his hands against his eyes. If Taropat knew . . . Tayven could not bear to think of it. The ultimate betrayal. Should Taropat discover the truth, their fragile new relationship would explode in flames and the quest would end in ruin.

The serpent laughed softly and a voice whispered in Tayven's ear. "Oh, we have a little honesty now, do we? All the time you fraternized with Almorante, didn't you secretly wish it was Valraven? Could it not be said that your love for Khaster was nothing but a

substitute for the burning desire you felt for the Dragon Lord? Your
relationship with Leckery was a foolish delusion to get close to someone who was close to Valraven. You were just a hopeful whore who
wished to belong to the dark king and become the light to his darkness. Now, you think noble thoughts, but the truth is you just want
him. And with the Dragon's Breath, you could have him. That's it,
isn't it? You are no chivalric knight, Tayven Hirantel. The idea is
laughable. Palindrake is only the king of your heart because of your
own greedy lust. What makes you think the Dragon Lord of the
empire could be the true king? He kills, he ruins, he is without compassion. Is he really fit to wear the Crown? No. This quest is a lie.
None of you speak the truth to one another. You have no hope of
succeeding. Why not just end it now? Come to me. I can end it for
you now."

Tayven shuddered. How could he dispute the serpent's words?
He saw his heart pulsing within his chest: a black, rotten core. He
should take out his knife and cut his own throat, end it now: the lies,
the deceit, the corruption, then the others might survive. His fingers
groped toward his belt. Then Merlan's voice rang through his head.
"Don't give up, Tayven. You are the one. We know the truth. You
were meant to have the Dragon's Breath. The love you felt for Khaster was pure. The love you can give now is pure. Take back the hope
you tried to give to me. I relinquish it. I am no longer afraid."

Tayven looked up expecting to see Merlan's face, but his gaze
fell directly upon the eyes of the serpent. One of its heads, that of
the sly young boy, was inches from his own. "Yes, you can love,
Tayven, but only yourself," it whispered. "You are the whore, the
schemer, the vain fool doomed to age and wither, the bitter assassin."

"No" Merlan's voice pierced the air, strong, firm and clear. "You
are beautiful, Tayven, but within, you are also hope and love and
courage. You have been the light to my darkness. I am behind you.
I can see you. Listen to me."

Tayven looked behind him, but all he could see was a filthy mist.
"Merlan?" he murmured.

The serpent hissed, laughed. "Wishes, dreams," it purred.

Merlan's voice came again, urgently. "Hear me, Tayven. The

demon cannot touch me. I've already defeated it, because I saw the truth of myself. I'd already denied all that I thought I was. It doesn't lie when it says you are an illusion but, like I did, you must deny yourself. You must. That's the secret. That's what Almorante couldn't do. Do it now. Leave all that you were behind. Let go of the past. Shed your skin and the breath of new life shall be yours."

Was that really Merlan's voice? Tayven couldn't be sure. Perhaps, ultimately, it was his own.

The serpent bellowed and raised its arms. "Come to me, bard. I will embrace you. You are mine. You belong to me utterly."

Tayven raised himself from the mud and threw his arms around the writhing beast before him. Its flesh was colder than the depths of Malarena. Tayven felt as if his brain were pierced by a thousand splintering darts of ice. The creature hissed and twisted in his grasp, its fingers clawed at his face, but he would not let go. "I embrace you," he cried. "I conquered fear at Malarena. I take you into myself. I face myself."

"Tayven!"

Tayven turned his head and saw Shan standing among the trees nearby. He held out the Dragon's Claw on its leather thong. "Take it, Tayven! Use it!" He threw the Claw and with one hand, Tayven reached out and caught it. Without pausing, he thrust his arm down the throat of the sly serpent-boy. He would use the Claw to rip out its dark lying heart. He surrendered himself to fate, uncaring of whether he lived or died, sure only that the serpent should be destroyed. His arm was enfolded by a cold, glutinous mass that squeezed his bones. He could feel something moving beneath his hand and plunged the Claw into it. As he did so, his arm was thrust back by a mighty force. The serpent's face hung before him, its mouth three times as large as it had been, dripping a stinking black ichor. Its eyes were mad with rage and pain and it expelled a hurricane of foul-smelling breath, which punched into his mouth. It was a hideous parody of when Taropat had passed his essence to Khaster. Tayven felt the serpent's breath writhing madly within him. Pulses of energy coursed through his flesh. He felt as if his body would burst. He was not strong enough to contain it. Then, with a final thunderous hiss sizzling in his ears, Tayven was thrown backward. His spine collided painfully with a tree trunk and dead branches rained down onto him. He was choking on something, which was lodged in his throat. He could not breathe. He must expel it.

Tayven fell forward onto his knees coughing and retching. Something flew from his mouth and landed in the mud before him. It gleamed wetly: a perfect blue pearl. He looked up, desperate to see the result of his actions. Had he done the right thing, or had he merely compounded the darker aspects of himself? He fought his way free of the dead wood and struggled to his feet. The serpent was nothing more than a pile of shrivelled skin before him. Its life force had left it.

A figure came out of the trees. Was this another illusion? Merlan stepped forward and put his hands upon Tayven's shoulders. "It's over," he said. "I feel it."

"Merlan?" Tayven asked. "Is it you? *Was* it you?"

Merlan nodded. "I am here. You did it, Tay. You conquered the serpent."

"*We* conquered it," Tayven said. "But for your voice I would have been lost. And the Claw. Shan threw it to me. I used it to pierce the serpent's heart." He lifted his hands, flexed the fingers. "The Claw . . ." He looked round. "Where is it? I've lost it. Where's Shan? He was here."

"I didn't see him," Merlan said. He stooped down and picked up the blue pearl from the mud. "What's this?"

Tayven touched his throat, swallowed, then took the pearl from Merlan's hand. "It is a symbol of the Dragon's Breath. It's in me, Merlan. I can barely describe it. It's as if my dark self, all my self-doubt, has been transformed. Through the Breath, I can enable great men to overcome their own darkness. I *am* the bard of the king, Merlan. I have become an avatar of hope, the light I believed myself to be before. I can be the light to Valraven's darkness." He laughed coldly. "And it won't be about sex, I promise you. This might all sound insane, but I feel it completely."

"*Is* Valraven the king?" Merlan asked.

Tayven stared at him for some moments. "We both know it, Merlan."

Merlan sighed and shook his head. "It would kill Taropat. How can we do this to him? He is helping us assist his greatest enemy. How can this quest succeed based on such deceit?"

Tayven shook his head. "Taropat is governed by his bitterness. For a great magus, he lets too much of his past incarnation color his present one. Khaster may loathe and detest Valraven, but I'm hoping that Taropat will eventually see the truth."

"Oh, so now you're the expert in letting go of the past, eh?" Merlan said, grinning. He began to laugh, and the laughter was infectious. Tayven reached out for Merlan and they embraced. For a moment, Tayven felt the true joy of spontaneous unity between them. They were surrounded by an aura of innocence and relief.

Tayven drew back. "You were with Valraven in Caradore, when he went to the old domain. Has he really changed, Merlan? Is he really the true Dragon Heir once more?"

Merlan did not answer immediately. "I saw him wake up," he said, "that's all. The man who went to the shore that evening to invoke the Dragon Queen was very different than the one who left it. He and Varencienne went into a trance. Their experience was private. I'm not close to him, Tay. He didn't tell me what happened. I can't give you the reassurance you want. Maybe all we have is faith. I just hope we're not deluded by wishful thinking." He sighed and gazed around the tiny island. "We are all changing. Perhaps we can become the worthy men we aspire to be. I had no hope, I was willing to die, yearning it even. But here I learned that Rubezal is the mirror of the soul. My vision was true of this place. We were separated, lost and wandering. But what I didn't realize was that it was an essential sequence of events. A person has to face the guardian of Rubezal alone. There is no other way."

"How did you conquer it?" Tayven asked. "What form did it take for you, Merlan?"

"It was always myself, just that. Inertia, pessimism, fear. I was alone with myself, almost satisfied that I was lost in an eternal hinterland. But it didn't come to me, Tayven, and then I realized that this was simply because I had no desires, no illusions about myself or this quest. It wanted nothing from me nor I from it."

"But what made you come for me?"

"Because in my mind, I saw you wrestling with a great beast of many faces. I saw your strength trickling away. At Malarena, and since, you tried to give me your hope. It was as if it was in my keeping, in a way. I had to give it back. I had to become involved again, and in doing so, fought the lethargy within me. But for you, I would have been lost, because I was unwilling to continue."

"But for you, so would I," Tayven said, "so perhaps we were not as alone at this place as you foretold." He looked around himself again. "Was Shan really here? Did I really have the Claw? We should go and look for the others, find out."

"If it is over for them," Merlan answered.

They walked to the shore of the island and saw that the mist was now only a thin veil over the water. A great bloated sun of crimson red hung among the mountain peaks beyond the vale of Rubezal. It hung in a dull white sky.

"The sun sets," Tayven said. "We have to leave here."

They made their way as quickly as they could toward the far side of the swampy lake. There was no sign of Taropat or Shan, or even the mad guardian. Then they saw someone sitting among the trees beside the shore and made their way over. It was Shan. He looked dazed and was wet through, his hair dark and matted against his head and shoulders. When he saw Tayven and Merlan his expression changed.

"Thank all the gods!" he said. "I thought I was the only one. Merlan, it pleases me beyond measure to see you again."

"Where is Taropat?" Tayven said.

"I haven't seen him yet," Shan answered. "Do you think . . . ?"

"We wait," Tayven said, "but we don't have much time. I feel strongly we need to leave here before nightfall."

Shan nodded. "I agree."

Tayven sat down beside him. "What happened to you, Shan? Can you tell us?"

Shan took a deep breath. "I had to fight myself. I was a black
knight, but no great hero. I was full of resentment, convinced Taropat
and the rest of you were using me. I wasn't being trained to be a
great warrior, just a lackey. I felt I, of everyone, had the right to be
king, and that all of you knew it, but were trying to stop it happening.
I found myself back at Doon Pond, where I acquired the Claw. King
Morogant hung in the water, taunting me. He told me I could never
be king, that I was not even a warrior, just a bitter man's menial. A
poor peasant boy. Peasants don't become kings except in fairy tales.
I was so angry, I took the Claw from my neck and threw it back
into the lake. I screamed that I didn't want it, that I'd find my own
way, independent of everyone else. I could be king of my own life,
and that was all that was important. I realized that the secret fantasy
I had of conquering the Malagashes and becoming king was an illusion. I wanted to be so much more than I had been. I was haunted
by the past, feeling that it was some kind of trap, waiting to take me
back into itself, hold me there forever. I imagined being an intelligent
mind bound within an ignorant one, looking out. A scholar trapped
inside a peasant, mute and powerless. It was ridiculous. I can be
whatever I want to be. We create ourselves constantly." He smiled.
"So, my less than noble origins no longer matter. I can face being
my father's son again. I could return to Holme and take up my life
there, enriched by all that happened to me. I would still be who I am
now." He shook his head. "My lesson here was that I had to overcome
my vanity. Once I'd relinquished that, I opened my eyes and found
myself back here. I thought I'd lost the Claw, but it was still in my
hand."

"You lent it to me for a while," Tayven said.

"What?"

Tayven explained what had happened to Merlan and himself.

As he finished the tale, a voice said behind them, "We all fought
illusion!" Taropat had joined them. His clothes were dry, but his
expression grim.

"Where's that damn madman," he said. "We must leave here at
once."

"Don't you want to know what happened to us?" Tayven asked. He held out the pearl. "Look, the Dragon's Breath. A real artifact."

"Of course I want to know," Taropat replied, taking the pearl and examining it in a cursory manner. "But I still feel strongly we should converse on the way. I'm uneasy about remaining here."

"Can't you just tell us a little about what you saw?" Tayven said. He folded his arms. "We won't move until you do."

"Deceit crowned and throned," Taropat said shortly. "My worst fear. That's all you need to know. Come on, now. On your feet." He handed the pearl back to Tayven.

"You must tell us more than that," Merlan said.

Taropat sighed impatiently, spoke briskly. "First, I met a dozen trickster serpents, who foxed me with intellectual riddles, all of which I answered. When this ruse failed, I was beset by incubi wearing faces I knew. These I dismissed. Then I saw it. The Crown. It was on the head of an enemy, and no matter what I did or thought or felt, the image would not change. In the end, I simply walked away from it."

"That sounds a bit . . . strange," Shan said.

"Who wore the Crown?" Tayven asked.

"No one," Taropat said. "A phantom, a lie."

"Who was it?" Tayven persisted.

Taropat hesitated, then said, "Some things it is best not to speak aloud. I will not give that preposterous illusion reality by uttering the words to form it. It was obviously my greatest fear and I conquered it by negating it, and that's that."

Merlan and Tayven exchanged a glance, and Tayven blinked slowly to indicate he knew what Merlan was thinking. His silent message was: don't speak, not yet.

Shan was frowning. "I don't understand," he said. "How could you just walk away from the serpent, without being engulfed or swallowed up?"

Taropat sniffed. "I came prepared, of course. A true magician always has some means to overcome a menace. That's the difference between us. It's why you are still an apprentice and I the master."

Shan's expression darkened and he opened his mouth to respond, but Merlan quickly interjected, "You must share your methods with us, Taropat. I've never heard of negation being used as a weapon before."

Tayven linked his arm through Merlan's, aware this might make Taropat squirm. "There's more to consider. As the serpent represents a person's self-delusion, perhaps you should rethink your actions, and whether they were actually appropriate."

Taropat, clearly uncomfortable, responded with false levity. "What, by the living flame, do you mean?"

"Well," Tayven replied, "you might have just negated yourself." He couldn't contain a grin. Beside him, Merlan snorted with laughter.

Shan slapped his thigh. "He's right! You walked away from yourself."

It wasn't funny at all really, but Merlan, Shan and Tayven couldn't stop laughing. Their amusement clearly irritated Taropat further. "You're behaving like children," he said. "Take control of yourselves. I knew what I was doing, and I have not negated myself." He put his hands on his hips and gazed around himself. "We must leave this place immediately."

"But where's the guardian?" Shan asked, wiping his eyes, and composing his face into a more sober expression. "Goodgog was going to take us to Pancanara."

"We must go without the mad fool," Taropat said. "Make our own way. We have little time."

"And which way should we go?" Merlan said. "Do you have any idea?"

"Follow our instincts," Taropat replied curtly. "Use the die if necessary."

"That'll get you nowhere!" The guardian came splashing toward them, apparently having materialized out of thin air.

"Well, we survived intact, as you see," Taropat said. "You said you would show us the path to Pancanara. We are ready to walk it."

"In all my years, I've never known anyone cross to the opposite shore," said the guardian. "The serpent let you pass."

"We conquered him," Tayven said. "We know his face. We

guessed his secret. And look, he gave us the Dragon's Breath." He held out the pearl.

Goodgog wouldn't take it, but squinted at it keenly. "You are mighty heroes, then. But what is the secret of Pancanara, eh? Do you know? Does anyone know?" The guardian cackled. "No one's ever got there, so it's all a mystery. Are you ready to climb the path? It's all uphill from here."

"How can there be a simple, actual path to the seventh lake?" Tayven said. "If there was, others would have found it before us. People who were ignorant and unaware, to whom the lessons of the lakes meant nothing. Physically, they could have got there, surely? We can't walk the path with our bodies."

"You think so, pretty boy?" said Goodgog. "These mountains have been here since the beginning of time. They know how to hide their secret paths. You need me now, because the mountains know me. They let me pass. And I need your silver coin, because I'm hungry."

NIGHT DID NOT FALL so much as creep all around them. Goodgog led the way, striking the ground with its staff. Now it was Taropat's turn to be subdued and fretful. He would not speak to the others and answered their questions only with monosyllables. Merlan, Tayven and Shan wanted to talk about their experiences, but even though Taropat listened, he did not join the conversation. Goodgog regaled them with tales of those who had failed at Rubezal, the often hideously mangled corpses that had been left behind. The group, apart from Taropat, was in a mood bordering on delirium. It was the product of their immense relief. They had faced Rubezal and survived. They had gained another artifact. Surely, there was nothing else to fear now.

Merlan was surprised at how healthy and vigorous he felt. Several days now without proper food. Merlan no longer felt terrible pangs of hunger, but was aware this deprivation had changed his state of mind. It was surely unnatural not to crave food? The thought of it now actually made him feel slightly nauseous. The hours following his experience at Malarena and emerging from the mist at Rubezal seemed as incoherent and unreal as a dream. He sensed that roles within the group had shifted somehow. He felt akin to Tayven, yet wary of Taropat, and could never have imagined that happening. It was clearly because he and Tayven had become conspirators. He hated the deceit, but felt powerless to do anything about it. The truth would only end the quest.

Merlan could not guess what was to come, and in some ways wondered whether it would all be rather an anticlimax. He found it difficult to visualize what might exceed the strange experiences of Malarena and Rubezal. They were the lakes of trial and torment. Pancanara, by contrast, was reputed to be the site of ultimate serenity. Where would they find the Crown? Would it simply be in another meditation, or would it manifest in reality as the Dragon's Breath had done? Despite everything that had happened, Merlan could not imagine that they'd leave Magravandias with a physical crown in their possession. During their quest, they'd faced fears and aspects of themselves. They'd acquired knowledge, but were they really any nearer to understanding the mystical qualities of the Dragon artifacts, or what they represented? Were they any nearer to being the magical company that Maycarpe envisaged? It seemed their own weaknesses had been emphasized too much.

Goodgog took them up a steep, gravelly path that wound between high walls of rock. The landscape appeared barren now. There were no plants sprouting from the chasm walls, no creatures scuttling away through the dust. In some seasons, perhaps this path was a waterfall. It was cut with deep fissures, which appeared to have been made by water. The further they climbed, the more difficult it became to breathe easily. Merlan was not the only one who had to keep stopping to catch his breath.

"Come on, come on," Goodgog urged, thumping its staff against the path. "Have you got all night? Have you?"

The guardian led them beyond the path into a landscape that seemed to belong to a different world. High crags of black rock loomed around them, illuminated by cold distant starlight. There was no mist here. Merlan couldn't see any pathways among the precipitous flanks of stone. The rocks might well have been the tumbled ruins of cyclopean buildings, erected millennia past by a lost race who had long since turned to dust. It was an eerie place, totally devoid of human life.

The group stood on a narrow platform, and ahead of them was a sheer drop, with no discernible route down, up or to the side. The opposite crag was not that distant, but without a bridge, it might as well have been a million miles away. They could see another platform on the other side, lower down.

"How do we proceed from here?" Taropat asked wearily.

"Easy," said the guardian, "if you've spirit that is. Many haven't. You have to swing across."

"Swing across?" Shan peered over the edge. "Am I right in thinking you mean with these old ropes?"

The others looked where he indicated. A number of hairy ropes were attached to a spine of rock that stuck out from the cliff.

"That's it," said Goodgog.

"They don't look very safe," Merlan said. "When were they last used?"

"How should I know that?" Goodgog snapped. It hesitated. "What a bunch of lily-livered boys you are. Let Goodgog help. I'll give you a gift, every one of you. Will you take it?"

"Yes," said Taropat stonily.

"My balance and deftness," he said. "I'll kiss it into you. Will you take a kiss from Goodgog?"

Given the guardian's earlier remarks about the company, Merlan couldn't help feeling this was just an excuse for it to play with them all.

"We've done many strange things to reach this point," Taropat said. "This is just one more."

"Flatterer," Goodgog said and took Taropat's face in its hands.

Merlan winced, as the kiss seemed to go on for too long. He could not imagine what Taropat must feel and think about it. When the guardian released him, Taropat fell back against the rock, wiping his mouth. He looked more dazed than before.

"Next!" screamed Goodgog.

One by one, they submitted to the guardian's kiss. Merlan steeled himself to do it. He would imagine it was someone else: Varencienne Palindrake. But Varencienne did not have a whiskery chin; neither did her breath smell so foul. Yet as he submitted to it, he was reminded of something Lord Maycarpe had said to him years before. In order to know the white goddess, you had to kiss the black. Was there any parallel here? He remembered the goddess inside him, the daughter of Purryah. All this time, he had not thought of her once.

Goodgog drew away. "By the peaks, this one's a good kisser!" the guardian cried and cackled loudly. "You must go first now."

Numbed, Merlan sat down on the edge of the platform, his legs dangling into space. He took hold of one of the ropes in his hand, hardly aware of the others around him.

"Swing!" cried Goodgog. "Swing out into the void."

Looking down, Merlan could see only blackness. He eased himself down, felt a surge of vertigo. Then he was hanging, pressed against the rock, clinging to the rope.

"Climb down," Goodgog told him, "and when you have a length, kick out."

Merlan glanced up once and saw the pale faces of his companions peering down at him. He had to trust. The rope slipped painfully through his fingers. He could fall right to the end of it. Now there was nothing above him or below. Uttering a cry, he pushed off from the rock face with his feet and found himself swinging out in a great arc. He was no longer conscious of the rope, although he knew his hands must have been gripping it in terror. At any moment, he must come slamming back against the rock.

Out of nowhere, wheeling black shapes came screaming down upon him; three immense vultures. Claws raked his body, wide wings buffeted his head. Merlan shut his eyes tightly. He must not let go of the rope. The birds smelled of ancient dust and dead meat left out in the sun. Their cries were the laughter of hag goddesses. Remember Merytet, daughter of Purryah, Merlan thought. Her cat aspect was the archetypal enemy of the bird. He imagined her within him, somewhere in a deep corner of stillness. Even as the vultures raked his flesh, he concentrated on bringing her forth. She was his flesh, his sinew. Merlan opened his eyes and expelled a loud, yowling cry. It reverberated from rock to rock, dying away in a feline wail.

There were no birds around him, perhaps never had been, but he was swinging now over the opposite platform. The experience had taken only seconds. He let go of the rope and dropped onto the rock. Crouching down, he turned and saw his companions on the other side of the gulf, punching the air, smiling over at him. If they made a sound, he could not hear them. His ears were ringing with a strange whistling wind. For a few moments, his vision blurred with boiling specks of light. He became aware, with a startling clarity, of a gulf between himself and the others. It was more than a physical space between them. Then Shan was climbing down to take hold of the rope and the moment passed. No. They were together in this. They were one.

A PATH LED from the platform, which was so overhung by dark rock, it was almost a tunnel. Gradually, the path became narrower and steeper, until the company was forced to climb, hands gripping spurs of stone, feet slipping on friable scree. Goodgog had not accompanied them from the platform. Now, they were on their own. The only sound was that of their ragged breathing, the smothered oaths as a footing was lost, the crunch of trodden stones. The cliffs around them were of deepest black, shot with opalescent veins that glittered in the harsh light of the stars. Nothing grew there. Merlan was conscious of every breath he drew. The action was no longer automatic and could not satisfy the body's craving for oxygen. Higher, higher, toward the sky. Merlan saw a white, ghostly staircase leading up to the moon. He blinked and it was gone.

Taropat, who was in the lead, came to a halt above the others. Slowly, they clambered up to join him. It seemed to take an eternity. Merlan fell to his knees beside his brother. A spiky crown of black peaks, which formed the crater of an extinct volcano, surrounded them. Below them was a stretch of water, which even in the dark shone so deeply blue it was as if a pool of midnight sky had fallen and lay trapped there. Pancanara. Stillness and silence were absolute.

Without speaking, Taropat began to slide down the rock toward the shore of the lake, which was no more than a rind of polished obsidian. The lake was held within this hard setting like a precious jewel, motionless and perfect. Here was the end of the quest, and it was mute and blind. No guardians. No lesson. Just Pancanara itself.

Merlan's body went limp and he tumbled down the slope toward the water, coming to rest on his back, next to Taropat who knelt staring out across the serene expanse of blue. Shan and Tayven joined them, and the four sprawled without speaking, simply breathing, slowly, raspingly. What now? Merlan thought. We have no strength. We are witless with exhaustion. The lake is dreaming. It does not know we're here.

"We must not sleep," Taropat said, with great effort, but already Shan was unconscious beside him, and Tayven was blinking so slowly, it was clear he would not be awake for much longer. Taropat reached for his brother's hand. "We must . . . wait . . . watch . . . not sleep."

We will sleep, Merlan thought, and it seemed as if he spoke the words aloud. Perhaps it will be the eternal sleep. No one has come here and returned to speak of it. No one.

24

THE CROWN OF SILENCE

TAYVEN WAS AWOKEN by a sound that had ebbed to silence by the time he opened his eyes. Slowly, he raised himself on the rock. His companions still slept beside him and the perfect cerulean blue of Pancanara dreamed on undisturbed in the light of dawn. He could not remember falling asleep, and his slumber had been unbroken by dreams. His body ached from the previous day's climb, but now the air did not seem so difficult to breathe. He felt neither hungry nor tired, but completely alert. Had there been a sound? He felt a strange vibration shudder through his right hand and up his arm. Uncurling his fingers, he was surprised to see the blue pearl nestling in his palm. It had been in his backpack when he'd gone to sleep. Had he sleepwalked to retrieve it? The sound came again: a strange tonal hum that was almost a human voice. Tayven closed his eyes and surrendered himself to the experience of the sound. There were no words to it, but in his mind, it seemed to say, "Follow me."

Tayven opened his eyes and the vibration ceased. The stillness of the atmosphere was a palpable force that pushed itself into his body.

It was a drug stealing through his veins, conjuring euphoria. He hardly dared breathe, because the sound of it was too loud, a brute human intrusion into this sacred place. Was the air above the crown of peaks shimmering? He squinted up, sure that something moved just beyond his perception. Silvery ribbons flashed at the corner of his eye. A sense of presence was building up around him. The others must wake up. He reached out and touched Taropat's shoulder, whispered his name, but Taropat only mumbled in his sleep and did not stir. Tayven shifted into a crouch, staring out over the water. Another sound came suddenly: a low, thrumming bass note, followed by a soft ripple of higher tones. The sounds seemed to emanate from the air around him and the pearl shivered in his grasp, as if in response. If this was music, it could only be the spiritual symphony of the mountains themselves. The shimmering above the peaks was clearer now, as if the air were dancing.

A ball of light suddenly shot out from the mountain opposite and hung poised over the water. Presently, it was joined by another, and another, until over a dozen spinning spheres of radiance created a living constellation above the lake. The others had to see this. Tayven had to wake them. Still, he dared not speak higher than a whisper. "Merlan, Shan, Taropat . . ." He shook each of them in turn, urging them to open their eyes. Merlan was the easiest to rouse. He looked into Tayven's face, who put a finger to his lips and murmured. "Look, we have company . . ."

Merlan turned onto his side, muttered, "By Madragore, what is that?"

Taropat woke up and physically jumped when he saw the spheres. "Earth lights!" he hissed.

"What are they?" said Shan, pushing hair from his eyes.

"Manifestations of the earth's energy, its intelligence, its power to create," Taropat said.

"Something's coming," Tayven said. "Can you feel it?" The air felt electric now, as if invisible lightning struck all around them. Tayven noticed the hairs on his arms were standing up.

It seemed that once the spheres knew they had the attention of the humans upon the rock, they began to put on a display. At first, they moved lazily around one another and the almost inaudible tones in the air became louder. The music was slow, stately, but gradually built in speed and intensity. The spheres danced with greater wildness, spinning around one another in complicated patterns.

"It's as if they are alive," Shan said. "Are they elden? Where's the music coming from?"

"Don't ask, just experience," Taropat said shortly. He got to his feet.

Abruptly as it began, the dance ended and the spheres dropped like stones into the lake, causing barely a ripple. For some moments, all was still. Tayven and his companions looked at one another, speechless. Tayven longed to ask questions, but could not bring himself to speak, and sensed the others felt the same. Eventually, Shan opened his mouth and Taropat raised a hand quickly to silence him. Simultaneously, the rock beneath them began to shake. Taropat was flung back to his knees. There was no music now, only a thunderous crashing sound, as if the mountains were breaking apart. Tendrils of steam rose from the lake and the air became filled with an acrid mineral stench. Tayven feared that the volcano was coming back to life and that presently magma would erupt from the lake. They would die beneath a deadly hail of ash and molten stone. He felt that the lake was angry. Something was wrong. Should they have said or done something to the earth lights? He reached out and grabbed Taropat's arm, and pulled him close against his body.

Suddenly, a bright light flared up in front of Tayven's eyes. It emanated from Taropat's right hand. Instinctively, Tayven knew that Taropat held the Dragon's Eye within it. He looked up into Taropat's face and saw that his mouth was gaping wide in a scream that was smothered by the cacophony around them. Two burning white rays lanced out from the artifact into Taropat's eyes, which had begun to film over. What was happening? Tayven heard his own name being shouted aloud, then realized it was only in his head. The Dragon's Breath was calling to him. The moment he realized this, a pulse of pain ripped through his body, emanating from his hand, which held the blue pearl. It was how he imagined being struck by lightning would feel. The Dragon's Breath roared with power, a sound that might dissolve his brain with its vibrations. Every fiber of his body shuddered to its resonance. He feared he would break apart. Doubt swept through him. It must all have been vanity, after all. He was not worthy of the gift and now, as punishment, the dragon would kill them all.

Do not decry yourself, whispered a voice in his mind. The gift of the pearl is within you. What need do you have for the bauble that represents its power? Do you not see? Do you not understand? The dragon must know you accept its gift.

Yes, he could understand now. A final sacrifice. Tayven tried to stand up, desperate to reach the waters of the lake, but could not raise his body. It felt as if his bones were fragmenting within his skin. Every muscle and sinew sizzled at the searing frequency of the pearl's vibration. He had to crawl, slowly, tortuously, like a baby learning to use its limbs. He was no longer aware of his companions around him. All that existed was the smoking, bubbling surface of the lake that drew him to itself. At the water's edge, he struggled to his knees.

"Dragon, hear me!" he cried. "I am your servant. The pearl is yours. I return it to you. It is my sacrifice." With a shoulder-wrenching arc, Tayven threw the pearl into the air. It soared out over the lake, where it skimmed across the surface three times before plunging into the roiling water. At once, the destructive vibrations ceased within his mind and body. For a moment, he stood beside the water, gasping, his hands upon his knees. His ears were filled with the hiss of boiling steam. Then, he straightened up and turned to his companions. Other sounds crashed back into his awareness. He could hear a frantic voice, terrible cries of pain. Merlan was standing over Shan, who lay upon the rock, his body writhing into contortions, his face a mask of agony. He clawed at his chest. Tayven could smell burning meat.

"The Claw!" Merlan cried, seeing Tayven coming toward him. "It's burning into his skin. He won't let me touch it."

"Take him to the water," Tayven shouted. "Shan must relinquish the Claw, Merlan. He must return it to the Dragon. Make him throw it into the lake."

Merlan nodded. "I'll do what I can. See to Taropat."

Tayven could see Taropat kneeling upon the rock some distance away. He was motionless, acidic beams of light still pouring out of the Eye toward his face. Tayven squatted down and attempted to wrench the Eye from Taropat's grasp, but it was as if his fingers had turned to iron. "Taropat, can you hear me?" he cried, shaking the man's shoulders. Taropat didn't appear to have heard at all. "You must let go of the Eye. The dragon demands it back." He tried again to prize Taropat's fingers away from the dazzling artifact. Then the shrill of piercing screech from behind him distracted his attention. He turned in time to witness Shan throw the Claw into the air, the torn cord dangling from his blackened neck. The artifact spun through the steam above the lake, and then splashed into the hungry water, amid a roar of flame and sparks. Shan slumped to the ground, his hands dangling in the water. A ragged scream close to Tayven's ear forced him to attend once more to Taropat. The man was shaking his head from side to side. "Merlan!" he cried. "Brother, do not forsake me!"

Merlan came running to Taropat's side. Even though Tayven had been unable to move Taropat's fingers, Merlan pulled the Eye from his brother's grasp. At once, its cruel glare faded away. Merlan cupped it gingerly in both hands.

"Taropat, you must relinquish the Eye," Tayven shouted. The roar and crash of splintering rock and foaming water made it almost impossible for him to be heard. "Speak now! Make your sacrifice."

Taropat, his head hanging, only uttered a groan.

"Go to the lake, Khas," Merlan said. "We'll help you. Once you are there, I'll give you the Eye again. You must throw it into the water. Tell the dragon you return it."

His words appeared to penetrate Taropat's mind. As Tayven had done before, he began to crawl forward, still shaking his head. Then, he reared up to his knees and began to strike the air with floundering arms, all the while uttering stark cries. His hair fell back from his face.

"By Madragore," Merlan cried, "he's blind, Tayven. Blind!"

Taropat threw back his head and roared at the sky. Tayven could see his eyes now, milky white, dead orbs. Without thinking, Tayven began to drag Taropat to the lake's edge, ignoring the glancing blows from the flailing arms. Taropat half fell into the water, his white eyes rolling madly.

"Give me the Eye, Merlan!" Tayven cried.

Merlan handed it to him. Behind him, Shan had got to his feet and now stood watching the others, an expression of horror and revulsion on his face. Tayven pressed the Eye into Taropat's hands. "Now, speak. Make the sacrifice. We are here with you."

Taropat gripped the Eye firmly. His voice was a ragged croak. "I give you my magician's sight. That is my sacrifice. Now give me the Crown!"

"No!" Tayven cried. "Throw it, Khaster. Throw it. Relinquish it."

"The Crown!" roared Taropat, spittle frothing from the corners of his mouth.

Merlan pushed Tayven aside and ripped the Eye from his brother's hands. He ran into the water a few paces. Water seethed around his ankles, a black and eager element. "Take this unto yourself!" he cried and hurled the Eye across the lake. When it reached the center, there was a stark flash of light and the waters came immediately to rest. The roaring sounds subsided, until all that could be heard was the sound of ragged breathing.

"Is it over?" Shan murmured.

"Seems to be," Merlan answered. He knelt down next to Tayven beside his brother, put a hand on Taropat's shoulder.

Taropat raised his face. His eyes were still blind. "The Crown," he gasped. "Where is it? Do any of you have it?"

"No," Tayven said. His throat was constricted with sorrow. Taropat hadn't been able to make the sacrifice. He had paid for his pride with his eyes.

Taropat drew in his breath, slowly, painfully, but before he could speak, the rock beneath them began to shake once more.

"No," said Shan. "Not again. What must we do now? Has he ruined it all? Has he, Tayven?"

"I don't know," Tayven replied. He could barely keep to his knees.

"Perhaps we should try and get out of here," Merlan said. "Let's carry him, Tay."

"I don't know," Tayven said. "I really don't know."

"We can't wait," Merlan answered. "We can't . . ."

The rock suddenly gave a violent jolt and the group was thrown away from each other. Rolling over onto his stomach and coming to rest at the edge of the water, Tayven saw that the surface of the lake had began to surge once more. The noise of grinding stone was again deafening. Taropat was lying nearby. Tayven saw his mouth moving, but could not hear the words. The ground was shaking so violently, all they could do was lie still and grip the rock, hope the tremor would pass. Merlan and Shan managed to crawl to Tayven's side. They drew Taropat to them, clung together.

Was this how their quest must end, in death? Was this the secret of Pancanara? Perhaps Merlan had been right at Malarena after all. Tayven closed his eyes and pressed his forehead against the rock. His teeth were vibrating in his skull. He felt he should pray, but to what? Let it be quick, then, without pain. He felt Merlan's fingers digging agonizingly into the soft flesh above his shoulders, heard him shout close to his ear. He could not hear the words, but his tone made Tayven lift his head.

Something was rising from the lake. Something immense. A mountain. A mountain of crystal. It rose slowly, inexorably, water cascading from its flanks. Were they dreaming? Was this real? The physical sensations did not feel like a dream. Tayven shook off the hold of his companions and scrambled to his knees. Only then did he realize that the earth tremor had diminished. The air was filled with a mighty roar and a hot wind coming off the lake made it difficult for him to keep his eyes open. But he had to see. Even if death followed, his last sight would be of something extraordinary and wondrous. The roaring sound died away and the last crashing waterfalls fell back into the lake. Tayven stared in disbelief at the edifice that dominated the center of Pancanara. Not a mountain but a fabulous city. He saw minarets and towers rising high toward the pulsing sky. They caught the rays of the rising sun, which was reflected with blinding brilliance. Tayven's ears were filled with the music of an unearthly chorus, as if a company of angels sang amid the towers. He could see them now, undulating spectral shapes that clung to the spires of crystal. He turned to the others, pointed wordlessly.

Shan nodded slowly. "I know this place," he said, his eyes strangely unfocused. "It is the city of Sinaclara's shining angel."

A glittering causeway had appeared, which led up to the coruscating walls. Tayven saw the phantom inhabitants beckoning him, calling out to him with their siren song. He could see them more clearly now: women, with long elfin faces, slanting eyes and waving silver hair. He got to his feet, unable to disobey the summons of their voices.

Taropat reached out and gripped his arm. "Don't leave me. What's happening? What can you see?"

"The city of angels," Tayven said. "If Shan is right."

"Sinaclara told me of it," Shan said. "She said it was the cradle of our civilization. I've seen it in dreams."

Taropat uttered a sob, pawed at his blind eyes.

"There are no dragons here, brother," Merlan said. "Come, take my arm. Come with us to the city."

"No!" Taropat cried. "I cannot see it. It might be a trick to lure us to our deaths. I cannot guide you. We have failed."

"It's all right," Shan said, putting an arm around Taropat's shoulder. "We will be your guides now."

"Yes," Tayven said. "We must see this through to the end, all of us together."

"Climb onto my back, master," Shan said. "I will carry you there."

Tears, whether of emotion or merely a physical reaction to his pain, slid down Taropat's face. But he allowed Merlan and Tayven to hoist him onto Shan's back. Ahead of them all, Shan began to wade into the water. Tayven stepped off the rock behind him. He half expected to be able to walk across the lake's surface, but after a few steps, the bottom fell away beneath him and he sank. Strangely, he was not afraid. An unnatural blue light surrounded him. He began to swim, and found his body moved quickly through the mineral soaked water. His companions were beside him and the siren song was a line reeling them in.

There was solid ground beneath his feet now. He was walking upward, out of the lake, along the shining causeway to the city. There was no gate, but a portcullis of crystal spears was raised to allow them ingress. Tayven was first beneath it. Beyond was a wide ceremonial way leading upward. The buildings around him were indistinct. Sometimes, they looked like natural rock formations, at other times like splendid palaces and temples. The song that surrounded him was so high-pitched, he felt it would melt his brain. Yet he was driven to walk forward. Something was approaching, a tall glowing shape. It glided like a ghost, surrounded by immense wings. The brilliance of the light bleached all color from the scene, but as the strange figure drew closer, Tayven saw that it was male and that his wings were white peacocks' tails. His hair was the darkest purple, the color of night-blooming, poisonous flowers. Valraven, he thought, but then behind him, he heard Shan cry, "Azcaranoth! The peacock angel."

The figure held a glowing object in its white attenuated hands. This he appeared to be offering to the city's visitors. Tayven fell to his knees. The great angel hovered over him, his face terrible and beautiful.

A voice thundered out from him, although his mouth did not move. "Who summons the etheric form of Kharsanara, city of the Elderahan?"

"Seekers, lord," Tayven murmured. "We have undertaken the quest of the lakes. Our sacrifices summoned you. We seek the lesson of the Crown of Silence."

Sparks of indigo light spat from the angel's eyes. "I am the father of humanity, reviled and worshipped in equal measure. It is I who gives knowledge to the world, that which breaks the endless sleep of the human soul. If it is my knowledge you seek, then speak now in truth." The angel's form was in constant motion, as if he were made of light or fluid.

"We come in truth, lord," Tayven said. "We seek your knowledge for the good of humanity."

Azcaranoth's voice rang out like the clash of a mighty bell. "Then answer this. Who does the Crown serve?"

Tayven took a deep breath. He had to speak what was in his heart. "It serves the true king, lord."

Azcaranoth raised his wings and the whole city shook to a deafening rumble. "There can be no king without the Crown of Knowledge," he roared. "Without wisdom, without awareness, without mercy, without will, the king does not exist. All these qualities are within the Crown. They are the vital elements of kingship, and when they come together in the flesh of the true king, silence covers the sky, the waters and the earth. Are you worthy custodians for this precious gift?"

"Judge our hearts, lord," Tayven murmured, his head lowered.

"I am not!" Taropat cried. "Smite me now. I am not worthy of this company."

"Ah, pride," said the angel. "You must learn to live with it, temper its excesses. I'll not smite you."

"I no longer want life," Taropat said desperately. "I cannot live without sight."

"You are blinded by your own folly," said the angel. "You were unwilling to make the sacrifice, because of your ignorance. Yet your brother made it for you. You eyes are not blind, Taropat, though your heart may be."

"We are only human," Tayven said, "flawed and ignorant. Yet we undertook the quest in good faith. It was all we could do."

"Look upon me," said the angel.

Tayven raised his face. Before his eyes, he saw the Crown, cupped by the angel's fingers. It was a simple high coronet of delicate spines, as if made from living coral, emitting its own radiance. It was the manifestation of all that was noble within humanity. Tayven could not bear to look upon it for long. His eyes were streaming.

"Take it," said the angel, "if you accept my words as truth."

"I do" Tayven said. "I do now." He sensed movement behind him, which he knew was Shan reaching out to take the Crown. Instinctively, Tayven reached for it first. He felt an icy cold burn course up his arms as his fingers curled around it. At once, he fell. The city was falling, water pouring over him in mighty waves. He was engulfed. Strong currents grabbed hold of his body, throwing it around like an insignificant piece of flotsam. He was being sucked downward into the darkness, the only light coming from the Crown. Tayven would not let go of it. His lungs were bursting, and his head was so crushed by pressure he was sure it must explode. But he would not let go. The descent seemed interminable. Tayven drifted in and out of consciousness. Each time he awoke, he could not comprehend that he was still alive. He felt he hadn't drawn breath for hours, but although his chest was on fire with pain, he did not give in and try to breathe. Something sustained him, perhaps the Crown itself. But he was weakening. He could sense it. Why prolong the agony? Why not just open his mouth and let the water fill him? There was to be no rising. It was impossible. He had gone too deep.

No! he screamed in his mind. We got this far. The Crown is in our grasp. No! I am hope. I will not let despair take me.

The moment these thoughts had formed, a vision splashed across his inner eye. He was sitting at the feet of Valraven Palindrake, who was seated upon a great throne, the Crown of Silence upon his brow. Shan stood on the king's right side, dressed in silver armor. Taropat was at Valraven's left, resplendent in the purple robes of a magus. The image lasted only an instant, before breaking up into myriad flashing colors. Tayven was ejected from the water as if he were an irritant it was compelled to dispel. Blinding sunlight filled his eyes and he sucked in a searing lungful of air. Waves crashed over him, pushing him under for a while, but then he rose again. This was not Pancanara. There were no mountains around him, but what appeared to be sea. He tasted salt in his mouth. How had this happened? Magravandias was not close to the ocean. How had they got here? He paddled round in the water and saw that land lay close by. On a broad sandy beach, he saw Shan crawling slowly from the foam. Merlan lay among the rock pools, covered by a blanket of weed, and Taropat sat next to him, staring out to sea, his eyes restored.

Tayven swam toward them, and it was only when they saw him and began to shout his name that he raised his arm above the water, and saw the Crown shining there, still gripped in his numb fingers. The Crown of Silence.

25

PARTING OF THE COMPANY

LADY SINACLARA DRIBBLED incense into a bowl before the statue of Azcaranoth. All day, her heart had beat too quickly in her breast. They would be here soon. She had waited so long for this moment, and this was only the beginning. There was no easy path to what was right, what was truth.

She heard Nana come into the temple, recognizing the soft graceful tread of her assistant. "It has come," said the Jessapurian.

Sinaclara turned and for some moments looked into Nana's eyes in silence. She felt like weeping rather than laughing. Joy filled her, but also terror and sadness.

"It is a burden you chose," said Nana.

Sinaclara nodded. "I know. And if I have regrets, it is not that."

THEY WERE WAITING in her sitting room, all of them looking gaunt and tired. It had been a long journey and it had changed them. Sinaclara could sense that they'd travelled guided only by instinct, numbed and shocked by all that had happened to them. She had been with them in spirit, unable to intervene, sharing their anguish, their hope, their weakness and their strength. Pancanara had revealed its secret and given up the Crown. They had been sucked into underground channels, reborn in the Magravandian inland sea, Magar's Stretch. Sinaclara could see that, even now, they were unsure how that had happened. They were disoriented, separated, even though they were also securely bound by their shared experience. A bond they did not want, perhaps. Whatever moments of unity they might have shared when they came out of the water had gone now. Secrets estranged them, unspoken words. Sinaclara's servants had given them something to eat and drink, but their plates appeared untouched.

"Well?" Sinaclara said, addressing Taropat.

He stood up and gestured to Tayven, who unstrapped a large leather satchel between his feet. From this, he withdrew an object wrapped in several layers of linen.

"Give it to me," Sinaclara said.

Tayven glanced at Taropat, who nodded. With some reluctance, he held the object out. It was hard for them to surrender it, she knew. Within each of them, even the one who was so clearly Taropat's kin, burned the desire to take the Crown for themselves. They could not help it, for they were only men, and the allure of the Crown was strong. But upon the head of any but the true king, it would be a force of chaos, no matter how good or true the owner of that head might believe himself to be.

Reverently, Sinaclara unwrapped the Crown and held it up before her face. Just an artifact, fashioned in an ancient time, hidden for centuries, perhaps longer. She turned it in her hands. There were marks upon it, scars of earlier battles. Each dent upon its surface was a relic of humanity's ignorance, for even those who had aspired to wear the Crown had not always lived up to its potential. Perhaps she was wrong now and the path she had unveiled was that of a lie. How could she tell? The allure of the Crown was strong. Sinaclara sighed, and placed the artifact down upon a table. The men gathered around her.

"You must tell me of your experiences," she said. "Please, refresh yourselves. This may be a long day."

She listened without commenting as they related the story, even though she knew they left many details out. They could not speak of the embarrassment and pain of their individual lessons and experiences, but despite that, she could see it shining from them.

Taropat spoke bitterly of his temporary blindness at the last lake. The experience had marked him. Sinaclara could smell his anger and resentment at not witnessing the city of angels for himself, an experience he wholeheartedly believed he had deserved.

At the end of the story, Sinaclara said, "You surrendered the prizes that had become most dear to you. I am sure it was this act alone that allowed you to attain the Crown."

"We have not lost the prizes," Tayven said, touching his throat. "They are within us. We do not need the artifacts anymore." He turned to Taropat. "The gift of the Eye is within you too, no matter what happened at the lake."

"You have your brother to thank for that," Sinaclara said.

Taropat nodded, his face pinched. "I know that." He sighed and smiled sadly at Merlan. "Perhaps I do not deserve it. Perhaps the gift is rightly Merlan's."

Merlan shook his head. "I don't believe so. We all have our part to play, and one aspect of mine was to be your strength."

"Do you understand the significance of the city of angels?" Sinaclara asked, looking from Merlan to Taropat. "There is a link here with your native sea dragons."

Taropat frowned. "I have a feeling they come from the same source." He shook his head. "No, if I had the knowledge once, it eludes me now. What do you know?"

"Azcaranoth once had an alliance with the dragons," she said. "It is a very ancient story, perhaps history, perhaps allegory, who knows? But the legend goes that the king of the angels sent the dragons of every element to destroy Azcaranoth and his conspirators. They were to be punished for consorting with mortals, helping them create civilization. Azcaranoth passed to humanity great knowledge that was sacred in nature. For that indiscretion, he must die. However, the angel king had not counted on Azcaranoth's persuasive nature. He managed to charm the dragon spirits to ally with him. Together they built great cities, one of which was Pelagra, beneath the ocean. Here the Ustredi were spawned, the sea people, who were the ancient ancestors of the Palindrakes."

Taropat's mouth turned down into a sneer. "Do not taint the day with that name. It should not be spoken before the Crown."

Sinaclara paused, judging the moment. Then she said, "It is only a story. I thought you might be interested in it." Merlan, she could tell, was anxious to hear more, as was Tayven. Shan, Taropat's apprentice, shared his master's prejudices. She could feel the black waves of hatred pulsing out of him. He should learn to think for himself. Sinaclara's heart felt heavy within her breast. There would be a severing here. It was inevitable. Strange the way it would go. Tayven and Shan so alike physically, as were Taropat and his brother. The pairs would be like warped reflections of one another.

"Did you believe we could do it?" Shan asked in a husky voice.

She nodded. "Oh yes. I was both afraid and hopeful that you would."

"Who will you Crown, now that you have it?" he asked.

She heard the hope in his voice, the determination and mettle. She could feel the burn of Taropat's desire to make a better world, scoured of monsters. She could feel Tayven's uncertainty warring with a sense of purpose, and she could hear the murmur of Taropat's brother's troubled soul, because he feared he knew her answer. And he did.

She turned to them, drew in her breath. "There is only one man in this time," she said. "He is the sum of all of you. I know that during your journey to me, three of you have come to feel the Crown is yours. One of you is afraid that is the case, while two of you desire it to be so. But you are all wrong. The fourth companion knows the answer." She looked into Merlan Leckery's dark eyes. "Will you tell them?"

He shook his head, turned away. "I know only what others think," he said.

"What do you mean?" Taropat asked harshly.

The tension in the room had heightened. I shall break this company, Sinaclara thought. I do not want to, and it will be wrong, but my words will break them. "Valraven Palindrake," she said.

For a moment, there was silence, then Taropat laughed. "I might have known," he said coldly. "Wrap the Crown, Tayven. It will not remain here."

Tayven hesitated, then reached out to take it, but Sinaclara stayed his hand. "You will not," she said.

"Take it, Tay," Shan said.

Merlan had turned away from them, walked across the room.

"You are not thinking," Sinaclara said. "You are just reacting, driven by your own fears. Taropat, whatever your feelings for me, I know you trust my judgment. Remember our alliance, how we planned this quest together."

"I knew it!" Shan cried. "It was planned all along. You used us!"

Sinaclara fixed him with a level gaze. "Never that," she said. "The quest was planned only in some respects, Shan. You must believe that. Taropat and I spoke it just before he left for Mewt." She turned back to Taropat. "And you would not have succeeded if I had not told you what to expect, and what to do, at Recolletine. You must accept I speak the truth."

"I will never accept that," Taropat said.

"Nor I!" snapped Shan. "You lied to me."

Sinaclara turned to him, her hands outspread. "Shan, don't be so naive. The days of divinely picked heroes have gone. I did what was best."

"It makes a travesty of all we've been through," Taropat said. "None of us survived the lakes to be told an incarnation of evil should attain the fruit of our labor. I would never have confided in you if I'd known your secret desire. All you want is for your dark angel to become flesh. I should have known better than to trust a woman again."

Sinaclara couldn't help bridling at that. "If we are speaking of secret desires, perhaps we should discuss your own. You want to possess the Crown as the ultimate revenge on Valraven. You believe he bettered you in the one thing that mattered."

"Meaning?" Taropat said dryly.

"Bedding his own sister, your wife, Pharinet. You cannot forgive him for the love she bore him."

Taropat laughed coldly. "How wrong you are. I care nothing for that conniving whore. Khaster is dead in me. Your insults mean nothing. I am strong now. I may not be fit to wear the Crown, but I am eminently more suitable than a dissolute wretch like Valraven Palindrake. The Crown will not stay here with you, madam, and your strength is no match for ours."

"No, it isn't," Sinaclara said quietly. "However, beyond my door, a dozen of my Jessapurian colleagues wait for my command. They are armed. If you touch the Crown, you'll never leave this house alive. I'm sorry. It's what must be. I cannot let personal feelings sway my judgment. There are greater matters at stake."

Again, Taropat laughed coldly. "So, it has come to this. You have used us for your own foul ends. You are part of all that is wrong with the world. What fools we were!"

"*You* are wrong Taropat," Sinaclara said. "Your own shuttered mind prevents you from seeing the truth. Only two of you have spoken. What is your view, Tayven? Can you look into my eyes and say that I am wrong?"

Tayven drew a hand across his face. "I know that some factions believe Palindrake should be king."

"I'm asking you what you think, what you really think?"

He shook his head. "I'm not sure. That is the truth. I can sense what might be, but I'm faced with what is."

"And you, Merlan Leckery," Sinaclara said, raising her voice. "Tell your brother your thoughts. Tell him how you convinced Varencienne Palindrake to take her husband back to the old domain. What was your argument, eh? Have you kept so silent on this matter?"

"Merlan, what does she mean?" Taropat said.

Merlan's face was utterly white. "Maycarpe thinks that Valraven is the one."

"Rather more than that," Sinaclara said. "Merlan convinced Varencienne she should help Valraven reawaken the sea dragons, reclaim his heritage. Is that not so, Merlan?"

"I was working under Maycarpe's directive," Merlan said.

"I can't believe this of you," Taropat snarled. "After all that has happened to our family. No wonder the quest took its toll upon you."

"I am not wholly convinced, believe me," Merlan said. "But I do not think personal concerns should enter this matter."

"Merlan, are you mad?" Shan cried. "Palindrake is the embodiment of the empire's power. He is the destroyer."

"He is many things," Merlan said. "All that you say and more." He made an anguished sound. "Damn this, I won't keep silent. Taropat, there is something you should know."

"Shut up, I don't want to hear it!" Taropat snarled.

"Of course you don't. It might compromise your righteous anger! Hasn't the lesson of your blindness taught you anything about your stubborn pride? I know the full story of what happened between you and Tayven, because Shan has told it to me."

"Shan!" Taropat glared at his apprentice, who shrugged in embarrassment.

"I felt he should know."

"Don't blame him," Merlan said. "The fact is, after hearing that story, I understood so much. Something you have failed to do. You hate Valraven most for when he would not help you save Tayven. You resented feeling so powerless, so in need of his aid. You hated him then for not being the great savior that he'd always been for you. But, in a way, you have always hated him; for being stronger than you, for bettering you and saving your skin."

"Thank you for this lesson," Taropat said in a strangely sweet tone. "I'd not thought of it before."

"Oh, don't play with me!" Merlan cried. "It is the truth. I can see now that you wanted the Crown for yourself, so you could be the stronger and better man for once. You can't bear to think that Valraven is like the rest of us—a mixture of attributes, both good and bad."

"Oh, tell me some good!" Taropat said, throwing up his arms. "I can't wait to hear it."

"I can do that," Merlan said softly. "You've never known it, but after you ran away from all your problems, Valraven did try to help Tayven. He went to Bayard as you asked. He didn't do this for himself, but for you."

"*He* took me out to battlefield and left me there?" Tayven asked in a horrified voice.

Merlan shook his head. "No, he was too late. Bayard's people had taken you away by then. Valraven had his men search for what he presumed would be your body, but it was never found. We know why now. Valraven told me this the last time I saw him in Caradore."

"*If* what you say is true, it makes no difference," Taropat said. "That's just a convenient excuse. He didn't go when he could have made a difference."

"He has tortured himself about it," Merlan said. "He knows he acted too late."

Taropat uttered a sound of contempt. "Poor Valraven. How that must hurt him. He should have seen what happened—to both Tayven and me. Then he might understand pain."

Merlan made an angry sound. "Is your damage so sacred, Khaster? Are you so privileged? Other people have suffered at the Malagashes' hands. Have you ever stopped to consider what changed Valraven from the friend you loved into the cold creature that could kill without thinking?'

There was a brief silence, then Taropat said softly, "So, it all becomes clear. My dear brother was the viper in our midst all the time. No wonder Maycarpe wanted you to accompany us to Recolletine."

"No, it wasn't like that!" Merlan said.

"We should have left you at Malarena," Taropat said and looked coldly at Tayven. "And you were the one to convince Shan and me otherwise. You haven't truly revealed your thoughts yet, Tayven. Are you with Maycarpe, or with us?"

"It is one and the same," Tayven said. "We are the company."

"I will never serve evil," Taropat said.

"Nor I!" Shan echoed.

"You are dividing yourselves," Sinaclara said. "Think clearly."

"There is no company," Taropat said, "not anymore." He crossed the room and hefted his backpack onto his shoulder. "Shan, come here."

"Don't leave," Sinaclara said. "It would be the worst thing you could do."

"I will fight you," Taropat said. "Don't ever doubt it. I hope you're ready for it."

"Taropat, see reason," Sinaclara said. "We must talk about this. We must exorcise the past, for it's clouding your judgment."

"You know nothing," Taropat said. "Come, Shan. If we have to fight our way out of here, so be it."

"Shan," Sinaclara said. "Don't listen to him. Stay. Listen to me. Let me tell you the truth, so you may judge for yourself."

Shan shook his head. "I know what's right," he said and went to Taropat's side.

Merlan appealed to his brother. "Khaster, remember who you are. Remember the beginning. That is what you must fight for, not bitterness or anger."

"Khaster is dead," Taropat said. "He was killed by the man you would have me serve. You are all under his spell. I pity you." He looked at Tayven. "I'll give you one last chance. Come with us. Help us fight for justice."

Tayven was silent for a moment. "You shouldn't go," he said at last.

"You had me fooled," Taropat said and marched to the long windows that led to the garden. Merlan ran after and tried to stop him, but Taropat threw his brother aside with little more than a flick of his hand. A table went over. China and stone shattered as some of Sinaclara's precious artifacts crashed to the floor. At that moment, the door opened and a group of Jessapurians poured into the room.

"Stop!" Sinaclara cried, more to her people than to Taropat, but the Jessapurians did not appear to hear her. They rushed toward the windows and Taropat and Shan fled away into the gardens.

Sinaclara pressed her fingers briefly against her eyes. "This must not be," she murmured.

Merlan had got back to his feet. "They mustn't be harmed."

"They won't," Sinaclara said. "Taropat will get away."

"Let him calm down," Merlan said. "We can leave it overnight, then Tayven and I will go to his house tomorrow. Maybe he'll talk to us when he's had time to think."

Sinaclara shook her head. "Too late," she said. "They'll be on their way to Cos by then."

"Cos? What are you talking about?"

"They will seek out Helayna," Sinaclara said. "She and Taropat will fashion Shan into a rival of Valraven. I've seen this. I've dreaded it happening."

"Then you must stop it," Merlan said. He appealed to Tayven. "You must know where Helayna is. Go after them. They have the power of the Eye and the Claw. What will happen if those powers fall into the hands of what's left of the Cossic resistance?"

Tayven turned to Sinaclara. "Lady, is that my function? Must I go after them?"

Sinaclara swallowed with difficulty. Her throat felt as if it were gripped by an iron hand. "It is not our place to end past conflicts. Only Valraven Palindrake can do that."

"I will go to the Dragon Lord," Merlan said. "At once. He must be told of this."

"It is not yet time," Sinaclara said. "You can't. It would do more damage than good. You must trust me on this."

"Then what should we do?" Merlan demanded. "Clearly, we have to do something."

Sinaclara reached out and gently touched the Crown. "We have this," she murmured, her fingers running over the delicate tines. "That was the aim of your quest."

"But what of the company?" Merlan said. He punched a fist into his open palm. "Oh, I have to go after them. It can't end like this!"

"Stay," Sinaclara said sharply, then more gently, "You have to let them go. It is their choice. They have yet to find their own silence."

The Jessapurians were coming back to the house now, muttering among themselves, angry at having lost their quarry. "We must wait," Sinaclara said. "We have waited before. The Crown has been given

428   —⟡ Storm Constantine ⟡—

back to humankind. That was the purpose of your quest. Valraven Palindrake must seek the way of light, for only then can past wounds be healed. Only then . . ." Her voice trailed off.

"I will return to Akahana," Merlan said abruptly. "Tayven, will you come with me and report to Maycarpe?"

Tayven nodded. "Yes."

"And after, will you go to Cos?"

Tayven paused. "I feel it is out of my hands." He pulled a die from his pocket. "Six options, Merlan. Will you name the first?"

26

HOLME

ON THEIR WAY TO Cos, Taropat and Shan passed close
to the village of Holme. Shan asked if they could visit the
site of his family home.

"Are you sure of this?" Taropat asked.

Shan nodded. "Yes. Here, my story began. Now I feel as if
another story's just beginning. I want to face the past."

They rode past Shan's old home. The site had been claimed by
another family, who had built a new house on it. A woman sat in the
garden with her baby, peeling potatoes. *That could be me,* Shan
thought, *me and my mother.*

The woman looked up at them and smiled. Shan was about to
say he used to live there, but for some reason didn't want to bring
that dark memory into her innocent, summer garden. He would not
be the shadow at the gate for the child playing among her skirts. "Is
there an inn nearby, madam?" he asked.

The woman pointed up the road. "The Roan and Furrow, just
five minutes away. Have you travelled far, sirs?"

Shan nodded. "Yes."

"Come on," Taropat said and clucked to his horse.

The villagers had done much to restore their homes since Shan had left it. No one recognized him as he dismounted his horse in front of the small tavern. The church had not been rebuilt and children played, shrieking, among its ruins, which were covered in bright yellow weeds. Poppies grew there also, and foxgloves.

Shan and Taropat went into the tavern and sat drinking cold ale in the shadows. "This is a different place," Shan said. "I don't know it."

"You could find yourself here if you looked hard enough," Taropat said, "but I don't think you should."

"How do you feel?" Shan asked, the first time he'd dared ask the question since they'd run from Sinaclara's house.

Taropat took out his pipe and stuffed it thoughtfully. Shan thought he wasn't going to answer, then he said, "When I took you away from here, I had plans for you. Formless, vague, idealistic, perhaps, but not without potential. Seeing Tayven again, the betrayal by my brother, these things were just trials to test my courage and determination. Part of the lakes quest. Part of all we have to do."

"But we've attained the Crown for *them*," Shan said. "It's such a waste. Will you try to get it back?"

"It will never be theirs," Taropat said. "I have that much faith. I could have given myself to Tayven again so easily. It's what he wanted. Power, control. But some part of me resisted. I'm glad of that now."

Taropat had left his house in Nip's charge. She had been confused by their rapid departure, but Taropat would tell her nothing other than that they had business elsewhere and didn't know how long they'd be away. He seemed serene and confident, but Shan wasn't sure how reliable this image was. "If you are hurt, you should say so," he said carefully.

Taropat gave him a hard glance. "That's enough of that, boy. I'm not the lily-livered Khaster who used to mope around, hoping that someone else would make his life better. Merlan and Tayven wanted me to be that, but I'm not and that's all there is to it." He lit his pipe with abrupt and jerky movements.

"If we find Helayna," Shan said, "if you can help her build an army, Merlan and Tayven might be your enemies. What if you had to kill to take the Crown?"

Taropat laughed. "What is this? Are you trying to be my conscience?"

Shan said nothing.

"We will both do what we have to do when the time comes," Taropat said.

When they rode away from the village, a woman stepped out of a farmyard into their path, trying to shoo a dozen young ducks away from their horses' hooves. Shan experienced a sickening jolt of recognition. The woman was his aunt. She looked so much older, and one side of her face was drawn down and paralyzed, but he still knew her. She looked up at him. "Excuse me, sirs, the gate was open. They got away."

"Do you know me?" Shan said.

The woman frowned. "No, sir."

"She doesn't," Taropat said. "Come along. Quickly." He urged his horse into a trot and Shan's animal followed.

"But . . ." said Shan, pointing behind him. "She's . . ."

"Don't look back," Taropat said. "People are never how you remember them." He kicked his horse to a gallop, and they were flying up the road, away from Holme, from Bree, to the wild lands of Cos.

ABOUT THE AUTHOR

STORM CONSTANTINE is the author of Tor's *Wraeththu* Trilogy as well as a number of other fantasy and science fiction titles. She lives in England. Readers can reach Storm Constantine at: http://members.aol.com/malaktawus.